S0-DNM-864

THE GOLDEN ISLE

BOOKS BY

FRANK G. SLAUGHTER

The Golden Isle

In a Dark Garden

A Touch of Glory

Battle Surgeon

Air Surgeon

Spencer Brade, M.D.

That None Should Die

THE

Golden Isle

FRANK G.
SLAUGHTER

GARDEN CITY, N.Y.

Doubleday & Company, Inc.

1948

PRINTED IN THE UNITED STATES OF AMERICA
AMERICAN BOOK–STRATFORD PRESS, INC., NEW YORK

Foreword

THIS *is a novel, not a history—and the author offers no apology to the pundits for the telescoping of certain events in the Spanish Floridas, on the Island of Amelia, and in the town of Fernandina, during the year 1817. However, the motivations, and the actual conduct, of Gregor MacGregor's bizarre invasion (and the more sinister rule of Jared Irwin and Luis Aury that succeeded it) stem directly from the records of that turbulent year.*

The three persons just named are presented in The Golden Isle *as actors in its larger framework. And it is a matter of local record that a witch named Felippa lived in Fernandina at this time and worked strange miracles among its citizens. All other on-stage participants are imaginary. Any resemblance to persons living in that era is purely coincidental.*

Contents

THE GOLDEN ISLE

I

The "Dos Amigos"

DECEPTIVELY soft in the iron winter night, the warm murmur of the sea drifted through the coach windows; the lone passenger roused from his doze and thrust his head out to seek its genesis. The Dover Road, chalk-white under a high midnight moon, had begun to spin downgrade at last. The coachman's whip, flicking ahead of the four post horses straining at the poles, seemed to point their destination like the tongue of a questing snake—a landlocked harbor, gleaming under the moon, sensed rather than seen across the pale sweep of moors.

Dr. Michael Stone leaned back with a sigh and admitted that he was wide awake at last. From this point on excitement would build in his veins as he puzzled over the operation that awaited him.

The whip cracked again; the coach roared into the level straightaway at the same breakbone speed. There was no doubting the skill of the giant black on the box above: Michael heard the man shout at the horses in a singsong guttural and remembered how expertly he had driven the coach through every post station in this long spin across the sleeping fields of Kent. From the moment they left Temple Bar, he had known he would reach his destination intact. This was hardly the first time he had dozed in wildly rocking coaches on his way to save a life. And accepted commissions from old Holly (to be blunt about it) without asking too many questions, or disputing the fee.

Dr. Felix Holly. He could see the aged satyr as clearly as a goat's head in an allegory of heaven and hell. Holly had been Michael's mentor since his father died. A colleague of the elder Stone's, and one of London's busiest surgeons, Holly had always kept an attentive eye on the fortunes of his unofficial ward. Both doctors had rejoiced when Michael took up the scalpel, the moment his fingers were wise enough. It had been his father's legacy that had seen him through his father's own college at Cambridge; he had learned his profession as Dr. Felix Holly's apprentice; and it had been Holly's influence at the Admiralty that secured him his first appointment as a ship's surgeon.

Youth (said his mentor) could do worse than season itself with tomcatting on the seven seas. There had been other voyages, and other argosies. He had burnished his skill in the service of the great East India Company—on jungle rivers, in princes' palaces, in the glare of desert noons. A ship's doctor could take most summonses in his stride—when his scalpel has earned two trips around the world. A ship's doctor (temporarily at liberty on terra firma) should think nothing of driving sixty breakneck miles to use that scalpel one more time.

The coach thundered across a causeway at the same reckless speed, though the moors had begun to give way to marshland on either side of the narrow roadbed. His instrument case nudged his ribs as a wheel danced over a stone; he shifted to a more comfortable corner, letting his fingers caress the mahogany rectangle. In the wash of moonlight those fingers were almost as dark as the wood beneath them: he had brought that tan away from his last ship when she had dropped anchor in the Pool. London bucks might shun the life-giving rays; Dr. Michael Stone had always stripped when he could, and kept his body a deep saddle-brown.

In its way, that mahogany burn had set him apart from his fellows more effectively than his hard schooling. He watched the brown fingers as they continued to stroke the mahogany. It was good to remember how they enjoyed their work. He had trained those hands in strange byways, but they had come by their skill honestly. As honestly as he had inherited this surgical case from his father before him.

His fingertips lingered on the silver name plate and traced the letters they knew by heart:

GEOFFREY STONE
Queen's College, Cambridge
June 18th, 1774

His father had been graduated from that cloister on the Cam over forty years ago. It was hard to picture the event from the vantage point of this young man's century. His memory of his parents had dimmed long ago. His mother had died at sea, between Halifax and the Port of London; Geoffrey Stone had followed her when Michael was still a boy. Why should he blame himself for this feeling of remoteness from his origins—as though his very birth had occurred beyond space and time, as though his country was the world? *Queen's College, Cambridge*. It was not their fault, or his own, that he had emerged from that same cloister ten years ago—with a career at his fingertips and no desire to pin down his destiny.

During that momentous decade he had roamed the seaways and refused to submit to molds. No corner, however exotic, had held him for long; no love had endured beyond its happy-go-lucky moment. A man who would soon turn thirty (he repeated the truism solemnly) must find a loyalty beyond himself. Yet his vagabond urge was unappeased, despite those two circlings of the globe. His interest in the land beyond the next landfall had all the brash intensity of seventeen.

II

Overhead the whip cracked once again and the coachman raised his barbaric chant to the moon. Dr. Michael Stone came back to the present—or, more accurately, to the consulting room of Dr. Felix Holly, some eight hours ago.

If Michael's parents were no clearer to him than a painting in a forgotten corner of one's attic, Dr. Holly's offices were always garishly real. It was here that the younger doctor repaired to settle his accounts between voyages; on this deep Turkey carpet he had paced out more than one lecture, while bailiffs waited in the anteroom. Michael seldom quit London without leaving debts behind, and his last voyage had been no exception. As usual, the gentlemen with the cudgels had awaited him at the gangway.

Oddly enough, old Holly had offered only the mildest of scoldings this afternoon; the two bullies in the anteroom had merely been paid and sent about their business. Michael, settling in the doctor's spindly armchair with his mouth agape, had had time to note that Holly's offices had grown even more splendid. The Louis Quinze suite, which the old rascal had acquired years ago from a French émigré in lieu of a fee, had been richly upholstered in petit point. A flamboyant portrait of the surgeon himself (done by Mr. Lawrence) now graced the overmantel. Yet prosperity alone could hardly account for Holly's deceptive gentleness; the elder doctor had never been noted for philanthropy where Michael was concerned.

At the moment, as he nursed his wig on his knee and settled in his brocaded wing chair, Felix Holly resembled nothing so much as a shopworn vulture. It's the shaved skull that does it, thought Michael (it was quite like Holly to cling to a powdered wig long after Mr. Brummel had made one's own hair fashionable), to say nothing of the agate-gray eyes, the aura of the autopsy table that still clung to the two stubby paws. Michael (who worked in smallclothes when he could and scrubbed himself after each operation) had adjusted himself to the other's odor long ago. A gamy stink was still the surgeon's badge along with those rusty splotches of blood that graced the lapels of Holly's beautifully cut coat, the spurt of yellow that gleamed like a faded topaz on the otherwise immaculate stock. A dandy's pustule, lanced too late, thought Michael. Or the aftermath of a curettage that turned out to be hemorrhagic after all? He stirred restlessly in his chair while he waited for the vulture's first croak.

"Tell me the bad news, Uncle. I'll try to bear it."

"I'm not your uncle, praise God. If I pay your debts, it's only for your poor dead father's sake."

Michael had ignored the false tremolo. "You mentioned a commission just now. A hundred pounds, I believe."

"Precisely. A county case. It will repay most of the guineas those rascals just took away."

"If the fee's that large, why don't you take it yourself?"

"Unfortunately, my client has asked for you personally."

He remembered how Dr. Felix Holly had smiled at that utterance, as though he were nursing a joke he could never share with anyone. "Perhaps you don't realize how famous you've become. Especially since your service in Bengal."

"Tease me all you like, Uncle Felix. You've bought the right."

"I was never more in earnest. Mr. Adam Leigh's janizaries have investigated your record thoroughly. They don't do things by halves, it seems."

"And who is Mr. Adam Leigh?"

"I'd forgotten you'd been away." Old Holly's lips resembled the mouth of an avid purse. "Your man's a Croesus on more than one front. Colonial planter under the Spanish Crown. Headquarters in the Floridas. Blackbirding station on the Gold Coast, with a branch in Angola. Warehouse in the Pool and private docks somewhere in Kent. That's where you'll operate. How soon can you start?"

"I've not yet consented to operate, Uncle."

"The fee is already banked, and I've deducted my usual percentage. Of course, if you'd prefer to lodge awhile at a sponging house, I can still call back the bailiffs."

"Have I refused a commission so far?"

"You seem to balk at this one."

"Only to make you tell me more. Naturally I'm only too happy to open Mr. Leigh at any point."

"It isn't Leigh you'll operate; it's one of his servants. An overseer or factor, I'm not sure which. Name of Numi Rey—or King Numi, take your choice. At all events, a valuable man. So valuable, Leigh wants to send him out on his next supply ship."

"Suppose I can't deliver that miracle?"

"Leigh is paying for your reputation—and gambling on the result. It sounds a ticklish thing, but you should manage it nicely. Swelling in the popliteal fossa——"

"Is a doctor in attendance now?"

"Leigh's own estate man. He's already recommended surgery."

Michael leaned back in the flying coach and held the sharp-nosed image of Felix Holly in his mind's eye. It was obvious that the old man had enjoyed the air of mystery he had created. His next remark had puzzled his unofficial ward most of all.

"You know, it's high time you settled on a permanent post. If Leigh should make you an offer, think it over."

"I don't care much for permanence, Uncle."

"Think it over, just the same."

The coachman's whip snapped one more time. Michael found that he had twisted away from the sharp report, as though that explosion of leather had threatened his own flesh. He was on trial tonight; that much seemed evident. Of course a doctor is always on trial, from the moment he picks up his knife. Why should he insist that this night was but the overture to a larger adventure whose end he could not see?

Why, when he had ridden out from London a dozen times to wrestle with death, should he go to this case with foreboding in his heart?

III

An hour later—after a second glass of claret, a second helping of guinea hen—he saw that his premonition had been groundless. The manor house had been just what he had expected to find: even the emptiness that echoed in its formal rooms was comforting—a ghostly reminder of the absentee landlord that blended with hooded chandeliers, the curt flame that danced on the library hearth where he was supping. So was the silence that folded the room in its cloak; so were the two Negro footmen who served him with catfoot skill. So, for that matter, was the bulk of the estate doctor in the facing armchair.

He had known in advance that the man would be fat as a bursting hogshead. That type of colonial (with a slave at each elbow and too much time to drink) had a way of going soft before his time. The hard, steady eyes were Dr. Keith's special attribute. From what the man had said so far, he seemed more than competent—and inclined to rest on his laurels. Already he had admitted that he was retiring a rich man, after a long service in Africa. The intimation had been that he had more than earned his retirement in lives saved.

"I gather your employer is both planter and slave runner?"

Keith's pale eyebrows just escaped arching; Keith's voice assumed a polite, dead monotone. "In Africa his factories process Negroes—if I may use the verb in that sense. The processing is completed at his estate in the Floridas. The finished product is sold throughout America."

"Your pardon, Doctor. But we're beginning the year 1816——"

"I'm well aware of the date, sir."

"Surely the importing of slaves is illegal in America?"

"It's still winked at, Doctor. Winked at openly in the United States—and throughout the Indies. In the other Americas there's no barrier whatever. Why should the question concern you?"

"Is the man I'm to operate a Negro?"

"They don't come darker."

"Is he in England legally?"

"Upon my word, sir——"

"I was merely thinking of our reputations. Naturally we must make a full report."

"King Numi has been a freedman for years," said Keith. The heavy voice seemed to draw itself to attention. "Mr. Leigh has had him made a Spanish citizen. His passport is good anywhere."

Michael touched his lips with a crested napkin. "Then I suggest we examine him now."

"If you're sure you've recovered from your journey——"

A black footman had already whipped up with a candle sconce; another sprang to open the double doors that gave from the snugness of Adam Leigh's library to the glacial immensity of his entrance hall. No one spoke as they ascended the stair well and turned into the passage at its head. The moonlight, splashing the cold flags with its radiance, made the candle flames quite needless, but the footman led the way with all the rigidity of a parade marshal. It was a grotesque procession, not without dignity. Michael found that he was part of it despite himself—and not in the least startled when a door opened at the head of the passage, as though an unseen hand had sensed their coming.

Their patient lay in the center of a four-poster in the enormous room. Save for the bed table and its night light, there was no furniture: even the valance of the bed was gone, and the posts themselves, thrust up into darkness, gleamed in the candlelight like thick spears. Once again Michael heard the echo of the absentee landlord. Adam Leigh, he gathered, was a man who could take luxury in his stride—and turn his back on its shrouded remnants.

He stepped to the dais and bent over the high mattress. The man beneath the quilted counterpane was shockingly small, a mere ebony dot in the immensity of the bed. He slept deeply under an opiate; the hand on the counterpane was relaxed as a child's. And yet, when he looked more closely, Michael saw that the fingers were long and curved; the nails were filed to a peak, like the claws of some strange bird.

"A pygmy king, Doctor. From the Congo basin. Don't be deceived by his size. He's really quite valuable."

Michael had begun to turn back the bedclothes before he realized that the voice was new—that it had ghosted up to the bed as quietly as its owner. The eyes that met his above the counterpane were both burning and remote. The eyes of an ascetic, he thought quickly, or a fiend. Perhaps a blend of both. The man was thin and hawk-proud. Even by candlelight his skin had a worn yellow sheen. Another white who has ventured too deeply in the tropics, added Michael—and bowed to Keith's rumble of introduction.

"Señor Ríos, Doctor. Mr. Leigh's chief factor in Africa."

The Spaniard inclined from the waist. There was only the flick of an accent when he spoke again: in that light he could have been any age, race, or creed. Once again Michael knew that Ríos's eyes were appraising him intently, weighing him in a cold scale that had nothing to do with the values of everyday.

"Is there a chance of saving him, Doctor?"

"I'll answer that in a moment." He forgot Ríos as he began the examination, forgot the group that had begun to cluster about the bed. Coal-black faces, most of them, that seemed to serve as immobile pedestals for the circle of candles that met his eyes whenever he raised them from his work. At such moments a wall of concentration was a blessed thing. He was but half conscious of Keith's hands as they turned the pygmy face down.

"A problem *in parvo,* if I may use the term."

"Precisely."

"The edema in the left limb, as you see, is pronounced. He's been off his feet for three days now."

"What is your diagnosis, Doctor?"

"An abscess or a tumor in the popliteal fossa. You will notice the pulsation there. It appeared with the swelling, possibly from pressure upon the artery."

Michael's fingers had already outlined the hollow behind the knee joint—or rather the violent swelling that had distended the skin above that area almost to the bursting point. The obstruction was round and tense and seemed to purr with a small heart of its own. No one stirred as the visiting doctor took a tubular-shaped object from his case and bent above the tiny patient. And yet he could feel the tautness in that wall of black flesh that all but encircled him now. He ignored the concerted sigh—and applied the small tip of the wooden tube to his ear and the funnel-shaped end to the swelling.

"Laënnec's stethoscope," said Ríos softly. "It's the first I've seen. You keep abreast of the times, Dr. Stone."

"May I return the compliment, sir?"

"I'm a physician of sorts myself," said Ríos. "One picks up the knack in our trade. In fact, I've already rejected Keith's diagnosis. To my mind, that swelling is a simple aneurysm, nothing more."

Michael nodded. "The purring sensation is characteristic. I would say that such a swelling could come from no other cause."

"Which means, in turn, that the artery wall is weakened and distended from the pressure?"

Keith took back his authority in a deep bass rumble. "Perhaps you'd also care to operate, Señor Ríos?"

"Dr. Stone is here to demonstrate his skill, my friend. Naturally I'm gratified that he sides with me."

Keith did not budge. "Let's admit your guess may be correct, gentlemen. I still insist on my prognosis—amputation."

Michael frowned, with his fingers still testing the arterial pulse. "There's no doubt that surgery is indicated."

"Amputation will save his life, if there is no sepsis. He'll be at sea this time tomorrow: the sea air always minimizes that risk—— "

"Numi is a headman at the Boca," said Ríos. "Of what use is a one-legged headman?"

"We'd preserve his essential organ," snapped Keith—and Michael wondered at the estate doctor's sneer even as he grasped the wordplay. He cut smoothly into the argument before Ríos could answer the burst of British choler.

"I'd hoped to save the leg."

"You can't incise," said Keith. "The hemorrhage would kill him."

"I can ligate."

"And stop all blood flow?"

"John Hunter has shown that there are other passages through which blood can serve a limb. In fact, it will flow better when the pressure of the aneurysm is relieved."

Ríos had listened with his sleepy-lidded stare unchanged. "Operate when you're ready, Dr. Stone. I'll endorse the result."

Keith said, "I must report this to the Royal College."

"Report away, sir. From this point on Dr. Stone and I are above the Royal College."

Michael spoke carefully, with his eyes on Keith. "I wouldn't quite say that, Señor——"

"Permit me to say it for you, Doctor. As for you, Keith, you are still in Mr. Leigh's employ—and mine. You'll assist this operation. With Dr. Stone's courtesy, I'll observe."

The hooded eyes had pinioned the estate doctor long ago. Keith, reflected Michael, was the Spaniard's tool as completely as the inert black homunculus sprawled between them. His own part in this strange trio was still unclear. He put that puzzle aside in favor of the business at hand.

"Permission is granted, Señor Ríos. Though I'm not accustomed to observers when I operate."

"But this is a test, Dr. Stone. An important test."

"I'm afraid I don't quite follow——"

"I'll explain that too, at the proper time. How soon can you be ready?"

"As soon as I've honed my scalpels."

"Dr. Keith will help, if you like."

But Michael only bowed to the glowering surgeon across the bed. "Thank you, no. This is one task I must do alone."

IV

When the operation was over—and he had retired to the bedroom assigned him for what remained of the night—he reminded himself that one is always alone at such a moment. The other hands that serve you, moving just outside the area where you are battling for a life, are mere obbligato to your own desperate gamble. Tonight's procedure (and he admitted it freely now) had been another gamble based on instinct rather than experience. The fact that he had succeeded completely was due to luck as well as deftness.

It was good to rehearse that operation now: the first raking sweep of the steel across that iridescent skin; the quick, merciless search for a point of attack in the fascia; the unmasking of the femoral artery, pulsing beside its companion vein. The aneurysm had already filled the entire fossa; it had taken steady nerves to trace the line of the artery, to place the ligatures well above the focus of danger. Yes, it was gratifying to recall that high moment—and forget the screams of his tiny patient, pinned by a dozen black hands to the blood-smeared table. Primitive as man's first human despair, Numi's howls had broken through the opiate like jungle banshees. Michael had steeled himself to ignore those animal bellows. They varied little, whether the man under his knife was a Chinese mandarin, a West End peer, or a pygmy from the Congo basin.

Now, at last, he could take time to wonder at the eyes of the Spanish factor—and how they had followed every move. At Keith's irascible good night, his abrupt departure the moment the last dressing was strapped in place. At the concerted adoration of a dozen slaves in claw-hammers when the visiting doctor quitted the table, as though he were Mumbo Jumbo incarnate. At Ríos's own deep bow in the doorway:

"You have passed your test brilliantly, Doctor."

"Your servant, Señor."

"*Yours,* Dr. Stone. Now and always."

Why had he sensed a light mockery behind those words? Why should he turn now, with the last glass of the evening shaking in his hand, and stare at the door of his bedchamber with a wildly pumping heart? After all, it was natural that Ríos should walk in on him with only the lightest of knocks.

Hovering above the operation, the Spaniard had been no more than a pair of probing eyes that missed nothing. Here in the faint halo cast by the night light he could have passed for Beelzebub in an unguarded moment. A worn but urbane devil, eager to spread his cards. Michael moved warily as he bowed his visitor to a seat. He had faced the devil in several languages and lived to tell the story.

"Our major-domo insisted you had not yet retired, Doctor. So I took the liberty——"

"Will you join me in a nightcap?"

"I seldom drink, Doctor. Never when business is afoot. Most of my colleagues remark that I've no visible vices." Ríos made a prayer book of his hands—as though reminding Michael that the devil can quote Scripture. "Nor do I enjoy a false air of mystery. I fear that several unanswered questions have formed in your mind tonight. May I strive to answer them?"

"I'm a surgeon, Señor Ríos—not an investigator for the Regent."

"Surely you are curious about Numi Rey. Or do you dissect pygmies every day?"

"There was no particular problem involved. As Keith remarked, it was merely an operation *in parvo*——"

"Did you know that Numi is a rich man today, thanks to Mr. Leigh—and myself?"

"I can believe that too."

"Mr. Leigh has bought him Spanish citizenship. He has twenty thousand pesos banked in Madrid. How many Africans can say as much?"

"Few are so fortunate, señor, when they join forces with the white man."

"True enough. But you must admit that most of these blacks were born without brains, as we use the term. Most of them are truly beasts of the field. If we pen them—if we tame and sell them —who can say we do wrong?"

"Are these questions rhetorical, Señor Ríos, or would you prefer an argument?"

Ríos studied his arched fingertips, as though he had not heard. "When the Arab trader brought Numi to our compound, he was only a small chieftain from the backlands. I could have sent him to the pens with the others—but it amused me to train him as my house slave for a while. To tame him personally, as it were." The fingers made gentle circles in the air, as though they were molding invisible clay. "When I saw that he possessed a brain of sorts, I risked educating him as well. Later I made him a kind of clerk at the barracks. Later still he was made headman in the compound itself, in charge of the native guards. I've sent him on a dozen hunting trips——"

"Hunting trips, señor?"

"Into the backlands," said Ríos patiently. "We don't always wait for the Arabs to bring us our stock in trade: the Negroes have slavery in their own tribal units and enjoy bartering as much as we. Numi developed a talent for dealing with the chiefs. No one could drive a shrewder bargain than he. No headman has kept better order at Boca de Oro——"

"The Mouth of Gold? An African river?"

"And a poetic name for a slave compound. But a true one. Numi Rey, as you may have gathered, has also been worth his weight in gold. Even without his stud."

"Your pardon, señor?"

"*Your* pardon, Doctor. I'm afraid I've shocked you at last. You mustn't let Numi's size deceive you. In his time he has fathered more than three hundred sons and half as many daughters. Mostly I bred him with middling wenches from the Ivory Coast or the Cameroons. It makes a sturdy, runty stock. The best house slaves in the world, from the time they reach their growth. Top price in Brazil or Mexico. Eventually Mr. Leigh's agents will make them fashionable all over America."

Michael recovered his aplomb. "You're telling me this with a purpose."

"Naturally. Ours is a growing trade—and a fabulous one. We reward our workers well. If an ex-slave at the Boca can retire a rich man, what of the estate doctor who presides there?"

Michael sipped his wine. "Keith seemed proud enough of his earnings——"

"Keith was a valuable man, to a point. I'm convinced that you can surpass him, Dr. Stone."

"Are you offering to make me his successor?"

"The post is yours, as of tonight."

"I'm afraid it doesn't interest me."

"An annual wage of three thousand pounds will be paid your agent, Dr. Holly—to be held in London against your return. A bonus will be paid on each boatload that reaches Florida with less than a dozen dead. If the climate is not to your liking, you may leave us in three years' time."

"Are you making this offer seriously?"

"I'm always serious, Dr. Stone. And I try not to waste words. Believe me, you would find the Boca a surgeon's paradise. Our equipment is of the finest. Both Mr. Leigh and I have respect for the—shall I say, the health of our stock? You would go often with our Arabs into the backlands. It would be a young man's education in every way. When you returned to London, a fortune would await you." Ríos lifted a detaining palm. "Naturally I realize that it's a glittering prospect. You should sleep on it."

"But I've given you my answer!"

"I refuse to accept it. So will Mr. Leigh, I'm confident. So confident that I'll take my leave——"

"Sorry as I am to offend you, señor—or your employer——"

"Mr. Leigh wishes you to sleep on his offer, Doctor. Mr. Leigh is a rich man, accustomed to his own way. In this instance I think we should oblige him."

"And I tell you that I'm a ship's surgeon and a traveler. I've no thought of settling anywhere. Least of all in a——"

"Say it, Doctor. In a slavepen that traffics in human cattle?"

"That will serve for now."

"Of course we differ there. I've already told you that I do not class the black with humanity. At the Boca you'll find him just human enough to—how shall I put it?—burnish your skill. A pleasant rest, Doctor."

He resembles the devil more than ever when he arches his back at me, thought Michael. He was still a bit dazed by the Spaniard's coolness. So dazed, in fact, that he returned Ríos's parting bow without a word.

Once again a door opened noiselessly on its oiled hinges. He had a glimpse of a black silhouette in the hall and knew that the man had remained to watch his door. The houseboy, sleek as a wasp in his satin smallclothes, who emerged from the shadows of the valanced bed with a nightshirt on his stiffly extended arms was only an added precaution.

"Will the master retire?" The Spanish was all but flawless, lacking only the lisp of true Castilian.

"Precisamente."

"Does the master desire a woman for his bed?"

Michael found that he could laugh aloud after all. *"Gracias*—not tonight."

He recalled another night in the Levant—not too far from a grateful sultan's harem—when he had received a similar offer and accepted with an eagerness born of too much wine. A sloe-eyed Turkish houri with fluent, lyre-shaped thighs—or an ebony Juno from the heart of darkness. Twin rewards for services rendered. What was the essential difference to a citizen of the world? He felt his laughter die. Somehow the question seemed indecent on English soil. Almost as though he had surrendered to Adam Leigh in advance.

Composed for sleep at last—and lying virtuously alone in the vast bed—he knew that his personal houseboy had settled on the step-down as naturally as a dog. That, too, was part of this opulent pattern: the guests of this nabob could take such details for granted—whether they slept at Leigh's Florida estates, in his African compound, or in the chill austerity of his country house in Kent.

Heavy-lidded in drowsy contentment (and ignoring, for the time, the threat of the morrow), he drifted between sleep and waking. He knew that he should question that threat closely and plan ways of avoiding it. Instead he found himself thinking of Mr. Chen, a merchant of Canton.

Mr. Chen, who maintained contact with the East India Company from his neat wharfside office on the Pearl, was a friend of years' standing as well as an amateur philosopher. When the Company's business brought him to Canton, Michael had formed the habit of dining at the merchant's: Chen Yui's excellent rice wine had been a perfect prelude to their arguments on the verities. The garden on the Pearl had been a happy rendezvous for a young man without ties; the wisdom the elderly Chinese offered was no less stimulating than his wine—though it came back at odd moments to mock young Dr. Stone when he least expected it.

"You use the word 'wanderlust' to excuse your vagabonding. It is a good English word. But you should let your mind sink deeper in your past—if you would find the true reason for your voyaging."

"Explain my mind to me, Chen Yui. It is a worthy effort for a philosopher."

"You wander the world seeking your father's face. Or should I say, your native land? Until you find it, no shore will hold you for long. You will have adventures, but no true happiness. You will grow wise, after a fashion, but the wisdom will turn bitter in your mind. You will grow old—as a gnarled tree on a windswept headland. Stubbornly, and without grace."

"What is the remedy?"

"You must seek the remedy in your own heart. You must go back to your beginnings and learn why you are alive. No man can be the architect of another's future. But I will give you this much advice. Return for a while to the land of your birth. To America."

"I was born a British subject, Chen Yui. In Halifax. Just after our American colonies won their independence."

"Then your father was an American?"

"A British colonial, who was loyal to his sovereign. He left Boston for Halifax when the Revolution began, to prove his loyalty. There were many so."

"I understand. You say that you have no memories of America. Perhaps they exist in spite of you; perhaps your own father repented his choice. Did you ever feel that?"

"I think not. My father began life in England; he emigrated to Boston to practice medicine. All this is legend, you understand. He wasn't the sort of man who confided in his young: and I was only sixteen when he died."

"Your mother?"

"I can't even remember her."

"So you wander the world, hoping to find them again. The search of a son for his father—for a tie that really binds. For an origin, a reason for being."

"Perhaps I'll find that someday, Chen Yui."

"Perhaps is another good English word that has ruined many lives. To find your destiny you must search; it does not rise up unbidden, like the sun at morning. How old are you, Dr. Stone?"

"I'll be twenty-eight in May."

"You will remember these words when you are forty."

He remembered them tonight—not yet thirty, at his ease in a

strange bed despite the nameless threat just outside his door. A vagabond, with no plans for tomorrow. It was odd that a Chinese should give his life a focus it had always lacked. That Chen Yui should advise him to seek roots in a country neither of them had ever seen.

America. The New World. So far they were mere bright-colored patches in an atlas to Dr. Michael Stone. He had touched the Indies in his voyaging, and the teeming Latin ports of the South; he had once signed as doctor on a Boston-bound packet—and canceled the contract in favor of a quick passage to the Orient. Now, at long last, he determined to take Chen Yui's advice. With cash on hand in London, he would sail for the United States as a gentleman should. Touring its cities (and, perhaps, its more accessible frontiers), he would study this America at his leisure—until he could measure its New World virtues against the old.

Nursing his plan as he dropped into slumber, he bowed to Mr. Chen across the years. The old man's wisdom was worth a trial. Even as he repeated that conviction, he was deep in sleep and rocked in a familiar dream. One of those dreams that is not quite a nightmare, though it hangs on the verge.

He was aboard a great, square-rigged ship, fleeing across the blue ocean plain with a gale on his quarter. At the wheel, driving the vessel into a sunrise without ending, he was alone with the singing cordage and the white hiss of the waves; he was waiting for the sun to lift completely above the horizon, so that his blinded eyes could mark the landfall beyond. . . . But tonight there was a new feature in the dream. The sun had changed to a dark, leering moon that seemed to stare back at him with eyes of its own. When he dared to look more closely, he saw that the moon was really a giant Negro's head—that the baleful iridescence in the eyes was hate incarnate.

V

He wakened to the white light of day. Even before his lids could open, he knew that the slender houseboy was bending above the bed to draw its mulled curtains wide. The dark moon of *that* youthful face, he noted wryly, was masked in deference; the eyes were modestly lowered as Wasp-Waist awaited the master's word.

On the carpet beyond, two other slaves stood at attention beside a huge enameled bath that exhaled a grateful steam, prodigal as a dragon's breath in the frosty morning.

Michael dressed leisurely, soothed by the deep comfort of the bath, the cup of pre-breakfast tea laced with blackstrap rum. It was only when he was settling his stock that he missed his portmanteau and instrument case. Both, he remembered, had stood neatly at the foot of the bed last night—and both had vanished now. The house slave's bland smile was unchanged as Michael turned to question him.

"Perdone, señor?"

"Why have my effects been removed?"

"They are downstairs, *Señor Médico,* with the other baggage. We close the house today——"

"What of King Numi?"

"He is already aboard the *Dos Amigos."*

"The *Dos Amigos?"*

"The supply ship for the Boca, señor."

"I wanted a last look at him——" Astonishment had brought the words to his lips. Obviously it was ridiculous to discuss the state of Numi's operation with a servant. "Where is Señor Ríos?"

"The *comandante* breakfasts in the library, Señor Médico. He requests that you join him."

Michael shrugged into his greatcoat and stamped downstairs Already the well of the great hallway seemed to exhale emptiness, as though Adam Leigh's estate was settling, not too regretfully, into its dust covers. Only the library preserved its air of cheerful warmth. Ríos, taking his ease at table and discussing a broiled kidney with relish, seemed oblivious of his visiting surgeon's glare.

"Do sit down, Doctor. You'll take tea, not coffee?"

"Where are my things, Ríos?"

"Tea for the doctor, Jaime," said the Spaniard to the hovering major-domo. "After all, we're still on British soil."

"Why have you taken my things?"

"You will find your portmanteau in the lodge, Doctor. And your surgical case. As you must have observed, we're leaving this morning. Sailing with the tide. in fact. I feared they might be overlooked."

"And Numi?"

"Numi Rey? He's resting, quite comfortably, aboard the supply ship. Dr. Keith saw to that early this morning. Before he drove back to London with Mr. Leigh."

"You should have wakened me."

"Granted. But we all felt you'd earned your rest."

Michael strode to the windows that overlooked the park and fought for calm. The threat of this bizarre establishment was real now; he could feel it in the black butler's eye—in Ríos's contained silence. Yet it would be fatal to rage against the Spaniard's politeness. If I'm really his prisoner, thought Michael, I must cover that knowledge carefully. I must continue to pretend that this is an ordinary English breakfast in an ordinary manor house.

He stared hard at the deer park. Snow had fallen in the night; the boles of the yews looked lonely as a dry-point etching against the sky. His eye followed the lines of footprints that dropped down the slope to the south. The Channel, he noted, was much nearer than he had suspected: the estuary that led to open water seemed to lap the walls of the house itself. The tall, square-rigged ship riding at anchor in that blue patch of harbor seemed moored to the land. The fact that such a vessel could anchor in Adam Leigh's park seemed only natural by daylight.

"The harbor is part of the estate, as you'll observe," said Ríos. "The barony once owned the wharves and most of the town. We've kept the former and turned the village into a storage depot. Most of Mr. Leigh's flotilla put in here. We've found it simpler to provision them on the spot. London chandlers, as you know, are a race of robbers."

Michael had already settled at the breakfast table, to accept a dish of tea from the major-domo's salver. Your cue is silence, he warned himself. Let the Spaniard talk on, and weigh your chances. He forced himself to look direct at Adam Leigh's factor. In that hard white light Ríos resembled a death's-head with a strangely mobile grin.

"Mr. Leigh wished me to offer his compliments on a brilliant bit of surgery. I am also to repeat last night's offer, in the confident hope you'll accept."

"May I see Mr. Leigh before you sail?"

"I told you he'd returned to London."

"I must examine Numi, at least."

"You'll have every opportunity for that examination, Dr. Stone."

The moment was not conducive to appetite, but Michael forced himself to butter a scone and drink deep of his tea. The grateful warmth lifted his spirits somewhat. Perhaps I'm imagining this threat, he told himself. Yet he was positive that the Negro, who hovered so deferentially at his elbow, would pinion him instantly if he strove to gain the hall again.

"The ship has begun to make sail."

Ríos nodded affably. "We can hardly miss the tide. I hoped you would sail with us, Doctor. So did Mr. Leigh."

"I'm afraid my mind is unchanged on that offer."

Ríos tossed a letter across the table. Michael kept his eyes blank as he recognized Dr. Felix Holly's scrawl.

"Mr. Leigh's coach brought this down from London. As you'll observe, the business is settled—so far as your agent there is concerned."

Michael scanned the letter. Dr. Holly, he gathered, was serene to the point of cynicism as he considered his protégé's great opportunity. Few young men, he indicated, had been blessed with such a chance as this. Only a young man with a donkey's brain would dream of refusing.

"I might add a pious footnote, if only for the sake of Propriety. Like all forward-looking men, I abhor slavery in all its forms. Mr. Adam Leigh is well aware of my views. And yet, as his doctor, you would be saving life: it would be in your power to make the lot of these black devils more tolerable. Mr. Leigh has assured me that he would spare no expense to implement your reforms. . . ."

The tone, Michael saw, was quite genuine: it was painfully evident that Leigh had outlined his offer in detail—and given old Holly to understand that Michael had accepted on the spot. His eyes darted again to the letter:

". . . so it's *ave atque vale* once again, my boy. It will be difficult for me to imagine you stationary for three years' time. But you have made a wise choice, so far as your future is concerned. Mr.

Leigh's down payment (which I have already acknowledged) will discharge the last of your London debts. The payments to come will buy you a practice anywhere in the world. . . ."

He dropped the letter on the cloth and drained his cup. Even now he was proud of the steadiness of his hand, though it took forcing to keep his voice even.

"Mr. Leigh, I gather, is accustomed to seeing his wishes fulfilled instantly."

"It's a habit of Croesus, Doctor."

"Do I understand that he's made a down payment for my services—*before* I accepted his offer?"

"What could be more logical, since he takes acceptance for granted?" Ríos touched the letter with a fingertip: for the first time Michael measured the strength in the Spaniard's bony hands. "So does your estimable foster father. Don't think he'll let the commission on nine thousand pounds slip through his fingers."

So Holly had disposed of his services as casually as that. Michael weighed the fact for a moment and wondered why he was not more deeply shocked. A strange lassitude had fallen on his spirit as he read the letter. Holly's betrayal (for a fee) was merely the final touch of gray. Gray was just the word, he added; a thin mist between me and the world. . . . He shook off the fancy as he rose. This was England: he was a free agent. He whirled on the black major-domo, daring him to intervene—and laughed aloud as the man fell back, with his deference intact.

"May I wish you good morning, Señor Ríos?"

"It's a long walk to London, Doctor."

"There's a post station just beyond your gate. I'll take the stage there, if you insist."

"Don't be a fool. Come with us."

"Good morning once again!"

"Try it, if you insist," said the Spaniard. "You'll never reach the door."

Michael sent his chair spinning and lunged across the carpet. Already his weaving legs told him that Ríos was quite right. The hall doorway, turning in slow, insolent circles, was a red wilderness away. Through the growing haze he heard the voice purr on:

"As you see, we took no chances. Good doctors are hard to come by in Africa. Yes, you're correct if you assume your tea was drugged. . . . Don't be alarmed, Doctor. Merely a strong sedative. Quite tasteless. No aftereffects. We've used it a thousand times at the Boca——"

There was more, but the words had blurred. He reached the doorframe on hands and knees just as the light changed from red to whirling black. Perhaps he could gain the hall if he drew himself erect on the lintel. But he knew the effort was useless just before he pitched forward into the major-domo's arms. Darkness, empty and soothing and never-ending, rushed up to claim him.

VI

His bed had been rocking for a long time. He turned to his other side and burrowed resentfully in his pillows; it was only his dizzy head that deceived him. And then, without transition, his whole being was staring wide-awake. His head, he discovered, was actually clear as a bell. Yet the bed continued its queasy pitching in rhythm with the lantern suspended from the whitewashed beam above.

He watched a white cloud whirl past the window in the far wall, saw it congeal and star the glass with diamond points of moisture. The window was round and clamped down with brass screws. Michael sat bolt upright, shaking off the last dregs of sleep. This was a ship's cabin. The white cloud of spray feathered the glass of the porthole once again, and he added a second fact to his painful orientation. The ship was at sea and riding out a spell of heavy weather. With that point settled, it seemed only natural to lapse into drowsiness again. A heavy, normal sleep that had nothing to do with drugs or a Spaniard's death's-head grin.

When he wakened in earnest he felt himself part of this world. A bit weak (as a man would normally be after a long fast) but more than ready for impending battle. His head swam a little as he dropped his feet over the side of the spacious bunk—that, too, was part of the vertigo that comes with extreme hunger.

With no surprise he noted that he was wearing his own nightshirt, that his portmanteau and surgical case had been lashed down beneath the bunk. The cabin itself was a generous square—deep-carpeted, and fitted with a table desk and a sea shelf filled with books. There was a medicine cupboard; beside it stood an armoire filled with suits of white drill. He was still fingering the fabric cautiously when the cabin door swung wide.

The man behind the dinner tray was squat-brown with the eyes of a friendly animal. At first glance he resembled a not too grotesque chimpanzee. The voice went with the image, a husky basso profundo that seemed about to end in a growl and yet was oddly gentle. Michael had seen few uglier men in his time—and few he was more disposed to trust at first glance.

"Tola, *jefe*. Servant——"

The words came out haltingly, a grotesque attempt at English. Michael smiled and replied in quick Spanish.

"What have you brought me besides tea?"

The saddle-brown face opened in a sudden grin. Clearly, Tola had not expected such instant communication. He placed the tray on the table desk, lifting the silver bell covers with a flourish.

"Eggs in cream, Doctor. *Arroz con pollo*——"

Sleet had begun to frost the glass of the port, but it was snug in the cabin. Michael let himself revel in the food; sustenance, for the moment, seemed more important than thought. He submitted gratefully to the luxury of being shaved and wondered if Ríos's drugs had dulled his brain. For the present it was enough to be at sea again, with the prospect of a fight ahead. He'd relish it, even if it was lost in advance.

"Would you answer if I ask where I am?"

"But certainly, jefe. This is the *Dos Amigos*. Bound for Boca de Oro. Two days out of England——"

So he had slept the clock around twice. Ríos was right: the drug had been powerful.

"I referred to this cabin, Tola."

"This is the doctor's cabin." The other's stare betrayed his surprise. "You are the doctor, *verdad?*"

m the doctor."

"All of Mr. Leigh's ships carry a doctor. Even a brig like ours that brings supplies."

Tola's aplomb was perfect. To judge by his tone, the *Dos Amigos* might have been a merchantman on a routine voyage. The Boca (and it was hard to think of that slave camp as a prison now) seemed as respectable as London on Tola's lips.

"So I'm already in my quarters." The words had emerged naturally: he could hardly pretend he felt as resigned as he sounded.

"The clothes are for your use, Doctor, when we reach the Boca."

Michael sipped the last of his tea, letting the picture build in that grateful aroma. A prodigal spread of palms, the fronds whispering in the river breeze. Himself, in a broad-brimmed hat and baggy cotton, counting an endless file of dark bodies that shuffled past in the dust. . . .

"You will have your own house in the compound, jefe. I am your personal servant, as you see. You will have Dr. Ledoux to assist you; you will have also, in the medicine stores, a Dr. Fulton from Philadelphia." Tola had offered these facts with a flourish. Now he subsided under Michael's scowl.

"So I'm to have a staff. I didn't expect that."

He hardly wondered why he was considering his future with a servant. Already he had a feeling that Tola was his friend, though he could not have said why.

"Did you also serve Dr. Keith?"

"To the best of my ability. It will be an honor to serve you as well."

The friendly eyes had lost none of their candor, but there was no mistaking the spark that glowed in their depths. Without words Tola offered his loyalty; without verbal warning he had told Michael that the wise servant at Boca de Oro walked warily.

"I am honored as well." You could say these things in Spanish—and let the overtones make their own point. Tola bowed deep in the same ritualistic manner.

"What are the doctor's first orders?"

"I must see Adam Leigh at once."

"Adam Leigh is in England, jefe. Ríos is comandante now."

"Ríos must do, then."

"He works in the chartroom, Doctor. If the doctor will follow me——" Alert brown hands folded Michael's greatcoat about his shoulders; gnarled legs scurried to open the cabin door for the Boca's new doctor.

Reality roared about his ears again with the icy winter gale when they stepped into the companionway. His cabin, as he had surmised, opened directly to the poop deck; he stepped into the buffet of the wind with a sharp relief. A glance told him that the *Dos Amigos* was a snug, well-found ship, an English square-rigger, despite the anachronism of the Spanish flag that whipped at the forepeak. The watch that swarmed to the crosstrees to shorten sail were as British as the *Dos Amigos's* holystoned decks, her gleaming brass. Adam Leigh and his lieutenants might blackbird with the worst in the trade. There was no feeling of bondage on this clean deck as the brig fled before the storm.

Michael paused at the weather rail and let the wind sweep the last cobweb from his brain. The ship seemed alone in that smoking immensity of gale-lashed sea, threatened constantly by the graybeards that seemed about to overwhelm her. Yet he had no sense of loneliness or of fear: he could turn his back on those following combers, secure in the knowledge that the *Dos Amigos* would ride them out. This was his world; it was good to come home again, even as a prisoner of sorts.

A prisoner, he told himself, should feel his shackles and strain against the iron. But that, too, was a threat without meaning in this wind-drunk moment. Facing down the stair that led to the waist, he leaned with the gale—rejoicing that his sea legs assured perfect balance. Turning the corner of the deckhouse that nested between the mizzen and the mainmast, he spread both arms wide and leaned on the wind in earnest, like a gull that has found his element.

They crashed in a head-on collision that rocked him on his heels and all but sent the girl sprawling. He steadied her with an instinctive arm, while his free hand groped for support along the rail. He was blinded by tumbled dark hair; the tall, lithe body that swayed in his arms did not shrink from his embrace. For an instant they stood thus, while a following sea (bearded like Neptune and gray as death itself) clamored at the scuppers. The girl drew back as the ship righted, though she still lingered in the curve of his arms. He breathed deep of her nearness; her perfume teased his senses, even in the sea-washed air. Wide hazel eyes met his and held them. Her eyes stared deep, as no woman had dared to stare before.

"Perdone, señora——"

"The fault was mine, Dr. Stone."

She left him on that, before he could quite find his breath. He stood dumbly, watching her vanish into a bath of warm blond light that filled the deckhouse. A maid, severe in a white coif, had already come forward to close the door.

Tola's hand steadied him at an elbow as he took a step forward to plumb this enigma.

"It is the Lady Marian, Doctor."

"And who is Lady Marian?"

"The daughter-in-law of Adam Leigh. She takes this voyage for her health's sake."

His fist (it was already clenched to hammer the deckhouse door) dropped to his side; he walked slowly forward, out of the shelter of the wind. In the lee of the main deckhouse he paused to let his thoughts overtake his racing pulse—and fought to shake off the familiar whiplash of that perfume, the feel of a body that had molded to his own as naturally as Eve's first teasing promise. Lady Marian Leigh. He spoke the name to the rushing wind and waited for Tola to complete the picture. But Tola had already darted ahead to point the way to the chartroom.

Michael walked into the Spaniard's presence with his fist still clenched. He had remembered his anger just in time. He must establish it now, he knew—even if the worst of that rage had been dissolved in a more potent alembic.

The chartroom of the *Dos Amigos* was a snug compartment, complete with baize table and a hundred pigeonholes crammed with neatly tied papers and ledgers. At first glance it seemed more an office than a navigator's workroom at sea. Ríos, elbow-deep in work at the table, completed the picture. The horn-rimmed spectacles on that bony forehead belonged to a countinghouse ashore; so did the ink-stained fingers, the febrile concentration on the column of figures growing under the pen. But the Spaniard's manner was completely casual as he glanced up from his task. No welcome could have been more sincere than the smile he offered.

"Inventories can be tedious things, Dr. Stone. I'm glad you intruded on this one."

"Haven't you some apology to offer?"

"Only my felicitations—now that you decided to sail with us after all."

Michael pounded the table with a fist, if only for the sake of form. "You'll suffer for this kidnaping, and you know it."

"Kidnaping, Doctor? You've a contract to function as the chief doctor at Mr. Leigh's compound in Africa. Three years, with payment in advance to your London agent, Dr. Felix Holly. I have the paper here."

Michael glared at the square of foolscap the Spaniard offered. "It's a contract, right enough. I find no signature."

"You'll sign, Doctor, when your anger has cooled a bit. I promised Mr. Leigh that much the day we left England."

"I'm here against my will. I'll sign no contract in the service of a slaver. If you insist on making me your prisoner——"

"Do you give me any choice?"

"Very well, Ríos. Kidnap me to Africa and lock me in your compound. As a doctor, I'll mend your sick slaves when I'm able. I'll promise that much freely. Just as I'll promise to escape you at the first opportunity."

"I'd prefer your signature."

"Your servant once again. But there are some things Adam Leigh can't buy."

"Whether you'll admit it or not, we've bought your skill and paid well for it. Will you examine your patients now, in the sick bay?"

"Of course."

"We'll argue your contract afterward—and its legal aspects. After all, you'll have weeks to change your mind."

Michael found that he was calm at last. Calmer than he had hoped to be in this cold spider's presence. "Will you lead me to my patients?"

"With pleasure."

They retraced the route that Michael had just followed from

the poop deck, with Tola dogging their heels. At the door of the deckhouse amidships Michael found that the desire to smash the panel had vanished completely. In that bitter moment he could believe that he had imagined Lady Marian—despite an unmistakable stirring behind the lattice.

The sick bay was a whitewashed cubicle with two tiers of bunks. Numi slept in one, his tiny body sprawled in pleasant abandon. Michael saw instantly that the danger point of the operation was behind them. The blood channels around the aneurysm had begun to function long ago. Testing the skin tone down the length of the pygmy's leg, he found no hint of the telltale coolness that advertised impairment of the circulation. The sac itself had disappeared completely. Numi Rey would be walking before the ship was in the trades.

The only other patient was a seaman still hazy from morphia, his forearm prisoned in a neatly knotted splint.

"One of our apprentices," said Ríos. "A simple fracture of the humerus. I set it myself, as you'll observe."

Michael, checking splint and bandage, nodded a candid approval. "You need no doctor aboard."

"I beg to differ. Until we fetch our first landfall, I'll be busy with my ledgers. We're loaded deep, Doctor: when one works for a Scotsman, one accounts for every penny. Not that I expect any real test of your skill while we're at sea. We've a healthy crew, and the ship is ratproofed."

"Would you repeat that?"

"Surely you've noted the reek of chloride in the companionways? It's far stronger under hatches——"

Michael stared at Ríos with a new respect. Inhuman or not, the man was on his mark. The notion that rats might spread disease was part of the wisdom of the Orient: he remembered the stench from the smudge pots, and how it had swept up the harbor at Canton, when Chen Yui's junks (prudently anchored in midstream) had been cleansed of their last rodent before a voyage. Most British shipowners, as Michael knew to his sorrow, considered such precautions a waste of sailing time. The thought that cleanliness was the enemy of death—or that rats and the plague might hunt together—had been dismissed as arrant nonsense. Yet here was the

Spanish agent of a blackbirder who subscribed to the selfsame gospel.

Perhaps there was a level where his mind and the Spaniard's might meet; perhaps his very trade might be a giant laboratory where he could perfect his skill. Michael held the thought at arm's length, distrusting its glibness. Staring down at the sleeping pygmy, he reminded himself that he had saved that life for just one purpose—that Numi Rey might continue to father pint-sized servants for the auction block.

The picture was an unhappy one. Perhaps such thoughts were ahead of his century. Slavery, for the masses, was an ancient institution. The business of a doctor was to save life, not to pass judgment on its excesses. Ríos had offered his hand. As a collaborator, Ríos would probably be honest enough, so long as their interests coincided.

But his mind rejected that sophistry, even as it shaped a tentative routine for working with his captor.

"My compliments, señor. May I congratulate you on a healthy ship?"

"The ratproofing? That is nothing. We have a fortune in trade goods aboard, besides a year's provision for the Boca itself. Naturally I prefer to sail with clean holds."

"What of the slave ships?"

"We've a nice problem there, one which I hope you'll illumine later. Most of our cargoes are transported in the natural state, if I may use the term. Hosed down, of course, and healthy: the Arabs know better than to bring us short weight or yaws. If sickness develops in the pens, the sickly are weeded out."

Ríos paused, his mind deep in a picture that Michael found himself sharing well enough. "Still, our Negroes must be shipped out wild, as it were. And wild animals must be confined, lest they become rabid. How close that confinement should be—how tightly the cargoes may be packed—is a subject on which slavers differ. I'm eager for your advice. To be frank, we've no greater problem than loss of life at sea."

"Will I be required to accompany your slavers to America?"

"If the compound runs smoothly, and you consider your assistants worth their salt. Your findings would be invaluable."

Once again Michael drew back sharply, killing that show of interest on the threshold of his mind. "Suppose I refuse to make these crossings?"

"But you won't, Dr. Stone. You'll sign that contract long before we fetch the Boca. We're going to get on famously."

"I've told you I'd never sign!"

"May we discuss this further in your cabin?"

The doctor's quarters, Michael found, were only a bulkhead's remove from the sick bay. He let his anger carry him in without a backward glance and sat down on the bunk, hoping he did not resemble a petulant schoolboy about to be punished by a master. Ríos came into the cabin with his silky calm intact. Without glancing up Michael knew that Tola had stopped on the threshold and closed the door.

"I'll hear your reasons, Dr. Stone."

"You've heard them. I don't submit to coercion. I choose my own work and my own employers. They don't include petty kings like your Mr. Leigh."

"If I were you, I would not dismiss Leigh so glibly."

"How else would you describe him?"

"Very well. Let us dub him a king, in a small way. In his own right. I can assure you that he's carved out a true kingdom in the Floridas."

"I don't dispute that. I've simply no wish to become a subject."

"Most of us are subjects of some king."

"Not in America."

"But you are an Englishman."

"A world citizen, if you don't mind."

"A romantic, Doctor. Democracy is still an ideal—like the Christian faith we both profess. Don't believe for a moment that it exists in that infant republic in America. Already the United States harbors its own small kings in its cotton states——" The Spaniard opened his hands eloquently, a gesture of chaos in the making. "There will be more in time. They will war among themselves—and clamor for a wiser king to unite them. But that is a concern beyond our lifetimes. For the present, Adam Leigh has made me a rich man. He will do as much for you——"

"Haven't you used that argument?"

"It bears repeating."

"Then I, too, shall repeat. I'm aboard your ship because I couldn't help myself. I'll escape you at the first convenient moment——"

"So I must keep you under guard?"

"Is that necessary at sea?"

"Hardly. At this moment the Portuguese coast is some fifty leagues off our weather bow. I don't think you'd try to swim ashore, Doctor." The Spaniard glanced at the frost-rimed port-hole. "Still, I must remind you that I'm captain of this vessel—and captain-general at the Boca——"

"You aren't captain of my soul, Ríos."

"Your soul, Doctor, has nothing to do with your usefulness. I merely wish to make sure that you're available as needed. In the meantime I must establish my authority. You won't sign your contract?"

"For the last time——"

"For the last time, then." Ríos got up briskly. "I'm behind in my bookkeeping, so I'll take my leave. You'll be confined to these quarters until you change your mind. At the Boca you'll be locked in your house with your servant and exercised under guard——"

"Like any back-country prince who refuses to be your slave?"

"The comparison is perfect. All I ask is your name on this bit of stamped paper. As a man of honor, I'm sure you'll live up to your signature."

"As a man of honor, may I wish you good morning?"

"So be it. Go with God, Doctor."

"Go with God."

But the Spaniard paused with a hand on the cabin door. This time, for some reason, he did not meet Michael's eye.

"Lady Marian will be disappointed. I've all but promised her your company at dinner."

"You'll convey my regrets?"

Ríos arched his brows, but his eyes were still fixed on the carpet. He was sure of himself a moment ago, thought Michael. Now, as he speaks of this woman, he has turned into a lackey. "My officers and I are poor company for her. It will be a long voyage, Doctor—and the lady is lovely."

"Surely her husband will console her."

Ríos seemed shocked for the first time. "Sir Forrest Leigh? Did you think *he* was aboard?"

"Isn't it customary?"

"Sir Forrest is in England, recovering from his wounds. Surely you knew that he was knighted after Waterloo?"

"My apologies. As a citizen of the world, I don't read the lists."

"Sir Forrest insisted that his lady take this voyage to recruit her strength. He hopes to join her later, when his own health permits."

"Why do you tell me this?"

"I'd hoped that your gallantry might outweigh your stubbornness, Dr. Stone."

The Spaniard's pale, hot eyes lifted at last. But Michael found it easy to stare the man down. "Convey my regrets once again. Tell Lady Marian that the skipper of the *Dos Amigos* is a soulless martinet. Tell her that thanks to him I'm pining in my cabin for another glimpse——"

The door clicked shut. Michael did not stir as he heard the bolt shoot home. For a long time he sat motionless on the bunk watching the sea gnaw at the porthole with a gray tongue. At least he had dismissed Ríos with the final word. Ríos would never know how hard that dismissal had been.

VII

"Il faut cultiver votre jardin."

He closed the volume, letting it rest for a moment on his knee as he blew out the candle. Through the porthole (it was open now, in the hope that a breeze would be stirring by dawn) he could see the prodigal wash of moonlight on the oily ocean's face. A thick golden arrow of moonlight, pointing to the heart of Africa. There was no shadow of land on the horizon, but he could all but sense its presence in the hot, spicy darkness.

Tola had said they would sight the Palos Verdes tomorrow, given a following wind. When that headland was noted on the chart, a few days' sailing should bring them to the bar that masked the Boca de Oro. He weighed that inevitable fact of geography as he breathed the heady invitation of the night. It was good to know that he had clung to his purpose during these weary weeks at sea.

that Adam Leigh's contract still lay on the chartroom table, unsigned. The thought brought scant comfort tonight. He had lived too long with his virtue to enjoy it now.

"Il faut cultiver votre jardin."

His fingers stroked the calf-bound book on his knee, though he could not read the print in that moon-dappled darkness. He had read *Candide* often this past month. Often enough to know that final page by heart. Voltaire was right, of course; his formula offered man the only lasting solution. Unless he had a garden to cultivate (with mind and hands and heart), unless he had an accomplishment in which he could take pride, man was lost indeed. The trick merely lay in finding one's garden before it was too late.

He had been fortunate there—and he admitted as much in this half-restless, half-resigned moment. Even during these weeks of semi-prison he had not let the hours drag. Books and more books from the well-stocked shelves. Lessons in Bantu from Numi Rey—with Tola to supplement the pygmy's birdlike chatter. Ríos had come often to his cabin to check the medical inventories, to sketch the extent of his duties at the Boca. Twice they had gone under hatches to examine the bales of foodstuffs that would be unloaded at their destination. He had visited the sick bay often—to dose the inevitable fever cases, to lance a felon, to stitch a knife wound that was the inevitable aftermath of a fo'c'sle quarrel.

Throughout the voyage his admiration for Ríos's mind had grown apace, though it was hardly matched by his feelings for Ríos as a man. His own captain aboard the *Dos Amigos*, as well as his own chief clerk, Ríos had run his ship by the book. His chartroom office already hummed with plans for the future. The Spaniard managed the African compound on a commission basis. Accounts, kept in the ledgers on both sides of the Atlantic, were balanced at the end of each voyage, and Ríos received his percentage on each healthy black delivered to the Florida pens. Michael had opened his eyes wide when the Spaniard had traced last year's total with a crisp quill:

"Leigh's Florida plantation must be larger than the moon."

"Punta Blanca? It's a Spanish land grant some twenty miles south of Fernandina. Hardly more than seven hundred acres overall. Much of that is salt marsh unfit for agriculture."

"Yet you delivered over five thousand slaves on his doorstep in 1815."

"Only because Mr. Leigh is a dealer first and then a planter."

"A dealer in the Floridas? But most of that peninsula is a howling wilderness, if I may believe the books."

"True enough. But the United States of America lies only a day's march to the north."

Michael had shrugged off the Spaniard's intimation that blackbirding was the most natural business of mankind and the young American republic a boundless market. He had learned by now that it was useless to argue with Ríos—or to question his ruthless code. After five weeks at sea he had learned a great deal about the captain of the *Dos Amigos* (and every soul aboard) simply by listening with genuine interest—and dropping a few questions at the proper time.

Tola, of course, had been his chief source of information, though Numi, surprisingly enough, was a close second. He had learned from the latter, for example, that Ríos was really the son of a Moorish lady who had mated with a renegade don at the court of the Sultan of Algiers. That Ríos's whole life (and it was uncanny how the small African's mind had probed his former master's weakness) was dedicated to amassing a fortune, that he might repossess his grandfather's bankrupt estates in Estremadura. Ríos had begun his career as a clerk in Leigh's warehouse. Now that he was rich, he was determined to purchase a grandee's title.

"It is something no man can buy," said Numi Rey. "One does not explain such matters to the *comandante*."

Michael smiled tonight as he recalled the pygmy's disdain. Naked as a diminutive Adam, his nostrils flared in their disks of bone, Numi had sat cross-legged on the carpet in the doctor's cabin. He had offered the aristocrat's age-old rebuke to the parvenu with an urbane smile.

"And what will you do with your riches, Numi, and your freedom?"

"You are wise to tie the words, Doctor. Without riches, freedom has no meaning."

"Will you settle in Estremadura with your *comandante?*"

"Ríos has seen too many dark faces. When he returns to Spain, he'll want no reminders of his past. . . . I shall visit America, now that the white worlds are at peace. Philadelphia, perhaps—the city of love." The pygmy's English was all but flawless, when he chose to use it. "The freedom of the United States might be worth sampling."

"They'll make you wear clothes and give up your title."

"One pays a price for everything, Doctor. Even for freedom."

Tola was more cynical in his appraisal of the fledgling Union. "They'll rob him of his fortune and put him in a circus tent. He should continue to plow the wenches at the Boca. Or buy his way back to his own people——"

"Speak for yourself, Tola. Why are you working for slavers?"

But the story of Bartola Segovia was even simpler. Tola was a Balearic Spaniard from Minorca. The Minorcans, Michael gathered, had emigrated to eastern Florida shortly before the British returned the colony to Spain. A resident of the ancient walled bastion of St. Augustine, Tola had begun his career as a fisherman and ascended rapidly to a post of minor importance in the smuggling trade. Unfortunately, the coastal schooner on which Tola had served as pilot had run afoul of one of Adam Leigh's own ships. From that moment the Minorcan had changed masters, not too unhappily.

"Leigh should pay you, at least——"

"After seven years in the trade I am happy to be alive."

Tola had not made the statement humbly; he merely offered it as a verity no sane man would dispute. Michael had seen his servant clear in that moment of resignation. Illiterate, patient, honest with the brown wisdom of earth, Tola was content—or seemed so. Brought to America as a bound boy, his life had not been too different from the slaves in Adam Leigh's own fields.

"Wouldn't you escape this if you could?"

"Where could I go?"

"Why not to America?"

"As a Spanish citizen, they would only return me to Augustine."

"Tell me this: when Ríos said you were to care for me, were you pleased?"

"Of course, Señor Mike. I have always served the chief doctor at the Boca."

"Suppose I should leave the Boca? Would you come too?"

"If you needed me."

"I think you mean that."

"I have never said a thing I do not mean."

Again Tola had not spoken humbly. It was a dedication, offered with no cringing—and no heroics. I'm yours, the steady voice insisted. Give me my orders, and I'll see them through.

Even as he made that discovery, Michael wondered if Ríos had anticipated a change in allegiance on Tola's part. Surely the Spaniard was shrewd enough to realize that Tola would react instantly to a kind word, a genuine interest in his welfare. By the same token, Michael guessed that Ríos had discounted the risk in advance. When a man is an absolute tyrant in his own corner, he is apt to take subjection as his due. . . .

Brooding on these imponderables, he flung *Candide* across the cabin and fell to pacing his carpet. Twenty times to the bulkhead and back by way of the porthole and the moon-silvered sea. Usually he managed to avoid this imitation of a caged tomcat "Confined to quarters," as Ríos interpreted the phrase, had not been too confining. There had been daily exercise on the poop deck. The visits of Tola and Numi had done much to cancel out the tedium of wondering (not too wildly) if he could manage the tasks that awaited him, or of cursing the moral stubbornness that had been this wall between himself and the woman in the deckhouse amidships.

He had glimpsed Lady Marian just twice since their encounter outside her cabin door. Once she had been wrapped to the eyes in fur, pacing the deck in a sleet storm, with her maid a shivering shadow behind her. Again (it had been only a week ago, in a heat-drugged noon) she had sunned her hair brazenly on the roof of the deckhouse, while the same maid combed out the dark tresses. She had held her Irish beauty before her on both occasions —not as a shield, he added hastily, but rather as a blazon for all men to admire. She could even toss a smile at the Boca's new doctor as he paced out his own lonely constitutional on the deck above.

Yes, he knew now that she was Irish, the daughter of a county lord who had come to London and married well. He knew that she had been Lady Forrest Leigh for just three years, dividing her time between London and her father-in-law's estate in Kent, while her husband earned laurels on the Continent as a staff officer with the duke himself. It was a believable pattern for a back-country lady with looks of that caliber. It hardly explained her presence aboard the *Dos Amigos*.

Tola had reported that Sir Forrest had made a slow recovery from his wounds. Still in England, he was taking the waters in the hope of an early reunion with his wife in the more salubrious air of the Floridas. Lady Marian, it seemed, was pining for her first glimpse of the plantations her husband would one day inherit; she had sailed at this time (and taken the long southern route) to improve her own health, weakened by months of intensive nursing.

So much for hearsay: the living reality did not blend with that pious picture. The tall, confident girl who could pace a deck in a driving sleet storm was no invalid in search of southern airs. The hot hazel eyes that had dared him across that same deck had never wept for a distant spouse. Or so Michael reasoned as he took one more turn of his carpet and shouted at the discreet tap on his door:

"Adentro!"

He had expected Tola and another lesson in Bantu. Instead it was the slave they called Mozo, a brown colossus who always reminded Michael of Aladdin's djinn. Mozo lived up to the comparison tonight as he waited politely to be noticed, his great arms folded, his chest belled like a pouter pigeon in Brobdingnag. As always, Michael hesitated to speak—as though the wrong word might shrink the Negro to a plume of smoke and banish him to the tarnished lamp that swung above their heads. Mozo was Ríos's special handy man. It seem incredible that this dark silhouette had come to fetch him for a routine bit of surgery.

"The doctor is wanted forward."

"Whose head is broken this time?"

"It is the Lady Marian. She asks to see you in the deckhouse."

Michael paused with one hand on his surgical case. But Mozo had not vanished when he looked again. Bowing from the waist, he had merely stood aside to let the doctor pass.

They crossed the deck in silence and took the stair to the ship's waist. The full moon seemed to drench the idle sails. Michael walked quickly through that quicksilver bath, holding his unanswered question at arm's length. Here, even more unreal by moonlight, was the latticed door where he had paused long ago; here was the same coifed maid, opening demurely to Mozo's knock. Michael entered as casually as he could, conscious of a dozen half-opened trunks that spilled their finery on a thick carpet, of a shimmer of candlelight on a bed that seemed, at first glance, to fill most of the cabin. The door shut behind him. He heard the slap of bare soles on the deck outside and knew that Mozo had gone forward, leaving him unguarded for once.

The girl lay in a froth of lace; she seemed asleep, her hair spread in a dark halo. Michael sat down quietly at her bedside and noted that she was beautiful as well as desirable. A thoroughbred beauty that went far beyond the classic purity of features, the petal texture of cheek and throat. For a moment he sat without stirring and enjoyed her beauty without shame. He could not yet believe that he had stepped so easily from his prisoned world to this.

Lady Marian Leigh spoke without quite opening her eyes. "It was good of you to come so soon, Dr. Stone."

"What seems to be the trouble?" He found he could manage the banal question easily enough. Already he had sensed a subterfuge in her husky greeting.

"A palpitation of the heart," she murmured, with her eyes still modestly veiled. "Would you care to examine me, and prescribe a remedy?"

His hand found her wrist, ambushed in the foaming lace of her gown. Testing the pulse, he was not surprised to find the skin burning under his careful fingers: in his mind's eye he had already diagnosed the cause of Lady Marian's facile fever. Now he merely beckoned to the maid to bring the candle sconce closer. He finished the routine check with the light full upon the nest of pillows—turning back the girl's eyelid, depressing the tongue to search for a nonexistent swelling of the throat. Lady Marian submitted without a tremor. When he reached into his case for the stethoscope, she stirred faintly and opened her eyes wide for the first time.

"You are quite thorough, Dr. Stone. What is that strange instrument?"

"A device for testing the heartbeat. Your pulse seems quite normal. Now I will investigate the—shall we say, source of palpitation?"

She made no protest as he folded back her gown, to expose the warm valley between her breasts. His fingers were firm on those proud hills of flesh, testing the skin tone once again before he applied the stethoscope.

"The palpitations, as you call them, are quite pronounced—and quite normal."

"Normal or not, I'd like a remedy."

Sure of her now, he did not drop his guard. "In cases like these the remedy is simple. The patient has only to follow orders to the letter."

"You may leave us, Soledad."

Michael, with the cone of the stethoscope hard against the girl's left breast, did not lift his eyes; somehow he had not expected her to be so abrupt with the maid. Neither of them stirred as the slender black padded across the cabin with the candle sconce. He heard her set the light on its pedestal; he heard the door whisper shut—and kept his mask intact. Lady Marian's lashes had fluttered down again, though he knew that she was watching him intently from behind their dark screen.

He removed the stethoscope at last and waited for her to speak. In that instant he felt the ship stir down her whole length and knew that a breeze had come at last. The floor canted gently as the *Dos Amigos* gained way. He heard the shouted commands overhead, the creak of gear as the watch spread the last stitch of canvas. Somehow it was all part of a universe miles removed from this fragrant cave. His only reality was this dark-haired girl and the challenge she had offered. A challenge no less definite because its impact was muted, so far, in lace and innuendo.

"So you feel that my troubles are quite normal, Doctor?"

"What is it? Loneliness, curiosity—or both?"

She considered the question gravely, with her eyes still veiled. "Does that imply that there's nothing wrong with me?"

"You might answer my question."

"Answer mine first."

"There is nothing wrong with you, Lady Marian. Or should I say nothing that a little frankness won't cure?"

"When did you reach that diagnosis?"

"When Aladdin's djinn rapped on my cabin door."

"Should I call you impertinent?"

"Honest is a better epithet."

Lady Marian yielded the point with a small, withdrawn smile. "Very well. Let us say I'm curious about you. Let's go further and say that I should have thought of this ruse long ago."

"Did you say ruse?"

"A ruse to bring us together naturally. Yes, Doctor, you'll find that I can be honest too."

She opened her eyes wide as she spoke and looked up at him with complete confidence. There was no withdrawal in that look, no false modesty. No woman on earth, he insisted, had the right to stare into a man's eyes so deeply.

"Tell me about yourself, Doctor."

"Surely you have my biography from Ríos?"

"Ríos has supplied the essentials. I want more than facts." Her smile encouraged him, to a point. "For example, why are you so stubborn?"

"You're asking why I insist on being the prisoner of Señor Ríos—instead of his colleague?"

"I'm asking why you've stayed away from me so long. *That's* worse than stubborn; it's ungallant."

"Extremely ungallant," he said, and bent to kiss her hand. So far the approach was standard; in another moment he would assume the offensive in earnest. "Unfortunately, I could never call on you like this—of my own accord."

"And now that you're here at last?"

"May I thank you for your enterprise?" He released her hand slowly, placing it on the counterpane with the precision of an acolyte handling a sacred relic. "Naturally I'm still a trifle bewildered."

"A lady arranges to have you visit her cabin at the end of a long sea voyage. She admits that she's looked forward to that visit from the beginning. Is that too bewildering?"

"How could you have looked forward to—to meeting me from the beginning? You didn't even know me."

"I knew your antecedents. And I had a good look at you before we'd been a half hour at sea. While you slept under Ríos's drug, to be exact." Lady Marian smiled down at her hands, spread fan-wise on the counterpane. Her eyes had the same clear candor when she raised them again. "At that moment I made up my mind about you. Or should I say, about *us?*"

"Forgive me again, but I don't quite——"

"I wanted you then," said Lady Marian Leigh. "I want you now. I'm using the verb in its simplest sense, Dr. Stone. I want you—for those palpitations you just diagnosed so thoroughly. May I have you—strictly as a remedy?"

He was on his feet, staring at her as though he could not believe his ears—or his eyes. The girl nestled deeper in the pillows and offered him that same open smile. "As I say, I've waited quite a while for this visit. You can hardly blame me if I come to the point at once."

"But, my dear lady——!"

"Naturally you'd prefer to conquer me. Not vice versa. Perhaps I should merely have permitted it. As you see, I'm much too honest for that timeworn pretense. Let me prove my honesty and tell you everything. This is no opportune rendezvous. It's a command performance."

He recovered some of his aplomb. "A command performance requires two principals."

"I'm counting on your compliance, Dr. Stone."

"Compliance is an unfortunate word."

Lady Marian rose from her bed with all the vigor of a pouncing tigress. He found that he had put up an instinctive arm, as though he quite expected her to leap for his throat. But the girl ignored him completely as she crossed to the cabin door and shot the bolt. She did not return to her nest of pillows. He was obscurely pleased by this hesitation, until he saw that she had paused, quite deliberately, with the light of the candle sconce behind her. In that filmy gown her body had no secrets. Had she twitched the silken sheath aside and stood naked before him, she could not have teased his whirling brain with a more potent compulsion.

"Take a little time, Doctor," she murmured. "Women are seldom the obvious aggressor. You have every right to be confused."

"What do you want of me?" He cursed the hoarse croak in his voice. It made the question even more idiotic.

"Surely that's apparent now."

He forced iron into his tone as he took a resolute step toward her. Lady Marian held her ground. Since they were almost of a height, he couldn't precisely tower.

"Say it," he ordered. "If you can put it into words. I don't think you'd dare."

"What is your *modus operandi,* Doctor—when you feel in need of love?"

"When I want love, I take it."

"As I'm taking you. I'll give you just five minutes to live up to your reputation. If you fail me, I shall be forced to scream. Mozo will break down the door. I'll say you tried to violate me."

He stood in the deep shadows beside her bed, watching her cup both palms around the candle flame. In that soft bath of light her body came vibrantly alive—high, pointed breasts, a waist lithe as a willow wand, the tapering enticement of milk-white thighs, deep-shadowed loins . . . It was a body tuned to concert pitch, wanting only a touch to sing with love. He stepped forward wildly as the candle flames died under her breath, one by one. Quite calmly she stepped out of her gown as she turned to face him.

"Which will it be, Dr. Stone? A slave's fingers at your throat or me in your arms?"

He held his ground even now—making her come to him, forcing her to stalk him in the dark. For an instant, as she crossed the open port, the moonlight dappled her shoulders, reminding him that she was naked—and supremely unconscious of her nakedness. She had found him now, though he stood in the deepest shadow. Her fingers brushed his cheek, an imprint from nowhere. It was hardly a caress, as yet. Rather, he thought wildly, it was a kind of instinctive branding. As though Lady Marian Leigh had fixed him there in the darkness, anchoring him in a vise older than time.

"Of course I could be mistaken, Doctor. Perhaps you aren't a man at all——"

He claimed her then, brutally and completely. Just as completely, quite as brutally, she returned his embrace, a symphony of clinging mouth, burning breasts, rhythmic thighs. The bed, white with moonlight, surged up to meet them as the *Dos Amigos* heeled in the freshening breeze and raced toward Africa.

VIII

The ship rode at anchor in the mouth of the jungle river a safe distance from the bar. In the longboat Michael sat with folded arms and waited for Mozo to cast off. The *Dos Amigos* loomed above him; for the first time he saw how proud a ship she was. Lady Marian Leigh, smiling down from the sanctuary of the captain's deck, was part of that pride this afternoon. He avoided her smile with grimly lowered eyes, even as he waited for her to speak. Surely she would offer him some kind of good-by—even if he refused to acknowledge it.

For the last half hour he had sat thus as the supply ship completed her unloading. A dozen times he had just escaped rising in the thwarts as all his being urged him to break off this posturing, to extend a hand to her across the green glass of the sea. A dozen times he had remembered that they had spoken scarcely a hundred words since that first night in her cabin. Why should she trouble to wish him Godspeed now?

The words came back to him in this blind, choked moment. Hearing them one more time, he knew that he would remember them as long as he drew a breath:

"You live up to your reputation, Doctor."

"Is your cure complete?"

"By no means. Could you manage a second treatment tomorrow—at this same hour?"

She had offered him her hand on that precise note—with all the poise of a queen, despite the fact that she was still deep in that tumbled nest of pillows and still quite naked. And he had kissed the fingertips just as punctiliously. The faithful physician who knew just when to prescribe—and when to take his leave. . . .

In the nights that followed (they were only a wild blur in his memory now, but he knew that he would relive them later, to the last detail) she had been no less shameless—and quite as adept as he in the ancient ritual they were celebrating:

"Ríos tells me we'll anchor at the Boca on Friday. Can you cure me by Friday, Dr. Stone?"

"I shall do my best, Lady Marian."

"Your best is very good indeed. Shall we repeat this therapy each evening then?"

"It's gratifying to know I still have the case in my charge. Only——"

"Were you about to ask a question? I wouldn't advise it."

"I was only wondering at your choice of a physician."

"I had no choice. You were the only doctor on shipboard."

The only doctor on shipboard. It had been easy for her to mock him with that pious pretense. Easier still to turn his other questions aside on their third night together—and their fourth. She had been deep in his arms, clinging like a wily nymph, when they heard the anchor chain rattle down. They had turned to the port together, without even rising from her bed, for their first glimpse of Africa.

He turned in the stern sheets of the longboat and stared at the coast line to the east. In the blazing heat Africa was only a mirage: a sullen green immensity, unreal as an encyclopedia plate. Thanks to the light offshore breeze, he could not breathe the aura of rotting vegetation, the miasma that had already begun to rise from that dense rain forest and along the mud flats of the wide yellow river that was the only break in the wall of green. A felucca from the compound, her sail belled in the languid wind, danced into the river's mouth, seemed to hang against the jungle like a homing bird, and vanished into the haze. Ríos was aboard that felucca, along with the last load of trade goods. Riding easy in her ballast, the *Dos Amigos* would weigh anchor any moment now. . . .

"You seem in perfect health, Lady Marian. May I wish you a prosperous voyage to the Floridas?"

"Thank you again, Dr. Stone. Your prescriptions were most invigorating."

Such had been their formal farewell on deck. Her manner, as well as her method, had been beyond reproach: she had even given him her hand to kiss, while Ríos watched the loading of the felucca. If Ríos had caught an overtone of meaning, he had given no sign.

Those nights in her cabin had been closed deep in silence, so far as the ship was concerned. They had met and loved (though love was not the word) in an enclave all their own. Or had he merely dreamed that he had held this dark siren in his arms—and was this his awakening?

Awake or dreaming, he could not sit here forever—with Lady Marian Leigh at the rail above him, serene as a painted Lorelei in her white sprigged muslin, and just as detached.

He rose in the thwarts to shout for Tola. Mozo, leaning hard on the sweep, steadied the longboat's prow in the ground swell and called a soft-voiced warning. Michael nodded—and settled in his place again as he heard the Minorcan call from the deck above. After all, it had been he who had sent Tola aboard to recover Voltaire's *Candide* from his cabin.

The Minorcan swarmed overside with the agility of a cheerful monkey and dropped into his place beside Mozo. His face was creased in a beatific grin as he handed the book to Michael across the bent backs of the oarsmen.

"Cast away! *Adiós, compañeros!*"

The Negro at the bow dropped the painter; the crew that lined the rail, tired after the long chore of unloading, waved a few lazy hands as the longboat squared away for the land. Michael held his place, determined not to look back even now. She was quite right to stand there and ignore him; after all, she had given him nothing of herself. Watching the row of sweating brown backs lean on the oars, he told himself that he was not in love with her. That she was far too reserved (in the deepest sense) for any man's love, far too determined to keep that essential self inviolate.

Yet he would never be whole again until he had plumbed that mystery. Until he discovered if she was really the great lady she seemed—or the brassbound wanton he had known, however briefly. It was impossible to adore a mystery in any sense of that dangerous word. He could still want her—as he had never wanted food or drink or love. He could still boil with helpless rage when he remembered how casually she had used him.

As casually, and as competently, as Michael Stone had used many a complaisant female in the four corners of his happy-go-lucky world.

He had never been in love: that soft threat, praise God, had never sapped his judgment or his independence. He had merely taken his women as his spirit dictated. Enjoying them, he had done his best to give pleasure in turn. *This,* too, had begun as another bit of taking—another shipboard affair, agreeably spiced with danger. But it was he, and he alone, who had been possessed—and discarded.

Admitting as much, he found that he was strangely calm. He could even settle in the longboat and wonder about the hazards that awaited him ashore. Nothing mattered now but the resolve to confront her again. To strip her of her last secret; to husk her completely and force her to her knees. To make her his slave—as irrevocably as a Gold Coast queen, with a ring in her nose and terror in her heart . . .

"Dr. Stone!"

He bounced up in the stern sheets as they fought the chop just off the bar. Mozo righted the craft instantly. A quick order sent the oars into reverse, backing the longboat into the glassy ground swell within hailing distance of the larger vessel.

Lady Marian still stood at the waist before the door of her deckhouse. With one hand on the rail she had half raised her free arm to shield her eyes from the glare. He knew that he would always see her thus—slender as a dryad in that white sprigged muslin, virginal as a boy's first hope of heaven. Come what may, that picture would be poor insurance for the time ahead.

"You called?"

His voice was icy, for all his inner tumult. Call me back again, he said wordlessly. I'll risk anything to possess you one more time—if I, or any man, can ever begin to possess you. Aloud he said only, "I believe we said good-by?"

"True. I did feel I should wish you good fortune at the Boca. I did want to say again that it was a pleasure to have you aboard——"

He understood her completely then, including the last bit of wordplay. And he reveled in the pride that made him stand firm in the stern sheets and match her laughter.

"May I say that the pleasure was shared?"

"You may indeed," said Lady Marian. "Otherwise I'd never forgive you."

She had vanished from the rail when he looked again; the *Dos Amigos* was only a silhouette against the dazzling sky. He settled in his place as the blacks leaned on their oars in earnest—and drove the longboat toward the jungle wall that waited, with terrible patience, to engulf them.

II

The "Mariposa"

Here in the crow's-nest, high above the slaver's deck, the morning air was almost cool. It was a precarious perch (and a queasy one when the ship rolled in the light, teasing breeze), but Michael had chosen it deliberately. As voyages went, this had been an easy crossing for the Boca de Oro's doctor. And yet, as always, he had felt despair grip his spirit as they approached the Florida coast.

Over the long months of his servitude he had never quite conquered this despair. But he had found he could fight it best when he was alone: the crow's-nest was the only haven the *Mariposa* offered. As an added attraction, it was the corner farthest removed from the stench that was the slaver's hallmark.

The miasma pursued him even here, a good thirty feet above the deck. It was a complex stink that he could never break down. Black sweat and blacker misery? The exhalation of six hundred bodies packed like worms on the narrow shelves below? The filth that no amount of hosing could wash away? All this, and more, was fearfully apparent to the nostrils. But the blend was more subtle, more compellingly evil; a smell old as the animal effluvia that hung in man's first cave—and new as man's lust-inspired deviltry. It was monstrous that it should cling to the *Mariposa's* decks and rigging even at sea. That the ship's coming was heralded downwind almost before an approaching vessel could glimpse her topsail spars.

A light showed in the half-darkness dead ahead, a lazy cat's eye slitted in protest at the fading night. Michael leaned forward sharply as he sensed the presence of another ship on their port quarter, though her lines were only a vague blur. In this last dead half hour before sunrise the sea was an endless dove-gray plain with no visible limits; the faint capfuls of air that drifted from the land seemed hardly vigorous enough to propel a full-rigged ship into view. But the other vessel grew more definite with each breath. As her blinker continued to talk with the *Mariposa's* own lookout, Michael saw that this was their sister ship—the *Santa Clara,* outbound from Fernandina.

He let out his breath in a grateful sigh and settled to watch the *Santa Clara* come alive in the growing morning. Piracy was not unknown along the coastal bayous of Florida—even when a prospective prize was armed to the last port. It was a relief to have this proof that they were on their course—to know that their sister had survived her own voyage from Africa.

Both slavers were Italian barkentines. Adam Leigh's agents had purchased them at auction in Mallorca, outfitted them in the Clyde, and put them to sea under the flag of Spain. The renovation had taken place a scant two years ago. Already the records showed that both vessels had paid off their cost some fifty times. At this moment it was hard to think of the *Santa Clara* in commercial terms: in that gray light (it was changing to topaz now) she was a butterfly that all but skimmed the surface of the Atlantic—black as the freight she had left in Florida, black from martingale to forepeak.

Then, as the first glint of sunrise touched her skysails, she came alive completely. A lacquered sea witch still, she seemed decked in white and pure as a bride.

Pure only to the romantic's eye, Michael amended instantly. Already his nose caught the familiar stench from her hatches. It was no less pervasive, now that she carried only the memory of that dark cargo. Like many lovely things, the *Santa Clara* was rotten at heart. That stink would cling to her timbers when she was a sea hag limping on her last voyage. It would stain the ocean floor when she had plunged to Davy Jones. . . .

"*Mariposa* ahoy!"

He watched the *Santa Clara's* skipper swing into the ratlines with a speaking tube at his hairy lips: the two vessels were near enough to speak each other now. Michael clenched his fist and fought down the impulse to shake it openly. Yankee Sam Coffin was one of Leigh's best captains, a man noted for record runs.

Michael himself had inspected the *Santa Clara* a scant six weeks ago, when she floated down-river from the Boca on the first leg of her crossing. Michael had given explicit orders for the care of the slaves below. He knew that Coffin had a reputation for ignoring orders—unless they came direct from Leigh's Florida headquarters.

Ríos was leaning out from his own jib boom now to shout across the narrowing strip of sea.

"How many did you beach?"

"Five hundred and seven, Cap. Speak for yourself."

Even from that height Michael saw Ríos go taut with anger. The ships had left Africa at three-week intervals with six hundred Negroes under hatches, the capacity load that Michael had reluctantly endorsed after months of argument. Thanks to daily exercise, to nourishing stews (boiled in the great copper pots at the forecastle head), to frequent hosings, the *Mariposa's* health record had been kept. Only nine black bodies had gone overside this voyage. The Yankee skipper had admitted the loss of almost a hundred. One sixth of his cargo. . . .

Cargo. Michael let the word take shape in his brain, forgetting the two bellowing captains below. When had he ceased to think of Adam Leigh's stock in trade as human beings? When had he begun to check boatloads en masse? Turned aside from the branding, the whips, the hideous crowding—and planned merely to deliver a high percentage of living, healthy flesh?

It was quite true that no other attitude was possible at the Boca—if a man wished to keep his sanity. An impersonal viewpoint was imperative at sea, when those tight-packed holds were a threat to every white soul aboard. He recalled his first voyage, the blind horror that had gripped him when the howling began below. Some said that it was the full moon that started this endless ululation—the low, constant moan that was neither animal nor human, yet heartbreakingly part of both. He remembered his first visit below to single out the dying—a vinegar-soaked scarf knotted across mouth and nose, his eyes wide in the fetid gloom as he followed a mate's lantern, feeling hot hatred sear his back from a hundred eyes, feeling the strain of murder on leash, restrained only by the glint of the musket barrels at each hatchway.

On that first voyage he had risked the unheard-of experiment of opening the hatchways each forenoon. Once again he relived the terror of that black eruption, a living lava that threatened for an instant to swamp the decks. The crew, with bull whips in their fists, had beaten back the worst of it, permitting only a favored few to exercise at a time.

That morning (he recalled the incident wryly now) he had knocked down a sailor in the act of lashing a naked mother with an infant at her breast. Only yesterday, after the semiweekly hosing, he had walked into the shadow of the dinghy chocks—and stumbled upon another seaman in the act of forcing another naked Juno to yield to his Priapean embrace. He had turned aside without a word. Satyriasis was routine after a long voyage. Adam Leigh would hardly protest the gift of an extra mulatto infant nine months hence.

Why, when he was fed and housed and growing richer daily, should he question the pattern? He was powerless to alter it. His only real problem was how to continue as an essential part of this inhuman traffic and retain his own humanity.

II

The *Mariposa* spun into a long, sweet tack, cutting the wake of her sister ship to bear down on the land. Michael closed his eyes against the first hot thrust of sunlight and let his thoughts veer with the dip of the mainmast.

Five hundred and ninety-one prime blacks. Save for the expensive Mozambique princeling who had tried to stab himself a week ago (and was still lashed down in sick bay), the count was accurate. Living, breathing fortune, whole on the hoof. Adam Leigh could hardly fail to rejoice when such cattle flowed into his Florida pens.

There would be a bonus for the doctor, thanks to this banner crossing. Leigh's payments, made directly to Holly through his London bankers, had always been amazingly prompt. Leigh himself, and the self-sufficient cosmos he had created here in the Floridas, was still a stubborn myth. . . .

This was Michael's fifth Atlantic crossing, and his third call in Florida. He had never learned if it was Ríos's caprice or Leigh's own order that locked him in his cabin from the moment the *Mariposa* lifted her first American land. Certainly there was no mystery about the disposal of the slaves themselves. At Bahia, when they had called with an overflow consignment of untrained field hands, he had watched the auctioneer's hammer fall on the quayside; at Fernandina, when the *Mariposa* had warped into Leigh's own dock, he had stood at his porthole to watch clerks swarm from the warehouse, had seen the trade goods swing aboard as busy pencils flew over bills of lading. But his knowledge of the land had been confined to these glimpses. At Bahia, a tropic quay, stinking of marsh gas. A faded stone wall in Havana. A sun-bitten stringpiece and the sweat-stained backs of clerks were his only idea of Florida.

Perhaps they felt he was too valuable to risk in the open air when the slaver was in port. Surely Ríos knew that he would break for freedom at the first opportunity. In the meantime no man could say that he had shirked his work aboard—or at the Boca.

Boca de Oro. He closed his eyes again in the sun, letting the image of that compound build: saw-toothed stockade, hard-packed terreplein where guards marched by day and night, clay-daubed walls to repel the heat. It was a picture forbidding as most prisons. The compound stood on high ground, at a point a half mile from the river's mouth. On the land side the dense jungle mat seemed a green maze without ending. Only Ríos's headmen knew the trails that led to the slave road; only the head boatmen could mark the landings upstream.

Thanks to its location, the Boca was secure from attack save on the river side—and the ten-pounders mounted on the terreplein were ample insurance against visits from possible rivals. Ríos had permitted the traders' caravans to camp before the compound's gate while bargaining proceeded, but Michael's first reform had been the erection of a huge open-walled shed on an island a half mile upstream. Here the slaves could be segregated while they were still chained. Here, with three doctors to advise Ríos, it was a matter of hours to separate the culls from the healthy, ignore the curses of the Arab captains, and barter on that basis only.

When the winnowing was completed and the selections ferried downstream, Michael segregated the newcomers on a second island —under the guns of the stockade, yet well removed. Here the first processing began: daily hosings, adequate feeding to balance the traders' miserable rations, smudge pots to banish the last of the flies that always hung in clouds above these jungle gleanings. During this quarantine the doctors checked daily for yaws, fevers, the myriad ills that marched with every caravan. Only the proven healthy were admitted to the compound itself, where the pens were limed and rainproof. Here they were driven daily to separate latrines, bedded on stilted mats, fattened in earnest for the rigors of the ocean crossing.

Ríos had protested this routine until he had discovered that the expense of the delay was more than offset by the saving of lives at sea. It had been harder to beat down his prejudice when it came to loading the slavers themselves. Michael would never forget the horror of his first voyage: the daily mass burials overside, the callous probing between decks to separate the quick and the dead. On that voyage the *Mariposa* had carried nearly a thousand slaves in her hold. Ríos, as always, had packed them in tiers—seating each slave between another's legs, with a yard of headroom, no space to turn or recline, and no visible air to breathe. At Havana he had unloaded a mere four hundred and sixty blacks, thanks to an epidemic of dysentery that had raged through that slimy hell.

"Very well, Dr. Stone. I will admit a fearful loss of profit. We've still realized a sixty-per-cent return on the voyage."

"Smash out those shelves and build two tiers instead of three. Break out a bulkhead aft for a sick bay. Ship a doctor on each crossing. Sleep a hundred topside in clear weather. Exercise in relays and feed in the open air——"

"They'll still die like worms."

"Give it a trial. Let me prove you're wrong for once."

"We couldn't ship seven hundred head, with only two tiers."

"Ship six hundred on your next voyage. Give each grown man and woman room to lie flat without touching his neighbor. I'll guarantee to deliver more live hands and fewer yaws."

He had made good that promise on the *Mariposa* when Ríos sailed as her skipper. It was hardly his fault that he could seldom leave the Boca. Or that Ledoux and Fulton, his juniors in the compound, could not be trusted to carry out his orders at sea, though they were both able doctors. Or that skippers like Coffin were not above calling at other stations en route to pack their holds for the long Atlantic voyage.

Coffin, reflected Michael, summed up the spirit of the trade as accurately as Ríos. Both men were coldly efficient—to a point. Both were determined to take quick fortunes from Africa and washed their hands of aftermaths. Neither could resist a gamble for profit. The fact that human lives served as counters in that gamble was of small moment to either.

The resemblance ended sharply at the cashbox. Ríos, a cynic to his fingertips, maintained his own harem at the compound and shipped out its coffee-colored offspring as casually as he renewed his crop of wives. The Yankee's quarters, when he came ashore between voyages, were as austere as the salt box he owned in Nantucket; the Yankee's morals, where his dark freight was concerned, were above reproach. On several occasions he had lectured Michael's assistants for admitting his crew to the females' pen—and the doctors once again for maintaining harems of their own.

Michael had avoided Coffin's wrath on that count at least. He would never explain why he had refused to solace his loneliness with the most obvious of drugs. Certainly there was no sense of outraged morality, no feeling of repulsion. And yet when the traders proffered a particularly shapely wench (as a bit of lagniappe when the prodding of the flesh was over), he could only smile and shake his head. When one of Numi's own daughters had offered herself with all the easy grace of a kitten (it had been Numi's own inspiration, a pleasant way of repaying the doctor for saving his leg), he had returned the girl to her father with that same fixed smile.

He had paid for those quixotic withdrawals, and paid dearly. There had been sleepless nights when the cloying heat of the rain forest seemed more than he could bear. His doctor's instinct warned him that such self-denial could not continue indefinitely. On occasions (those rare breathing spells between caravans when the pens were all but empty) he had taken briefly to the bottle and cursed himself for a fool. At such times he had left his quarters and roamed the compound, if only to shake his fist at the moon—and the echoes of saturnalia that came from the house of the comandante, where Ríos rolled in dalliance with his coal-black concubines.

It was not loyalty to the deckhouse of the *Dos Amigos*. God knows those aching unions with Lady Marian had been no more than passion, shared to the hilt. He repeated that bitter truth as solemnly as he could. In the same spirit he renewed his promise of an appropriate revenge, when their paths crossed again. The promise had sustained him over more than fourteen months. It lifted his spirits now as he opened his eyes to watch the shadow on the horizon grow and take form.

The barkentine had made her landfall while he brooded in the crow's-nest. Before the lookout on deck could mark its contours he had his first real view of Florida. In the full glow of sunrise the land had changed in a twinkling from gray to gold. Even as he watched, the shadow became a reality—a long, low island, its palmettos a straw fire in the sun, its beaches aureate in that clear bath of light. A true isle of gold, shielding the approach to El Dorado.

Amelia Island, he told himself; it could be no other. Beyond, to the west, masked by wide marshlands and tidal reaches, was the low land mass of Florida proper. To the south (and they would fetch it on the next long tack) was Punta Blanca, their immediate destination.

Thanks to the maps he had pored over on other voyages, he could picture that promontory clearly, though he had never been favored with a glimpse. Punta Blanca, as the Spanish words indicated, began as a sandspit and ended in a nest of dunes. Leigh had sunk a long stone jetty to the north to mark the limits of the land grant he held by royal patent from Madrid. Thanks to the scour of the ebb, it made a fair anchorage for ships no larger than the *Mariposa*. If the surf was high, the slaves were taken off by lighter. In a calm they could be beached direct.

He had pieced out that much behind the locked door of his cabin. He had no idea what lay beyond that ridge of dunes. Of course he had pictured the great estate of Punta Blanca in its entirety—if only in his mind's eye. There would be an avenue of live oaks, deep in moss (all planters, his reading indicated, had just such an avenue). There would be a cream-white house with a pillared colonnade and window frames with jalousies like folded green fans. Perhaps, since this was a salt-water plantation, there would be a captain's walk between the two fat chimneys. He could hear Leigh's boots stumping away an afternoon on that eminence while he conned the horizon.

Below, in the drawing room, the parquet would be a gleaming lake, the spinet an inlaid jewel. Lady Marian would play at that delicate keyboard and wait for a certain English doctor to claim his reward. Only revenge was a better word, the only word. . . .

He heard a sharp hail from the deck and dropped both feet to the ratlines, even as he turned for a final glimpse of the land. The sea was a blinding cobalt now. Florida had begun to smudge in heat haze, its golden contours obscure. But he felt his heart beat faster as he dropped to the deck and turned by rote to his cabin. For a moment that bright gold had seemed near enough to touch with a questing hand.

III

As always, he tried to sleep away these hours of confinement. Sometimes it was easy to drop into a troubled slumber until the whip of fresh air at his cabin porthole told him he was at sea again. Today, however, he found that he was to be denied that sign: a thick tarpaulin, weighed with sounding leads, had already been lowered over the porthole from the outside—plunging his cabin into a kind of sepulchral gloom, filling it with a promise of airless hours to come.

He stripped and flung himself on the berth, determined to cling fast to the hope he had found in the crow's-nest. To say nothing of the plan he had hatched with Tola's aid.

If the Minorcan was given shore leave (at Punta Blanca or tonight when they docked in Fernandina), he would permit that crazy hope to build a little. The details were simple, once Tola had made his contact ashore; they had been rehearsed one last time, only yesterday, when Tola had brought his morning tea from the galley. So much for the prisoner who dared to burrow an exit from his pen. He had gone over those details too many times to savor their rehearsal now. Flinging himself face down on his bunk, he made no effort to keep Marian from his thoughts or his heart.

Marian. Lady Marian Leigh. Usually it was easier to re-create her in terms of that title. If he had used her Christian name while she lay in his arms, he could not recall it now. He pondered her remoteness from this life he was leading. He did not even know if she was now in residence at Punta Blanca—or if her hero husband had recovered from his wounds and joined her. Was it reasonable to assume that this headstrong beauty would be content for long with her colonial kingdom, however splendid? He had no background for his certainty that he had only to step ashore to find her. But he refused to admit, even for a moment, that she might prove inaccessible. Or that she had taken other lovers in the meantime. Or resolved to be true to her husband, wounded or otherwise. On that stubborn note, as always, he dropped into an uneasy dream.

Usually it was Lady Marian who ghosted through those dreams—warm-white as a summer moon and just as enticingly remote. Today it was Tola who danced in and out of the stagnant shadows that filled his cabin—and his brain. Tola, with a finger to his lips and a giant map flaring from one fist like a banner in a revolution. Then the Minorcan vanished in cotton wool. The map changed from white to cherry red—and, waking with a splitting head, Michael found himself staring at the round eye of his porthole, still blanketed in the tarpaulin and baking in the full glare of noon.

He heard the thud of naked soles on the deck even before he had quite opened his eyes. Beyond the tarpaulin the water boiled with thrashing limbs as the blacks went overside. The sea around the *Mariposa* had a strange, liquid vibrancy all its own, as though that part of the Atlantic had become a bath of dinosaurs. Michael, who had heard these sounds before, did not trouble to raise his head. He knew that they were inside the jetty at Punta Blanca, that the slaves, wading through the shoulder-deep sea, were already marshaled on the beach. With each wild burst of splashing, the barkentine seemed to lighten, to find a belated soul now that her 'tween decks were freed of their ballast. Michael found that he was smiling as he shared in that release from shame. From this point on he could turn his face to the wall and sleep in earnest.

He did not hear the tarpaulin swish away from the port. Breathing clean sea air again, he did not hear the anchor chains rattle down a second time. When he wakened in earnest he knew only that the sun-baked aroma outside was the true smell of land. That the scream of a winch, the hoarse shouts of the wharfside huskies, came from Adam Leigh's own freight shed in Fernandina.

Once again he did not trouble to rise and check the view. Whether the ship had warped in from port or starboard, that vista would be limited enough: A corner of the warehouse itself, with its faded label in red and gold:

Adam Leigh and Son

A bored clerk, perhaps, gnawing his quill at a portable desk. Behind a dusty window, another quill driver, equally bored. No more than that, and no less. He had yet to know what lay beyond that wall of yellow pine. Whether those two seedy fellows kept their ledgers in Spanish or English. Whether they hated their work or hoped to rise on Leigh's shoulders and become blackbirders on their own.

If the *Mariposa* was loading from her portside, the view would be more inspiring: a sweep of tidal harbor, a score of full-rigged ships at anchor or drifting in the current to await their turn at dockside. Ships of as many nations—the flags of Holland and Denmark, of France and the *opéra-bouffe* kingdoms of Italy; the Red Duster of Britain cheek by jowl with the candy-stripe flag of the infant American Union; the bizarre flags that proclaimed other experiments in rebellion to the South . . . But he was too dispirited to check his view today. The hope that had sustained him in the dawn had vanished in the siesta hush of afternoon. He burrowed deep in his pillow and courted sleep as the last light faded. It was pitch-dark in the cabin when he heard the lock turn at last.

Tola came in softly with a lamp on the supper tray. Through the half-open door Michael saw that Mozo was on guard as usual. Tola shrugged an answer to the unspoken question as he bent to place the tray across his master's knees.

"We must be quick, jefe."

The Minorcan spoke in the barest of whispers, without moving his lips: it was a trick he had taught Michael long ago. When he spoke again, his tone was quite normal.

"May I bring you anything from town, Doctor?"

"You're getting shore leave?"

"Until dawn. Rum from the ordinary, perhaps? Or a girl from Ladies Street?"

"Is this Ríos's idea or yours?"

Michael spoke normally for Mozo's ears and kept a sleepy scowl intact. It was common knowledge on shipboard that he accepted no favors from the captain.

"Mine only, Doctor," said Tola. "For your pleasure and your comfort. The comandante will permit it——"

Despite himself, Michael found that his heart had begun to pump with a half-forgotten rhythm. It would be good to hold a woman in his arms again, if only for an hour. Even if it were only a trollop from the town's notorious Calle da las Damas. He felt his mind blur on that image, even as he shook it off. There had been other dockside evenings here in Fernandina when he had paced his way to exhaustion—knowing the ship was deserted save for the guard outside his cabin door, knowing that the crew was wallowing in the bodegas not a stone's throw from the pier. It was incredible that Fernandina was only a spot on the map for Dr. Michael Stone. It would be good to hear more of Fernandina from a native's lips. Who could tell him more than a member of the world's oldest trade?

But he downed the temptation a second time, even as he recalled Tola's real purpose. His lips shaped another soundless question.

"Is a woman needful to our plans?"

"No, Señor Mike." The Minorcan's taut lips offered the travesty of a smile. "When I return, I will know everything. Talk will be safer then." The smile deepened. "While you waited, I thought you might need company."

"I'll do without that sort of company a little longer." Again he spoke aloud for Mozo. "Isn't Ríos afraid you'll jump ship?"

"The comandante is wise, Señor Mike. He knows that the dog can stray awhile. But the dog returns to his master."

Tola went out on that note with a quick, cringing bow. Mozo, impassive as ever, waited in the open doorway until Michael had pushed aside the meal, took up the tray, and locked the door as he backed out of the doctor's presence. Michael lay back once again and stared at the low ceiling beam without seeing it at all.

It was a perfect moment to burnish his geography. His picture of this corner of Florida, acquired after endless map reading, was accurate enough. He repeated the fact solemnly, even as he began the review. Accuracy was vital to the plan he had just set in motion.

At the moment (given his freedom and a good pair of eyes) he was within sight of the United States of America. If he could climb to the crow's-nest and look north, where the Amelia River mingled with the St. Marys in Cumberland Sound, he could mark the line that separated the Spanish Floridas from the sovereign state of Georgia. So much for this junction of decaying empire and vigorous republic. He traced the map in his mind's eye, marking the precise location of Fernandina itself—on its neck of land in the northeast corner of Amelia Island. He noted Fernandina's fine, deep harbor—opening to the south until it was one with that long tidal estuary known as the Amelia River. Meandering through its marshy flats, the Amelia divided its namesake island from the mainland. Some fifteen miles to the south it joined with Nassau Sound, another of the endless salt-water bayous that divided these coastal islands from Albemarle to the keys.

The *Mariposa* would almost surely take this water lane as the first lap of her return voyage. Just as surely, she would complete her loading tomorrow and slip her cable with sunset. Slavers, as a rule, preferred to hug the inland bayous for the first few leagues of their journey and whisk into the open ocean via a convenient inlet. Such a course masked their movements from too curious eyes at sea—whether the Nemesis was a pirate captain from Augustine or an American gunboat from St. Marys, the first Georgia town across the Cumberland.

Ríos might stand out to sea by daylight. Even if he followed the inland waterway, he might keep Michael in his cabin until they were clear of land. It was a chance they could not avoid—just as they must pray that Ríos would still be drunk when he weighed anchor. This had been the Spaniard's custom during their other departures from Fernandina: Ríos never drank at the Boca, and almost never at sea, but these lapses were regular enough to seem deliberate. Tomorrow, it would seem reasonable to hope, he would continue drinking in his cabin, relying on his leadsman to call the soundings—and on Dr. Michael Stone to keep him amused.

Once in Nassau Sound, with Amelia astern, the *Mariposa* would be dead on Talbot Island. Michael stared hard at the chart in his mind's eye. The island was an elongated sand bar backed by marsh; Ríos had always used it as a navigation point to set his course. Once that course was set, he must continue to make southing to avoid the shoals on his port quarter.

Michael's fist pounded the bunk as he let their ruse shape its own climax. At this moment Tola was at the ordinary, bargaining with his cousin from Augustine. Pablo (a waiter who had renounced smuggling for the nonce) owned a sloop tidy enough for a single man to handle. Both Pablo and his vessel could be commandeered, for a price. Unless Tola's persuasions failed, his cousin would be idling inside the bar at Talbot Island when the *Mariposa* entered Nassau Sound tomorrow. A shot across the slaver's bows, a bonfire floated into the channel, should convince Ríos that a pirate was in the offing and ready to pounce. Crowding on sail, the Spaniard would presumably dash for the open sea—a signal for Dr. Michael Stone to drop overside.

As plans go, thought Michael, ours has the virtue of simplicity. Drinking (as always) in Ríos's cabin as the slaver entered Nassau Sound, belaboring the Spaniard (as always) with his heartfelt curses, he would have every excuse to stamp out for a breath of air. When the signal came, he could be overside in a flash. Tola, who had swum before he could walk, would precede him to the beach. His passport and three hundred well-hoarded American dollars would make his emancipation complete when they reached St. Marys.

He slept fitfully that night, as his mind churned down to a gray nadir of exhaustion. Mozo brought breakfast at sunrise; a sailor appeared, shakily enough, with Michael's dinner tray at noon. He felt the hush aboard, framed by the constant whine of winches on the quayside. The seaman, he noted, was drunk to the point of collapse. Even Mozo (a good Mohammedan when it came to spirits) had a suspiciously bleary eye. The spell of Fernandina, thought Michael dourly. Invading the ship like a tipsy dryad, it had always led the crew into strange byways.

At four o'clock (the ship's bell had just sounded amidships) the bolt flew open once again, and the mate himself, a Yankee with a Triton's beard, staggered into the cabin. The boatswain drooped like a sack at one burly shoulder; a trail of blood marked their progress from the deck. Michael was already suturing his needles while the mate stripped back the man's jersey, exposing the deep gash from collarbone to diaphragm. It was a routine aftermath to their Fernandina visit. Probably a razor in an experienced hand, thought Michael: only first-rate steel could make such a wound.

He shouted for Mozo, but the giant black was already waiting with compresses and a basin of steaming water. He worked quickly, swabbing the wound, ignoring the man's howls as he joined the sundered flesh with neat, housewife stitches.

"No eyes so far, Saunders?"

"Not on *our* side, Doctor.

Michael nodded absently as he tied off the last strand of whipcord. Removing the aftermaths of a gouging had been another of the routines he had learned to perform without comment. Two of the crew had been blinded on their last visit: eye patches to mark a single vacant lid were common in the forecastle.

"I gather we won all our fights this time?"

"All of 'em so far. Frenchy here cut his man down to size. And there's a lieutenant of the Spanish Army who'll never fight again. Left him on the carpet at Madame Chica's, begging his own men to shoot him."

"Ríos will fine you for that."

"Bless you, sir, but it was the comandante's own knife. Just between us, I never saw Ríos quite so happy. Course, this was a record run, but——"

Michael opened his eyes in earnest. He had realized, long ago, that Ríos enjoyed the torture chamber as well as the cashbox. But the Spaniard had never dared to indulge those warped passions so close to Adam Leigh's own estates.

"You're positive it was Ríos who did the stabbing?"

"I saw it happen, Doc. He'd hired two of the madame's best girls at once. One to bed and one to tease. You know the skipper's idea of teasing."

"Too well."

"I smelled the flesh burning from the next room." The mate looked down at his red-veined hands; his jaw had set in a hard line. "Ríos was smoking a cheroot, and drunk as any man can be. Had his fist twined in one trollop's hair, while he was working over the other. So help me, he was burning a circle on the first one's back with his cigar and howling like a hyena on an anthill."

The mate shrugged, with the air of a man dismissing a bad dream. "Course the don had to come running with the others to see what was wrong. He clipped the skipper's jaw—just once. Next thing I knew, he was tumbled on the carpet, along with his guts." Saunders swallowed hard. "Even that was easier to watch than what had gone before. If I make myself clear, sir——"

"The picture is too clear for comfort. When do we sail?"

"With the tide, Doctor. If you ask me, it's high time we were at sea again."

The mate lurched out, with an arm around the boatswain's waist. Tola was already bowing from the doorway to let them pass. Michael felt his heart stop when the Minorcan met his eyes.

"You are wanted on deck, Mozo. Captain Ríos has just come aboard."

"What of the doctor?"

"Captain Ríos will see to the doctor."

Mozo shrugged, looked thoughtfully at the unlocked door, and hurried out. Tola closed the door quickly and spread his hands in a gesture that combined apology and despair.

"Usually he does not come aboard so soon, jefe."

"There was a knifing on Ladies Street. I suppose he'll stay under cover until we sail."

"He is coming here, Señor Mike. To your cabin."

"Then speak quickly. Did you see your cousin?"

"All goes as we planned. Pablo's sloop will wait for us at Talbot Island. But you must be on deck when the signal comes."

"I'll manage that somehow. And you?"

"It is you they will try to stop, Señor Mike. Not I. Once you have gone overside, I'll find a way to follow."

"We can't swim ashore together?"

"True. We could never find each other in the dark. You must head for the surf and let it carry you in. The tide will be at the flood: there is no undertow. Sleep among the dunes. We can meet by daylight."

"And your cousin?"

"Pablo promises to hide his sloop in the marsh behind the island. With morning, he will show his sail in the sound. We will swim out together and go aboard. He will bring clothing and food——" Tola had spoken in the barest of whispers: he swallowed the last words as the cabin door banged open and Ríos stood swaying on the threshold.

Save for his rolling gait, the Spaniard seemed quite sober: the silken stock at his throat, the pearl-gray coat he always wore ashore, were both immaculate. But the eyes betrayed him completely. Such eyes had no right in a human skull, thought Michael. He knew that the brain behind them was coiled to strike, to destroy. The whip in the man's fist was only an outward symbol. Michael flung himself forward and snatched the knotted leather from Ríos's hand just before it could lash down on Tola's back.

Captain and doctor stood frozen for an instant. Michael watched the spark in Ríos's eye explode like a coal in a grate, until it seemed to suffuse the whole iris. Then the Spaniard chuckled: his face seemed to come apart, like a papier-mâché mask melting in the sun. Michael saw drunkenness strike his brain with a sudden hammer blow. He had watched that hammer fall before, when Ríos came up the gangplank from Fernandina.

He stepped back and let Ríos tumble to the floor. Mozo came forward calmly, slung the captain over his shoulder, and carried him out.

Tola said, easily enough, "He heard nothing, Señor Mike. And it meant nothing. When he is deep in his wine, he wants to hurt someone. Anyone will do. You should have let him beat me. I have been beaten before."

"Let's hope you've been beaten for the last time, Tola."

A hawser slapped the deck outside. Michael let the rest go as he thrust his head through the port. He was in time to see Leigh's warehouse spin from view as the *Mariposa,* accepting the nudge of the outgoing tide, moved easily from quayside to open harbor.

Tola said, "There is no cause for worry, Señor Mike. We anchor in the roadstead, to wait for the turning tide."

"And to be in the clear, if that officer from Fort San Carlos has friends."

"Ríos thinks of most things. Even when he is drunk."

"But we can still outthink him."

"I hope we can, Señor Mike. God guard you."

"God grant me strong muscles, you mean," said Michael. "I won't worry about yours."

He was still at the port when Tola left him. Already there was a wide strip of cloudy green water between quay and barkentine. Michael had watched that barrier grow before now and yielded to despair. Tonight it was only a challenge to be met.

Fernandina, as seen from the porthole, was still only a splinter from a kaleidoscope—a log house atop a bluff, the peeling white shoulder of another warehouse, a burst of scarlet hibiscus at the foot of a stair. But he felt part of it for once. Florida, at long last, seemed to await the imprint of his foot.

It was too early to wonder if he would be welcome.

IV

Honing his scalpels all through that dying afternoon, he still refused to wonder. He had used this routine often to cheat his boredom, while he waited for the *Mariposa* to put to sea. The routine served him well today. It soothed brain as well as hands, even as he admitted he was handling these tools for the last time.

Three hundred American dollars in the waistband of his smallclothes; a passport in that same oiled wallet; a single scalpel folded into the waistband itself. It was all a man could hope to take overside on a mile-long swim to the Florida surf line.

Tonight he weighed his surgical case between his hands and stared down one more time at the shining rows of steel. Forceps and probes, ratchets and retractors, neatly sized scalpels. Each instrument was an old friend to his fingers; each had been fashioned to his order by Monsieur Ali, a Levantine who dealt in the choicest Damascus metal. Even the forceps had been forged in Ali's furnaces. Kept for years as a monopoly by the surgeons of the Chamberlain family in England, they had not yet come into general use. Yet they had saved a life on this voyage. His mind returned to that sweltering night in mid-Atlantic when he had delivered the howling black infant, who had chosen to come into the world, as savage babies rarely did, with the head pointing backward. Most doctors would have lost both baby and mother in such a complication. The Chamberlain forceps (turning the unborn child into a normal position for delivery) had saved Adam Leigh two lives that night.

Michael found that his eyes had roved to the cabin door, which Saunders had locked once again. Perhaps he was letting his hopes outrun his common sense. With Ríos sleeping off an alcoholic collapse, the mate was in charge of the ship. Saunders, a competent officer with a strong sense of discipline, might keep him confined until the Spaniard was on his feet. He shook off that fear, even as he began pacing the cabin floor—and yielding to the tug of excitement when he felt the ship heel and knew they were under way.

Tola answered his echoing knock—so promptly that he felt his spirits bound.

"The captain will see you when you like, Señor Médico."

This, too, was part of the invariable routine of putting to sea. First, the tap (or the pounding fist on the door panel). Next, Tola's cringing scuttle. Finally, Michael's own pacing, the length of the barkentine's decks. It was *de rigueur* that he curse, and continue cursing, as he drew his first breaths of sea air. He yielded wholeheartedly to custom tonight.

"Caramba contigo, Ríos! May you rot in the milk of your grandmother!"

He took three complete turns of the deck before he glanced at the captain's door. At each forward turning he paused to sniff mechanically at the great riveted stewpots—though he knew they would be spotless now that the *Mariposa* was free of her human cargo. At each turn aft he thumped the binnacle with his fist—if only to let the helmsman know that Dr. Stone's rage was expending itself as usual.

Even in the pitch black of the Florida night he did not turn for a glance toward land: in sober truth, he did not dare. The barkentine was deep in trade goods: she handled a bit heavily, even with a steady northeast breeze. When she heeled, he noted, the scuppers were almost awash. A man could go overside without a sound and vanish like a minnow. He choked the impulse one more time: Tola had made their plans. In another moment he would face Ríos in his cabin and lift the ritual glass to their homing voyage.

Thanks to her trade, the *Mariposa's* decks were stripped to the bone: save for the bulk of the forecastle, the holystoned surface was unbroken from capstan to afterhouse—a three-cabin structure that sheltered Ríos, Saunders, and Michael, in that order. The Spaniard's cabin, by far the largest of the three, was still little more than an oblong box, with a latticed door to let in the breeze as well as rumbles of riot from below. Tonight the lattices were opened wide, spilling a ladder of light along the deck. The light indicated that Ríos was far from sober even now. The *Mariposa* usually ran into darkness with all lights doused, relying on the cat eyes of her leadsmen to bring her into open water.

On the fourth turn of the decks Michael slowed his pacing, knowing that he had devoted enough time to this pantomime of a free lion roaming outside its cage. One more turn of the binnacle; one more glance ahead to estimate the nearness of Nassau Sound. Then he leaned hard on the captain's door—and walked in, as always, without knocking.

Ríos lay deep in a cane-backed chair with his immaculate legs crossed and rum at his elbow. He was smoking a long roll of Havana and staring thoughtfully at the inch of unfallen ash. The hand, Michael noted, was as steady as the ice-cold eye.

"Don't look so bewildered, Doctor," said Ríos. "As you know, my powers of recovery are unlimited."

Michael stood foursquare in the doorframe and continued to study the Spaniard with level-eyed contempt. "I'd have cared for you myself if they'd let me out."

"I needed no care. Only what Saunders gave me. A sovereign remedy, prepared by a herbalist in Fernandina. Officially it has no name: the Indians call it the black drink. I might add, in confidence, that it's the world's finest purgative."

"So fine that you're ready to start over?"

"The hair of the dog, if I may use an American phrase. Surely you'll join me in a toast to the voyage?"

"Only if you insist."

"I'm afraid I do, Doctor."

They touched glasses with glacial formality. Michael took down his three ounces of burning Jamaica at a draught—proud that he had resisted the urge to empty the glass into the pale face below him. The insults would begin any moment now: the mutual damnation that was part of this ritual of putting to sea.

"Tell me this, Doctor. Why are you so seldom drunk—and never in company? Why did you refuse a girl last evening? Why, in short, do you refuse to be one of us?"

"Why do you keep me a prisoner?"

"Don't answer one question with another: that's a Yankee trick, and beneath you. Or, if you insist, permit me to guess the true answer. You consider us devil's spawn. All of us. *Está correcte?"*

"Verdad, Comandante."

"From myself to the last freedman who ever plowed black velvet on my orders—or without them."

"Black velvet is seldom plowed at the Boca without your orders." Michael spoke evenly, since he was only stating a clinical fact. "Wenches are clocked by your black midwives and kept penned until the most fertile days of their cycle. Then, and only then, you unleash your freedmen, and your crews——"

"True. Is it something to argue over?"

"Not at all. It's merely a part of your trade. But don't pose as a philanthropist. You're a breeder who's never wasted a moment—or a man."

"Your eloquence is my reward, Dr. Stone. But why hate me because I'm wise in the ways of earth?"

The white hands made a gentle, all-but-pleading gesture. It included the slaver's deck, her hatchways; it embraced the land beyond the starboard bow. By a strange legerdemain it seemed to outline the land beyond the Floridas—that infant republic the *Mariposa* had served so well.

"Continue," said Ríos. "Flay me alive. You know I enjoy it."

"I'm stating a fact, nothing more. You've chosen to live without friends. So does every man who feeds on society. You've made yourself a Leigh in miniature——"

Michael paused on that phrase. It had an odd, almost a prophetic ring. As though Adam Leigh himself were hovering, somewhere in that velvet-soft dark, watching his minion brandish a fist at his fate.

"An atavism," said Michael. "A shape from the past that grows fat beyond its time. You and Leigh. Each in your fashion. I don't doubt that he's your inspiration—and the better man."

The Spaniard looked down at his rum. "And what do you call yourself, Doctor? The future, in shining armor?"

"By no means. So far, I've drifted—without answers. With no moral sense whatever, since you insist. At least I try to understand the future—and my place in it. I don't turn my back and live on other men's flesh."

"But you've done precisely that for the better part of two years. You've grown rich at it."

"Only because I can't help myself."

"True again. Your virtue, as always, is beyond reproach. Still, you'd have been wiser to accept my friendship. I might have shared a secret with you tonight. I might even have explained just why I ran amok in Fernandina. Who knows? You might have believed me human after all—and not the devil's stepson."

Michael smiled around his growing anger. "Let me see if I can guess that secret. Leigh has increased your bonus. So you chose a —shall I say, a peculiar way to celebrate?"

The Spaniard downed his rum and filled two more glasses. "I think I'll tell my story after all. I must tell it to someone—and you're the only other gentleman aboard."

"I am honored by the bracketing." Michael bowed mockingly from the waist. Even as he inclined he watched Ríos narrowly, saw the familiar spark glow and die in the Spaniard's eyes.

"Yesterday Adam Leigh paid me in full for my—my long services. He tore up my contract—at my request. This is my last voyage to Africa. Next month I sail for Barcelona to resume my true place in society. Does the news startle you?"

"Not at all. I'd wish you success, if I could."

"But you feel sure that nobility is something I'll never buy—in Spain or elsewhere?"

"Put that another way. I don't think you can buy forgetfulness."

"So you think this life will haunt my dreams?"

"As it will haunt mine. Can you keep it out?"

"Why not? And why can't you grasp the fact that I believe in slavery as the natural lot of man?"

"We've covered this ground before I believe. You still insist that life is a weed——?"

"A weed that must be pruned endlessly, lest it choke the earth."

"And you enjoy the pruning?"

"And the transplanting. Even weeds are useful in their place."

Michael clung grimly to the metaphor. "And you'd include me in the pruners—or should I say the transplanters?"

"I'm offering you my place, Doctor, now I'm retiring. I'm suggesting that you assume full charge at the Boca, with Adam Leigh's blessing—and mine."

The Spaniard's words sank into an immense silence which Michael made no effort to break. The Spaniard's lips twisted into a pale grimace. Michael would never be sure if it was a smile of pure mockery—or a genuine fumble at friendship. "Coffin is in *de facto* charge—or will be, when he's made his crossing. It would give me real pleasure to depose him in your favor. I'm sure that Adam Leigh would confirm my judgment."

"You must be even more certain that I'll refuse in advance."

"With your special skill you could save Leigh a hundred lives on every crossing. If he paid you my percentages—and I'm sure he will——"

"The Boca is another name for prison in my book. How often must I repeat that?"

"Where has this defiance led you? Are you any less the prisoner for refusing to sign Leigh's contract?"

"At least I've kept my honor." Michael regretted the bombast instantly. Already he was positive that the Spaniard was playing with him with all the assurance of a well-pleased feline. A tomcat who has had his romp—and can enjoy a bit of lazy torture.

"Honor is a beautiful word, Doctor," said Ríos. "It is deplorable that only the wrong people take it seriously. The best men have always known that *power* is the only word with universal meaning. I have just offered you power. Command over thousand of lives. Refuse it, and that renegade Yankee will succeed me. And bungle a job you could do magnificently."

"I think that's more than enough. Don't you?"

The white hands spread eloquently. "As you wish."

"You'll forgive me if I turn in?"

"Surely you've rested enough for one day?"

"With your permission, Comandante."

"With my permission, Señor Médico. Go with God."

Michael stepped from doorjamb to deck and prayed that he had made that transition casual. At the rail he dared to pause for breath. They were in open water now. The green haze of marsh that covered the approach to the Amelia River was definitely astern. Ahead, to the south and east, Nassau Sound was brisk with cross chop. He shivered in the dark at the thought of vanishing among those whitecaps. . . . Ríos's voice still held him fixed. It would be fatal to show the slightest haste, now that he was planted for his plunge.

Instead, he leaned on the rail and watched the spout of surf along the dim reaches of sand bar ahead. The barkentine was moving easily, with that threat well to port. Still more distant, a mere ghosting of white on the western horizon, the surf of Talbot Island had begun to take shape in the blackness. There was no sign of Pablo's sloop, or Pablo's promised bonfire. He could not picture Tola's cousin at this moment or the threat he represented. Ríos had been talking for some time. He came back to the reality of the deck.

"Why don't you take a header, Doctor? It might solve your troubles nicely."

Using all his will, Michael held his back rigid—and spoke with his eyes on the *Mariposa's* wake. "Would you stop me?"

"Answer one question first. What would you gain if you reached shore alive?"

"Freedom, I suppose. Or is that only another word to you?"

"The most deluding word of all. Assume you could weather the surf on Talbot Island. And that you lived to reach Fernandina. How would you use your freedom?"

"Don't make me think too far. You've just put the idea in my mind."

"Forgive me again, Doctor. But I'm quite sure you're lying."

You're still teasing me, thought Michael. You've no inkling of Tola's deception or of mine. Perhaps it's the climax of that cat-

and-mouse dance you began over the rum. But he held his peace and kept his eyes on the dance of whitecaps.

"One more thought and I'm done," said the Spaniard. "Freedom is worthless without power. Even if you could eke out a living, Leigh would hunt you down. Or hadn't you thought of that?"

"I'm a British citizen with a passport to prove it. Florida is a dominion of the Spanish Crown." Michael's fists had anchored him to the rail. It was all that kept him from plunging, before he damned his chances with an unwise word. "Don't tempt me too far, Ríos."

"You are tempting yourself, Doctor. And I'm enjoying the show."

"You'd stop me, of course."

"You asked that once. Repetition proves you are nervous."

"You promised an answer, I believe."

"You'll have it in just sixty seconds. Will you take it between the shoulder blades—or between the eyes?"

Michael turned at last. Had death itself poked his ribs with a bony finger, the transition could not have been more shocking. Ríos sat as before, deep in his chair, sipping his rum. His free arm, swinging just above the floor, was part of that lazy repose. The snub-nosed derringer in his fist was strangely out of place. But Michael knew how effective that toylike pistol could be at close range. Only this voyage he had watched the Spaniard drop a freshly branded slave at the rail. Oddly enough, the black had been about to plunge from this same part of the deck. He remembered the jab of flame, the heart-stopping scream. His own emergency operation, that had found the bullet just in time. And he remembered how Ríos had watched with flaring nostrils as the Negro writhed under the steel and all but howled away his life.

"So you planned this too?"

He was facing the Spaniard directly now with his arms spread-eagled on the rail. Six feet, he reflected, was too long a space to leap. The derringer would stop him in his tracks.

"I've planned to hurt you for some time," said Ríos. "As I say, life has been hard for me. I have fought for all I have. You, with talent at your finger ends, have enjoyed life from the start. No, Dr. Stone, you have not been hurt enough. It pleases me to correct that equation with a thunderbolt all my own."

Ríos was taking his time now and savoring every word. "On second thought, I'll give you more than sixty seconds. But I'm afraid I must kill rather than maim you. Personally, I'd prefer the latter. But you have friends aboard. Too many friends—even if they are devil's spawn like me. They might not believe you were shot while attempting to jump ship."

"I'm still asking you why."

Michael had kept his voice level with a great effort, though the words seemed to clutter his throat like marbles. If I break, he thought, he'll shoot me out of hand. I must keep as cold as he pretends to be. That's what he enjoys—for the present.

"Shall we say five minutes instead of one, Dr. Stone? Surely it's time enough to defend your right to live."

"But I've no *raison d'être* that would appeal to you."

"Quite so. You're a romantic in a killers' world. Your sort has always menaced mine. Given too much time, you'll ruin everything with your pale Christian kindness. When the world belongs to the weak, its days are numbered. It would be far simpler to return it to the apes. Or to those black limbs of Satan we've been selling so profitably in America."

Ríos let his breath escape in a gentle sigh; Ríos's lambent eyes opened wide as a child's. Michael watched the flame die in the irises—abruptly, as though a hand had snuffed the light in the Spaniard's brain. Only then did he note the thin trickle of blood at the man's neckcloth, the knife quivering haft-deep in his throat.

Ríos sighed again as his body collapsed in the chair. His lips kept their smile, but it was frozen now for all time. The seven-inch blade, skewering the top vertebrae, had plunged deep into the wood of the chair back, holding its target erect in death. Michael stared on, unmoving, as the derringer slipped from the Spaniard's fist and fell to the cabin floor.

"Do not move, Señor Mike."

"Gracias, amigo. I don't need that warning."

"Pablo's signal will come in a moment." Tola's voice was casual in the dark, despite the whisper. "You must be ready to answer it."

"When did you——"

"I watched from the beginning."

"And threw the knife when you saw——"

"And threw the knife."

"Did anyone notice that——" He would finish his sentences in another moment. For the present it was enough to breathe deep of clean sea air. To revel in the shuddering animal reflexes that told him how alive he was.

Tola's whisper was calm as ever. "The boom hid me from the helm when we came about. Saunders is forward with his leadsman——"

"Come out where I can see you."

"It is better that I stay hidden. You must go overside alone in another moment. There is no other way."

The voice seemed to recede with the final words, to blend with darkness. Michael found that he could close the cabin door with an extended toe without leaving his place at the rail. Staring blindly at the latticed pattern of light, he reminded himself that he was still a doctor, that even an enemy deserved a death certificate. But he could not risk entering the cabin a second time. Already the lookout had shouted a warning from the mainmast shrouds.

Once again Michael marked the thin white line of surf to starboard and the black void he must cross to reach it. Talbot Island, in that encompassing darkness, was only a shadow against the horizon: he had a sense of low dunes, of a dull pounding that told him the surf (which seemed only a penciled smudge from this vantage point) was heavy enough to threaten the swimmer. A musket cracked in the gloom, and he whirled to the sound with a great surge of relief.

"A sail, sir! Dead ahead!"

There, at last, was the gray bulk of Pablo's sloop, leaning with the wind on their port quarter. There was the floating bonfire he had promised—a mass of tarred kindling on a raft, spinning with the current until it seemed ready to burst against the barkentine's side. The sloop plunged across the Mariposa's bows and vanished into the night as though it had never been. There were two more musket shots to cloud the picture further: Pablo was giving a convincing performance. Thanks to the diversion of the floating fire, the path of the sloop's retreat was secured instantly. From the

Mariposa's deck it would seem that a flotilla of pirates was about to converge, now that the flames had outlined their prize.

Michael heard the wheel creak as the helmsman pulled the barkentine's nose away from the fire, with inches to spare. Crouched at the rail, he waited for the blazing raft to drift well astern. Already he could hear the slap of feet on deck as the crew sprang to stations. Saunders shouted from the forecastle head. Michael cursed his luck as he saw the mate lunge into view with a musket cradled in his arm, his eyes wild in the reflected glare. He had forgotten that Saunders would report instantly to Ríos.

"Where is he, Doc?"

There was no time for planning as the mate loomed above him. He kicked open the cabin door and waved Saunders inside.

"Dead to the world, I'm afraid."

The mate bent above the Spaniard's chair. Michael was upon him before he could lift his head. A straight, hard chop of the right fist, with all his weight behind it, connected neatly with the base of Saunders's skull. The mate crumpled, not at all neatly: it was a trick that the man had used himself to quiet rebellion in the compound.

Michael plummeted into the Atlantic without pausing for thought. He had swum free of the barkentine's side and was clawing his way up the slope of a following wave before he quite realized that he was overboard at last. The beacon fire, already dancing out to sea, picked out the slaver's spars with goblin fingers, even as the slaver's own night shadow cast him into deeper darkness.

No one had seen him take his header. Every eye aboard was probing the dark for the pirates that had sent their warning, then failed to join battle. He heard Mozo bellow for orders and laughed aloud as he remembered that the barkentine was without an officer at this critical moment—and would so remain, until Saunders emerged from his daze. Then it was his turn to panic—to sound abruptly, digging deep at the sea's heart as the ship, heeling in a sudden puff of wind, threatened to run him down.

He felt his senses whirl in the depths and swam even deeper, ignoring the ringing in his ears. Someone was shouting again when he broke surface. He blew the water from his head, conscious that the ship had roared over him without quite making contact with his skull. The dinghy, dancing like a water bug on her painter, just missed his head. The *Mariposa* roared on with every sail belled in the wind. He heard the click of cocked muskets at the weather rail and shook his fist at the vanishing silhouette. How could they know that Pablo, with his good deed done, was already racing for the land with his own sails spread just as wide?

Tola, he hoped, had gone overside long ago. His own badly timed departure had been delayed far beyond the margin of safety. Perhaps they had missed him and would still come about. Perhaps Saunders still lay spread-eagled at the captain's feet. He would have an answer in another moment.

Riding as high as he dared on the next following sea, he knew an instant of real fear as he swept the horizon for land and could see nothing but the angry teeth of whitecaps. The panic died when he heard the boom of surf on the Talbot Island beach—more insistent than ever, now that he was clear of the ship. He moved toward the sound, flailing both arms in a swinging overhand, swimming by ear rather than eye.

He was startled to note that the *Mariposa* had shifted position and was yawing violently, her trim lines disheveled by flapping canvas. Even at the distance he could hear the babble of voices. So they've found Ríos, he thought dully. Are they rushing to the doctor's cabin—or is Saunders telling them that the doctor is overboard?

He slid into the trough between two waves, leaving the question in mid-air. The detonation all but split his eardrums long before he could orient it; the sea itself seemed part of this sudden cataclysm, lifting him in a wild whirlpool, sucking him deep in its turbid vortex. An invisible fist struck his midriff a paralyzing blow. Thrust down by the weight of water, sucked even deeper in that nightmare whorl, he all but yielded to the combined pressures. Air streamed from his lungs in a cascade of bubbles; a black haze invaded his brain. Then, with no sense of relief, he felt his body burst into the air again. He found he was treading water in the midst of foaming backwash and staring at the spot where the ship had been.

Already the tall pillar of smoke and fire, a spout from some demonic whale, had begun to subside in the hungry mouth of the sea. In that flash he understood completely: Tola (it could be no one but Tola) had detonated the magazine. The Minorcan, who had watched their cargo come aboard at Fernandina, had known precisely how much powder they were ferrying to Africa. Quick as a marmoset between decks, and quite as mischievous, Tola had used this Draconian means to pay back old scores—as well as to cover their escape completely.

The force of the explosion, he saw, had split the barkentine into a hundred fragments. Already only a few dimly burning spots remained to mark its place. He watched these glow and die as his senses spun back to normal. Nothing (he repeated the thought grimly enough) could have lived in that inferno. A wave of nausea gripped him as he watched the oily slick widen into a monstrous, feebly burning mushroom. There would be broken bodies in that welter, and sharks aplenty, once their fright had subsided—the same scavengers that had clung to their wake on every crossing. It was ironic (and strangely appropriate) to think how well they would feast tonight.

He began to scramble wildly toward shore before the thought could take definite form. Every stroke was a hideous effort. Before he could swim a hundred yards, he rolled to his back and surrendered to the sickness that gripped him.

Thank heaven the tide was almost at its flood: even though he was only floating, it could not help but sweep him inshore. He trod water easily, letting his fingers test the muscles of his abdomen. They came away shaking with relief: there was no sign of a broken rib, none of the distention that told of blasted intestines. He had seen too many explosions to doubt the narrowness of his escape; too many bodies, scarcely marred on the outside, twisted in death agony as those unseen hands clawed the last life from the vitals.

But this was no time for aftermaths. With his own life to save, he could not pause to ponder the hideous fate of the barkentine. It had been Tola's idea of revenge, and, bizarre though it seemed at the moment, it had its own rough justice. He rolled to his face again in the chop and forced his stiffened muscles to their task.

V

Two hours later, still laboring in the troughs of the waves, still fighting the lulling urge to drift, he felt that he had always been alone in this wilderness of wind-harried sea. Sometimes, when he rose to a crest and stared desperately shoreward, he knew that he was making progress of a sort: the surf that fringed the beach was a reality now, though it was still fearfully remote. More often (as his eyes caked with salt and his lids drooped in the first prelude of exhaustion) he found it easier to surrender to a lassitude that went deeper than despair.

The tide was at full flood now. In another half-hour the Atlantic would draw him back to its depths as casually as it reclaimed its other denizens. Once again his brain lashed his muscles, urging them to another effort. But now he could see how puny that effort really was in the face of these endless hills of salt.

Was that roaring the surf on Talbot or the last spasm of an overtaxed heart? He struggled to raise himself enough to see ahead. The sea's face was black now, as a scud of rain clouds blotted the stars. I've lost my bearings again, he thought. I'm returning to that hideous blot of oil and flesh. Another stroke and I'll touch a sea tiger's snout.

He felt a stinging slap on one cheek and rolled with the blow. Gasping for breath, he took down a strangling mouthful of sea. Then he was engulfed in the first great comber. He let himself go with that dark wall of water, yielding to its downward shove, feeling the sudden gravelly pain of sand along his side as it pounded him deep in the spongy face of the bar. Just as naturally, he rode the roaring backwash that had sucked him to the surface again and sent him bobbing seaward.

Three times he rolled shoreward in the surf, only to be whisked back by the undertow. On the fourth try he rode as high as he could, feather-kicking with all his strength to hold his position on the glass-smooth shoulder of the wave. But the breaker, moving shoreward with dizzy speed, was too much for his flagging strength. As it broke in earnest, he felt himself surrender to that churning impact, knew that he was sinking like a waterlogged spar, to roll on the bottom once again. When he broke surface he seemed farther from shore than ever. Worse, he could tell that the tide had changed. Merely by lowering his toes between waves he could feel the backsuck.

His vital forces stirred for the climactic effort. When the next wave came he tried another tactic: without riding its surface or yielding to its ruthless downbeat, he made his whole body rigid, save for his churning feet. Taking the whole sea on back and shoulders, he held himself firm in the wave's heart, made himself one with its velocity. There was no time to breathe in that boiling spindrift. But when the force of the roller had spent itself, he knew that it had taken him a good fifty yards inshore.

The sea was still deep, but he dared to sound between waves, and found that he could just graze bottom with his toes in these moments of slack water. When the next roller came he was ready —riding its back with all his failing strength, flinging himself forward in a blind wallow as the water crashed and broke, riding once again like an arrow at its heart.

Now, he found, he could almost stand as the wave receded— though he spoiled that triumph instantly by collapsing in the slack water, and all but foundered in the backwash. But the feel of ribbed sand beneath his toes had given him the will to survive. From that moment his progress was crablike but steady—until the receding surf was boiling at his armpits, at his waist, at his knees. Again he lost his elation as he collapsed, face down, in the foam-flecked shallows. A wave passed over his back, and he fought off the last temptation—to lie here and breathe deep of death. To ignore the dry shoulders of the dunes just beyond. . . . Little by little, inching forward on hands and knees, he pulled himself out of real danger, though the backwash still threatened to float him free of his straining grip on land. Ten minutes more and he realized, dimly enough, that he was safe, though his trailing legs still lifted free in the tongues of brine.

On elbows and toes, panting like a broken bellows, he lunged forward once again. Now he lay in a swirl of foam where the tidemark ended. Now he was on dry sand, sprawled in a rack of seaweed, feeling rain stream on his naked back.

The shower was short and violent. Under his hands the beach

was still warm from yesterday's sun, even as the rain pitted it. He made a wallow for his body and lay there as instinctively as a tired dog. His mind just escaped a blank, though he remembered when the shower ended, when he wavered to his feet and began to climb the nearest dune.

This is America, he told himself. You're visiting it for the first time: go to meet it on your feet, like a man. He was not quite sure how or when he gained the summit of the dune, though he knew that the soft sand had absorbed the last wisp of his strength. He stared for a long time at barren tumbled white—at a green waste of marsh crisscrossed by tidal reaches. All of it was etched in starlight, a picture painted with a loose and prodigal brush. No land had ever seemed more welcome.

It was his last conscious thought before his knees buckled. Tumbled in warm sand halfway down the slope of the dune, he heard someone call his name. The shout repeated through the warm haze of his drowsiness, and he knew that Tola (waiting at the water's edge) had marked his silhouette against the stars.

He lapsed into the Minorcan's arms and found that they were gnarled as old palmetto roots, firm as the Florida earth itself. With that certainty to sustain him, he slept in earnest.

III

The "Resolve"

MICHAEL lay quietly, with his eyes on the age-stained timbers overhead. The first panic had subsided now—the certainty that time had done a grotesque back somersault and deposited him in the cabin of the *Dos Amigos*. There was no doubt that he was aboard yet another vessel. But this ship was strange to him—and this ship was blessedly landlocked.

He was lying in a roughly built corn-shuck bed; the rolled quilt that served as his pillow had never gone to sea. Looking farther, he saw broken timbers, a splintered gunwale letting in a glimpse of an enclosed sound wide and blinding blue in the sun. Beyond, a salt marsh, thickly tufted in bright greens and browns, ended in a filigree of palm fronds. Untidy cabbage palms against a sky as brightly blue as the sound. As he looked, a pelican dived from the heart of that bright blue, skated along the water with hardly a splash, and winged away with a fish dangling from its pterodactyl-like beak. It was just the touch of pre-history that the scene needed. Surely this hulk had drifted to its careening ground from the dawn of time. Was Dr. Michael Stone her only passenger?

He hesitated over that question, comfortably postponing the answer. His last full moment of consciousness framed Tola, and Tola's strong arms, as they lifted him from the sands of Talbot Island. The rest hovered between sleep and waking. Yet there were several vignettes—all of them crystal-clear, though he could not yet arrange them in sequence.

First and most vivid was the crone's face in the rainy dawn. He was lying in the bottom of a dugout canoe, with Tola at the paddle. The unwieldy craft bumped with the tide as it nuzzled the end of a rotting pier. The woman had stood there balancing expertly with one foot on the gunwale as she examined him. He remembered that her skin was the color of weathered walnut. The nose was prominent, a Roman nose that had outlived its century; the large, liquid eyes were just as incongruous in that frame of straight black hair. She had taken his pulse with casual skill. Her voice, it seemed, was as savage as her appearance, though she spoke a fairly accurate Spanish.

"He is not sick, amigo—only tired."

"You cure him, Maman?"

"Rest and food is the only cure he needs. Take him to the hulk. He'll be safer there. I will send for Dr. Hilary."

Before that apparition—and after—there had been endless green whispers of marsh grass against the canoe's sides. He was in this cornhusk bed when he wakened again, his cheek pillowed on the yielding firmness of a woman's breast. Slender tanned fingers stroked the brine-caked hair at his temples; a woman's hand spooned porridge from a bowl clutched between her knees. It should have been a strange wakening, but he did not feel in the least strange; somehow he knew that he had been fated to accept this bounty from the beginning; to relax against this firm young flesh and surrender to the greatest contentment he had ever known. . . . But when he tried to put his thanks into words, she had merely vanished.

The doctor came later, fitting neatly enough into his next spell of wakefulness. At first the doctor was only a rather untidy beard and a reek of Jamaica rum. There had been a few murmured instructions to someone Michael could not see, though he was sure that it was the girl who had fed him the porridge. Tola was in the background too. He was grateful for that square brown presence.

"Heard you had a sick man here, Dimity. This fellow's only waterlogged. And hungry. What have you fed him so far?"

"Corn-meal mush, Dr. Hilary." The girl had a pleasant voice, he recalled. An unschooled American voice—though he could not place the accent.

"Give him what he likes, and try to keep him on his back till evening." The doctor, thought Michael, had walked in Oxford cloisters. Only an Oxford man could bite his consonants so briskly.

Tola had spoken anxiously. "He'll recover, Señor Médico?"

"Naturally. With such a nurse how can he help himself?"

There had been more in those same quiet whispers. But even the whispering had faded as he slipped into drowsiness again. He had taken the girl's whisper into his uneasy dreaming—pleased that he could recall its cadence. It seemed quite in order that he should hear that same whisper now—if only as an assurance that he had wakened at last.

"Decided you've slept enough?"

She was at the bedside smiling down at him. He knew she was quite real now, but he touched her arm to be positive. The deep-tanned flesh was firm and cold under his fingers, as though the girl had just come from the sea. Her close-cropped blond curls made an aureole about an impish, attractive, unpretty face. Her real charm, he noted, lay in the wide, friendly mouth, the snapping blue eyes that were laughing at him now. Perhaps it was the tilted nose that gave her the air of an alert boy. There was nothing boyish about the small compact body, more revealed than hidden by a worn cotton wrapper.

"I thought I'd have a swim while you dozed. Guess I'm a poor nurse after all."

"Is your name really Dimity?"

"Dimity Parker. Doesn't it suit me?" She had challenged him instantly—a laughing challenge delivered with arms akimbo. He found it easy to join in laughter that came so obviously from this small person's heart.

"May I ask how I got here?"

"Don't you remember?"

"There was a canoe. A mahogany witch." He considered those memories. "You came after her. A long time after. Then a doctor with a beard who smelled of rum——"

"Dr. Hilary. So far your memory's first-rate."

"What about the witch?"

"Some folks in Fernandina say that Felippa works in magic. But I won't listen: she's a friend of mine."

"Tell it your way," said Michael. "I've nothing else but time, it seems."

"I'll tell you nothing until you've taken your lunch. Dr. Hilary said to feed you each time your mouth opened."

He watched her leave the cabin with the same gamin stride. On deck she paused just within his range of vision to investigate a saucepan simmering on a brazier. Sitting on her heels as she stirred the contents, she seemed oblivious of the fact that her wrapper had fallen aside, to exhibit a great deal of a body that managed to be both well muscled and slender. Everywhere her skin (high-lighted by the blaze of noon) seemed to be the same shade of golden brown. Michael closed his eyes, half expecting her to vanish when he looked again. But she was already seated on the bed and offering him a steaming bowl of fish chowder.

"First this. Then your medicine."

"No facts until I've had both?"

"No facts at all. You were a tired boy when you came in this morning."

He admitted as much silently as he spooned away the fragrant contents of the bowl. Dimity Parker was waiting with his medicine as he swallowed the last morsel. He watched her pour out the black concoction from a rum bottle that still sported a garish West Indian label.

"Felippa's special brew. She makes it for no one but the Indians —and Dr. Hilary."

He took the spoonful down and shuddered at the wormwood tang. But he recognized the blend instantly.

"Extract of Peruvian bark. How in the world——"

"That's what Dr. Hilary called it too. How did you know the name?"

"I happen to be a doctor myself."

The bright-blond head cocked in frank disbelief. "You wouldn't tease a girl you've just met?"

"The name is Dr. Stone. Dr. Michael Stone, late of the Royal College. Would you care to see my passport?"

"Mike is easier, Doc. And don't show me your papers. I never had time for much book learning."

He sat up quickly in the cornhusk bed, fighting his sudden fear, as his mind fumbled with the fact that he was naked under the tattered quilts. The passport, the scalpel, the three hundred American dollars—where were they now? Dimity answered the unspoken question with a smile and a reassuring hand on his bare shoulder.

"Your drawers are drying, Mike. Your man took your money into Fernandina to buy whatever you'll be needing."

"And my passport?"

"On that shelf above your head. Right under your knife. Are you really a doctor?"

"I suppose it's hard to believe, Dimity. *You're* rather hard to believe right now. May I get used to you gradually?"

The girl tossed her damp blond ringlets. "Take your time, Mike. Only I'm easy to get used to. You'll find out."

The blue eyes were luminous and friendly: like the hand on his shoulder, they had not wavered. Michael felt a great urge to respond in kind—and controlled it firmly. He spoke the first question that entered his mind—if only to cover that urge.

"You know Tola—the man who brought me here?"

"Never laid eyes on him before. There aren't many Minorcans on Amelia Island. Augustine's their stamping ground, and that's a good eighty miles down the coast. Why did he bring you here?"

Michael hesitated, resisting a no less potent desire for a confidante. "Why did you take me as a patient?"

"You've answered that. Felippa sent you. I told you she's a friend of mine. So's Dr. Hilary."

"Does this Dr. Hilary practice in Fernandina?"

"When he's sober. And sometimes when he isn't." Dimity chuckled at a picture all her own. "Full name's Dr. Hilary Tyler. A stranded Englishman, they say. Been here since the Spanish took back the Floridas."

"I thought the English made a mass exodus at that time."

"Come again, Mike?"

"Didn't they leave in a body from this very port?"

"Dr. Hilary didn't. Maybe he had his reasons for staying behind. So far as I know, he's the only Englishman on the island, if you don't count visiting sailors."

"There'll be two of us, for the time being."

"So you're English after all. I thought you might be an actor. Most actors talk like Englishmen." She regarded him musingly, but her blue eyes were merry. "Being an actress of sorts myself, I can speak by the book there."

Michael settled deeper in the cornhusk bed. So far her chatter had told him little, yet he felt completely soothed in her presence. Completely at ease in this battered hulk that was, apparently, her home. Contented, for the moment, to let her tease him in her own way.

"So you're an actress. Of course I should have guessed."

"Late of the Wharf Players, Charleston."

"Tell me more."

"You don't believe a word, do you, Mike?"

"On my honor, Miss Parker——"

"Then believe me when I say you need your rest. Try to sleep till sundown. Your man should return by then. Let *him* explain why he brought you to me."

"I'd rather have your version now."

"I'll tell you this much. You're in Dr. Tyler's hospital right now—and I'm in charge. So you'd better follow orders."

"Say that slowly, please."

"This is the brig *Resolve,*" said Dimity. "Late of His Majesty's Navy. Careened in a hurricane years ago. Dr. Hilary's supposed to have bought the salvage. He made me his nurse when I left the Players." Dimity was still smiling down at him, but he saw that her eyes were veiled now. "Aren't those enough facts for one afternoon?"

"Forgive me for being wide awake. Why should an actress become a doctor's nurse? And why is a nursing home located on a stranded British brig, fifty miles from nowhere?"

"Fernandina and the Amelia River are just beyond that screen of palms," said Dimity. "You must walk a mile across the savannah —and cross a creek that's only fordable at low tide."

"Why isn't the doctor's hospital in Fernandina?"

"The air is better here. In more ways than one."

"Are there other patients aboard?"

"Not right now. Maybe I'd better be honest and admit you're my first."

"Go a bit further. Admit you're an actress who ran away from something."

"Speak for yourself, Mike."

He let his hand cover hers and smiled as she blushed under her tan. "Perhaps you're right, Dimity. Too many questions could overtax my strength." She had not withdrawn her fingers. He turned her hand slowly in his own and closed a kiss in the palm. "That's for stopping me in time. You see, I can hardly remember when I've talked to a woman in my own tongue."

Dimity was blushing in earnest when she left the bedside. He lifted on an elbow to watch her go down the deck—and caught his breath at what he saw. Unaware that she was observed, the girl had already mounted a canted gunwale where the brig's bowsprit raked the sky. Apparently she had dropped her wrapper en route. Naked as a pagan princess, and just as unconcerned, she balanced on her toes for an instant with her arms taut. Sunlight poured down her slender thighs, high-lighting small, pert breasts until they seemed to glow with a light of their own. Then she plunged, vanishing overside without a splash. A moment later, as his eyes shifted to the porthole beside his bed, he saw those same slender arms cleaving the water far out in the bay.

Michael settled deeper in his impromptu mattress. Despite his weariness, his heart had begun to assume a familiar rhythm. This time, however, the rhythm was oddly soothing. So soothing, in fact, that he could slip into another drowsy half-dream with scarcely a pang. Even now Dimity Parker could be a mirage. He could still waken in his cabin aboard the slaver. In the meantime it was good to slip into this easy cat nap, to cling to the strange certainty that he had come home at last—though he had yet to give his home a dimension or a name.

II

It was late afternoon when he wakened, and Tola was seated at the bedside.

"Supper in a little while, jefe. The doctor said you could leave your bed when you wished."

Michael yawned prodigiously and knew he was himself again, even before he could smile at Tola. It seemed quite natural, now, to waken in a cornhusk bed—with a nightmare as his genesis and a golden nereid as his nurse.

"Tell this from the beginning, Tola."

"There is little to tell, Señor Mike. I could save only your boat cloak and the instrument case. The cloak dries now on the deck.

The instruments are in the doctor's house in Fernandina. He promises to scour them well—before the salt water can rust the steel."

"The *real* beginning, please. When you found me on the beach."

"You had swallowed much sea water. When the ship blew apart you were still too close. It is apparent that the explosion shocked you badly. It shocked my cousin Pablo still more. I had told him I would set the powder train and wipe them from the sea. And yet, when he saw the red fire against the sky, Pablo could think only of flight. Only now I hear that he is in Augustine."

Michael sat up in bed and hugged his knees. The Minorcan's face was masklike: there was no hate in the quiet eyes, only the righteous pleasure of a job well done.

"So you admit you detonated the magazine?"

"I had planned to do just that for a long time, Señor Mike."

"You might have warned me."

"You are a humane man. I knew you would forbid it." Tola leaned forward earnestly. "Now I beg you not to sorrow for the death of dogs."

"You don't look like an avenging angel." In his moral puzzlement Michael found he had spoken in English. "Still, you took the part beautifully."

"Perdone, Señor Médico?"

"Never mind the rest, Tola. Just explain how you got overside with my instrument case?"

"I was in the water ahead of you, Señor Mike. Your case was hidden in the dinghy astern. I cut the painter just before the fire could reach the magazine."

"We didn't come here in a ship's dinghy. I'm sure of that much."

"No, Señor Mike. Only as far as the southern tip of Amelia. In Fernandina it is already known that the *Mariposa* exploded and went down with all hands. If Adam Leigh learned that the ship's dinghy was still afloat, he might ask questions. So I hid the boat in the marsh and stole a dugout from a plantation dock——"

"Don't tell me that Leigh's in Fernandina."

"He remains at Punta Blanca for the present. But his sloop is often in the harbor." Again Tola considered carefully before he spoke again. "It is well that we could bring you to this hidden place. Better still, if you remain here awhile. Until you are really well."

"I'm well now, thanks to Dimity." Michael sat up in earnest. "Where is she?"

"She has taken my canoe, Señor Mike. To fish in deep water for your supper."

"Does she know who I am?"

"I have already told Felippa. If Felippa tells this girl, or Dr. Hilary, we should trust them too."

"Why can't we buy a sloop and leave at once?"

"Leaving is not so simple, jefe. The Georgia country is quite as wild as this. You would be forced to touch at St. Marys. Or wait for a coastal vessel to take you to Savannah or to Charleston——"

"St. Marys is Georgia, isn't it?"

"St. Marys is filled with American soldiers, Señor Mike. There is a garrison at Point Peter. Always there is a sloop of war in the Cumberland to turn back smugglers."

"I'm a British subject. My passport is in order. I've enough funds to prove I'm not a pauper. Won't these United States receive me?"

"Not without questions."

"Are you suggesting I'd be arrested because of my connection with Leigh?"

"You wish to become an American, Señor Mike. Well enough. But it is better to answer no questions at St. Marys."

"What other course can I follow?"

"Wait. Here on the hulk. Rest in the sun. No one will find you out. The girl will care for your needs."

"Say it, Tola. You're afraid that Leigh will snatch me back from St. Marys if I show my face."

"Adam Leigh has many agents. The Georgia customs guards are in his pay. If he wished to bring you back from the boundary, he could do so easily."

"I won't believe that." Michael spoke slowly, as though to gather conviction. "I'm a free agent now."

"So you turn to America, the land of liberty. Liberty is not to be had so quickly."

"Very well. Let us say I hide here like a fugitive. How long can I keep my presence a secret?"

"Until a coastal vessel calls at St. Marys. Cargo ships enter Cumberland Sound from all parts of the world. Some turn north to Georgia with legal cargoes." Tola considered his words, his face unsmiling. "Dr. Hilary Tyler will put your bribe in the right hands. You will go by sail from this bayou. Stand out to sea and board this cargo ship well beyond the land—after she has cleared St. Marys. At Savannah or Charleston Adam Leigh would be powerless to stop you. You could go ashore as an English gentleman who had wintered in Cuba."

"Can we trust this Dr. Hilary Tyler?"

Tola glanced at the cabin door. "He waits on deck now to prove his good faith."

"Why didn't you say that sooner?"

"The doctor is a man of tact, Señor Mike. He asked that I prepare you first."

"Show him in, with my apologies."

Tola whisked out to the deck and Michael, about to swing his legs from bunk to floor, remembered his nakedness just in time. Sensing that this was a part of Dr. Hilary Tyler's strategy, he wondered why he did not resent the trick. Certainly he didn't feel in the least trapped. Even before the bearded shadow loomed in the door, he knew that this man was his friend.

Dr. Hilary Tyler seemed more retired dock hand than physician; a quaking barrel of a man in loose ducks, with a gaily-striped sailor's shirt beneath the untidy gray spread of his beard. The aroma of rum blended perfectly with his attire. So did the eyes that blinked at Michael from that wilderness of hair, though the hand that tested his pulse was expert enough.

"You looked rested, sir. I'll go further: you look cured."

"We're well met, Doctor."

"I'll go further still. You're just what this godless corner needs. Upon my soul, if I could anchor you here, I'd do it."

"My man says you can help me to enter America." Michael consider the phrase: it seemed absurd to ask help for so simple a procedure. But Dr. Hilary Tyler rumbled instant agreement, as though he had waited for the question.

"Only if you insist, sir. As I say, I'm perishing for a partner. Not to mention a few patients——"

"Surely my man has told you why I landed here?"

"I know. You've worked in Africa for Adam Leigh. That's nothing against you. Most Fernandinans have taken his money in their time and come back for more. You, being a young man of stern moral fiber, are eager to escape him. *That's* not so easily arranged. Not if that stubborn Scotsman feels he can use you still."

"Surely I've earned my freedom."

"A man and his two fists aren't enough in this corner of Florida. You must buy your way—or join a group. Become a *condottiere,* if I may use an Italian word for an old Spanish custom. You must join Marsden here in Fernandina—or Aravello. Or Leigh—if you work near Punta Blanca. Or Kingsley, if you operate on the St. Johns——"

"I'm a bit behind you, Doctor. Just who are Marsden and Aravello?"

"Kingpins of smuggling in our fair village. Marsden is also the town's leading doctor. Aravello owns the Long Wharf: my quarters are in one of his warehouses, so I'm attached to his group. It's the only reason Marsden hasn't had me knifed so far. Instead, he's contented himself with stealing my patients one by one. Ever since he set up shop in that fine coquina house on the parade——" Tyler pulled up short and blinked owlishly at Michael. "Am I letting my tongue outrun my brains?"

"This smuggling you mention——"

"Our major industry, sir."

"Doesn't it conflict with Leigh's activities?"

"Not at all. Merely a rogues' agreement. Leigh and Kingsley operate with human freight. My friends in Fernandina handle all other contraband."

"Under the guns of Fort San Carlos?"

"Under the Spanish guns, Doctor. Colonel Morales merely turns the other eye. Adam Leigh's factors are another story. *They* keep an eye on every shipment—to make sure there's no live cargo. Have I made my point?"

"Myself, you mean?"

"Precisely, Dr. Stone. Yesterday I find you on Dimity's doorstep, as it were. As provocative a bit of flotsam as I've seen in these waters—and as dangerous. Mr. Leigh has mentioned you more than once when I've called professionally at Punta Blanca. Mentioned you with pride, sir. How would he feel if he knew you were tucked away here—and planning to escape him?"

"Are you implying that escape is impossible?"

"Ticklish is the word, sir. Ticklish—and middling expensive. Would you be agreeable to a hundred dollars—if I swore it would handle everything?"

"How far must I go to be safe?"

"Savannah would do. Charleston's better. Stay here for a fortnight and leave everything to me. I've friends among the military at Point Peter. A dengue and two chancres, to be exact. The port doctor and I have held more than one consultation. It'll be a simple thing to learn in advance when a vessel is putting in from Nassau or Havana. Simpler still to buy your way aboard."

Michael met Tyler's smile. "Would you like the money now?"

"Spoken like a gentleman, Doctor. Take my word, you won't regret a fortnight here with Dimity. That girl can hardly write her name, but its an education to know her."

"Is it true she was an actress once?"

"Call her my ward and let it go at that."

"Life isn't that simple, Dr. Tyler. Not when a man's about to get on his feet again."

Tyler weighed that challenge, with both fists twined in his apostle's beard. "Exception, sir. The word isn't ward—it's waif. Last fall she was washed ashore, along with the troupe she served. Now that you mention it, I do believe she appeared in a mob scene. With a spear—or a bed sheet, if the play was Roman——"

"Then the Wharf Players were real enough?"

"A strolling company from Charleston that took to salt water and were blown off their course. They did well enough in Fernandina until there was a brawl in the midst of a performance. Footlight candles were overturned, and the theater—or should I say the barn?—went up in flames. There wasn't another empty warehouse in town, so the troupe put itself on muleback and started north. All but Dimity. She was down with fever at the time. Felippa was nursing her. Naturally we insisted that she convalesce on the hulk."

"You haven't quite explained her place in the troupe."

"Let's say she was an understudy who did cooking and mending on the side. Let's go a step further and assume she was an apprentice who ran out on her articles. Is that any affair of ours?"

"None whatever." Michael chuckled under Tyler's benign eye. "You're quite right, Doctor. It's an education to meet people like Dimity—and you, if I may make so bold."

"The compliment is accepted."

"Where else would a shipwreck find asylum so readily? What European doctor would keep a nursing home for fugitives?"

Dr. Hilary Tyler rumbled with laughter. "I'm afraid our Dimity has gilded the lily a trifle there. I'm not that sort of doctor—or should I add, not that good a doctor?"

"Forgive me if I differ."

"That compliment I will not accept. And you must visit Fernandina to understand my mirth. Most of my patients are end products of some tavern brawl. Stitched scalps or missing eyes. Or a broken humerus, just for variety's sake. Occasionally I probe for bullets. Or do my best to tie off bleeders my old fingers can no longer find. In any event, the patient usually dies on my office floor—or walks out on his own legs."

"So this isn't a hospital after all?"

"Call it Dimity's personal asylum and you'll be nearer the truth. I bought the hulk years ago as a salvage risk. Felippa put her in this cabin to nurse her through that bout of fever. She's lived here since—on what she could filch from the sea and her neighbors' gardens. A child of nature, Doctor. A nymph who has found her true dwelling place."

"Never mind the poetry, sir. Why did Tola bring me aboard?"

"Felippa, I gather, decided you needed an asylum as well as Dimity."

"But the girl is alone here."

"Does that fact outrage your Anglo-Saxon soul? Perhaps Dimity feared as much. And invented the story of a stranded hulk that served as my hospital. Perhaps she felt that the story would satisfy an English gentleman until he was strong enough to ask further questions."

Michael found that he could match Tyler's grin, after all. "Am I strong enough now?"

"Try my shoulder, and we'll see."

It was absurdly easy to rise from the cornhusk bed. Easier still to take a turn of the cabin with Tyler's shoulder as a crutch. When the trial was over, Michael settled in a corner of the bed and smiled his thanks.

"It seems I'm recovered."

"Englishmen are hard to kill, sir. Look at me, if you want a fair example. Sure you won't reconsider and come in with me?"

"After what you've said of Adam Leigh, how could I?"

"Exception noted." Dr. Tyler sighed in his beard. "You're leaving us because you must. In the meantime, stay close to the hulk and answer no hail but mine—or your man's. I'll return in a day or so. Dimity will see you're well-fed in the meantime."

"Where is the girl now?"

"On deck—cleaning a drum for your supper."

Michael dived for a quilt to cover his nakedness. "You might have brought me trousers, at least."

"Simple precaution, my boy. Can't have you roaming too far afield until the time is ripe."

The English doctor strolled out on that as casually as he had come. Watching him go, Michael wondered why that raffish presence had been so reassuring—and why he was content, even now, to sit quietly in the cabin and breathe the delectable dinner aroma of Dimity's saucepans. Tola shouted a good-by from the water level, and he turned to the open port to wave. The Minorcan was sweeping his paddle in the stern of the dugout—if that ungainly craft could be said to boast a bow or stern. Dr. Tyler, a cigar glowing in the midst of his whiskers, waved an expansive farewell.

There was something Olympian about the gesture, something that blended perfectly with the peace that surrounded him. Once again he had a sense of benign destiny pinning him to the map at last.

III

He sat for a long time on the cornhusk bed, hugging the quilt about his knees and watching the dusk deepen on the bayou. He was thinking of Chen Yui—and an occasion not too dissimilar from today, when that estimable Canton merchant had offered him sanctuary. As always, Mr. Chen made an excellent stalking-horse for destiny.

It had begun at the Pagoda anchorage. Like most men in the employ of the East India Company, Michael had had enemies in Canton. He had entered a water-front brawl, with both fists flailing, to save a colleague's life. The colleague had sailed back to Calcutta scot-free, even as Michael himself was marked for extinction by one of the blood tongs. Chen Yui, who knew everything that happened in Canton, had merely hidden his favorite doctor in the attic of one of his warehouses. Food had been smuggled in by Mr. Chen's own amah, an ancient in a widow's kimono, who had soothed him in a language he could not begin to understand. Later (when the hue and cry had faded, and he was sure he would live again), Mr. Chen had replaced the creaking amah with a sloe-eyed Eurasian girl who could not have been more than sixteen. A sweetly rounded female creature whose very presence had cured his cursing, his wild-eyed pacing in that ambush of silk and rattan. A soft-voiced presence, the girl had known just when to efface herself—and when to touch his cheek with jasmine fingers. When to remind him that there are few problems that Lilith cannot soothe away. . . .

"It was wrong to take her as I did, Chen Yui. Why do you forgive me?"

"She was made to be enjoyed, Michael. Only the puritan mind would berate itself after such pleasure."

"What do you know of the puritan mind?"

"Only what you have taught me, young doctor."

"Aren't you confusing your labels?"

"Not at all. Like most Englishmen, you are puritan in your inmost soul. Of course I have known many others since the first Yankee trader dropped anchor in the Pearl. Most of them were bigots who drove hard bargains. Some were devils under their broadcloth—men who destroyed their essence with old lusts. You are the first puritan I have known who is also human. Cling to your humanity, Michael. When it bids you love, love with all your heart."

"You spoke of devils just now. Perhaps you're a devil too, for all those mandarin silks."

"Perhaps, as we said before, is a word that can lead the West to its doom."

There was no doubt that Chen Yui had saved his life. Recalling their discussion now, he wondered if the Chinese merchant had hoped to make his protection permanent. The daughter of Chen's amah (or was that fluent creature Chen's own daughter-once-removed?) had been sent to him as a solace, pure and simple. Had his friend hoped she would pin him to China's coast forever—a comfort to Chen's declining years? It was an unworthy thought. Chen Yui, that most unselfish of mortals, had offered him a deeper meaning, even as he offered this flower of his secret garden.

Had Dr. Hilary Tyler repeated the Canton merchant's wisdom, here in his corner of the American wilderness?

Michael put the question aside. Draping himself decorously in the folded quilt, he emerged on the deck of the *Resolve* and bowed to his hostess of the evening.

Dimity was still crouched above her saucepans, fanning the coals with a palmetto branch. She gave a faint gasp as he appeared, then settled on her haunches again with a chuckle of welcome.

"Dr. Hilary said you were stirring. I didn't think——"

Michael struck an attitude, with a hand thrust into the bosom of his makeshift toga. "Sorry if I frightened you. But I could hardly resist that overture to supper."

Dimity watched him narrowly as he crossed the slightly canted deck. "Sure you're strong enough to navigate?"

"Thanks to you, I've never felt better." He was above her now, looking down at the bubbling saucepans. "What have we here?"

"Fried okra and onions—with chopped pimiento. Sauce for the drum."

"Drum?"

"He was a twenty-pounder, Mike. They were running deep tonight, but I landed him."

Michael took the fork from her hand and prodded the thick fish steak broiling on the charcoal. "Don't tell me you gaffed this monster alone?"

"I'm stronger than I look, Doc. Just like you."

"Finish our menu, please. It's pure poetry."

"Red yams, green beans, and corn pone. And oranges, from the priests' own grove." Her wide eyes reproved his smile. "Only they weren't really stolen. There haven't been priests in Fernandina for years now. Only Father Ybarra—and he came up from Augustine with the garrison, for their souls' sakes. Dr. Marsden bought the monastery acres when he built his house. It's a pleasure to help yourself, if you don't like Marsden——"

"Never mind Dr. Marsden. Tell me about Dimity Parker."

The girl flashed him a quick grin, and blinked back the tears as wood smoke teased her eyelids. "You know enough about me now, Mike. That is, I asked Dr. Hilary to set you right."

"Item one, that you're a stranded actress?"

"A stranded wardrobe woman, God forgive me."

"And before that?"

"A Charleston barmaid who wouldn't take another beating," said Dimity calmly. "A stubborn trollop who ran away——"

"You aren't the only one who's run away, my dear."

"I guessed that much, on my own," she said just as calmly. "That's why I took you in."

Michael pressed her hand warmly. "May I say I'm more than grateful for the shelter?"

"Of course this isn't really a hospital, like I pretended."

"It's the finest hospital I ever visited. No other nurse has cured me of malaise so quickly."

"Malaise?"

"Lack of a reason for being," he said. "Incurable wanderlust. But you've cured that too, Dimity. Watching you at that saucepan, I never want to stir again."

Her eyes had held him steadily throughout this formal compliment. He broke their dangerous trust and went to the rail to stare across the sound—convinced that he was talking nonsense and positive that she must think him quite mad. But Dimity only chuckled in the growing darkness.

"I've had compliments in my time, Mike. But none as nice as that. Even if I can't quite understand it."

He kept his eyes on the graying sound. "Do you really know who I am? Or should I say, what I came from?"

"Dr. Michael Stone," she said softly. "The slavers' right-hand man."

"I didn't choose the role, Dimity."

"Of course you didn't. Why else would you cut and run?"

He didn't speak for a long moment, hearing only the soft hiss of the fish broiling over the glowing coals. Her quiet understanding had invaded his spirit with its own balm. One with the dove-gray evening, he could almost forget that he was a fugitive—whose safety depended on this bizarre waif, on the whim of a drunken doctor . . .

"What's that red glow to the north?"

"Probably a barbecue," said Dimity. "On one of the sandspits north of town. The sailors have them often, between voyages. Oysters by the barrel and whole kegs of wine. Guitars and garrison girls——"

"Aren't you ever disturbed?"

"Even if they were sober, they couldn't find their way through the marsh." She was beside him now with a steaming plate and a cracked earthenware mug minus a handle. "Will you dine in the open air, Doc? It may help your appetite."

"Tonight it needs no help."

Michael stared blankly at the empty mug, until Dimity reached overside, tweaked a fishing line from its mooring, and swung a bottle on deck. The white Spanish wine, chilled perfectly in its plunge to the bottom, teased his palate with memories of a world he had all but forgotten. He raised the mug to Dimity and thanked her silently for the renewal.

"Is this standard fare?"

"All but the wine. Dr. Hilary brought that."

The fish steak, succulent in its salt-water freshness, vanished rapidly. He dined where he stood, with the plate resting on the ship's rail. Dimity watched contentedly and filled the mug with a practiced hand.

"Don't let me eat your cupboard bare."

"You couldn't if you tried. And even if you could, I'd love it. All my life I've enjoyed watching men eat."

He held out his plate for more with his deepest bow. "May I go on entertaining you?"

This time she perched on the rail beside him, with all the agility of a pouncing kitten. "You're fun, Mike. Do you mind if I say that —so soon?"

"You're more than just fun to me, Dimity. You're salvation."

"It was lonesome here, until you came."

He watched her closely in the growing dark, but there was no hint of coquetry in her smile. "Somehow I can't imagine you lonesome for long."

"Listen to the quiet. Wouldn't it press down on your heart—if you didn't have someone listening beside you?"

Michael nodded as he sipped his wine. They sat there on the rail for a long moment, side by side, letting the dusk wrap them in its peculiar peace. The bayou was a dark mirror for the stars now; the ring of cabbage palms, remote as frowsy ballerinas in the night, seemed to sigh in a sleepy tempo of their own. Days later he would know that their unseen concertmaster was only the sea breeze that moved across Amelia Island at sundown. Tonight the image of remote dancing girls seemed an ideal simile. He settled deeper in contentment, letting those savage coryphees enclose him in their sanctuary.

"Why did you decide to camp here, Dimity?"

"It was Felippa's idea. She thought I should—well, live by myself for a while. Until I made up my mind about the future."

"Witch's wisdom, eh?"

"Aren't you glad you found me, just so?"

Again there was no hint of coquetry in her manner. He struggled to respond in kind, knowing in advance that he would fail. "If I told you how glad I was, you'd think I was making love to you."

"Felippa said you would," murmured Dimity, and he saw that her blue eyes were round in the dark.

"Make love, you mean?"

"She said a man would come to me out of the sea. That I'd nurse him back to health. She didn't mention love-making."

Michael accepted these statements with all the aplomb he could manage. "More of the witch's wisdom?"

"Felippa has the gift of prophecy," said Dimity. She spoke the phrase formally, as though it were strange to her lips. "You mustn't laugh at her, Mike. She *is* wise—even if you don't believe her now."

"I never felt less like laughing. And she's extremely wise to hide you here. From what I've heard of Fernandina, it's no place for a lone female. Especially a pretty one."

"Don't say I'm pretty, Mike. I'll know you're teasing me."

"I've yet to see anyone prettier—in the water or out."

Even in the dusk he knew that she had colored to the roots of her curls. "So you were watching. I might have known you weren't as weak as you seemed."

"I didn't mean to spy, but——" He decided not to be too contrite as Dimity laughed in the darkness. After all, he reflected, this was the world's oldest game. He had played it too often not to anticipate a few moves.

"Dr. Hilary says I'm to stay aboard for at least two weeks. We'll have time to be friends, I hope."

"We're friends now," said Dimity.

"Do you always make friends so easily?"

"Why not—when they talk my language? If you ask me, we're two of a kind. In lots of ways, Mike. Even if you did go to a Royal College once and can take off a man's leg before he can say knife."

Michael chuckled at the English locution—which he knew she had used for his benefit. "Thanks for putting me in your bracket, Dimity."

"You mean that," she said. "That's another reason why we're friends. When a man says a thing like that—and looks at me without a lopsided grin—I'll talk to him without secrets."

She offered her hand in the dark to bind the bargain. "You've been lonesome a long while, haven't you, Mike?"

"Too long, my dear."

"Longer than me, I guess, if the other side lives up to its name."

"Europe or Africa?"

"Take your pick," said Dimity. "I wouldn't have either for a gift. That's where I'm a step ahead of you—if you don't mind my saying so."

"I'd heard the Yankees were proud of their new experiment," he said. "I didn't expect proof so soon."

"Only I'm not a real Yankee. Or a nabob, either. Or even a poor white, as you'd use the word. I'm just a bound girl who ran out on her articles."

"I know that, Dimity. Don't talk about it if you'd rather——"

"Why shouldn't we talk about it? I'm glad I ran away—and skipped for the Florida frontier, like any redneck. While the food lasts, and the good weather, I'm taking my ease. I might even put down my roots, for once, and see what they find. You could do worse, Mike."

"At the moment I'm trying to escape Adam Leigh and all he stands for."

If she was disappointed, she gave no sign. "Do you have friends in the North?"

"I've no friends anywhere—save for a merchant in Canton whom I'll never see again. And an old rascal in London who looks after my finances."

"Don't leave me out," said Dimity. "I'll see you're comfortable until you're ready to skedaddle. Have you enough money to visit America properly?"

Again he listened in vain for a wistful note—a take-me-with-you hint that most girls of her class would have sounded at this point as delicately as a calliope at a county fair. *A girl of her class* . . . If America was truly a democracy, one did not use such labels, even in one's mind. Certainly he felt nothing but respect for Dimity Parker. The fact that she had decamped from a fog of dishwashing in a Charleston tavern was in her favor. The added fact that she could settle contentedly here, with no visible worry for the morrow, was more than enough to stir his envy. He grinned in earnest as he saw their traditional roles reversed. Ordinarily he would have teased her with pictures of the great world beyond her world—if only as a legitimate inducement, a prelude to taking her in his arms. To-night it was Dimity Parker who offered her own carefree cosmos—a gift to be had for the asking.

"What will you see first, Mike?"

"Boston, I think. Is that Yankee enough?"

"As Yankee as they come."

"My father lived in Boston once. Sometimes he even admitted he was an American." It was the last thing he had intended to say. Yet he was obscurely glad, once the words were out.

"Then you're an American too."

"Not yet. I was born in Halifax. That's British soil."

"Where you were born doesn't matter here," said Dimity. "It's who you are—and what you want."

"Here is still Spain, Dimity."

"It'll be an American territory next year. Or the year after. Most folk in Fernandina are Americans, if you don't count the rascals—and a few clans like the Aravellos." Dimity paused. He smiled in the dark as he noted how carefully she was shaping her little lecture. "Of course everyone must pretend to be a Spanish citizen to do business. And of course the rascals run things——"

"Surely the Spanish garrison keeps the peace?"

"Colonel Morales is here to see that the customs duties reach St. Augustine on schedule. He hasn't more than fifty men at the fort. If you ask me, it'd take a line regiment to police that water front. As for the back country, it's been wide open from the beginning. Seminole hunting ground, with a few log-cabin farms on the King's Road——" Again Dimity paused to choose her words. "North Florida's decent enough, underneath. It's just that it's an asylum for runaways of all colors."

"Including you and me?"

"Give us time," said Dimity, "and we could turn into citizens. Most of the rednecks like things as they are. If the smuggling stopped tomorrow, they'd have to go to work. If the gunboats at Point Peter could blast out the slavers——" She drew a deep breath and let the thought die. "Don't let me preach to you, Mike. You've the book learning. You should be telling *me*——"

"Telling you what, my dear? That it's dangerous to be on this hulk alone, with a stranger?"

"From where I'm sitting, you don't look strange at all."

Now was the time to rise with a gentlemanly yawn. If the girl rose too, you fastened both hands on her shoulders and kissed her, long and hard, on the mouth. If she lingered, you moved to the rail, for a last look at the stars—and waited until she joined you. Instead he leaned back against a broken stanchion and yielded to her logic. They had never been strangers: there was no need of subterfuge. No need to be startled when Dimity was the first to rise—with a full-bodied stretch that would have shamed Falstaff.

"Don't be polite if you're ready for bed. I am."

"Shall I make up a bunk out here tonight?"

"The dew would drench you in the morning."

"I can hardly rout you from your cabin."

"We slept together well enough this morning. Or didn't you even know I was there beside you?"

He did not stir as she vanished through the splintered cabin door. This was no time to remember another cabin that had opened wide to his approach—or the white arms that had claimed him in the dark. Dimity's arms were honey-brown from the Florida sun. Her mouth would be warm and comforting—as soothing, in its own way, as the easy words that had passed between them. If this was a gift, Dimity Parker offered it freely. Why did he hesitate? And why, above all, should he bring back a night aboard the *Dos Amigos*—when love had been a long hunger, feeding on another's flesh?

He had no memory of rising from the deck or crossing to the cabin door: he knew only that he had walked in with a singing heart. The cabin was dim rather than dark, lighted faintly by the reflected gleam of the bayou just outside the port. Dimity, already at ease on the wide bed, stirred contentedly as she saw his silhouette against the stars.

"There's usually a sea breeze just before dawn, Mike. Better keep the quilt."

He groped blindly, trustingly, until he found her. As he had hoped, her mouth was sweet in the dark. He kissed it for a long moment, letting time and the tug of the future wash over him unheeded.

"You're beautiful, Dimity."

"You don't mean that. You couldn't."

"I mean every word." His face was buried in her hair. Even now there was a salty savor to the close-cropped curls. "Every word," he repeated in a whisper, though there was no need to whisper. "You see, I'd forgotten how beautiful a woman can be."

"And I'd forgotten there were people like you, Mike."

"But we're two of a kind. You said that only a moment ago. We were lonely. Now we're together."

Dimity drew back a little and twitched her worn wrapper aside. Reflected, aqueous light gleamed on bare shoulders as she returned to his arms. Even before his arms could find her again, he knew that she was naked, and proud of her nakedness. Even before his flesh knew the challenge of her burning breasts, he guessed that she was as eager as he. This is too easy, he told himself solemnly. This is a dream you've dreamed too long. Now that it's come true in your arms, it's more than your senses can credit. Dimity's mouth moaned sweetly against his as she moved still closer, and he forgot to think at all.

Hours later (or was it only a matter of minutes, when he found that her body was a lute where he could harmonize at will?) Dimity stirred lazily in his arms, and shook her head when he murmured the question once again.

"Does it matter who I am?"

"It matters enormously now."

"Or what I was?"

"Tell me, please."

"Aren't you happy just so?"

"I've never been happier." He knew he was speaking from the heart: the emotion in his voice frightened him a little, but he went on regardless. "I want to thank you properly. The real you."

"Just because I took you in?"

"And gave yourself."

"You gave *yourself* too, Mike. Don't think I'm not just as grateful. And don't think you've ruined me. I'm glad that I could—well, that I could make this real again."

"You've brought me back to life, Dimity. Thanks for reminding me—how good life can be."

"I enjoyed the reminder too, Mike."

He smiled in the dark and drew her head down to his shoulder. Of course it was folly to spoil a perfect moment with words. But he could not hold the questions back.

"Tell me how you came here. All of it."

"You know enough now."

"I'm not just curious."

"I know, Mike. But a person's life can be so dull if she's poor."

"From the beginning. I insist."

"It won't take long. My mother cooked at the Concord Arms. An ordinary on the Boston Post Road. Don't ask me who my father was."

He waited for her to stiffen in his arms, but her small body was quite relaxed: the easy throb of her heart (so close to his own that the rhythm all but matched) was as steady as her breathing.

"Don't tell me she raised you in a posting inn."

"There was an uncle, when I was ten. A farmhouse in Connecticut. It smelled damp, even in summer; there were more rocks than fields. They made me do a hired hand's work from the start; even his own sons had deserted to go to the Western Reserve. I ran away the moment I was strong enough to run. When the New York sheriff picked me up, I pretended to be an orphan. They put me in work school for a while and articled me as a cook's helper. A city house this time. On Washington Square. Only it seemed just as damp as my uncle's—and just as cold in winter. By that time I'd learned my lesson. When a girl runs away for keeps, it's better to head south. So I walked down to the Battery one day and stowed away on the first coastal trader I could find."

"And came to Charleston, and the Wharf Players?"

"Baltimore first. They put me ashore there. I still insisted I was an orphan looking for a better climate. I'd changed my name, so they put me in another workhouse. This time I was articled to a bar kitchen on the water front, so it was easy to take another ship. . . . You know the rest. A barkeep's life in Charleston, until I joined the Wharfers. Savannah and Fernandina. Fever, and waking up in this bed, with Felippa swishing a palm leaf and promising me work the moment I was well enough."

"And now, a stranded doctor is your first chore?"

Dimity stirred in his arms with a sleepy laugh. "The very first. I guess both Felippa and Dr. Hilary figured I'd earned my rest. But don't you dare pretend I haven't done well by you. Course, most nurses are a bit more formal—if that's the right word. But——"

He silenced her with a kiss. "For a life story, that'll do nicely."

"The short and simple annals of the poor," said Dimity.

"Who told you that?"

"Dr. Hilary. He said it was poetry."

"English poetry. Sir Thomas Gray."

"It isn't true, you know," said Dimity. "Being poor isn't half as simple as being rich. And it doesn't seem short, when you're going through it. That workhouse seemed to go on forever."

"But it's over now. You aren't poor any more. You've friends in Fernandina. And you've got me."

"Only for the fortnight, Mike."

Her mouth had already sought his in the dark. Her alert body, sensing his need, moved with fluent ease to mold itself to his desire. Rocking in a rhythm older than time, covering those firm young breasts with his kisses, he forgot to reproach himself for his ecstasy. . . .

"Only a fortnight, Mike. I'll do my best to make you remember it."

Again he heard her warm chuckle in the pale aqueous light that filled the cabin. Her hands (they were both soothing and compelling as they caressed the small of his back) seemed to move in time to that laughter.

"Dr. Hilary said I was to help you get well in jig time. Course I planned on this, the moment you had your strength."

"On *this?*"

"The moment they brought you through that cabin door."

"On *this,* Dimity?"

"Why not? Is there a nicer way to get acquainted?"

IV

Deep in marsh grass, following the tide-scoured path with toes rather than eyes, Michael felt positive that he was screened from view on all sides. Nothing human would be stirring now in this plain of mud and tufted grass. Yet he had left H.M.S. *Resolve* on tiptoe, even though he knew that Dimity was fishing far down the lagoon.

For a week now he had looked forward to this venture with all the guilty anticipation of a schoolboy. The path had become part of his brain ever since he had leaned on the hulk's rail to watch Hilary Tyler pick his way among the green tufts, after the doctor's second visit. He was proving that knowledge now—with a few slips in mudholes and one heart-quaking moment when the bog sucked at his knees. Another hundred yards and he would be standing on dry land—if the wind-riffled water of these shallows did not conceal another quicksand bed.

He had planned his walk carefully. From what Tyler had said, he judged he could gain the outskirts of Fernandina in an hour—once he had entered the pinywoods of the island itself. The sailor's shirt he was wearing and the faded nankeen trousers were seagoing gear the world over. Certainly there was nothing about him to excite remark, if he encountered a stranger on the way. Thanks to a week in the sun and to Dimity's cooking (and Dimity's own engrossing presence) he was prepared to look any man in the eye without a qualm. Any man at all, he repeated grimly—including Adam Leigh himself. . . .

Knee-deep, now, in the cloudy green shallows of this tidal creek, he looked back at the *Resolve*. Despite her stripped spars and barnacle whiskers, the hulk made an impressive pattern against the pale afternoon sky. He remembered the day he had swum with Dimity along the line of the grounded keel. Plunging deep, bursting out to breathe, and plunging again, they had checked the crack at the bow that had waterlogged her. Yet he had a wild fear that the *Resolve* would sprout canvas as he watched and point her nose for open water.

The *Resolve* (and he admitted this freely, as the fancy died) had been the only real home he had known. Was he a fool to leave her so impulsively, if only for an hour?

He walked on, consulting the sun with a practiced eye as he prodded each step with his toes. It was perhaps an hour past noon, the heart of the Spanish siesta. Fernandina would surely be dozing in its own heat haze: the town would take no notice of a lone visitor on its outskirts. He would mark the location of Adam Leigh's wharf, and the warehouse he had stared at so often from the slaver's porthole. He would look into Leigh's world, and shake his fist, however briefly, at its menace. There was no explaining that urge to anyone. Least of all to himself.

Another yard, now, though the tidal suck of the creek still threatened his rolled trouser tops. From this point on the bottom was clean mud. A battalion of fiddler crabs deployed about his feet as he stepped from creek to sunbaked flat. A moment more and he stood in the shade of the first dwarfed water oak. Already his eyes had found the path that Dr. Hilary followed—a faintly marked trail among the pines, dusted prodigally with brown needles.

He settled on a palmetto root, rolled down his belled trousers, and unknotted the shoelaces that held his sailor's brogues suspended at his neckcloth. Ready for the road again, he paused to mop his brow with the same kerchief, and conned the mental map one more time. To the west the sound merged with the stand of cabbage palms that marked the line of the Amelia River and the thin neck of land that separated it from this great tidal bayou. Behind him, to the south, the no less formidable barrier of the tidal creek, spread fanwise to the edge of the marsh. Ahead, to the north, the aromatic shade of the pinywoods, laced with a yellow sea of palmetto scrub, tangled with thickets of bay grape, yucca, and wind-harried cedars. Here, at long last, was the solid sand of Amelia herself—the isle of gold.

The isle of gold, he reflected, could belie its name after a man had tramped its sandy paths for a sweltering half-hour. Save for the strangely marked snake he had killed as he left the creek's bed (an ominous overture to his excursion) he had seen no living thing below the treetop level—though the pines had been filled with the quarreling of birds, and he had marked more than one vulture circling deep in the blue. The sandy stillness, which had seemed so cooling when he entered it, all but stifled him now. Perhaps he was still too tired for such a venture. Perhaps it was only the breathless heat of early afternoon, the long uphill pull of the path.

Tyler had said that there were plantations the length of Amelia Island. He did not know that most of the cotton acres lay a good mile to the south. Or that this sweep of barrens had been a kind of *terra deserta* for years since the Spaniards had resettled the town on the island's northern tip. Or that the hill he was ascending so painfully was the highest point on the island—until he emerged upon its summit and settled under another of the wind-twisted cedars to sweep the horizon in earnest.

The hilltop was bald as an ancient's skull, with the sparse growth of cedars replacing the traditional last hairs. The limestone outcrop underfoot reminded Michael that this was a relic of some remote geologic upheaval, centuries before the first Indian moccasin had moved across the wooded flats below. From where he stood he could sweep the country for miles. He noted instantly that Amelia was golden only in name—the real reason for that poetical tag was the town at his feet.

He looked twice at that scar in the immensity of palmetto scrub, slate-gray tidal basin, marshland that seemed to close the horizon on all save the ocean side. Seen from this sweeping angle, the

Atlantic, and the white ribbon of its beaches, was the first vista to draw the eye. By contrast with this sun-weary land, the sea was a thing of clean beauty, a lure to the wayfarer. Dr. Michael Stone (who had succumbed to that lure for years) forced his eyes back to Fernandina. This, after all, was what he had trudged through siesta heat to see.

There was the road, just where Tyler had placed it—a ragged track of deep-rutted sand, laid down the island's spine like a ruler, dipping into blue sloughs, vanishing to the south in heat haze. There was the burnt-over scrub at the approaches to the town itself —a fitting prelude to the wooden stockade and the two blockhouses that flanked the entrance gates. The fort that stood on the bluff just beyond, a white-limed square with a fat ten-pounder at each port and the flag of Spain languid at its sentry box, completed the picture neatly.

Fernandina itself, at first glance, was disappointing as a child's checkerboard forgotten in the sand. Laid out in geometric squares, its sandy streets all but empty of life in the pitiless sun glare, it was a marked contrast to the romantic bower that Michael had pictured in his mind's eye. Most of the houses were mere wooden cabins. Others were only stilted shacks, their roofs like old hats clapped on as an afterthought. A few, he noted, were built of the same material as the fort, the burnt-shell tabby stone that the Spaniards had introduced from their older settlements. Two of the most pretentious structures faced each other across a kind of dusty parade ground at the fort's main gate. These boasted grounds, of a sort. There were clusters of China trees (a foam of mauve blossoms in the early Florida spring, oddly reminiscent of lilac) and a few stunted palms to mark the beginnings of lawns.

The walls of these two patrician dwellings were quarried from a substance that resembled pinkish-gray stone. Michael knew instantly that the house nearer to the fort was the residence of the commandant. The other belonged to Dr. Emil Marsden, the rival who had always caused Dr. Hilary Tyler to choke a little as he discussed the man's varied infamies. The foundations of both dwellings were products of the coquina quarry—primeval coagulations of sea shell, porous enough to chip under a fingernail, stout enough to withstand cannon fire. Dr. Tyler had described them in detail—

with a pious footnote on the labor necessary to transport the blocks from the nearest quarry, a good fifty miles to the south.

Michael stared at these twin monuments to wealth and tried hard to make them part of the pattern—a rallying point for a growing community, a fount where the whole town might draw sustenance and wisdom. But Fernandina remained a child's checkerboard, forgotten in the glare of afternoon. Those two proud coquina houses would crumble with the town itself—if Fernandina's reason for being should vanish in the stream of history.

He looked for that *raison d'être* and found it at the foot of the steep bluff that faced the Amelia River and the great harbor that opened beyond. Here were the stone piers where the slavers outfitted. Here were the warehouses, the chandlers' barns, the taverns that served those slavers and their crews. From where he sat he could see only the tops of the wharfside buildings, the tall spars of vessels warping into their berths for another cargo of trade goods—or another load of contraband for Georgia.

One of those roofs covered the establishment of Adam Leigh and Son. Michael shook his fist at that memory, even as he laughed aloud at the childishness of the gesture. Until he met Adam Leigh in the flesh (and cursed him as he deserved) there was little point in heroics. He took a last look at Fernandina, re-counted the thirty-two full-rigged ships at anchor in the roadstead. Then, like a boy who has outstayed his welcome, he turned downhill again.

Thanks to the steep pitch of the path, his return journey was much less arduous. He walked with bowed head, still troubled by the conviction that he had turned his back on a challenge, though he could not quite put that challenge into words. Leigh was part of it, of course, but the challenge went beyond the blackbirder and the mark he had put on Dr. Michael Stone. The town itself, he reflected, had a lure all its own. Now that it had drawn him to this distant view, there was an enticement to explore further. But he had turned his back firmly on that enticement once and for all; the lure diminished with each step he took on this pine-needled path. Dr. Tyler was right: he should have stayed under cover to the end.

Here was the last dog-leg turn in the path, the dead cedar that marked the slope to the tidal creek and the treacherous ford beyond.

Here, on the mud flat, was the twisted coil of the snake he had killed. Michael quickened his pace, aware of the westering sun even as he admitted his own sharp weariness. Dimity's hail (an echo on the rim of his brooding) was only another reminder that he had been away too long.

When she called again, he knew that her voice had come from the marsh. Stumbling down the sandy bank, he saw her at last, a slim figure in the creek bed, running with all her strength to join him.

"Mike!"

She thought I'd gone without a word, he told himself. She returned to the hulk sooner than she'd planned and found it empty. She mustn't believe that of me. When we say good-by, we'll say it honestly. He was running now, as wildly as Dimity—his hands outstretched in a gesture of welcome that somehow included a plea for forgiveness.

"Right here, darling!"

He had never used that word for Dimity: the fact shocked him almost as much as his betrayal of her trust. And then, winded despite himself, he leaned for a moment against a pine bole, watching her leap nimbly from flat to flat in the creek bed, framing the excuses he would offer when he took her in his arms.

Someone had begun to spin a top in the palmetto scrub. He turned to that strange sound just as Dimity began to scramble up the bank. In that quick change of focus he saw that the dead snake had taken on a sudden monstrous life, that there was not one snake, but two, that writhed in the girl's path. Dimly he remembered the adage that even snakes have mates. The snake he had killed an hour ago was now mourned by another—six feet of coiled death that sounded its warning just before it struck.

"Dimity! Wait!"

The warning came too late. He watched the girl swerve as the gray-brown coil unwound as quickly as a released spring. He saw her roll in the sand with that monstrous coil riveted to one bare ankle. He heard her scream as his own nerves exploded. He was beside her now, wrenching the snake away with bare hands, smashing out its life before the slavering fangs could find his own flesh.

When he turned back to Dimity, he could almost hope that she had fainted. But the girl was waiting for him with her eyes fixed on that wounded leg, her fists bunched at the calf, where four neat bluish punctures were already oozing blood.

"It was a diamondback, Mike."

"Don't talk, darling. Don't move a muscle. I'll handle this."

Thank God for memory, he told himself, with the scalpel already flat against his palm; thank God for the impulse that made me bring this knife along. He had saved more than one black at the compound when adders had invaded the pens. If he worked fast, he could save Dimity now.

The scalpel split Dimity's short sailor pantaloons from knee to thigh. He had no memory of removing his belt, though he could feel the welt rise on his midriff where the buckle had struck him in passing. Already the leather was around the girl's leg, as high as it would go. He made the belt bite home, cinching the brass tongue of the buckle until Dimity gasped with pain.

"It's the only way. We must stop the circulation——" He did not complete the sentence as his free hand fastened just above her ankle. But he remembered to meet her eyes before the steel slashed down—if only to ask for her trust.

"Will it hurt, Mike?"

"Break that palmetto. Bite into the pulp. It'll steady you."

He did not look up again as he went about his work. The scalpel outlined the four geometric punctures, even as it slashed deep above and below their points of entry. Blood welled at the neat rectangle, the capillary bleeding that no tourniquet can control. He cut deeper, crisscrossing the wound deliberately before he thrust his tongue into the incision. Sucking like a vampire bat, he used both hands to force Dimity flat on the sand. Her blood was warm and salty in his mouth. He spat and sucked and spat again, maintaining the frantic rhythm until the flesh was dry beneath his tongue. At that instant he felt her whole body go lax under his steadying hands and knew that she had fainted at last.

He tested the bite of the tourniquet before he tried her pulse. It was strong and regular, a sure sign that the poison had not yet reached the heart. There was no time to think of quicksand as he lifted her high in his arms and staggered across the creek bed. Marsh grass slashed his ankles when he stumbled into the dimly marked trail on the far bank, but he was too intent to note the pain. For a few blind moments he was positive that he had lost his way in that head-high maze. Then the green tufts parted, and he saw the barnacled beak of the *Resolve* against the sky.

For all her slightness, Dimity was lead in his arms as he stepped over the brig's gunwale, kicked open the cabin door, and laid her gently on the bed. He knew that she had come out of the faint, for she had stirred more than once on the last lap of that watery trail. Now he dared to look into her frightened eyes, to force a smile he was far from feeling.

"Better, darling?"

"My head aches, Mike. My whole body aches. Is that the first sign?"

"Don't talk. I'm ready for that." He had already taken a wicker bottle from the shelf overhead—a providential memento of Dr. Hilary's last visit. "Drink this down. Quickly. As much as you can take."

"Rum, Mike?"

"It isn't the best antidote. But it'll serve." He could hardly explain that he wanted to drive her body into a stupor in the shortest time. Laudanum was the drug he needed, but he could not produce the impossible. . . . Watching her bite the cork from the bottle, knowing that she was taking the fiery Jamaica in deep, heroic swallows, he dared to go on deck for a moment—to light the charcoal brazier and place the largest water pot above it.

"Don't leave me, Mike!"

Her voice stabbed at his heart; her fever-bright eyes, already a bit glazed with rum, stared up at him piteously as he knelt at the bedside.

"I'll never leave you, Dimity."

"No. You mustn't say that. I mean for now. If Tola comes with a sloop to take you away—make him wait. Am I a coward to ask that?"

"I'm your doctor now. I'm staying with you until you're well."

"The best doctor in the world," she murmured drowsily.

"Then obey his orders. Work awhile on Dr. Tyler's bottle."

"My foot's so numb, Mike." She drank with one hand, even as she brushed the laceration with free fingers. "Is the poison——?"

"That's only the tourniquet. I bled out the poison with my knife." He said it with all the authority he could muster. No tourniquet could dam off the worst of the venom, even if it were kept in place indefinitely. Already the leather had impeded circulation for the better part of an hour. To leave it too long in place would mean that Dimity might lose her foot from gangrene.

He put that knowledge behind him and forced his hands to complete the preparation for the coming crisis. A pot of grease from the larder, spare blankets, an extra pot to stand beside the brazier, in case the first should boil away before it was needed. The ancient hunting watch at their bedside had run down days ago. Time, he reflected, had lost its meaning in the lazy pattern of the life they had shared. That slow-moving hour hand was vital to his treatment now.

"Lie still, my dear. Don't stop drinking."

"But the bottle's half-empty." She gave a sleepy giggle, and he blessed the stupor that had stolen out of that wicker jug.

"No more aches now?"

"Feel wonderful, Mike. Not a bit afraid." She managed a drowsy grin. "Is that the rum talking, or me?"

"You, of course. You're a fine, brave girl. I'm going to ease the tourniquet now for a few moments. It'll hurt a little."

Blood pumped at the wound as he let out the notch of the belt. Dimity moaned faintly as the vessels in her leg resumed their function. Once again he sucked furiously at the wound, hoping that more of the venom could be drawn off, though he knew that it was part of her blood stream now. He verified that certainty after he had clamped the tourniquet and forced a few spoonfuls of broth between Dimity's lips. The girl tried hard to swallow normally, despite her semicoma. He drew in his breath sharply as he saw her throat muscles tighten in the first of the strictures that would torture her later.

Until that crisis overtook her, he could only wait. Crouched at Dimity's side (and hardly aware of his own tortured muscles), he watched the sun go down behind the row of palms to the west. At the moment he felt that he had lived aboard this hulk forever—that he had watched a thousand such flaming sunsets, with this small blond head cradled at his shoulder. Only last night they had sat thus, talking softly as the day faded. Only last night he had been ideally happy in this drowsy present, with no compulsion to face the future. He had not even wondered if his words were nonsense or the ultimate wisdom. They returned to mock him now, as though his own voice were whispering at his ear:

"Happy, sweet? I've never been happier."

"I won't ask you why, Mike. That might spoil it."

"I know why, Dimity Parker. So do you."

"Don't say it, please."

"How could I help loving you?"

"I love you too, Mike. I've loved you from the moment you came into this cabin, feet first."

"You see? We've said it at last. What's the harm?"

"You may be sorry later."

"Sorry that I found you when I needed you most?"

He repeated that last remembered tenderness now, with his lips against her fevered cheek. *I've found you, Dimity—when I needed you most.* Pray God it isn't to lose you, he added silently.

Conscious of that prayer and its sudden blessed relief, he let his eyes stray again to the red glory in the west. He had never quite thought out his religion: tonight, it was easy to believe that his prayer had been heard somewhere in that graying infinity beyond the sunset. . . . Was it cowardly to call out for help—to offer hostages to the power that encompassed all living things?

The prayer was gone, and he could hardly call it back. Or forget the promise he had made to Dimity, if it were answered.

V

It was after midnight when the first convulsion came. He marked the time precisely as he shook himself free of his doze and staggered to his feet with leg muscles screaming. Each hour of that vigil he had loosened the tourniquet for a few moments and roused Dimity from her stupor to feed her more of the broth, along with a liberal dose of rum. Now that the crisis was on her, he found that he was almost calm. The habits of years returned to steady his hands and his brain; this thrashing body on the bed was only another patient he must save.

Ignoring the wildly chattering teeth, the corded agony of muscles that arched her body like a bow, he tossed two blankets into the steaming cauldron on deck. When the immediate spasm had subsided, he forked them from the boiling water and beat them with a stick on the ship's rail. Wrung out, the cloth was still hot enough to sting his palms, but he could not pause to notice the pain. The pot of grease came into his hand, still warm from its long sojourn beside the fire. He had stripped Dimity long ago to control her thrashings. Now, as he larded her body, he could only hope that the grease would protect her from the burning poultice he had fashioned.

Deep in stupor though she was, the girl screamed as the blankets made their first contact with her glistening body. Her teeth fastened on his wrist: he was forced to hammerlock her head and neck before he could knot both blankets about her. Choked in this strait jacket, she fought back still, though her resistance was feebler now. Already the moist warmth had begun to have its effect.

Twice he was forced to pin her to the bed as her back arched wildly. And then, little by little, her muscles began to relax in earnest: her mouth sagged, and he saw that she was asleep. He hurried to deck to soak another pair of blankets in the boiling water—and wondered when she would rouse from this stupor—if at all.

It seemed hours later when he heard the footfall on deck, though his watch said that Dimity's last convulsion had passed only a few minutes ago. He looked up haggardly at the shadow in the cabin door. A tall dark woman with piercing eyes and a huge Roman nose that had outlived its century. Felippa, the witch—already kneeling at his side to test his steam packs with strong, wise hands. . . . He made no effort to greet her; for the present he was beyond surprise.

All that night and the long day that followed they spelled each other at the bedside—wringing out countless blankets, warming the soups and jellies that Felippa forced between Dimity's lips, soothing her convulsions as best they could. There was no blinking the fact that the girl was slowly losing ground. The weak, racing pulse told its own story: there was but one cause for the fever that seemed ready to melt the joining of soul and body. But even at this nadir of his hopes he had not yielded his place at the bedside. . . . It had seemed quite natural to accept Felippa's help as his due. Natural, too, that she touch his shoulder now with a soothing hand and address him directly at last.

"Tonight you will sleep. Leave her to me, *Inglés.*"

"This is my task, not yours. Don't think I'm not grateful for your help."

"Before you came, I nursed this girl through other fevers. I can save her now."

Michael found he was looking into the witch's face for the first time as they stood above the charcoal fire. Felippa's eyes were level and brooding: there was a steady blaze of confidence in their depths. For a moment he had the sense of falling into those hot pools—as though the woman's eye sockets were bottomless wells. Yet the sensation was not unpleasant. Rather, he felt lulled by strange rhythms as he spiraled downward.

He pulled back sharply from that illusion and stared at Felippa's spare, lined face (the color of ancient mahogany whose luster has vanished under repeated rubbings), her dead-black gown, the wink of an amulet at her throat. In Africa he had faced down the mumbo jumbo of medicine men. Surely this crone had no special powers of enchantment.

"This accident was my fault. It isn't that I don't trust you——"

"First we give her strychnia," said Felippa. "Then you sleep."

"Strychnia?" He found himself staring in earnest. What did this woman know of such drugs? Just in time he recalled the extract of Peruvian bark that had come from her hands.

"Dr. Hilary ordered it," said Felippa. "He was leaving on a country case, but he gave me what he could."

"You mean that Tyler sent you here? How could he know I needed a nurse—or strychnia?"

"It was not Dr. Hilary's thought." Felippa's gaunt face just escaped smiling. "Dr. Hilary was surprised when I said that you had summoned me. But he gave me the medicine just the same. It is in the bottle in my bag."

Michael bent forward as the woman lifted a leather pouch from the deck, but there was no time to check the contents. The bottle of nux vomica was already in his hand. Felippa, like a model nurse, had taken a freshly soaked blanket into the cabin and was swathing the feebly moaning patient.

"How did you know I needed you?"

"I know many things, *Inglés.*"

"Did you know that it was snake bite?"

"A diamondback, on the edge of the slough."

Michael almost dropped his measuring spoon. Obeying some obscure impulse of her kind, Felippa might well have followed the path to the hulk. Not even a cat's eye could have noticed the dead snakes in the blackness of midnight. Once again he shrugged off the implication. The strychnia was in his hand, that was the important thing. Forcing Dimity to swallow the dose while the woman held her lolling head, he wondered if the powerful stimulant would jolt her failing heart into one last effort.

Felippa's hand was steady at his elbow as he swayed above the bed.

"You have done all you could."

He nodded dazedly as their eyes met. Somehow it seemed quite in order that he should stagger toward a nest of rolled-up quilts in the corner. There had been no bed in that corner yesterday: he realized that Felippa had fashioned it for him during his vigil.

"I will watch till morning. It is time you slept."

"What if there's another crisis?"

"She cannot endure another crisis."

"You'll waken me if it comes?"

"I will waken you."

Her eyes compelled him, even as her hands soothed him to the floor: there was no mistaking the hypnotic power of that stare—or the completeness of his yielding. He was asleep on his feet long before his head could settle in the nest of quilts.

It was a deeper slumber than he had ever known. Later (when he tried to fill in the details) he could hardly believe that he had roused for a moment in the last dark hour before dawn. At the time, of course, his mind had dismissed the whole episode as a dream. . . . He had seemed to waken to a room alive with goblin shadows. As his mind cleared, he thought he could see a fire dancing in the cabin—and concluded that Felippa had brought the brazier in from the deck. Mesmerized still (and unwilling to admit that he was fully conscious), he had burrowed among his quilts, watching a clawlike hand toss some powder on the flames: he knew it was Felippa's hand, though the woman sat with her back to him and her head was covered with a dark hood.

The flames danced green and yellow as the powder ignited, casting a startling pattern on the ceiling, where Felippa's shadow hung like a homing bat. Only then did he dare to glance at the bed. Dimity lay there naked and glistening. At her head and feet tiny, waxlike images, naked like herself, picked up high lights of their own from the chromatic flames. A strange jargon poured from Felippa's lips—a prayer that was not a prayer, a supplication that was a votive poem and a barbaric chant heavy with iteration.

And now his brain insisted that he was dreaming—and clung to that insistence, for the sake of sanity. Felippa had just risen above the dance of the flames to pirouette on her toes like a banshee from a child's Halloween. She seemed enormously tall, a figure of evil elongated by nightmare. Her shadow, taller than she, fell across the bed and the golden statue that was Dimity. The strange chant continued as the witch moved across the room with both arms extended like a sleepwalker. The clawlike fingers hovered at Dimity's breast to make strange markings just above the heart. The pattern was clear in the firelight—a cross that was not a crucifix, though its pattern was oddly similar. A savage cross, etched in blood above the girl's heart. . . .

He wakened in earnest to the raucous crying of the gulls. Starting up on one elbow, he was sure that he was alone in the cabin. Felippa had vanished; there was no glowing brazier in the room and no golden statue on the bed. Only a frail mound beneath the blanket that might have been a body.

Michael knelt at the bedside and stared for a long moment at Dimity's pale face, composed in the blond aureole of her hair. She was clothed now in a long cotton night shift. There were no markings on her breasts when he opened the front of the gown—and the heart beat strongly underneath.

He knew that the crisis was over even before he counted her steady pulse. Dimity Parker would live again, thanks to the stamina of a young body—and Felippa's magic. His mind pulled back from that admission even as he discounted his dream.

"Satisfied with your patient's progress?"

He turned to the open door—and Dr. Hilary Tyler, squatting at the brazier, which stood in its accustomed place on deck. A savory whiff of steam assailed Michael's nostrils as the old man stirred the contents of a fire-blackened pot.

"Bacon and hominy grits, my boy. Not a breakfast by Dimity's standard. A bachelor can only do his best."

"How did you get here?"

"Your man ferried me over. He's taken Felippa to town. As usual, she has several country cases waiting. Do you take your tea strong? That's how I brewed it."

Michael turned back to the bed. A glance told him that Dimity had been freshly bathed. The blankets were fresh: even the corn-husk mattress had been changed. He checked the wound, knowing in advance that its dressing would be just as immaculate. The scalpel cuts had begun to heal nicely, and there was no hint of infection. When he looked up at last, Tyler stood beside him with a steaming mug of tea.

"Eat, my boy. You've earned it. I gave her an identical check an hour ago. She'll come out of this little misadventure nicely."

"You wouldn't have said as much last midnight."

"She has had inspired nursing in the meantime."

Michael glanced quickly at Tyler, but the old doctor's nose was deep in his tea. "You're quite right there. I'm eternally grateful to Felippa."

"Admit now that she's more than a witch?"

"Perhaps I've more respect for witchcraft. You've put Dimity under an opiate?"

"A light one. It will do her no harm to sleep till evening. And it will simplify your departure."

"You might say that again, Doctor."

"If you're sure that you're wide awake. It seems you may leave the Floridas a bit sooner than you expected."

Michael rose slowly from the bed. A few days ago his heart would have leaped at Tyler's words. Today, it merely steadied into a more confident beat. He had made his decision—so far as flight from Florida was concerned—while he held Dimity's head in his arms and whispered a promise into the sunset. He had not expected to implement that promise so soon.

"So you've arranged for a sloop to take me to sea?"

"Tola should be sailing it across the bayou now. One of those cruising yawls the natives use along these shores when they've a bit of deep-sea fishing in mind. So you won't be in the least conspicuous if you put out from Cumberland Sound today."

"North by northeast?"

"Precisely. You hold that course until you speak the *Martha's Vineyard*. She's weighing anchor now at St. Marys. Captain O'Hara. A thousand-ton merchant tub out of Philadelphia." Tyler's face had not lost its beatific grin as he sat with one foot hooked in a scupper, like an overweight archangel distributing largess. "Captain O'Hara has fifty of your American dollars in his pocket now. You're to hand him the rest when you go aboard. Full payment for transport to Charleston——"

"When did you arrange this?"

"Only yesterday, at St. Marys. O'Hara put in at the river's mouth with provisions for the town—and a fine stand of Havana tobacco. He's taking cotton from the gins and picking up more as he moves north. Incidentally, you're down in his log as a passenger out of Havana. O'Hara has visa stamps from every port in the Caribbean."

"No wonder you look like an archangel. You've behaved like one."

"I beg your pardon?"

"You have opened the door to a new world, Dr. Tyler—and bowed me in. I can't thank you enough."

"Let's hope you find that new world to your liking. Most of its visitors have." Dr. Hilary's whiskered calm was still beyond reproach. "At least they've lingered, and made the best of their chances."

"Precisely what I intend, Doctor. I'm particularly happy that Tola and I will be sailing our own yawl. I've wanted to see this coast under my own power for a long time."

"Give the bays a wide berth, once you're in Amelia channel. That yawl cost me a pretty penny in St. Marys. The former owner swears she wasn't stolen, but one can never be sure of those things. Particularly when one's in a hurry."

"Speaking of yawls, is that our vessel now?"

Tyler swung to the rail and shielded his eyes from the cobalt glare of the sound. Dancing toward their shore with the fresh morning breeze behind her, the trim schooner-rigged craft could have had no other destination but the *Resolve*. Even at that distance Michael could be sure that the helmsman was Tola—an exuberant Tola who was steering with his feet as expertly as a seagoing chimpanzee and executing a jig of welcome as he slipped into his last tack.

Michael smiled inwardly as he returned the wave. It would have been fairer to Dr. Hilary to explain his recent resolution here and now. Somehow he could not find the words as he turned toward the cabin door.

"We should leave promptly, since we're timing this rendezvous."

"I'm afraid you must, Dr. Stone."

In the cabin Michael pocketed his passport and slipped his scalpel into his belt. He had come aboard the *Resolve* all but naked. He was leaving her (but not for long, his heart sang) richer by a pair of soiled nankeen pantaloons, a striped sailor's jacket that had seen better days, a glazed sailor's boater to keep out the worst of the blazing Florida morning. Richer by a new-found purpose that had given his life meaning. Richer, above all, by Dimity Parker's love. . . . The yawl bumped gently against the side of the hulk. Michael knelt at the bedside and kissed the girl's relaxed lips.

"Hola, jefe!"

He went on deck without looking back. Tola's massive shoulders loomed at the broken gunwale as the Minorcan steadied the smaller vessel in the bounce of the tide. Dr. Hilary Tyler, more Biblical than ever at the rail, spoke softly as Michael hesitated in the shadow of the deckhouse.

"Time is of the essence, Doctor—when you're making a rendezvous at sea."

"You'll stay with her until Felippa returns? Promise me that."

"Word of honor, my boy."

"Then I'll take my leave. How long will Captain O'Hara wait?"

"He promised to heave to a league to the northeast of the Point Peter buoy. He'll wait 'till noon."

"That should do nicely," said Michael—and smiled at his own subterfuge.

"Let me have a letter when you're safe in Charleston." Tyler's blue-veined hand shook a little when he offered it. Michael wondered if this was age—or the aftermath of the drinks he had bought O'Hara yesterday on a St. Marys wharf. "I'll make your farewells when she wakens."

Michael hesitated, with the doctor's hand still in his. Perhaps it was unfair to Dimity to go like this. And yet, when he thought of the meeting he had planned—and the possible aftermath of that encounter—he realized that this was no time to justify his decision. Particularly at secondhand.

"Tell her she'll hear from me too. Sooner than she expects, I hope."

He jumped into the yawl on that note and took the tiller. Tola cast off expertly. The sail, tilting in the tease of the wind, canted the little vessel sharply as she coasted from the shadow of the hulk to clear water. Michael glanced back just once and waved up at Tyler's puzzled stare.

"Sooner than she expects—don't forget *that* part of my good-by."

"Good-by, Doctor."

He thinks I'm softening the blow, thought Michael. He's positive that we're looking into each other's faces for the last time. After all, it's a cynic's world. . . . He leaned on the tiller, letting his sudden release of energy ride with the following wind.

"Call the course, Tola."

"Straight for the tallest palm cluster, *jefe*. It is deep water all the way, now the tide is full. When we are closer, you will see the channel to the Amelia."

The Minorcan's tone was subdued, now that they were really under way. Abruptly Michael realized that Tola (even as Dr. Tyler) expected to say good-by in the next few hours. He opened his mouth to speak, and found that he needed all his wits to handle the yawl in that bouncing breeze. For the present it was enough to set his course for that wedge of open water that would lead him to the Amelia River and the sea.

Tola ran down the gunwale as they came about on their first tack, and lay flat with his hands cupped against the wind, his bare toes managing the guy rope.

"The surgeon's box is aboard, Señor Mike. And your boat cloak. Also a box of clothes which the old doctor bought for you in Fernandina. There is still more than a hundred dollars in the wallet."

"Never mind that, Tola. You know I trust you."

"It is only that we are saying good-by, jefe."

The boom swung, as the wind beat in from a new quarter. Tola ran forward to unfurl the flying jib. He knows how eager I was to be off and away, thought Michael. A lump filled his throat at that mute evidence of loyalty.

Devoting his whole mind to the handling of the yawl, he did not speak until they were in the channel that led from the sound to the wide estuary of the Amelia River. This broad bay, sparkling with whitecaps in the whippy morning, was separated from the sound by a low ridge hardly four hundred yards in width. Part of the island spine, this segment of Amelia was thickly studded with scrub cedar and the inevitable clumps of palmetto. The cabbage palms, which had seemed so distant from the deck of the *Resolve,* turned into a long, straggling grove, clustered on either side of the road that led to the southern tip of the island. The road itself, Michael noted, was no more than a sandy wagon track, bisected neatly by the channel they were sailing now.

"Can this cut be forded when the tide is out?"

"Yes, jefe. Now that the tide is full, we have draft to spare."

"That stranded brig didn't come this way."

"There is another channel, Señor Mike. Far to the south, where the water is deep." Tola looked his surprise at the question. His shrug said more than words: what can this matter to you, now that you are leaving it? Again Michael leaned on the tiller without attempting to explain his interest. Explanations must come in another moment. He might even tell the Minorcan of the plan he had just made for the *Resolve*. . . .

Sand scoured their plates as they bounced across the last shallow hurdle in the channel. Already the Amelia was wide open to their bowsprit. The wind, slapping their canvas with its full impact, sent the yawl into a dizzy tack. Michael let the little vessel spin away with the breeze and took his compass bearing. North by northeast, straight as a string. Nursing this first long tack, he could lay his course down the Amelia's mid-channel and fetch

Fernandina as they came about. Fernandina, and the wide sea beyond the Amelia's mouth. . . . They could be chasing their shadow across the ocean's floor before the *Martha's Vineyard* showed her topsails.

He laughed aloud and opened his arms to the blazing morning. Leaping to the after housing, steering with his toes as expertly as Tola, he brought the yawl about—so abruptly, that the vessel seemed to spin on her heel, like a dancer caught off balance. When she righted, she was running dead south with a bone in her teeth and the full impact of the wind behind her. Tola, who had spread-eagled on the foredeck to take a sounding, came sputtering aft.

"Norte, Señor Mike! Norte!"

"Sud, amigo mío!"

"We must fetch Cumberland Sound in the hour."

"Nassau Sound, Tola. Not Cumberland. I know the maps as well as you."

"The merchantman leaves St. Marys! You will be twenty miles off your course if you——"

"We aren't meeting the merchantman. I'm staying on in Florida. If the old rip takes me, I'm going to practice in Fernandina with Dr. Tyler."

Tola was staring as though Michael had taken leave of his senses. Michael roared with laughter—and let the sound bounce away with the following wind.

"I'll tell you more. If Dimity Parker is agreeable, I'm marrying her the moment I'm established. Wouldn't you say it's time I settled down?"

"But, jefe——"

"Naturally, I've a call to make, before I can really plan. That's why we're sailing down the coast to Punta Blanca."

"But, Señor Mike!"

"You're quite right to be startled. But how can I practice medicine in Florida until I've made a truce with Adam Leigh?"

VI

He knew the road by heart. In his dreams (those half-waking fantasies of revenge) he had walked the route too often to miss that first steep climb through the dunes, the first slope to the powder-dry savannah beyond. Now he was walking that road alone, the hero of his own nightmare. Like most nightmares, he found, the reality was less frightening than the dream.

Tola and the yawl were safely offshore now, awaiting his return to the beach—assuming that such a mad journey would end as easily as it had begun. Tola would nurse the wind and coast with the ground swell a good mile offshore. . . . A perfect servant to the end, the Minorcan had offered only routine protests when Michael stepped ashore.

"They are watching, Señor Mike. Always, they watch this landing place."

"Let them watch. I've come with empty hands. I'm striking a bargain with Leigh."

"Even so, you will be stopped. Before you reach the first pen."

"This is a free country. This is America."

"This is a colony of Spain, jefe."

"Have it your way. I'm still meeting Adam Leigh face to face."

Tola had said no more. Michael smiled wanly as he recalled the Minorcan's almost courtly silence when the yawl bounced into the dead water behind the jetty; Tola's gentle offer of a hand from gunwale to stone. . . .

"I will wait offshore till nightfall, Señor Mike. Then I will go to Savannah—and the British Consul."

"Never mind the British Consul. From now on I'll fight my battles outside the Crown."

He had said it confidently enough as he swung up the beach and took the well-worn path among the dunes. It was harder to recreate that courage now.

A generation of naked feet had worn this path from sea to land: he could sense that much, even had his eyes been blinded. Hard-packed as any track to Calvary, the trace was arrow-straight. A wide white-gray arrow, pointing the way to the savannah—and the corduroy road that vanished in a cedar grove to the west. Yes, his toes could find the way merely by testing the hot sand beneath. His nose picked up other signals—the stench of a passing brown wave, the droppings of a human inundation that was not quite human. thanks to this brutal channeling.

He crossed the savannah grimly, raking the cedar grove for the lookouts who had refused to take shape. Tola had said he would be stopped before he reached the pens. His nose told him that the pens were almost in view, but he had yet to glimpse a guard. He was among the cedars now. For an instant the dry, winy aroma of the trees themselves almost canceled out the reek of misery beyond, though he could hear the blacks now as well as breathe their presence at every pore. Another step, and he saw the first tall yellow shoulder of a stockade. A step more, and he had walked into the heart of Adam Leigh's empire, unmolested.

Much later he would know that these grading pens (the first in the long process that transformed savages to docile field hands) were a full thirty acres in extent. Laid out as precisely as the runways in a zoo, and just as ruthlessly enclosed, the pens were actually a series of circular corrals. Each corral was boxed in eight-foot palmetto stockades and wide ditches bristling with pointed spikes. Within (and he verified his first shocked impression as he stood atop the corduroy slope and surveyed the writhing black mass below) the slaves were thick as black sand and almost as immobile. Segregated by age and sex, these Negroes seemed to clot the Florida earth: too indolent to move, they merely waited for the next keen of the whip.

Here, then, was the result of his long labors at the Boca. Now that he was checking the end product of those labors, it seemed incredible that it had borne such monstrous fruit. He counted burry heads until his mind reeled: surely there were two thousand blacks in these enclosures alone.

Michael walked away from that dreadful arithmetic. The processing pens and the hosing shed were beyond and to the right. He recognized the low-eaved cluster instantly from the similar structures they had built in Africa based on plans delivered from Punta Blanca. The squarish building with the great copper bell in its roof could only be the training shed. Here the future headmen would learn the arts of leadership as practiced by Leigh's white counterparts. Here the slave assigned to a cotton row would limber his hands with actual bolls under the eye of a teacher. The favored few who had shown aptitude would train in the gin itself before they moved on to Leigh's cabins to learn obedience at first-hand.

Michael walked on with only a passing stare at the long white-washed files dotting the slope to the south. All the cabins seemed spotless at this distance and empty as the moon. If this were a dreamworld, he had at least found his bearings by instinct. The manor house would be dead ahead between this windbreak of oleanders and the stout coquina barricade that shut off the fields to the north.

Only a fool could come so far, he told himself. Only a brass-plated idealist would play out his luck—and walk through that half-open gate that so obviously divided the world of Adam Leigh's chattels from the sanctum he called his own.

He forced himself to pause, with one foot on the gate itself, and looked warily down the long path of crushed oystershell that led, with all the precision of a plumb line, through endless rows of truck garden to a white-painted storage shed. You can still pull out in time, he told himself (and wondered, even as his mind framed the alternative, why he was not more afraid). Thanks to those escape-proof stockades, Leigh can leave his raw Negroes unguarded. Thanks to the hour, the quarters are empty: a Scotsman can hardly permit his cattle to idle while the sun is up. Turn back now (the same voice whispered). Run for the beach, and Tola. You can still sail back to Dimity—and take her out of this.

But he was walking through the truck-garden gate with his head high. The die was cast, after all, long before he could set foot on Punta Blanca. Besides, he could hardly doubt that he was being watched, even though the watchers had not yet troubled to show their faces.

At the corner of the whitewashed shed he paused in the patch of shade—an actor who has walked into his setting alone and wonders if he will remember his first line. Surely he could not go much deeper in Leigh's domain without contact with a living soul. And yet, as he took his first step on the wide lawn beyond, he knew that he must play this cat-and-mouse game to the end.

Rehearsing his well-planned words, he found that he could cross the great green apron without a tremor. If the slave road in the dunes was a dreary anticlimax, the estate itself proved that reality, on occasion, could transcend illusion. . . . There was the avenue of live oaks, precisely as he had imagined—a noble avenue, bearded with moss, sweeping down to a sheltered bay. There was the house itself, tall, white, and proud: pillared portico, flaming flower beds, trim yew hedges as carefully molded as any English counterpart. And there, in the first hibiscus bed, was the spot of life he had missed in all the rest. A small Negro, kneeling to spade the rich earth. A frightened Negro who started like a rabbit at his approach and scurried for the safety of an open french window.

He walked boldly up to the portico and waited for the gunshot that did not come. He had lifted his hand to the gargantuan bronze knocker on the door when a voice called his name at last.

"Señor Mike!"

It was Mozo whom he had last glimpsed at the wheel of the *Mariposa* a few seconds before the slaver had spouted to eternity. Mozo, who had stepped easily from the shade of a tall Corinthian pillar to bar his path with the half-furioso, half-fawning air he recalled so well. He could feel the house come alive, as dark heads thrust from every window to view the interloper. The two gaunt figures that had ghosted to the edge of the lawn merely completed the picture. Even without the muskets, the gimlet stares that pinned him to the spot, Michael would have guessed that this brace of guards had trailed him from the beach.

He took a step toward the door. Mozo, a sulky djinn today, stood his ground.

"You needn't gape, amigo. I'm not a ghost. Can I say the same for you?"

"Why do you come from the sea, Doctor? Only our own ships come within the jetty. Visitors land at the bayside only——" The Negro's voice stuttered a little with surprise. His broad gesture included the avenue of live oaks, the dock at its foot.

"Convey my apologies to your master. Say that eagerness outweighed my manners."

"It is my day to guard the portico, Doctor. You will stop where you are."

"I demand to see Adam Leigh!" That, after all, was his opening line. He shouted it resoundingly against the great white sounding board of the colonnade—and rejoiced as the rows of dark heads vanished at his roar.

"Señor Leigh is always in the fields at this hour." Now that he had adjusted to Michael's presence, Mozo seemed to unbend a trifle.

"Tell him I'm here. He'll break a rule for once."

Mozo's hand had already dropped to his side. One of the guards came closer, stared briefly at Michael, and vanished among the live oaks. Michael watched his departure and felt his own muscles unbending. The fact that the second guard still stood on the alert, with two fingers hooked in the trigger guard of his musket, was quite in order now. He had expected that sort of welcome from the first. Mozo's presence was the only jarring note.

"Tell me this much. Were you blown clear when the ship exploded?"

Mozo did not budge: the question hung fire between them, as though the Negro had not heard.

"If you'd rather not answer——"

"I was blown clear, Señor Mike. And swam ashore. We thought no one else had lived."

"Tola survived with me. We reached Fernandina together. I've decided to settle there——" He let his voice trail off, chilled by the Negro's impassive stare. Already there was a stir of booted feet on the driveway. He held his ground as the short, squat overseer strode up the portico. The pattern of his arrival, he reflected, was taking definite shape at last. Even from the distance the newcomer's stumpy stride bespoke his authority. Here was the slave driver of legend, a man who reeked of his job from dusty boots to sweat-stained work shirt. The whip in his belt, the long-nosed pistols at each armpit, were needless confirmation of that picture. Michael met the fellow's black-browed stare and held his ground. Leigh's deputies could gather at will: he would await Leigh's own arrival before he spoke again.

The overseer stormed across the flagged immensity of the portico. His first words, delivered in Mozo's teeth, established his authority instantly.

"Who's this fellow, Mozo?"

"Dr. Michael Stone, señor. He comes from the ocean side to visit us."

"Don't wast my time, idiot. You know that Stone is dead at sea."

"Touch him, señor. He is real."

Michael found he had spoken, after all. "Will you take me to Adam Leigh?"

The overseer's brows knitted again above ice-blue eyes. For the first time Michael felt the probe that lurked in that unwavering stare. *"I'm* Adam Leigh," said the overseer. "And don't tell me I'm crazy too. You're down as dead in my books, Stone. If there's one thing I hate, it's altering a ledger."

"Mozo was blown clear when the *Mariposa* exploded. I was lucky too."

"Of course you could have set the powder train. I never thought of that."

Michael returned the glare. "Did you think me that sort of doctor?"

"To be frank, I never tried to picture you."

"May I remedy your neglect?"

Adam Leigh nodded briefly and stamped up the portico without a word. Mozo, with eyes still lowered, offered the master of Punta Blanca his deepest salaam, and indicated that Michael should follow that beetling exit, as a tall french window sprang open under the impact of Leigh's boot.

Side by side they strode through a vast, shuttered drawing room, across a hall only a trifle less magnificent, into a cluttered workroom that seemed to hold the afternoon's heat a willing prisoner. . . . Later Michael would remember that the drawing room was pure Georgian to the last wink of the brass firedogs; that the hall had come from Aberdeen, down to the last wall panel, the last gold-crusted ancestor sneering from the stair well. But Leigh's workroom belonged to the sweat-stained man who flung himself into the desk chair, pushed aside a stack of account books, and faced his visitor with a stare that hardly masked the curiosity beneath.

"I'll hear your reasons, Doctor. If you have any."

"For walking into your lair, when I've escaped you?"

"You don't look in the least insane."

"I'm glad I can surprise you. It's only turnabout."

"Say that again, Stone."

"You're the greatest surprise I've ever had."

"I, Doctor? I'd heard you were a traveled man. Surely you've seen planters in their work clothes——"

"But I'd always pictured you as a prehistoric monster. Like Ríos, only larger. Now I find you're real as sin. Here I sit, talking to you as though you were quite human."

"I'm a slave trader," said Adam Leigh. "What's inhuman about that?"

Ríos, thought Michael, would have defended himself with a flourish. He rather enjoyed Leigh's bluntness and the earthy challenge behind it.

"I could be wrong," said Leigh. "You may be mad as a loon, after all."

"I've never felt more sane, now that I've seen you at last. Now that the myth's a reality."

"What d'you want of me, man?"

"Only your promise that I won't be molested if I settle in Fernandina."

"I've no property in Fernandina save my chandler's wharf. Why should it concern me if you settle there?"

"People don't escape you that easily. Not when they can be useful to you."

Leigh flexed a big-knuckled hand, closing the fingers into a slow fist. Michael watched that fist beat an easy cadence on the desk top and knew that his fate was being weighed with that gesture. Leigh had called him a fool, but he did not regret this visit—or its face-to-face challenge. When the planter spoke at last, his voice seemed as remote as his thoughts.

"Why did you compare me to Ríos?"

"I've told you. When I was that devil's prisoner, I thought you were his apotheosis."

"A big word, Doctor."

"Big words suit you, Mr. Leigh." Michael weighed the admission for a moment and knew that it came from the heart. Surely it was not a sign of weakness. "Now we're face to face, I admit my error. You're another breed from Ríos. He was consciously evil and gloried in it. You accept your trade as part of the times. You don't even trouble to defend it——"

He paused in earnest on that and waited for the thunderbolt. Adam Leigh continued to pound the desk top with that same easy fist.

"The thing that troubles me is that naturalness in you. How easy it is to—shall I say, respond to your sincerity? God help me, I might have gone to Africa willingly, if you'd offered me the post yourself."

"Ríos informed me that you'd accepted the offer."

"Ríos was lying. Didn't you trouble to check his lie?"

"As my African factor he had full authority in my absence. I'd never had reason to complain of that trust." The fist ceased its pounding: Adam Leigh's stare was strangely mild. "As it turned out, both you and Ríos were valued members of my staff. Both of you delivered results. Why should I question his methods—or yours?"

"Did you know that he enjoyed torture for its own sake? Or that he murdered a man in Fernandina?"

"Slave runners are seldom gentle people, Dr. Stone. Murder is a commonplace word in Fernandina. That's one reason why I keep a small private army at the Point."

"I'll accept that as a rebuke to my inexperience. I'm still asking if I'm to be left in peace."

"Isn't that a great deal for any man to ask on a frontier?"

"I intend to hang out my shingle in Fernandina. May I have your promise that I won't be molested?"

"I make no promises until I'm ready to fulfill them. I know you're a superior man, Stone. And a stubborn one. You might become a power in Fernandina someday. You might even threaten my interests here. Obviously that would require action on my part."

"Aren't you looking a bit far ahead?"

"Foresight is important in my market. However, I'll make you one promise. I won't be sending you back to the Boca. The Boca is no longer mine: I sold out that holding a month ago."

Michael sat unstirring in his chair, even as he felt the weight lift from his heart. "Why weren't we told of this at the compound?"

"Why should I give you a chance to slack?"

"May I ask who's taken over?"

"The depot now belongs to a Yankee combine, headed by my ex-skipper, Captain Coffin. Naturally, they'll use their own staff, medical and otherwise. Ledoux and Fulton, your two assistants, are on the water now: they'll be in residence here, to superintend the Punta Blanca pens." Leigh's deep-tanned face relaxed briefly in the ghost of a smile. "Why are you staring, Dr. Stone? I assure you that I know just what I'm doing. And I bear you no ill will for that business aboard the *Mariposa.* She was fully insured at Lloyd's: they paid on the line."

"And your other ships?"

"They were included in the transaction. I'm keeping the *Dos Amigos* for plantation use. She's in Philadelphia now, bringing us a cargo of foodstuffs."

Michael let out his breath at last. The question had been purely mechanical. In a moment he would let the vista of his own future build and burgeon. It was enough, for now, to stare wide-eyed at Adam Leigh—to let relief wash over him like healing rain.

"Did Ríos know that you'd planned to sell the Boca?"

"Ríos was leaving my employ when he died. I saw no reason to honor him with my confidence."

"Yet you have honored me."

"Precisely, Dr. Stone. I'll do more. You can be useful to me in Florida as well as in Africa."

It was Michael's turn to stiffen in his chair. "Shall I pretend to be stupid?"

"Tell me this: have you heard of a Fernandina doctor named Emil Marsden?"

"Indirectly, yes."

"You'll hear more if you go into practice there. Marsden has been an inspector of my pens for some years. He's able enough—or seems so, to my layman's eye. But Marsden is not content to make doctoring his only occupation. Of late he's been developing a smuggling ring of his own in Fernandina."

"I've heard of that as well."

"Naturally, most natives do a bit of smuggling on the side. I don't interfere in that. But Marsden has been expanding his operations: he's away for long periods, in Charleston and elsewhere. Some even say he's planning a filibuster. Or made himself the advance agent for one." Leigh considered that thought for a long, brooding moment. "I'm only telling you this to give you my side of the picture: why I brought those two pill-pounders from Africa to keep a spot check on my pens. And why I'm offering you Marsden's post, if you'll have it."

The words sank into the hot silence of the room. Leigh waited quietly for his answer, though his fist had begun its restless drumming once again. Michael watched a bluebottle, stupefied by the hot crisscross of sunlight at the dusty window, spiral upward for a moment as though seeking an exit, then settle on the pane. Like that fly, he thought, I had an illusion of freedom for a moment. . . . He spoke quickly, before the thought could complete itself.

"This is rash of you, sight unseen."

"I know your record in Africa. The work would be much the same—and a great deal simpler. In the future I plan to buy from other runners and concentrate on my training. I needn't add that I accept only prime stock. Your task would be to keep them in that state, until I was ready to sell again."

"Suppose I say no?"

"I don't imagine you'll be so foolhardy. Perhaps I should add that your wage would be the same as that you drew at the Boca."

"My plan is to practice in Fernandina."

"Fernandina is only a morning's sail from my dock. Put aside two days each week for Punta Blanca. A sloop will call for you and return you to your patients."

"You'd pay my old fee for just two days?"

"I'd see that you earned it, Doctor." Leigh's fist banged the desk top in earnest. "Don't accuse me of generosity. And don't pretend you're in a position to bargain."

"I've had enough of blackbirding. More than enough."

"Blackbirding, as you call it, will continue to flourish here beyond my time—and yours. I've a dozen competitors on this coast alone, all of them eager to outdistance me. I fully intend to go on outdistancing *them*. Why shouldn't you help me to deliver healthy stock?"

"Are you suggesting that my help's essential?"

"Not at all. The Georgia dealers will take what they can get these days. I could scrape the bottoms of my pens, and retire in another few years. Or continue as a mere planter, like a thousand others. Perhaps it's unfortunate that I'm a fair man." Leigh's level blue stare was unflinching. "When I demand a thousand American dollars for a prime hand, I must give honest weight. My sick list has grown too long under Marsden. That's why I'm paying well for the best medical brains. *Your* kind of brains, Stone——"

"May I say once again that I'm honored?"

"Be moral, if you insist. Say you're helping me to reach the figure I've set in my mind. Say I'll give up blackbirding that much sooner, thanks to your help. I plan to do just that, when Florida is part of America. I might even retire now, if my son could take over. You knew I had a son, of course?"

"Of course. As it happens, I doctored his lady aboard the *Dos Amigos*."

"I remember that occasion perfectly. Lady Marian has spoken of you often since she came over."

Michael felt his heart give a great wild leap. He wondered if he had flushed under Leigh's dispassionate eyes. "Is Sir Forrest at the plantation now?"

"They came out from England a month ago. At the moment he talks of resuming his army career. That's nonsense, of course: he'll never ride again—unless his leg knits."

"And Lady Marian?"

"On her first visit she was afraid that she might not endure the climate. But her health has been perfect since she made me a grandfather." Leigh's stare was still bland, impersonal. "I tell you this, since my household would be among your patients. Especially Forrest's knee. I might almost say that he's made a career of it."

Michael let his laughter build its own ambush. "You make it hard for me to refuse. I must still ask the consequences if I do."

"Let's not discuss them."

"After all, you can't force me to use my knowledge as a doctor. What if I establish myself in Fernandina—and refuse to call at the Point?"

"But you aren't in Fernandina now. You are under the jurisdiction of the governor at St. Augustine. I might add that I'm his deputy here, with full powers."

"So you'd turn me over to the Spanish?"

"As a citizen-in-fact, I'd have no choice."

"On what count?"

"Murder, sir. The destruction of my slaver and its crew. Governor Coppinger happens to be as Irish as his name, with little love for renegade Britishers—and less for the denizens of Fernandina."

"Will you complete the threat?"

"It's a promise, Doctor. An oubliette at the Castillo. An oubliette deep enough to rot away your prejudices—along with your life."

Michael nodded slowly, but his eyes did not waver. He had known for some time that he would take the offer—even as he admitted it was generous. Yet he could not resist bargaining a moment longer.

"What are the consequences if I accept?"

"I'll stand behind you when you come to blows with Marsden—or Marsden's successors. When the scalawags leave Fernandina and American troops move in, I'll make you Florida's leading doctor."

"You are much too kind, of course."

"I'm paying well for what I want. Yes or no?"

"Yes, I'm afraid."

"You knew you'd accept. Why have you wasted my time?"

Michael permitted himself a small but defiant grin. "Perhaps to test your powers of persuasion."

"You found them convincing?"

"Especially the oubliette. You haven't said when I'd begin my duties."

"Now will do nicely, Doctor."

Michael rose. "Which shall I visit first? Your son, or your slaves?"

"The slaves, of course. Forrest's knee will keep. Fever won't."

They went out together, into the grateful cool of the stair well. This time Michael risked a quick glance upward—and dared to ask himself if Marian Leigh were somewhere in the dim reaches of the hall above.

Fever won't keep, he repeated. Adam Leigh had uttered a deeper wisdom than he knew. Fever won't down, when you are near the cause. . . . In that moment he admitted the real reason he had walked into this house to beard his lion singlehanded. And why his heart raced as he followed the master of Punta Blanca into the hush of afternoon.

VII

An hour later (standing atop a dune to wave Tola inside the jetty) he scrubbed himself dry with a towel and found that he had regained his composure, if not his peace of mind.

His tour of the pens had restored him to familiar ground. At times during that busy hour he had only to close his eyes to imagine himself back at the Boca—with Ríos flicking his rawhide just ahead and Ledoux (twitching after a night of saturnalia) at his elbow with a long-handled brush. This had been the inevitable spearhead of their first grim scouring: the pattern had been unaltered today. But there had been no cloying heat in these compounds as the long spring day faded into evening—none of the miasmic oppression. Only a clean, hot smell of dunes and the benison of the sea breeze. Only a sense of space, of freedom, of abounding peace. . . .

Freedom and peace. There was no freedom in view for the poor creatures in these eight-foot stockades. Whatever peace they earned —when their rigorous training was ended—would be bought with a lifetime of sweat in the service of alien masters under strange suns. He watched a platoon of estate hands lime the last square inch of earth within an enclosure. He saw Mozo at the corral gate, coiling his leaded bull whip as the long chore ended. He, Michael Stone, would check the dysentery that had raged through this pen. In time he would guarantee that each black who left the Point would go out to his long labors in perfect health. What right had *he* to stand in the fresh sea breeze and rejoice in his freedom?

These raw slaves were a far remove from Africa. Even a layman could grasp that fact at once as he surveyed the strong-limbed bodies within the palmetto walls. Well-fed and sheltered, they would make their transitions from grading pen to cabin. When they had learned obedience to word as well as lash (a smattering of English if they were earmarked for the States, Spanish if they were destined for a *finca*), they would work the cotton rows, in the rice paddies, in the turpentine forest to the west. Later still, they would be shackled for the last time and marched under guard across the pine barrens to the assembly points where the traders made their bargains.

The traffic would continue until the reservoirs of both Americas were filled. Michael knew that that day was far down the horizon. He could see these same men's grandsons, backs bent in the self-same toil, eyes void of hope. Slaves, and the sons of slaves. Most of the African gangs, he knew, were slaves in their own tribes, and sold as such by their black owners. Even the Mozos and the Numis had come to the Boca in collars as spoils of some jungle war. . . . The sophist could argue that they had merely exchanged masters —that this New World bondage was a vast improvement on the old. It seemed to Michael that men in a new world—all men—deserved an equal chance.

Was that a visionary's utopia, a democracy too pure for its century? He sighed, and turned to watch Tola drop anchor in the shallows and stump up the dune for orders.

The Minorcan was still gaping at Michael's news as they walked down to the corral. "You should have called me in at once. At the Boca it was I who went into the pens. Your clothes are ruined now."

"I've washed away the worst of it. There'll be fresh things waiting for me at the house."

He let his mind dwell on Adam Leigh's dinner invitation, and avoided the hope that had grown, unbidden, in his heart all during the afternoon. There was still much to be done. This was a poor time to plan the things he would say to Lady Marian Leigh.

"Do we stay the night, Señor Mike?"

"We'll always sleep at the Point on these visits. Until Ledoux and Fulton take over, at least. This fellow Marsden has left an Augean stable behind him."

"But we *live* in Fernandina?"

"We live in Fernandina."

Michael spoke the words firmly and let that picture build to the last detail. The *Resolve* would float easily, once her sea cocks were closed and the crack in her bow sealed off. Pumped dry and towed into deep water, she would make an ideal home—and perhaps a floating hospital as well. He would warp her into the Amelia, float her down to Fernandina with the tide, moor her near one of the harbor piers. Dimity could not ask for a better establishment. Of course there would be no time for a honeymoon. Honeymoons could come later, when his practice was flourishing.

Dimity Parker, as Mrs. Michael Stone. His heart told him that she would accept the change in title as easily as she had accepted Michael Stone himself. Dimity, in short, would make the ideal wife for a country doctor. With her help he would translate quixotic choice to solid reality. Lady Marian might insist that he was quite mad. But he could take Lady Marian's opinions in his stride.

Roger Farrar, the head overseer, was waiting for him at the gate of the training compound. At first glance the man seemed a snuff-brown mole, oppressed by the weight of the pistol at his belt; it was hard to imagine Farrar as Leigh's second-in-command, the absolute master of three thousand blacks when their owner was absent. But Farrar's quiet authority soon emerged—along with an even deeper assurance that his slightest order would be obeyed without question.

"Did they send enough lime from the stores, Doctor?"

"More than enough. I've left orders to repeat the washings daily for the next fortnight." Michael's nose wrinkled as they paused at the gateway to the first training compound. "Judging by the aroma, we'll have to repeat it here."

"Only in a few cabins, I think. There's a communal latrine in each pen, of course. But we've found it impossible to train the raw material. If you fellows had housebroken them in Africa——"

"I'm afraid that's a word you can't translate into Bantu."

They walked through the gate into the growing stink. Farrar flicked his boot with a whip end and smiled his apology. "Not that I'm passing on the blame. We trusted these details to Marsden."

"Can you spare a dozen men to lime these quarters daily?"

"You can have all the men you want."

"We should have inspectors working inside the cabins. See that they're kept clean by the Negroes themselves—and punish every violation. How near is the water?"

"No more than three hundred yards away. You can see it from the rise—beyond that yucca windbreak."

"Is it open sea or creek?"

"It's the tidal reach that opens to our anchorage."

"Then you could march the field gangs there in relays, when they return from work. Let them bathe daily."

Farrar raised his brows. "Do they? I wouldn't know."

"In their native regions these Africans bathe frequently, in streams and ponds. Are there many sick in this compound?"

"Spotted here and there. Here's one quarantined cabin."

Michael braced himself as Farrar kicked open a white-chalk door. Inured as he was to such visits, he felt his stomach recoil at the odor that swept out to greet him. Torpid as snakes in the half dark, the three blacks stirred faintly, raising imploring eyes. A glance told Michael that two of the trio were in the last stages of dysentery and quite beyond hope. The third man, who seemed to be suffering from an enteric fever, was not so desperately ill, though he made no attempt to raise his head as the new doctor bent to examine him.

"This is the worst cabin in the compound," said Farrar. "There aren't more than a half-dozen others."

"The fever case can be saved, if it's isolated. How long since these men have had medical care?"

Farrar scowled at the question. "Marsden never made reports. He said that a certain loss from sickness was inevitable."

"And you believed him?"

"It's always been true before."

Michael nodded soberly. The picture was clear now. Despite his evident competence, Farrar was an overseer of the old school when it came to the doctor and the doctor's place in his planning. Dr. Emil Marsden (a pig in any language, Michael added, sight unseen) had been hired by Leigh to insure the health of this yeasty mass of humanity. So long as the blacks poured out of their compounds each morning, so long as their field work was satisfactory, Farrar would hardly jibe at the stench that hung over that outpouring. Naturally he would take the doctor's word—when a few fell sick and howled away their lives.

"Have you a large building near by we can use as a sickbay?"

"The south storage shed is not in use at present."

"That will do, until we can build a hospital."

Farrar's whip made a wide, hissing circle. "A hospital—for *this?*"

"Why not? Don't you segregate your pigs when there's sickness in the pen?"

"Give me your orders, Doc. They'll be carried out."

"I want all the sick removed to that shed, even the cases that seem hopeless now. Assign house slaves as nurses. The sick must be kept clean and their bedding changed daily. They must be fed broths at first. Then tender meat, if they can take it."

"No dosings?"

"Dosing won't help this sort of flux. I'll write out a simple medication for the fever cases. Fulton is our medical man. He'll arrive with a pharmacopoeia as long as your arm. Meanwhile, I'll settle for that sickbay and enough chloride. We'll hold your lost man-hours to a minimum."

That, thought Michael, should turn the tide. Put the thing on a dollar basis, and you've won an ally in advance. Aloud he added only, "You'll refer this to Mr. Leigh, of course. It will be an expensive undertaking."

"Mr. Leigh has already given you a free hand here," said Farrar. "Say the word, and we'll rebuild the compounds from scratch."

"The general layout is admirable. It's only the policing that's at fault."

Michael glanced around the training compound once again. He had spoken no more than the truth. Replicas of the quarters that the Negroes would someday inhabit in the slave states to the north, the cabins were built of whitewashed tabby stone; the thatch of the roofs was sound, the windows unusually wide for these latitudes, where most of the natives believed that fever entered one's bedroom with the night air. Within, the floors were well shored; the brick hearths and iron utensils were more than adequate; the wall bunks, while crudely built, were equipped with rope mattresses; there was ample bedding to protect these forced emigrants from the tropics.

Most of the slaves, he observed, had fitted naturally into their new habitat. Family life had taken on its inevitable pattern. A score of smoke-wreathed chimneys told of suppers in preparation, now that the wives and smaller children had been permitted to return from the fields. But the primitive terror of disease still persisted: the sick had been merely shut away and allowed to sweat out their sickness. The visiting doctor from Fernandina (rather than lose time in policing all the cabins) had allowed tribal custom to run its course—and pocketed his fee.

Here, then, was the one missing link in the conveyor belt that delivered prime field hands to a hundred eager markets. One doctor, scamping on his assignment, had failed to make the belt perfect. With Scotch thoroughness the master of the Point had now called in three doctors to close the gap. Doctors from Africa, wise in the ways of slaves.

"Don't spare the hands," said Farrar. "As you've observed, we've an army in residence."

Michael nodded his thanks—and hoped that his smile was not too troubled as he recalled the quarters that housed Leigh's private police. A barracks that was more fortress than dwelling, it perched on high palmetto stilts in the southern curve of the point itself, commanding the whole sweep of slavepens from its flat roof. Guards marched here by day and night to supplement the guard who sat, patient as Cerberus, in the sentry block above each pen. Counting field overseers and their helpers, Leigh's private force was almost a hundred strong—or twice the garrison maintained at Fort San Carlos in Fernandina. Farrar had quoted the figures proudly, and Michael knew that Farrar could be taken at his word.

Most of these men doubled as teachers for the blacks, in workshop, forge, and field. Recruited among the rednecks and the scattered poor whites of the back country, they had struck Michael as a mongrel lot. But he conceded, even now, that these mongrels knew their task by heart. It was hard to believe that he had walked through these well-policed acres without stopping a bullet. Only a born romantic (blinded, for the moment, by his own stubborn purpose) could have missed these lynx-eyed lookouts in their ambush of palmetto log and Spanish bayonet.

"I needn't keep you longer, Doctor," said Roger Farrar. "If you're dining at the big house, you'll just have time to change. Besides, Mr. Leigh will be wanting you."

"I thought Mr. Leigh would be in the cotton rows till sundown."

"Mr. *Forrest* Leigh. Or should I say Sir Forrest? You won't be the first surgeon who's tackled that cavalryman's knee." The overseer's voice had a strange clipped timbre. Did it cover pity, contempt—or a blend of both?

"I understand that Sir Forrest was wounded at Waterloo."

"Been more or less invalided ever since, it seems. And fighting mad to get on a horse again. Deliver *that* miracle, Stone, and the estate's yours."

Michael pondered that last remark as he walked west in the gathering dusk. Somehow, it was quite natural that a Waterloo officer should await his ministrations in that vast white house beyond the oleander hedge. That he, Dr. Michael Stone (a man whose private destiny was stabilized at long last), had seduced that officer's wife—and felt no pangs at the seduction. No pangs at all, he insisted—and no fear of aftermaths. Tonight he would minister to Sir Forrest Leigh (late of His Majesty's Life Guards) as casually as he had attended his father's slaves. Just as he would face Lady Marian—and outplay her at any game she might devise. Assuming, of course, tht Lady Marian was in the mood for games.

With that resolve he walked firmly on. Already it seemed that he had taken this path of crushed oystershell a hundred times, between the vast storage barns that shut off the last of the slave quarters from the plantation proper. The blacksmith shop on his left and the vast, echoing depths of the gin were familiar as the contours of old friends.

Beyond, the path ruled the large truck gardens into two equal segments. He paused in its midst to check the geometrical rows. There were beans and Irish tubers, and Indian corn already knee-high in this seasonless sun. There were beet and okra (that newly discovered vegetable). There were endless tomato frames. . . . The tomato, Farrar had just explained, had come to this garden via Morocco: Adam Leigh was convinced that these rich red globes were an essential ingredient in the meat stews he served at each nooning. Strange, that Leigh should devote personal attention to his slaves' diet—and entrust their health to a rascal. Stranger still that the rascal's successor should hesitate (in the heart of Leigh's domain) and feel his muscles stiffen under the thrust of a fate he could not name.

Why (when he had decided he could face Marian Leigh without a tremor) did he yield, however briefly, to a belated onslaught of fear? Why did his heart insist, however faintly, that he was still a prisoner, in spirit if not in flesh?

VIII

He shook off the absurd notion and marched down the path with all the arrogance he could muster. The gate swung wide under his hand. This time he did not even pause as he walked from the world of black sweat and cat-eyed guards, of okra and love apples—and crossed the pale-green carpet of the lawn.

At this hour the manor house and the hand-tailored acres that surrounded it were drenched in a pellucid beauty all their own—a beauty that was part and parcel of the afterglow that lay, heavy as mist, on the sweep of tidal river to the west. In that light, Adam Leigh's mansion was a gigantic white bubble floating against the sunset, fresh-blown from the pipe of Aladdin's djinn. Mozo, magnificent in burnoose and turban, did nothing to spoil that elaborate metaphor as he waited with folded arms on the portico. The house slaves who rushed out to shepherd Michael's progress from lawn to colonnade, from baronial doorway to stair well, were merely lesser janizaries, conjured from the same fable. The pine-knot torches, passed from hand to hand on the lawn, echoed in the great candelabra of the stair well, were stars that marked the path to Scheherazade's bower.

Just in time he recalled that he had entered this magic world to examine the leg of a Waterloo officer. There would be no threnody of dulcimers in the dark tonight—and no Scheherazade.

The footman who met him on the first landing was part of the picture. The man's sweeping bow did much to restore his balance, though the fellow's side whiskers and canary-yellow livery were fabulous enough.

"Service, M. le Docteur. Je suis Guillaume, le valet de Son Altesse."

"Bonsoir, Guillaume. Où est ma chambre?"

"Par ici, monsieur."

The burst of French brought Paris into that sub-tropic stair well. He followed Guillaume with a lighter heart: *son altesse,* he gathered, was the valet's hyperbole for Sir Forrest Leigh. If Sir Forrest had assigned his own man to the visiting doctor, it would only mean that the doctor was important to Sir Forrest. Michael walked into his own spacious bedroom as debonairly as a man can walk when his boots are caked with the leavings of the slavepen. Guillaume's age-old cringe had made him feel civilized.

"D'abord, le bain?"

"Mais si! Où est-il?"

But the brace of house slaves (slim-flanked youths stripped to smallclothes and attentive as otters) had already pushed back the double doors. Michael entered a tessellated bath that exceeded his wildest dreams—a room gleaming with soaps and lotions, prodigal of mirrors and deep sunken tub. He noted the perforated shower tank in the ceiling, saw that it was dripping a welcome of its own as he stripped off his last soiled garment and stepped beneath it. For a long time he stood in that life-giving flood, hearing the water gurgle away beneath his toes, soaping and rinseing and soaping yet again. Guillaume stood aloof from it all, snapping instructions at the houseboys—who stood on facing ladders to sluice hot and cold buckets into the perforated tank.

Enough clothing for three men was spread on the vast double bed when he stepped out of the houseboys' chafing towels at last and went to make his selection.

"Tonight," said Guillaume, "we settle on a size. When the doctor visits us again, there will be a real choice."

In loose white linen and flowing black stock, Michael found the sense of belonging had enclosed him as snugly as a silkworm in its cocoon. Standing at the cheval glass to admire the sheen of his newly glazed boots, surrendering to Guillaume's magic with a wine-red waistcoat and a matching hibiscus at the buttonhole, he knew that he could face Scheherazade—or Marian Leigh—on equal ground.

"The dinner bell will sound in another hour, Doctor," said Guillaume. "May I take you to Sir Forrest now, or will you rest a moment?"

"Now will do nicely, if Sir Forrest is prepared to receive me."

"In that case, shall we say *Major* Forrest from this point on?" The Frenchman just escaped winking. "And may I say that we are both happy you are here?"

"You may indeed."

"The major has waited for hours, and cursed me while he

waited." Guillaume chuckled discreetly, though his cringe was intact. "The major doesn't take too kindly to the world since they forbade him the saddle." The valet paused, as though he would say far more. Then he led the way through a pair of french windows to a gallery that seemed, at this angle, to open into airy space.

The gallery, Michael noted, was really a catwalk that extended across the upper portico, connecting the bedrooms on that floor, and offering a welcome breezeway to the occupants. He had a sudden breath-taking glimpse of field and river under the dying day—the fields a pale-gold blur, the river a dreaming rose riffled by a school of mullet with a cloud of gulls in hot pursuit. He paused for a moment, drinking the beauty of the Florida sunset. Somehow its magic gained in potency, now that it was framed in the proud white of the portico.

"Here is the major's window, Doctor. As you see, he is only a step away."

Michael walked into the heir's bedroom and braced for a shock that did not come. Without quite knowing why, he had expected Marian to be in attendance on her husband. He had even looked forward to blushes and averted eyes—the makings of a scene he would carry off triumphantly. But this spacious apartment bore no marks of a woman's hand. The mahogany, the brassbound soldier's bed, even the vague aroma of leather and unguents were all male—and just as hostile to feminine intrusion. So, for that matter, was the claret-colored man in the old dressing sack, who sent a book sailing across the carpet and half rose from his chair with both hands extended in welcome.

"It's high time, Dr. Stone. I've been fuming here since noon. Damning my father when he let you go to the quarters, instead of sending you straight to me."

Michael found he was still gaping as he took the extended hands. He had expected anything but this in Marian's husband. Depending on one's viewpoint, Major Forrest Leigh could have passed for a saber rusted in its scabbard—or a near-invalid settling inexorably into fat and peevish boredom. A glance answered Michael's first question in advance, but he reserved his verdict as the valet eased Sir Forrest into his armchair again.

"I came as soon as I was presentable, Major."

"Don't blame yourself, sir. Blame a family that insists I must go on resting—when I'm bursting to be outdoors."

"Mr. Leigh said your leg would keep."

"It's kept since Waterloo. Damned badly, if the patient may express an opinion of his own. And double-damn all the quacks in England who wouldn't operate. Your Dr. Marsden is of that ilk, of course. Or isn't he *your* Dr. Marsden at all?"

"I'm Marsden's successor here."

"So you are. The servants told me as much only this morning. Father tells me what he feels I should know, and nothing more. But I've heard all about your miracles in Africa. Be a good chap, and build me a new knee?"

"I'm afraid I'm only a surgeon, Major. Not a magician."

"Is it too much to ask? This land's a horseman's heaven. I can see as much from that balcony. Don't think I'll sit here forever with my nose in Smollett. That was all well enough in Cheltenham, when I was an invalid—and admitted it. Damn it, sir, I'm an active man who wasn't burdened with a brain. I'd rather die than chew my navel."

Michael, with the valet's help, had already turned back the silken hem of Sir Forrest's dressing gown to expose the pudgy limb beneath. Rocking the kneecap between his palms, noting the fatty degeneration of the whole member, he confirmed his first melancholy verdict even as he listened to Sir Forest's litany of despair.

"What did it, Major?"

"A dragoon's saber on Mount St. Jean. We made history that day, I'm told. But a butcher set that knee when it was over. You can see for yourself that the cap's grown back askew."

Michael kept his eyes on the scar. Still livid after two years, still pouting at the edges (where the raging infection had burst into the open and spent itself at last), the long saber slash had split the leg from kneecap to groin. The damage had not ended with the leg. Doctor and patient sat quiet for a long moment, while the doctor stared at the mutilation that had destroyed the patient's manhood.

"Don't say it's an odd place to be wounded," said Sir Forrest "I've thought as much myself."

"You're lucky to be alive."

"Not if I can't ride again as well as any man. Never mind the other. I can bear that, now my wife has given me an heir."

"In time's nick, Major?"

"In time's nick—since I'm talking to my doctor."

"The issue should be a comfort to you now."

"The issue is in England, with his nurse. A nine-pound boy, Doctor—and his mother's image."

"May I congratulate you both?" Incredibly, Michael found that his voice was dead calm. Still more incredibly, he was enjoying this moment—and fighting an all-but-uncontrollable impulse to burst into laughter.

"Lady Marian insisted on bringing me to Florida for my health's sake. She insists on remaining until I'm mended."

"The child was born in England?"

"Some eighteen months ago." If Sir Forrest Leigh had noted the abruptness of his doctor's query, he gave no sign. "We all felt he should grow a bit before he risked a sea voyage."

"A wise decision."

Michael's voice was still dead calm—even as the demon of laughter capered in his brain. *The man is lying,* that antic fellow whispered. *What's more, he knows that you know he's lying. Just as surely as you know that his heir is still a babe in arms. He knows you fathered that infant aboard the* Dos Amigos. *He knows that old Adam himself planned that bit of studding—that the girl in the case was a willing accomplice.*

Aloud he said only, "As you may know, I met your lady aboard the *Dos Amigos*. In January of '16, to be precise. When I first entered your father's employ."

"I was unaware that you'd met."

"Strangely enough, your father remembered."

"My progenitor has a passion for detail that I lack."

"I'm sure your lady will remember me. May I say that I look forward to seeing her?"

"You may indeed, Dr. Stone."

Once again the man in the armchair did not betray his emotion by a flicker. Michael did his best to match that mask-like smile. *He knows he's safe,* whispered the same antic demon. *He's relying on the fact that there are certain things gentlemen don't say to each other. Now that you've pushed this subject to the limit of decorum, he knows that you'll retreat first. Yes, Doctor, you'll both keep your honor, even though you cuckolded him as thoroughly as any husband was ever cuckolded.*

Aloud he said carefully enough, "We were considering your knee—and the chances of an operation. It seems we have strayed from the subject."

"Deliberately, I'm sure."

"Why deliberately?"

Sir Forrest's pear-shaped body shuddered—a long, despairing sigh that should have been pathetic and seemed merely grotesque. "Because you've nothing to say on the subject of my knee."

Michael rocked the joint between his fingers one more time. "Let us be frank, Major. Your leg will never be whole."

"Which means I'll never ride again?"

"You can walk, with the help of a stick. But the stiffness will never work itself out: the joint will always be rigid as a board. As you can see, there's no articulation whatever."

"Damn your book words, sir. What d'you mean?"

"I'm telling you that you can thank God you escaped gangrene on the field. You are fortunate that you can walk at all."

Sir Forrest heaved up from his chair with a great effort and steadied himself on his good leg while he groped for his cane. As Michael had said, he could walk, after a fashion, if he put his mind to the task. An active man and an impatient one, he had obviously refused to perfect—and, far less, to practice—a crab-wise gait.

"Guillaume! Dominique!"

Michael stood aside as the valet and a broad-shouldered house slave rushed into the room. At sight of the cane they crossed arms automatically to make a chair of their hands. Sir Forrest sighed into this improvised carrier without even a backward glance. Sir Forrest, reflected Michael, would always settle back—and expect a chair of sorts to be waiting. He would always prefer to ride thus, rather than walk on broken bones.

"Sit with me while I dress, Doctor. We'll discuss this further."

"I'm afraid there's no more to be said."

"And *I* insist that I'll ride again."

"That is your privilege, Major. It's my duty as a surgeon to say I can do nothing."

Their eyes met and held. Cradled in his domestics' arms, Sir Forrest resembled a monstrous baby on the point of a tantrum. "I thought you'd be different from the others, Stone. I was sure you'd take a risk."

"It isn't a question of risks. The position of the joint is hopeless: the malformation has knit for all time. Of course if you'd like another opinion——"

"Look at me, Stone. Am I a tub of lard that's had its day?"

"No, Major. Just a cavalryman who must be content with the ground."

"Damn your ground, sir. The ground was made for shopmen's plodders. I was born to ride."

"Have it your way. If you put that knee in a saddle, I won't endorse the result."

"Will you patch me when I fall?"

"Since it's my vocation, Major——"

Sir Forrest's angry eye had not wavered. Now he pulled himself into a travesty of a salute, ignoring the straining muscles of slave and valet.

"Very good, Guillaume. Take me where I can curse in comfort. You'll join me in a brandy-and-water, Doctor? I always drink brandy while I dress. Helps me forget I had a figure once."

"Thank you, no. I must report to your father."

"Turn your stubborn head, sir. You can report to him here."

Michael swung toward the hall door, and saw that Adam Leigh was standing there—a bit larger than life in his loose white linen, a cheroot smoking between his lips. At the moment Leigh was surveying his son with ill-disguised contempt. But Forrest Leigh only chuckled under the paternal glare.

"Tell him your verdict, Doctor. He's used to it."

The heir of Punta Blanca was still chuckling as he went out in his human chair. His father took a step into the room with a dragon's snort. Curried for evening, with a diamond sunburst in his stock, Leigh was still more bull than man. A solemn bull that knows his strength, added Michael. An unhappy bull at this instant, as he surveys the result of his paternity.

"So there's no hope for his leg?"

"None whatever. I thought it wiser to tell him straight out."

"You can't tell Forrest something he doesn't wish to hear. He merely closes his mind."

"His field surgeon bungled the job at Waterloo. The kneecap could have been rescued, I'm sure. Of course with the threat of gangrene, and a suppurating wound——"

"Let's be frank, Stone. You must have seen that a hopeless knee joint isn't his only trouble."

Michael nodded soberly. "It's a miracle he didn't die from *that* wound."

"Perhaps he should have died."

"You don't mean that."

"I'm a practical man, Doctor: I don't mind saying that I've never regarded my son highly. That's why I let him spoil himself at Oxford and Sandhurst. I needn't add that he had his commission in the Guards by purchase. The Gazette will tell you that he earned his title, but it cost his father a pretty penny too. Not that I'm complaining, you understand. He *is* my son, so I bought him the life he wanted. Like a thousand others he planned to be a gentleman in uniform and make a career of it. Who'd ever dreamed the Guards would be ordered to Belgium in '15?"

Leigh puffed savagely on his cigar as he considered that quirk of fate. "I asked but one thing of him: a worthy marriage and a grandson I could cherish. Am I speaking too frankly?"

"I find your frankness refreshing." As he spoke, Michael offered the planter a wary smile. If it was true that Forrest Leigh was a gentleman (in the stuffiest sense of that word) it was equally obvious that Adam Leigh was not. A self-created nabob, an absolute tyrant in his world, Leigh could afford to be blunt. How far would bluntness take him now?

"Naturally, we chose my son's wife with care."

"Naturally."

"Lady Marian is a daughter of one of the oldest families in Ireland —and one of the poorest. The marriage contract was made by my London agents. It provided for male issue in five years' time. There was a down payment on the principal: the balance is payable only when the child is safely through its first year. I need hardly add that I expected Forrest to do his part; the girl's a tearing beauty, and he'd bedded enough wenches, in uniform and out, to know what he was about."

"I gather this wasn't a love match."

Leigh scowled over his cigar at the irrelevant query. "They met just twice before the ceremony with lawyers from both sides present. The girl came to Forrest to save her family estates. Forrest took a wife because I'd promised him twenty thousand pounds the day he presented me with a grandson. Naturally the collaboration was enthusiastic while it lasted."

"Naturally."

"You needn't echo me on that point, Doctor. And while you're about it, you needn't pity Forrest for—shall I say, his personal Waterloo? He was married two full years before he smelled powder on Mount St. Jean. It's my considered judgment that he was sterile on his wedding day."

"You speak with authority, sir."

"Explain that, Doctor." Leigh's brows were a solid line above his cheroot.

"I was only complimenting an expert. And may I pity *you*—since I can't pity the major?"

"I'm afraid I don't follow."

"Your trade depends on the fertility of your subjects, doesn't it? Surely it's ironic that your own offspring should be found wanting."

Adam Leigh flung his cigar through an open window and watched it vanish in the night like a miniature comet. Expelling the last of the smoke, he seemed to throw aside his choler in that same breath. Michael could not be sure whether the planter was smiling as he began to pace the carpet. But he felt that boldness had saved him from annihilation—for the present at least.

"Think what you like of me and mine, Dr. Stone. I am indifferent to opinions. Common sense has put me where I am today. Common sense tells me that I'm the future here. But I've gone as far as a man can go alone. I wanted an heir. My son failed me."

"Therefore, since you always get your way——"

Adam Leigh paused in his pacing and shook his fist at an invisible foe. "You're right about me, Doctor. I do get what I want, and I make a virtue of necessity. Above all, I wanted an heir who would appreciate what I left behind. A man who would use his inheritance, not squander it. Forrest, I know, would have done precisely that. Therefore, Forrest is written out of my will. How could I be sure that his offspring would not do likewise?" The fist banged a table top. "Today, thank God, I've no doubts. The grandson Lady Marian has given me will be worthy of Punta Blanca."

The planter bit off the words with the air of a man who has tasted an unknown fruit and found it good. As he spoke, he bowed to his doctor from the waist. Dr. Michael Stone returned the bow.

"May I ask a question?"

"Try me."

"How many people share our secret?"

"Naturally Lady Marian knows that you sired my grandson. It's a fact she accepts without blinking."

"I can believe that."

"Her contribution to this business has been admirable. I'll go further: she's a girl after my own heart. She'll be a perfect mother to young Forrest when the child is brought here from England."

"Boys need fathers too."

"My son is a fool who'd rather ride to hounds than think. But he is not a complete loss. When he stops raging at his inactivity, he'll settle down as a passable frontier squire. My guess is he'll be a passable father as well. That he'll love the boy as naturally as though he'd really fathered him."

"Does he know that I——?"

But Michael found that the outrageous discussion had gone too far after all. Trying in vain to complete his question, he found that he was fighting down another insane burst of laughter. This time, he knew, the laughter would be for himself alone. Aloud, he said finally, "Of course he knows. How could he help but know?"

"My son can't help realizing that his lady went outside their nuptial chamber to assure the succession. And what of it? I'm told it's been common practice among titled English gentry for centuries. Especially among the blue bloods who have gone to seed. *Noblesse oblige,* you know. Thanks to his knighthood, my son considers himself of noble lineage."

"Then he can't—name names?"

"No, Dr. Stone. The most he can do is suspect. And he will never dare put his suspicion into words. Our little secret is quite safe among Lady Marian, you—and myself."

"How can you be so sure of me?"

Adam Leigh smiled in earnest. "I could appeal to you as a gentleman, of course. Or mention your professional code. I find it simpler to trust you."

"There was no need to tell me anything."

"You're forgetting that you are now my son's physician. With a perfect knowledge of the timetable of generation." The planter quartered the carpet once again and spoke without turning. "Besides, I don't enjoy working in the dark. Nor, I suspect, do you."

"So you're giving me my orders?"

Leigh's wolf grin deepened. "It's a pleasure to see quick wits in action. Yes, Dr. Stone: I *am* giving you your orders, once and for all. I'm telling you that there will be no shadow on my grandson's blood line. When I am gone, he will live on here, as the master of Punta Blanca. Until he marries, his mother will be the chatelaine. I can assure you it's precisely what she bargained for."

"And Sir Forrest?"

"Sir Forrest will make the best of his present equipment—and thank God for an indulgent father."

"And your doctor?"

"My estate doctor is a first-rate man. I've every confidence in his ability to keep my cattle—and my household—in rugged health."

"Suppose he fails?"

"He would find failure an expensive luxury."

"Will you put him to the test?"

"Gladly. They're waiting dinner now. Shall we pay our respects to Lady Marian?"

Adam Leigh had already opened the hall door. With that flourish he put on formality like a coat. Michael matched him, stride for stride, as they descended the noble spiral of the stair well. Tomorrow would be time enough to regret this shameless discussion, to weigh the implications behind Leigh's words. Even now he could not doubt the planter's ultimatum. Valuable as he was, he knew that he would be destroyed, as casually as a fly, if he threatened the pattern of Leigh's future.

"Will Sir Forrest join us at dinner?"

"His slaves carry him down the service stair. It's a shorter haul."

"So you even conserve the muscles of your houseboys?"

"Do you quarrel with that regime, Doctor?"

Michael drew in his breath without answering as they paused in the high white arch that opened to the formal salon. He knew that he should keep up this debonair fencing to the end—that Leigh would take silence as a sign. But he could not quite hold back the gasp (or the wild rush of relief) when he looked into Marian Leigh's eyes again—and found she was a stranger.

He had pictured her at the spinet, deep in Mozart. Or rising from a tapestry frame, with her dark hair unbound, to offer him a cool hand in greeting. Tonight she was seated calmly in a tall-backed love seat with an open book in her lap. Framed as she was in that high, cold archway, she seemed as unreal as a Lawrence canvas and as remote. Her eyes lifted at last. She offered him the smile he had waited for through heat-drugged eternities. And he knew that this, too, was a romantic dream image that would fade with time.

Surely this tall woman in a white sheath of China silk, with a scarf of spun gold at her waist and hair like black glass at neck and shoulder, was an ideal chatelaine for Punta Blanca. Surely she was offering him her hand to kiss for the first time. The voice that had just murmured a polite welcome had never chanted unending savage rhythms at his ear. The slender body that rose so gracefully from that tall-backed love seat had never been one with his—or strained for a more perfect oneness in Eve's timeless cradle.

"It is good to see you, Dr. Stone. To hear you're in Father Leigh's service once again."

"May I say that the pleasure is mutual?"

Fifteen months ago, almost to the day, he had used those very words on the deck of the *Dos Amigos*. He used them again tonight, knowing she would hear the echo—and knowing (with a small private chuckle) that she would never guess that they were the open sesame to his emancipation.

Adam Leigh, twirling a fresh cheroot into flame at the french window, flashed him a quick glance as he stepped back, and Michael realized that the planter had caught his meaning instantly. So be it, he told himself. If I'm to forego the revenge I swore against her, let me make the most of it. Emancipation is worth that surrender, Marian, now that I can see you for what you are. Now that I've grasped your entire game, I'll grant you this queening in your barbarous kingdom.

A stir at a side door pulled his eyes back to the room. Sir Forrest Leigh (magnificent now in a dress tunic of the Guards and sausage-tight doeskins) teetered on his valet's arm and groped testily for the cane that Guillaume had just offered him.

"Late again, Marian. Dr. Stone insists I should practice walking. Shall I humor him?"

There was a strong whiff of brandy in Michael's nostrils as his patient began to cross the desert of gleaming parquet unaided, and with all the grace of a heartsick crab. Marian's chin had risen regally at the greeting, but she did not stir until her husband stood beside her. In the double doors that gave to the dining room a major-domo waited to be noticed. Behind him Michael heard a wine cork pop, as a small regiment of slaves bustled over the vast rectangle of cloth—lighted now by a score of candles, gleaming with plate and a vast golden épergne heavy with all the fruits of the Floridas.

The rich backdrop blended and blurred, and he knew there were sudden tears in his eyes.

Marian turned at last and favored her husband with a lingering smile. Had she, too, noted the hunger in Sir Forrest? Understanding that hunger with all his heart, Michael could gauge the man's torment tonight. It was a long time now since he had permitted himself to feel pity. It was ironic that it should go to the helpless hulk he had deceived so casually—and so competently.

Lady Marian spoke, with her eyes still on her husband. Michael caught the tender note in her voice and marveled. Of course that tenderness might only be part of her poise.

"You're just in time, my dear. Jaime is about to announce dinner. Will you take me in?"

"If you'll give me an arm——"

Husband and wife led the way to the dining room. Walking side by side, they made a handsome couple, despite the major's red-faced *embonpoint*. Lady Marian Leigh had a supple strength of her own as she moved across the parquet. Watching the white arm at her husband's elbow, Michael remembered how firm that flesh could be. It was a guilty memory. He branded it as such, even as he dismissed it.

"Shall we follow the happy couple, Doctor?"

He came back to his surroundings with a slight start. Adam Leigh, still grinding his cigar in the french window, was watching him with his wolf grin intact.

"One more question, and I'm done."

"Make it short, man. I'm hungry as a field hand."

"Why did you keep me here tonight?"

"Why did you come?"

"To settle my account with you—and with her as well. Now that I've seen her in her element, I'm sure that it was settled long ago. Only a hopeless romantic would have borne a grudge."

"From where I'm standing, Doctor, you don't look in the least romantic."

Again they exchanged curt but formal bows. "You can depend on that," said Michael. "From this point on I mean to be part of the country. I'm marrying a girl in Fernandina tomorrow—if she'll have me on such short notice."

"May I offer my congratulations?"

"You may do more than that. A new doctor in Fernandina will need all the practice he can get."

"I've promised you that."

"And I promise to obey the rules at Punta Blanca. All of them."

Planter and estate doctor struck palms in the dining-room doorway. Then they entered, side by side, to join the chatelaine.

IX

It had been absurdly easy to make that promise. Easier still to match Lady Marian's bright talk across the vast gold-and-silver plain of the dinner service without a single qualm. Easiest of all to bounce to his feet when the long repast ended and bow her from dining room to salon—as though he had dined at the Point a thousand times. . . .

Now (in the glow of the new day, as he stood in the bow of the yawl and conned Tola into their own bayou) he puzzled one more time at the ease of that renunciation. He had not expected to burn with all his old desire when they met again. And yet, in his secret heart, he had missed the echo of that desire. More important, and more chilling, he had missed it in Marian as well. He admitted (now that it was over) that he would have enjoyed a reminder, however slight, that the fire she had once kindled in his blood had been more than matched in her own. Or, at the very least, some curiosity anent his year in Africa.

Lady Marian had treated him with faultless manners. The casual observer would have seen only a woman of the world, presiding expertly at her own board, and exchanging correct small talk with the doctor at her father-in-law's estate. Her light chaffing of her husband, the grave attention she bestowed on the observations of Adam Leigh himself, were other facets of her poise.

All this, he admitted, was no more than logical, in the circumstances. Marian Leigh had simply blended with her setting—as inevitably as the generations of women who looked down from the heavily gilded frames in her salon. Marian had merely made up her mind to join the dynasty, to establish its colonial branch for all time. If she had taken a time-honored means to accomplish that end, who was he to censure her?

Or so he brooded (pleased, once again, that he could brood so tranquilly) as he stood with one foot on the yawl's dancing bowsprit and waited for his first glimpse of the *Resolve* across the shining water mirror of the bayou. No man could have chosen his land, or his destiny, more deliberately. No man was more eager to carve his own niche in this wilderness. Now, thanks to his inevitable alliance with Leigh, the wilderness seemed ripe for conquest. Why should a final question linger in his brain, irritating as the grain of sand in the oyster?

He knew the answer, of course. It had been easy enough to think of Dimity Parker as his wife when his fate at Punta Blanca was still in the balance. It had been easy to tell Leigh of that marriage plan. To accept the planter's grave toast at dinner, between the terrapin and the roast. To realize (with only a small pang) that Lady Marian's congratulations were no less sincere. This bright morning, when he stood clear-eyed on the threshold of his first honest proposal, it was inevitable that he should hold back a moment more.

There, at long last, was the dark silhouette of the hulk against the sunrise. There, framed in its ragged scroll of palmetto and pine, was the setting for his future. He measured the lines of the brig (still proud, despite their barnacles) and assured himself that she would float free with little persuasion. Only last night he had discussed the project with Adam Leigh over claret, while Sir Forrest snored like a porcupine in his chair. Obviously the *Resolve* would never put to sea again: she would still make a snug, floating home for Dr. Stone and bride.

He could still turn back. A word to Tola would bring the tiller up and point the yawl's nose for the north. Adam Leigh (understanding that flight perfectly) would find another doctor in time. Lady Marian could interpret it as she chose. As for Dimity herself —well, that good-by had been understood from the beginning. If he meant to break out of Florida, this was his final chance. Once he had mounted that ragged rope ladder that led to the brig's deck —once he had held out his arms to Dimity—he could never let her go.

The bowsprit quarreled with the saw grass as Tola nosed his way into the tidal creek. Already they were in the hulk's shadow: he could see the last familiar splinter of the broken mainmast and hear the hiss of bacon broiling on deck. The hemp of the rope ladder was a rough challenge to his hand; he found he had swarmed over the broken gunwale without pausing to think.

But it was Felippa, not Dimity, who squatted before the brazier this morning. The witch's stare was quite impassive, but he could read welcome in her eyes.

"Buenos días, Inglés."

"Am I late for breakfast?"

"Two places are set in the cabin. The girl still sleeps. She is happy in her slumber. I said you would return today."

Felippa made these pronouncements quite calmly. Now she bent over her fire to test the thick fish steak dripping above the coals. Michael stood above her, and wondered why he was not more surprised. Somehow this reception seemed quite in order, as though he had expected it from the beginning.

"How could you know I'd return?"

"Dr. Hilary said you went north. He said I must tell the girl when she wakened. I told her nothing. Only that you had gone to make your peace with the earth."

He watched the mahogany-dark hands move easily at their task. *Peace with the earth.* The phrase had the ring of clairvoyance. Now he saw clearly that his whole long odyssey had sought that dedication from its very start. That this was the haven he had sought, the peace he had only begun to find.

"Perhaps I've made a bargain with the devil instead," he said slowly.

"It is a way men have, when they seek their fortunes young."

"At least I'm staying in Fernandina. Doing the work I can do best. Or did you know that too?"

Felippa kept her eyes on her work. "I have told Dr. Hilary to clear his office on the Wharf. I have said that you would become his partner before this day is ended."

"Of course he didn't believe a word."

Felippa's laughter, when it came at last, had a rich, warm timbre. He found himself joining in that laughter quite naturally. "Dr. Hilary has used me for nursing a long time now. He has faith in my words. He has gone to tell Señor Aravello that the rent will be paid at last."

"And who is Señor Aravello?"

"Your landlord, and the owner of the Long Wharf. A rich man of Fernandina, thanks to his fleet of smugglers. A good champion, Inglés. When he learns that Adam Leigh is also your champion, he will protect you from Marsden."

"Say that slowly, please!"

"You will take away Marsden's practice, Doctor. All of it. Do not question your right to do that. The man is a pig."

"And my bargain with Leigh? Do you approve that too?"

"When a man begins to establish himself, he cannot always choose his allies. Adam Leigh will back you for reasons of his own. Accept that backing. You will repay him before his history is ended."

"Tell me this, Felippa. Will he conquer, or will I?"

"The evil that Adam Leigh brings to America will be a long time dying."

"Then it will outlive him?"

"It will outlast him by centuries."

He tested her one more time—if only for the record. "Will this evil outlive Leigh's progeny?"

"He will leave no progeny. It is a judgment of creation no man escapes. Evil triumphs—for a time. Often it makes a desert of the world. But evil carries its own death in its heart. Only the good is immortal."

"Are you sure we aren't talking nonsense, Felippa?"

"It is a hard lesson, Inglés. Pray you learn it young."

"Give me my marching orders. I'll accept them."

"You have chosen your path alone. That is the only choice with meaning."

"I'm going to marry Dimity, if she'll have me. I suppose you know that too?"

"Father Ybarra will publish the banns tonight, in Fernandina," said Felippa tranquilly. "In three days' time he will marry you in the chapel of Fort San Carlos."

"Is there anything you don't know?"

"I know you are a good man for the girl, Doctor. I read that knowledge in your face when we fought to save her life."

He turned away from the witchwoman's lambent eyes and stared hard at the sunrise on Amelia.

"Will we be happy?"

"Answer that for yourself. She sleeps like a child after a quiet night. Waken her with a kiss and tell her that you love her. Promise to stay at her side until death. She has had little enough of love—and no constancy."

Doctor and witch faced each other across the glowing coals. But it was Michael's hand that touched Felippa's shoulder—Felippa, who took the mute thanks as her due. She did not even look up as he walked through the cabin door.

For a moment he stood on the threshold and stared into the sun-shot dimness. It was enough, for that moment, to listen to his own strong heartbeat, to know that the die was cast for all time.

"Is that you, Mike?"

"I've come back, Dimity. Didn't you know I would?"

She half rose in the bed, and the sun made a dim glory around her. Without transition, without conscious thought, he found that she was in his arms—and the wild thud of his heart was only an echo of her own.

"Didn't you know I could never leave you?"

He kissed her hard on the mouth without waiting for an answer. He knew that this was a beginning, not an ending. The peace he sought would take a deal of winning—but the incentive was in his arms at last.

IV

The "Hirondelle"

QUIET as monoliths from another age, ramrod-stiff in their knee-length buckskins, the four Seminoles loomed above the operating table as Michael concluded his examination. He lifted his eyes to those copper masks and bowed to each in turn, as usage demanded. Chief Hospetarkee Emathla. Coacoochee his sense-bearer. The two princelings who were Hospetarkee's sons—and chiefs in their own right in the fastness of the Okefenokee. Last of all he bowed to the boy who thrashed feebly on the table, though Hospetarkee's youngest son was deep in coma. In the past month he had saved more than one Indian's life—on this same table, in this same bare room on the Long Wharf. Ritual, he had learned, was almost as important as his surgery.

"Your son is very ill, Emathla. We must cut deep to release the evil."

"If you cut him, he will die."

"Perhaps. If I do not cut, he dies twice as fast."

It was a routine argument—and a routine case, though a desperate one. Infection, spreading from a week-old cut in the boy's heel, had now invaded the entire leg: the original cut was hardly visible, so great was the swelling of the member. Even in that coppery skin the red harbingers of death were visible from ankle to groin. Yes, the picture was complete, even without the racing pulse, the forehead blazing with fever. Once again Michael let his fingers trace the foci of danger: the sense of fluctuation in the calf region was unmistakable. The dugout had come down from the swampland just in time.

"The evil must be let out at once. There is no other way."

"There is white magic."

"No magic can save him now. Only the knife."

Michael opened his hand as he spoke, and showed the scalpel nested in the palm. The steel picked up a spark from the hot afternoon sunlight that fell through the window of Dr. Hilary Tyler's surgery; Michael watched another spark glow in the Seminole's eyes. The other Indians stood unstirring with their eyes on the chief. The doctor bowed again and drew back from the table to permit the decision to take shape.

In a case of this sort, he reflected, a great deal would depend on his reputation: he could not be sure that his name had spread into the back country so soon. Most of the Indians he had operated had been strays—water-front stevedores, or occasional deckmen aboard the coastal runners. Yet there had been a hunter from upriver whose arm he had set only a week ago. A Mickasukie squaw from the Oklawaha, who had writhed without a whimper under the knife that had delivered her baby, whole and screaming.

The muted wrangle continued behind his back. He moved out of its orbit completely and stared through the window at the late-afternoon bustle on the Long Wharf. Ships were banked solidly along the stringpieces, their bowsprits all but grazing the eaves of the chandlers' warehouses. The commotion of the winches, a part of his life these days, hardly penetrated to his brain.

There was the warehouse of Adam Leigh & Son, shuttered now that Leigh's fleet was in other hands. There, in an imposing frame of black and gold, was the sign that proclaimed José Aravello and Aravello's warehouse monarchs of all they surveyed. There (in clear water a good hundred yards offshore) was the solid bulk of the *Resolve*—resplendent in new white paint and dry as a bone after her long tow up the Amelia estuary. If Dr. Hilary turned up sober enough to take over the morning calls, Michael could begin to commission his floating hospital tomorrow.

He watched the plume of smoke rise from the amidships deck, and knew that his wife was beginning their supper, in the hope that he would row out on time tonight. It was good to stand in one's consulting room after a long day and know that one was strong enough to go on for hours, if need be. Good to realize that Dimity Parker (who was now Dimity Stone) was humming at her work while she waited for the return of her lord and master.

"Señor Inglés!

"Si, Coacoochee?"

"Will the English doctor risk the curse of Outina if he fails?"

"I have risked that curse before, as you know."

"The Chief Hospetarkee will pay well, if the cutting succeeds."

"There is no need for pay. This last hour of the day is my clinic."

"Clinic? The word is strange, Señor Médico."

Michael swung back from the window and fumbled in earnest at the grab bag of his Spanish vocabulary. It still seemed odd that this Indian's Castilian should be as pure as his own.

"The time when the doctor operates for the joy of operating."

"In our nation, the medicine man receives his pay, no matter what the hour."

"Will the Chief Hospetarkee Emathla permit me to do this cutting *por favor?"*

Michael watched the scowl gather above Hospetarkee's brows, saw it echo on the face of each princeling. Coacoochee spoke instantly, without waiting for a formal protest.

"We take no favors from white men, Señor Médico."

The buckskin sack had already clattered on the operating table. Michael weighed it politely between his palms before he returned it to the sense-bearer with another ritualistic bow.

"The affair is understood. Shall we begin?"

"When you wish."

"It is my custom to operate alone."

"It is the Seminole's custom to stand at his son's side when his life is in danger."

Michael shrugged. He had conceded that point in advance. "You will hold him, then, if he moves under the knife?"

"A chief's son does not stir under the knife."

Again the white doctor conceded the point, as he turned to his scalpels, laid in a neat row on a side table. Automatically he tested each blade and let his eye outline the probable limits of the incision. Sponging the area with water from a kettle on the corner range, he turned back to the buckskin-clad quartet. Not a man had stirred. Only the small patient turned in his delirium. Hospetarkee Emathla spoke a few sharp words to his son. Michael saw that they had penetrated through the child's coma, for the stirring ceased instantly. He took his place at the table and stood with the knife poised. The boy's long-lashed eyelids fluttered, but he had already braced himself for the first bite of the steel.

"When you are ready."

"We await your magic," said the sense-bearer.

Knowing that it would be a grave mistake to touch the child, save with the scalpel itself, Michael still hesitated for a moment. Rough surgery was not unknown in the Seminole villages: he had heard of amputations performed successfully by the tribal doctors, to the throb of the medicine drum. Surely there had been anchors on the patient at such a moment, to guard against irreparable damage. Yet no one stirred as he made the first long, slashing outline of the task ahead. The boy did not flinch as the steel bit home: Hospetarkee Emathla, standing with folded arms at the table's head, merely watched—from eyes as empty as a stone idol's.

Hesitantly, then firmly, the knife went about its work—moving in sure strokes as though guided by a force beyond the will of the pale-faced surgeon who managed it. Four pairs of Indian eyes watched the blood spurt between the surgeon's busy hands, saw those hands tie off the bleeder and sponge capillaries into temporary submission. The patient himself was still immobile. The child's mouth, set in a hard line, seemed the only living thing in that diminutive death mask.

"Why do you pause?" said Hospetarkee Emathla.

The words were spoken in dialect, but Michael grasped their import. He had told these primitives that evil was locked in the boy's body: evil must be produced with a few more strokes of the steel, or the Seminoles would mark him as a charlatan. He forced the scalpel to bite deeper; this time there was a spasmodic intake of breath from the small patient. The skin had parted in earnest down the whole length of the incision; there was the tissue below, pale from inflammation, dancing with a gnomic life of its own. There, as the knife dared to continue its exploration, was the first faint warning to the surgeon's brain—that sensation of freedom which comes from the scalpel itself as it penetrates an open cavity.

Michael stepped back for an instant, letting the spurting pus paint a picture that even the mind of Hospetarkee could grasp instantly.

"As you see, the evil begins its escape from your son's body."

One of the princelings coughed in the background: it was the only visible sign that the white man's lesson had sunk home. Foul reddish fluid continued to pour from the incision: Michael did not pause again, now that his diagnosis was established. The scalpel bit yet deeper, enlarging the area of free drainage. Then, reversing the knife, he explored the cavity he had opened with the blunt handle. Years in the clinics of the world had told him that there was no other way to destroy the partitions which often formed during the crisis of an infection—hidden caves among the fascia which could dam the pus into separate pools.

"Evil and yet more evil, Hospetarkee Emathla. As you see, we must liberate all of it."

The operation was not yet ended. He turned the boy on the table and opened a smaller incision on the opposite side of the infected limb. As he had expected, another sizable pocket was uncovered here as well. With the drainage established on both sides, he swathed the leg in a length of cotton cloth, scrupulously boiled in Hilary Tyler's kettle that morning against just such an emergency. Blood stained the dressing, but he made no attempt to stanch the flow, knowing that he must count on such minor hemorrhages to complete the scalpel's work.

"There was much pus, as you have seen. But the boy should recover."

"This pus. Is it an English word, Señor Médico?"

"Humor," he said, playing his role to the hilt while it lasted. "A Spanish word for evil. Can you take him where he will rest for several days?"

"He will go now to Felippa's," said Coacoochee.

"Good. I will see him there tomorrow. Or, if I am busy, Dr. Hilary will come for me." The princelings had already come forward as one man, to lift their brother from the table. Michael made no protest as they transferred the boy to a rough litter and bore him from the office; he had learned how gentle the hands of an Indian could be. Besides, there were no empty beds in the temporary hospital he had set up in the storeroom downstairs. Felippa could be relied on to nurse this sort of overflow.

The buckskin bag clattered on the table between them. "Do not forget your fee, Doctor."

"Permit me to return the boy to health, *por favor?*"

"When you say he recovers, we believe you. We pay for our belief —now."

Michael bowed to the accolade. In the door, Hospetarkee Emathla raised one hand, palm outward, the time-honored gesture of peace since man carried weapons in his fist. Michael matched the salute and knew that the ritual was complete. Thanks to a talent with razored steel, he had accomplished yet another miracle—as miracles are reckoned on the edge of a wilderness.

As always, gold was his reward. American eagles, clinking in leather bags, or silken purses—or counted out, coin by coin, from horny palms. He emptied the Seminoles' gold into his strongbox without pausing to reckon the total. So far, his luck had balanced his skill. Hospetarkee Emathla's expansive flourish was only another proof that he had come to Florida to stay.

So far, he had been too busy to ponder the risks he had assumed —or the consequences, if he had failed.

II

On a lean-to porch outside the dispensary he scrubbed himself clean and donned a fresh suit of cotton drill. He had performed four operations this afternoon, not counting the lacerated scalp he had stitched in the bodega at the wharf's end. A long morning had preceded them, spent in dosing the cases of dengue in their hospital, policing the vessels loading at José Aravello's dock. Tuesday was Dr. Hilary's day for country calls, so Michael had taken on the entire routine of the office.

Today, he had managed without Tola; the Minorcan had sat at the paddle of Hilary's canoe. Word had come of a broken leg to be set in a plantation far up the St. Marys, and the old doctor would need assistance. Combing his hair in the cracked mirror, Michael hoped that Dr. Tyler would return to the dock in a reasonably coherent state. There was a deal of checking to do aboard the hulk, and he had no desire to be routed out for an emergency.

Besides (in theory at least) he was still on honeymoon with his bride. No one but Dimity herself would know how thoroughly he enjoyed those evenings on the *Resolve*.

He brought his mind back to the work he had chosen. Two of this afternoon's operations had been simple routines of bone setting—one, the aftermath of a shipboard fall, the other the no-less-inevitable product of a water-front fracas. The third operation, just as inevitably, had involved the removal of an eye—or what was left of that organ, after a gouging. Hospetarkee's visit, then, had merely concluded an average afternoon.

The total receipts for this work alone would run close to a thousand American dollars. Fernandina (spilling over with smugglers' gold) was grateful for expert medical care, and Fernandina paid on the barrelhead.

Most gratifying of all was the eagerness these frontier folk showed to put themselves completely in the doctor's hands. Only a few nights ago (with Tola anchored to the fellow's midriff and Hilary hammerlocking the jaw) he had probed for a bullet—and extracted it, a hairbreadth from the throb of the carotid artery. In London old Holly would have poulticed—and prayed. Even at the Boca he could hardly have risked a slave's life in favor of a quick cure. But this young bearded captain was eager to be at sea again. The captain's officers (even as the Seminole retinue) had stood owl-eyed at the table while this new wonder-worker removed the threat of gangrene with one whisk of a probe.

But these, of course, were only the high points in a crowded month. His biweekly visits to the Point, the aches and agues of a subtropic community, his endless checking of ship's crews for a threat of epidemic—such were the usual chores that filled his days. And he was finding that he enjoyed the work mightily, even as the files of fever-wasted bodies, broken heads, and bleeding eye sockets threatened to people his dreams.

It was routine now to stitch a torn ear on the deck of the hulk while Dimity cooked breakfast in the galley that Tola had installed amidships. To rush ashore behind a brace of flying oars to tie off a spurting artery on the bar of the Silver Dollar or the Mañana de Sol, Aravello's two thundering grogshops under the bluff. To purse together another twelve-inch gash . . . To wash away, as best he could, the fire that raged through more private organs after a sailor's visit to Ladies Street.

"Ladillas, Señor Médico? Esta posible?"

"See for yourself, *amigo.*"

"But Madame Chica swore the girl was no more than fifteen."

"Apparently she was well traveled."

Madame Chica herself had visited him shortly after he had moved in with Hilary—a demure little woman in bombazine with a cream-white fichu and a cameo as respectable as her downcast eyes. But those same modest eyes had snapped with good humor when they were alone. Madame Chica, as Michael soon gathered, was a true Tinker, and Spanish only by adoption.

"I understand you've had complaints about us, Dr. Stone?"

"One must expect such things in our trade. As an old ship's surgeon, I'm more than accustomed to——"

"Why don't you pay us a visit? *Professionally,* of course."

Michael bowed his thanks at the compliment. Madame Chica was a power in Fernandina; the fact that she ventured abroad by daylight and looked each citizen in the eye was proof positive.

"Last week I was called in by Colonel Morales to treat his wife for diabetes. Three days ago Señor Xavier Canova, your oldest citizen, asked me to examine *his* wife's goiter. And now you invite me to inspect your establishment. Madame Chica, my cup runneth over."

"Blasphemy, Doctor!"

"The sentiment came from my heart. So you feel your young ladies could use a doctor's care?"

"Saints preserve us, it's all I can do to make 'em wash. But if a man like you would advise them, now and again——"

"—or confine a few to quarters until their health improved?"

"That, too, if you say so. My young ladies come from the best exchange in Havana, but——"

"A word that covers many sins, madame."

"Would I be arguing? Why else am I here? And when will you pay your first visit?"

"Your street happens to be in Dr. Marsden's section of Fernandina. It'd be worth my life to trespass."

"Are you a man to jibe at risks where a lady's health is concerned?"

"Control of this town is divided between Dr. Marsden and Señor Aravello, my present landlord. But why should I tell you something you already know?"

"Marsden takes his percentage of my profit," said Madame Chica. "That is well understood. And I can't deny that I'm protected, after a fashion. So far this year there hasn't been more than a killing a month on Ladies Street." Madame Chica pursed virtuous lips over that record. "Still, I'd be easier in my mind if my customers were happy afterward. Next thing you know, my houses will be getting a bad name on the wharves."

"Surely you can complain to Marsden. It's his job to keep his half of the town well."

"Dr. Marsden is too busy getting rich to doctor Ladies Street."

"Can't you make it worth his while?"

"I'm employed from Havana, Doctor. There's no provision for medical expense. If a girl get sick, I'm supposed to send her packing."

Michael nodded soberly. Here, then, was a slave trade of quite another sort, a bondage that destroyed its devotees no less ruthlessly.

"Bring your girls here, two at a time, over the next fortnight. I'll do what I can to keep them well."

"But I said I couldn't pay for office visits."

"Bring them in the last hour of the day. I'll include them in my clinic."

Madame Chica hesitated discreetly. "Most of our doctors took their fees in trade, if I may make so bold——"

"I appreciate the courtesy. As it happens, I'm a married man. A happily married man," he added hastily, when his visitor's Irish eye had fixed him with a cynic's quirk.

A happily married man. He repeated that conviction in the gathering dusk. A man who could hardly wait to rejoin his beloved in their floating paradise. But there were still odd tasks to perform before he could close the office. The recheck of the dispensary, the final entries in the account book. Brooding on those names and house numbers, he saw the geography of the town again as clearly as though the map lay under his hand.

It was quite true that the better element of Fernandina had come to him from the start—from both sides of that mythical line that José Aravello had mentioned so emphatically. Don Xavier (to name the most distinguished example) had walked down the sand-rutted streets alone to request that the new doctor examine his wife. Colonel Morales had escorted his lady to Dr. Hilary's consulting room and rejoiced publicly that Fernandina boasted a real doctor at long last. It was pure coincidence that he had been able to correct Doña Morales's ailment in a single visit—and assure her, only yesterday, that she was on the way to a complete recovery. Digitalis (which Felippa had produced from her herbarium with her usual quiet competence) had been indicated from the start; the bleeding which Dr. Marsden had advocated had been abandoned in favor of this simple specific. In another fortnight his patient would walk again as well as any lady in Fernandina.

The account book told him how deeply he had raided Marsden's practice; it was hardly reasonable to hope that the man would yield with good grace. Michael pictured himself in a like situation: kingpin of a brawling frontier town, estate doctor to the region's richest planter—and deposed, in both departments, by an upstart no better than a castaway.

But Marsden was in Charleston on business, so he had been unmolested so far. True, he had yet to cross the line of demarcation, even in his rival's absence.

Aravello had summed up that division, neatly enough, when they had shaken hands for the first time. "Naturally I was here ahead of him, Dr. Stone. There were Aravellos in Fernandina when the first garrison came up from Augustine."

"Then why give half the town to Marsden?"

"It was a mistake. I admit as much freely. Marsden came from the States with men and guns. Not quite enough to stamp him as an invader. He would have been blasted overnight, had Coppinger heard in Augustine. At the time Amelia still bore scars from the last American war—when filibusters made it their capital."

"So his was only a rival gang that was strong enough to challenge yours?"

"As always, you have put things in the nutshell."

Aravello had smiled around the circle, as though apologizing for the English idiom. They were seated in Aravello's own office, with the hot midday bustle of the pier spilling in at the open windows. Michael could still remember the stares of the Spaniard's lieutenants. Armed to the teeth, these young smugglers could have called themselves pirates with ease and made their own laws. He noted the hawk-proud attention that each man had given the remarks of this reckless visitor from Albion—and warned himself to walk carefully.

Aravello seemed less perturbed than the youngest of his retinue. A plump young man in faultless linen, an almost cherubic young man who threatened to burst from the vast band of scarlet silk that confined his midriff in lieu of waistcoat, Don José justified his rolling name to the last syllable. Here, thought Michael, is the curse of inheritance, with no inner drive to make the inheritance permanent. Here is a man who knows the ritual of ruling, without the strength. He muted his next question deliberately.

"May I ask why I cannot cross Sevilla Street, either as a doctor or a citizen?"

"It is the division we made long ago. The gentleman's agreement."

Aravello had spread the map of the town on his desk top with that admission. He made his point with one well-fed hand. "As you see, Sevilla Street descends, by this stair, from the bluff to the water front. On the south lies Long Wharf, and perhaps half the town. On the north, the Sugar Wharf and the rest of Fernandina."

"Yours—and his?"

"Life is simpler so, *verdad?*"

"But if you were here first——"

"At first he posed as a man of peace. A doctor who was also a planter, with a retinue of slaves and overseers." Aravello shrugged again. "The slaves were Haitian blacks, who learned their sailing from the pirates of the Tortugas. The overseers were smuggling captains to the last man. Within a year he forced me to sell him the Sugar Wharf——"

"But how?"

"By taking up my notes in Charleston banks. By convincing me that there was business enough for all. He has many friends in Charleston, Doctor. Some say he lingers there now to plan another coup for Fernandina—and for us. At that time I drew a line down Sevilla Street. I gave him the water front on his side, the rents in the town itself, the right to take tribute at the *bordellos* of the Calle de las Damas. Today you see the result. But Marsden was right in another way. There is business for us both. More than enough."

"Does that make you friends?"

Aravello spat deliberately. "I would have great pleasure in killing him, if I could risk it. Often I feel the urge to cross this line which I myself drew—and fight it out. But what would you have? Between us we have made the town strong. If I drove him from the island, another might come in his place. A stronger one, who would devour me."

"Isn't that a chance worth taking?"

Michael had looked around the room as he spoke and read assent in hot young eyes. But Aravello's hands, fluttering upward from the map, silenced the murmurs.

"You come to me as a tenant, Doctor. To ask my permission to expand the quarters of Dr. Tyler on the Long Wharf. And already you talk of battles."

"Surely it's bound to come someday."

"Beyond a doubt. In the meantime, we will keep our heads and grow yet richer."

Their first meeting had ended on that note. In the month that followed Aravello had proved himself an excellent landlord. Hilary Tyler's small office had been enlarged; the hospital in the storage shed had been equipped within the week. Last and best, the *Resolve* had been reconditioned and floated into the Amelia by one of Aravello's own crews, to become a respectable addition to the water front. A sea dog whose days were done, she could still serve as home for Dr. Michael Stone and bride, since there was not an empty house in all of this teeming town.

Michael locked his door and carried his strongbox to Aravello's front office at the great warehouse door. Across the way the wide-open doors of the Silver Dollar roared with song and drunken laughter. A dozen voices shouted invitations across the dockside, but he ignored them all as he strode toward his own haven. There was Willi, the half-Negro, half-Indian servant that Aravello had assigned him as boatman in Tola's absence. There was his skiff, bobbing in the strong, blue-green wash of the tide. And there, as the little boat danced across the harbor, was his bride—with her hands extended in welcome. The same Dimity, though she was all but civilized now, in a calico house dress and voluminous apron.

The hulk was bright with sunset as Willi's oars bit into the cross rip. The sun had gone before they could quite gain her side. In a flash the great tarnished block of the man-of-war, rocking gently in the tide, seemed more prison than paradise—and Dimity herself a white wraith that waited amidships. But Dr. Michael Stone ignored that metamorphosis, even as it chilled his bounding spirits. This was the first home he had known, and he had fashioned it with his own brain and hands. This was the wife he had chosen. His strong-beating heart drummed down the brief burst of logic. This was his destiny—and he had chosen well.

III

"Why, Mike?"

"Why," he said, "is the riskiest word in any language. Don't use it, if you can't take the consequences."

"Why did you marry *me*—out of all the people you could have married?"

He teased her cheek with a light kiss. "Do you really want to know?"

Dimity settled in his arms and looked up contentedly at the stars. "Why would I ask you every night at this same time?"

"I loved you, needed you, wanted you."

"But you *had* me already, Mike."

"I'd made up my mind to settle in Florida as a frontier doctor."

"When did you decide that?"

"When Felippa and I were pulling you through that siege of snakebite. I made a private arrangement with Heaven. If you got well, I made up my mind to become a solid citizen. To make us both respectable, if it killed us. Naturally the first step was to take you to Father Ybarra's chapel."

"I could have kept house for you, just as we were."

"Granted. But I hope you're happier as Mrs. Michael Stone."

"I've never been happier, Mike. But I'm still asking why."

It was his turn to stir sleepily in their embrace and study the stars for wisdom. They were resting in their favorite nest, the forecastle shrouds of the *Resolve*. Without raising his head from Dimity's breast, he could look back at Fernandina—pin-pointed with lights from warehouse and tavern. Even at that distance he could hear the brawling voices, a peppering of shots, that told of another water-front feud pushed to its inevitable climax. Tonight it was good to know that Fernandina and its feuds were a safe quarter-mile away. The brig shivered in the changing tide, then sighed gently against her mooring buoy. Precisely as I've settled at mine, thought Michael, with an answering sigh.

Dimity spoke in the same gentle whisper: "Don't answer if you'd rather not."

"If I say *I've* never been happier, will you believe me?"

"You're a gentleman, Mike."

"That's a big word for the frontier."

"You've education, money, and a career. You could have settled anywhere in America—if you insist on being an American. Why do you stay on in Spanish Florida? Don't pretend it's for love of me."

"Why else would I stay?"

He closed her lips with a long kiss before another question could escape. They had played this game of questions more than once in the last drowsy half-hour between dinner and bed. Tonight he found he had most of the responses by heart.

"Isn't it enough that I love you? That it's for always?"

That, too, was part of the ritual, Dimity's doubts—which he soothed by time-honored methods. His own protestations—which were all the more welcome, because he could mean every word. Tonight he answered her question silently for the first time. I married you, Dimity, because I belong here, as I've never belonged before. Belonging to *you* has made it all real. But don't think I married you out of gratitude. Or because I saw that you had always been as lonely as I. This is a bargain for all time, just as I've told you. I'll fulfill my part to the letter.

Aloud he said only, "We're part of this now. Just as I'm part of you. If that doesn't dispose of your question—how can I answer it?"

It was a traditional finale for what was, by now, an ancient family argument. When Dimity spoke again, her voice was drowsy with tranquillity. The cynic buried in his heart (in that odd corner where cynics have always lurked) was scarcely troubled by her words.

"When do you go to the Point?"

"Wednesday and Saturday are my visiting days. You know that."

"You said you might cut down your visits, now those two doctors have come on from Africa."

"So I did. The place is clean now and ticking like a clock. But I've contracted for two weekly visits. I can't change my schedule until Leigh returns from Havana."

"Do you *enjoy* those trips to the Point, Mike? Is it a breathing spell from this?"

"I don't want a breathing spell from this. Now ask me if Lady Marian Leigh is beautiful. The answer is—I wouldn't know. I'm too much in love with my wife to notice."

"You mean that too," she whispered. "I'm glad you mean it. But Lady Marian *is* beautiful. I've seen her more than once in Fernandina. She used to sail up from the Point with her father-in-law. On his sloop, the *Hirondelle*."

"Are you afraid she'll lead me astray? Would you prefer I gave up the Point altogether?"

"Certainly not, Mike. I know how much the Point means to your future. Can't I tease you a little too?"

She chuckled with her lips against his cheek and drew back to offer him her best smile. He could not see her eyes clearly in the dark, but he knew that they were wide with trust, humid with happiness. This is my final proof, he told himself. Could I mention Marian Leigh so casually if I hadn't put her memory behind me once and for all?

"Come with me on my next trip. Farrar is in charge, now Leigh's in Cuba. He'll put us both up over night."

"No, Mike. I'd much rather stay right here and wait for you. It's too much fun—making a home of the *Resolve*."

He drew her even closer, enjoying the implication back of those words. "You're a born homemaker, Dimity."

"Just as you're a born doctor. We *do* make a team, don't we?"

"A perfect team."

"I guess I'm luckier than I know. Having a man who enjoys his work. That's half the battle for any wife."

He saw that he had avoided the question of the Point neatly enough—and resisted a perverse impulse to push that question to the limit. The stronghold of his marriage, he repeated, was impregnable. This business of healing the sick in Fernandina was the most engrossing task he had ever undertaken. Would he enjoy it as much if Adam Leigh sold out his estate and left Florida tomorrow? If Marian Leigh (and the bizarre ruin she had married) whisked back to England on the next ship, never to return?

Obviously the question was academic. Marian would never leave Punta Blanca: she had made her plans too well. Now that her child would be Leigh's eventual heir, she could have no other dwelling place. He recalled his bitter inward grin when he had gone to the Point for his second inspection tour and learned that Lady Marian was already en route to London to bring back her son—now that young Forrest had weathered his first winter without a day's illness. Naturally Adam Leigh's putative grandson must lose no time in solidifying his inheritance: the boy's living presence, on his grandsire's knee, was an essential no intelligent mother would overlook. It seemed no less natural that Sir Forrest Leigh (late of His Majesty's Guards) should lock himself in his room and subsist on a diet of brandy and curses. Sir Forrest (and Michael saw this clearly now) missed Marian in a way no ex-lover could. . . .

So much for this strangely assorted family and its future—so precariously balanced, despite Adam's millions. So much for the fact that he must soon look his own son in the eyes and deny his paternity. Young Forrest had been born a Leigh—and he would die one. He would protect the boy—and the boy's mother—with his silence. God helping him, he had no other course. One more time he assured himself that Marian Leigh had had no part in his decision to stay on in Florida. That Marian was only an enigma he had made up his mind to solve with time.

"We won't stay here forever, will we, Mike?"

He came back gratefully to the living, breathing reality in his arms. "Only so long as I'm really needed. Or until I can buy a plantation on the St. Johns."

"When did you think of that?"

"Only this moment, if the truth is told. Aravello has a number of land grants he'd dispose of at bargain prices. There's a place called Cowford, where the King's Highway comes up from St. Augustine to cross the St. Johns. It'll be a seaport when the country opens up in earnest. It could be the largest city in the state someday—when Florida becomes a state." He wondered a little at the enthusiasm in his voice, to say nothing of his long-range view. "Felippa isn't the only one with second sight. We might even farm a quarter section, or put in an orange grove, while we waited for a practice to grow up around us."

He felt her stir in his arms and knew that her contentment was genuine now. "I've always wanted a farm, Mike. How did you guess?"

"After that New England uncle?"

"That wasn't farming; that was just ingrown hate."

He closed his eyes on the image of Dimity in a sunbonnet before a cabin doorway and found that she suited that background perfectly. "Of course we must stay in Fernandina for now."

"For quite a while, Mike. You can't farm without money. Whole fistfuls, in fact."

"Don't say we aren't getting rich fast enough. I could put down an option with José tomorrow, if I liked."

Dimity sat up abruptly. He raised himself on an elbow and grinned up at this sudden show of determination. "Money isn't the only reason, darling. I know Fernandina is just a smugglers' paradise now. It'll trim down to size when the Americans take over. But it's still a town."

"What on earth are you driving at?"

"Only that I'll feel safer in a town when my time comes."

It was Michael's turn to sit up abruptly. "Do you know what you're saying?"

"You said you were part of me just now. Do you know how true *that* was?" She was laughing softly in the dark. Like any happy woman's laughter, there was a hint of tears at its heart. "Imagine having a doctor for a husband, who doesn't know you're pregnant."

"You're sure, Dimity?"

"Maybe I should have been more delicate. But I had to tell you sometime." A quick shadow crossed her tone as he sat unstirring beside her. "Are you sorry, Mike? That it happened so soon, I mean?"

He made his kiss take the place of words until his mind could adjust to this new concept. "Why shouldn't I be glad, since it's the one thing that's lacking here?"

"You mean that too, don't you, darling?"

"Let's hope he'll be born an American. Perhaps I should send you to St. Marys to be positive."

"We'll take care of his citizenship later," said Dimity. "Anyway, I'd planned on a girl, for the first time." She got to her feet with a happy laugh. "I'm glad I told you this way, even if it did surprise you."

"A father is always surprised, I'm told."

Dimity walked to the rail without quite meeting his eyes. "Of course I didn't dare say a word until I was sure."

"Of me?"

"Of this. God forgive me, Mike, but I couldn't make myself believe this marriage was real—until tonight."

"What convinced you?"

"Cowford," said Dimity, with her eyes on the dark harbor. "Your plan to buy a quarter section. A man doesn't buy land without planning to put down roots too. If that doesn't include a family, what does?"

He sat where he was—quietly, enjoying her contentment. He had not expected life to overtake him quite so rapidly, yet that was a way life had when you surrendered to its compulsion. As he had surrendered with Dimity. He would pay the price gladly, he told himself—and felt his heart tighten that such assurances should be necessary, even in the corner of his mind he shared with no one.

"You're sure you don't mind, Mike?"

"Life moves fast when you're riding with the current," he said. "That's how I want it. That's how it must always be."

"I can go to Felippa, even now, if you think we should wait. She'll give me something to——"

"Don't even say that, Dimity."

"I told myself I'd have it, even if you left me," she said. Her voice was oddly calm when he considered the import of her words. "Probably I'd have changed my mind long before the time came."

"How dared you think I'd leave you?"

"You had every right," she said, in that same dead tone. "I've never made claims on anyone. Why should I begin with you?"

"This marriage is for always. I won't tell you that again—now that you've given me the proof."

But she avoided his embrace with light-footed ease, dodged nimbly around the stump of the mainmast as he pursued her, and ran forward to the bowsprit, where she stood poised against the stars—and daring him to follow. Michael paused with one foot on the anchor flukes, the other on deck. Experience had taught him that Dimity would be out of her cotton print and overside in a twinkling if he took another step. It was a game they had played often on moonless nights, if they were in the mood for a swim before bedtime.

"Of course I could leave *you,* Mike. Did you ever think of that?"

"Just try to get away!"

A white cotton cloud whirled into his face, blinding him briefly. When he tossed it aside, his wife stood at the bowsprit's very tip, balancing precariously on her toes, her body an arched golden bow. Even in the velvet cloak of night there was a radiance about her, as though that lithe, alert person contained a light of its own.

"I could go overside now and swim out to sea. You'd never catch me, if I put my mind to it."

"Don't you dare!"

"Don't worry, Mike. I'll stay with you now, as long as you need me."

She plunged with the words and vanished in the dark without a splash. He leaned far out from the rail, sure that the night had swallowed her. Then her sleek head broke surface far out in the harbor. Instantly her body was outlined in another kind of radiance as her thrashing limbs picked up phosphorescence from the bay itself. He whooped a warning, even as he kicked off his own clothes and followed her.

"Who says you can outswim me?"

He knew that she had slowed her pace a little, so that he might overtake her with honor. They met in a wild phosphorus whirl, letting their bodies meet and merge in a kiss that seemed to have no ending. Much later he would remember that the salt of her tears had mingled on his cheek with the warm lap of this great tidal bay; that her broken laugh, when he released her at last, was still a little frightened—as though she had half meant her threat. For the moment he was too happy in her nearness to feel the chill behind her words.

"Don't do that again, Dimity—even as a joke."

"I won't, darling. This is my last swim, now I'm a mother-to-be."

"I'll see you keep that promise too," he said sternly. "Remember, I'm your doctor as well as your husband."

"What's your prescription now, Doctor?"

"Once around the channel buoy, and then to bed."

They swam easily, side by side, letting the warm void of the bay enclose them completely. When the channel buoy loomed ahead like a great ghostly bird riding the soft lap of the tide, they rounded it in a long circle and began the swim back—still silent in the faint bath of starlight, still content in their silence. When Dimity spoke at last, her voice was warm with a new-found trust.

"Somehow, I didn't want that to end—ever."

"Nor did I."

"I love to swim with you, Mike."

"Just to *swim?"*

"This is no place for your low jokes." But she surrendered her lips to his for a long, heart-stopping moment. "Treading water like this, we might as well be swimming in a quicksilver bath."

"Does it matter, since we're alone?"

"We aren't quite alone any more, Mike. There's a boat coming out now, from the Long Wharf. I can hear the oarlocks."

He did not dispute her word as they rolled apart and sprinted for the *Resolve* together. More than once he had marveled at the keenness of her hearing when they had sat on the brig's deck and guessed the identity of the small craft ghosting by in the night.

"If this is a race, I'll win it."

"Not this time you won't," said Dimity firmly. "There are men at those oars, and they're rowing fast."

He disputed her for the first hundred yards, then acknowledged defeat with a good-humored chuckle. Feathering the surface with long, easy strokes, Dimity's slender body had eaten the distance between them and the rope ladder; it seemed only a matter of minutes before she swarmed up the rungs and vanished overside, though Michael himself was still panting far behind. Glad that she was safe aboard, with the approaching boat only a dim threat in the distance, he rolled on his back and floated quietly for a moment, while he waited for his heart to resume its normal beat. For the first time he was conscious of the commotion ashore, a babble of voice and dancing torches that seemed to include the wharves and a good section of the bluff above them. His mind swung back abruptly to the spatter of gunfire he had heard earlier that evening. Was it possible that this melee was the aftermath of a burst of violence, unusual even for Fernandina after dark? And was this long, gray-white skiff (darting to meet him now like an agile water bug on the black floor of the harbor) a messenger from his own surgery on the Long Wharf?

He swam to his rope ladder and drifted there easily, with one foot twined in the lowest rung, while the skiff took form in the dark. Already he could recognize her trim lines: he had seen that little boat a dozen times, bobbing like a crazy chip in the wake of the *Hirondelle,* when Leigh's own sloop had put into the Amelia. Tonight, he noted, a brace of Leigh's best-muscled Negroes were making the oars hum. The small, erect figure in the bow could be no one but Roger Farrar.

"*Resolve* ahoy!"

"Speaking, Roger."

The skiff nuzzled the brig's side as the blacks reversed their oars. Farrar leaned down to stare at Michael. Even by starlight there was something in the head overseer's face that froze Michael's grin of welcome at the source.

"I thought you were pinned down at the Point."

"I was—until Mr. Leigh returned. Things have happened fast since then. Too fast for comfort, if you ask *me,* Doctor."

"Did Leigh come up with you?"

"He's at Marsden's now. What d'you think the shouting's for?"

"So my rival's returned at last?"

Farrar made an impatient shooing gesture that brought Michael from water to ladder in record time. "Marsden's retired in Charleston on his moneybags. Mr. Leigh has taken over his practice, and his house, in your name. How soon can you be dressed?"

"My things are on deck. I'll go as I am, and dress en route."

Farrar clucked approval from the dark. "Of course there was a little trouble when we crossed Sevilla Street and took over. Some of the good doctor's confederates didn't believe he'd sold out. Not even when I produced the deed of transfer."

"So I've patients from both camps now."

"The broken heads can wait," said Farrar. "You've a more important patient to handle first. In fact, he's lying on your table now. Old Tyler is trying to soothe him down with brandy."

The skiff bounced violently as Michael dropped from the deck and straddled a thwart, with his clothes bunched in his folded arms. "Don't tell me Adam Leigh is ailing?"

"Adam Leigh has never been sick in his life. It's the cavalryman's leg. This time it's broken for fair."

The skiff was already leaping across the bay as the two panting blacks leaned on their oars. Michael settled against the thwart for an instant and stared hard at the frenetic pattern of torches along the bluff. The pin points of light seemed to spell out a welcome of their own. His mind, struggling with Farrar's news, could not grasp the full import of that welcome.

"Sir Forrest, eh?"

"He said he'd ride again, or know the reason why. Of course he was drunk when he tried it, and rolling in the saddle. We brought him here as fast as canvas would take us. Didn't I say things were happening too fast for comfort?"

IV

Hilary Tyler spoke softly, with his eyes on the ragged pattern of torchlight at the surgery window. "I served with Cornwallis, boy. I give you my word, I never saw a stranger wound."

"How did it happen?"

"He insisted on riding a hunter and took the first fence at a gallop. If you ask me, he was suffering from hallucination at the time. No sane man would strap an English army pistol at his belt with the trigger cocked. When he tumbled, the gun didn't discharge; it would have been better for Sir Forrest if it had. Made a cleaner wound, as it were. Of course he would pack in twice the charge of powder the bore could carry. That's why the barrel exploded slam against his thigh."

Michael nodded and folded his hands in the towel that Tola stepped forward to offer him. He had been scrubbing mechanically for the past moment, while his mind sorted the details of the task that lay ahead. Just as mechanically he stepped to the window now and stared down at the hullabaloo on the Long Wharf.

The torches picked out high lights on a dozen musket barrels, as the unit of Leigh's private army herded stragglers about their business. Michael knew that these picked huskies stood at each street corner in Fernandina, at each stair that led down from the bluff. Leigh had taken no chance on a miscarriage of his plans—whatever those plans might be. The fact that a desperately injured son had accompanied this expedition (like so much excess baggage) was only incidental, it seemed. He stepped back from the window, glad that there was no chance now to brood on Leigh's unpredictable ways.

Sir Forrest Leigh, hunched like a grotesque beast in swathings of heated blankets, began to mutter brokenly under the opiate Dr. Hilary had already poured into him along with the brandy—a low, monotonous mutter familiar to Michael as his own breathing.

"Where's Stone? Promised—save leg. *Made* him promise——"

Tyler glanced pointedly at Michael as the two doctors moved over to the table. Tola had already whisked into the lean-to to resume his carpentry on the traction splint.

"Did you make such a promise?"

"Never in this world. It's just a wish he's buried in his brain. For all I know, it's what made him saddle that hunter." Knowing in advance what he would find, Michael set his jaw in a hard line as he began to cut away the shredded riding breeches that clung like a second skin to Sir Forrest Leigh's overstuffed leg.

"Obsessions play strange tricks in a man's mind when he's fuddled with drink. Would you call me mad if I said he'd broken his leg on purpose—to *force* me to operate?"

"He's done worse than that," said Dr. Tyler.

Michael nodded his agreement as the knife bared the area where they must work. The powder burns, mushroomed over a wide segment of flesh and mingled with clotted blood and wisps of torn cloth, made a formidable wound in themselves. Already, without even exploring the bone picture, he saw that this would be a task to try any surgeon's skill.

"It's a compound fracture of the thigh," said Tyler. "Why waste Tola's time on a splint? You know you'll have to amputate."

But Michael spoke as though he had not heard. "It's the good leg that's broken this time. Unless it's mended somehow, he'll never walk again—even with a cane. He'd have to go on crutches, Hilary. The man is too proud for that, God help him."

"God help you if you let him die of gangrene. Leigh will have your heart for breakfast."

"I saw Leigh on the Wharf. He gave me carte blanche."

"So you mean to take the risk."

"I saved two blacks on shipboard. Both were almost identical cases. It was simply a matter of removing the bone fragments, starting traction, and maintaining it in a cradle splint."

"With Cornwallis, it was knife and bone saw. Better a gimp than no man at all."

The old doctor was speaking the truth of his times: only the most reckless of surgeons would dare to shrug it away. Michael merely nodded soberly as his fingers explored the distended skin, searching for the pulsation that would tell him the femoral artery was undamaged. If there was the slightest leakage there, amputation would be inevitable; with a free flow of blood, there would be a chance. How much, he did not know.

On the top of the foot there was a faint throb beneath his probing fingers. Definitely faster than his own pulse, it told him that the artery was open and safely out of the field of injury.

"We'll police those powder burns and set without amputating," he said firmly. As he spoke he glanced at the instrument table and risked a faint smile. "I see you've set up for both."

"I haven't assisted you five weeks for nothing," grumbled Tyler. "Nor has Tola, for that matter. Here's your splint, ready ahead of time."

Michael tested the double incline of the box that Tola had just placed beside the table. Tailored to fit Sir Forrest's gouty limb, it would support the broken bones neatly when the operation was finished. Later, traction would be exerted by attaching weights to the ankle.

"Can you anchor him, Tola?"

"If you will strap his other leg, jefe."

"Take care of that while I go over these burns. The tissue here is narcotized."

He spoke with more assurance than he felt as he attacked the injured area. To his gratification, he found that the condition was less serious than he had feared. The thick leather facings of Sir Forrest's riding boots had protected the skin to some extent—and it was now apparent that the pistol had exploded most of its force into the free air, probably at the very moment the foolhardy rider parted company with his saddle.

"Ready when you are, Doctor."

"We'll go in now. Take his head, Hilary. Tola will manage this bag of bones."

Even to a surgeon's eye the breakage was formidable. The jagged end of the thighbone had made a ragged laceration through the skin; blood began to seep here in earnest as Michael tested the opening with a tentative flick of the steel. Without hesitation he enlarged the wound, parallel to the bone. The scalpel, uncovering successive layers of fat, seemed to float in white suet for a moment, as it revealed the full extent of Sir Forrest's divorcement from the world he loved. And then, as the steel bit deeper, new blood welled forth from a myriad severed vessels—a free flow indicating that the circulation was still good. With the last precise stroke, Sir Forrest screamed just once, before his head lolled in Dr. Hilary's iron grip.

The scalpel reached the white sheath of the fascia; with each bite the strokes became sharper, more mercifully quick. The wound was pumping blood in earnest now. Michael clamped the larger vessels as he proceeded, ligating with whipcord from the neat stack on the side table. Then, with fingers and scalpel joined, he separated the muscles above the bone itself, probing for splinters that might have disengaged from the periosteum. A loose fragment came into his hand, and then another. He dropped them into the basin at his elbow and continued his exploration—deep in his work now, too intent to consider anything but the injured tissue beneath his hand, the throb of flesh as the knife flicked a nerve, the next hard fragment that seemed to burrow perversely in the wound.

"Steady does it, Tola. This is lead, not bone."

He knew that the Minorcan's forehead had beaded with sweat as he threw all his weight across Forrest Leigh's body, steadying the patient with a last supreme effort as Sir Forrest seemed about to roll from the table in his thrashing agony. Still burrowing in the wound, still groping for that elusive leaden pancake, he knew that Tola would not fail him now. Aboard the *Mariposa* he had seen more than one foremast hand collapse at just such a critical moment; the Minorcan was made of sterner clay.

The muscles under his fingers were writhing like captive snakes when he found what he was seeking at last and filched it deftly from the moist depths. For an instant he paused there, with the mushroomed lead pellet in his palm, and met Hilary Tyler's eyes across the table.

"Apparently the pistol discharged after all. This could only be a bullet."

Back in the wound again he explored thoroughly for several fast-paced minutes without uncovering another foreign substance. The muscles still twitched from time to time as he touched a nerve, but the patient's flesh seemed quieter now as the scalpel moved into its finale—separating the tissue to search for future pockets of infection, incising any torn segment that did not seem normally healthy. At last he straightened the leg and nodded to Tyler.

"The splint, please, Doctor."

Even now they moved gingerly and with all possible speed, lest a final lurch on Sir Forrest's part might undo their therapy. But the Waterloo officer seemed inert as mutton now; the broken leg, collapsing into the splint box like a discouraged sausage, might have belonged to a cadaver. Pacing his movements with Dr. Hilary's, Michael wrapped the whole limb snugly in bandages while the older surgeon knotted the cloth ends in a series of snug knots. The upper part of the leg was now fixed against the boards; the lower segment would be movable in but one direction, the long plane of the splint itself.

With crude ship's glue Michael painted the lower leg on each side of the ankle and up the calf. He could wish for isinglass or the new adhesive plaster now being used in England, but there was none available here. Strips of cloth, anchored in the glue, would serve him well enough. Dr. Tyler was already attaching the corded weight that would depend from the splint itself and keep traction constant.

"We can move him to his litter now. It's best to transport him before he wakens."

Tola opened the door to the anteroom. Four of Leigh's estate guards marched in with the wordless celerity of automatons and placed the injured man on the litter. The canvas slings groaned under Sir Forrest's weight, but the men managed their burden well. Michael tested the splint and saw that it was riding comfortably.

Dr. Tyler pursed his lips. "Are you sure it's wise to move him at once?"

"It was Leigh's wish that he go aboard the sloop. If he mends he can return to the point tomorrow, or the day after. If not, he'll be anchored just off the wharf—and we'll do what we can." Michael tested Forrest Leigh's pulse and noted that it was no worse than it had been before the operation. "As you know, wounds of this sort stand a chance, if they mend on salt water."

"So I've observed. I don't see why."

"There are some things we must leave to fate, Dr. Tyler. This leg is one of them."

The old doctor watched in silence as the litter went creaking down the stairs. "I still say we should have sawed. If that's old-fashioned, make the most of it."

"Common sense is on your side, of course. It's a better than even chance that that wound will be gangrenous within three days."

"Yet you insisted on a bone set?"

"Only because I was thinking of the patient. He'd go mad on crutches."

"My thought exactly, Doctor. Unless, of course, he's already mad."

Hilary and Michael turned sharply as the voice boomed from the doorway. Adam Leigh strode into the room with his arrogance intact, his shoulders defiantly squared in a dark boat cloak. As always, he seemed to breathe out an almost visible vitality, along with the plume from his cigar.

"I'd have come sooner, but this has been a busy night in Fernandina."

"I gather my own work is just beginning."

Leigh grinned around his cigar. "Don't worry, Doctor. No one has been seriously hurt tonight. Though I'll admit that several are rather badly frightened."

"Surely the Marsden men put up a fight?"

"A token resistance only. Most of them took to the woods when they heard we were coming. I seldom interfere in the affairs of Fernandina. When I do pay the town a visit, I try to make my wishes stick." Leigh shrugged off the interruption as he walked to the window of the surgery. "You'll find the town is quiet as a church, I think. If not, Farrar will hear from me in the morning."

Michael, washing his hands in the lean-to, glanced wryly at Hilary as the older doctor scrubbed down the table. Leigh, brooding at the window on business of his own, might have forgotten their presence completely. Foursquare as some barbaric idol in the lamplight, he seemed indestructible as time—and quite as determined to have the final word.

"I think we can trust your overseer."

"So do I, Stone. Was the operation a success?"

"A complete success. Thank you for asking."

"If you're implying that a father should show more concern, spare me the homily. I'd told Forrest what would happen if he put his feet in stirrups again. So, for that matter, did you. Don't waste pity on him now."

"May I thank you for offering the sloop as his private hospital? We've been crowded here from the start."

"I expect to be awhile in Fernandina. I've always slept aboard the *Hirondelle*. I felt it was safer to have my son on the water."

"Safer *medically,* Mr. Leigh?"

The planter glanced pointedly at Hilary Tyler, who straightened from his work with a ceremonial bow. "If I'm intruding on a confidence, Mr. Leigh——?"

"What I'm about to tell Dr. Stone will be common knowledge tomorrow. Still, I'd prefer you to go aboard the sloop with the stretcher, and make sure my son is comfortable." Leigh ground out his cigar on the window sill. "If you stay, you'll ask long-winded questions and waste my time."

"Your servant, sir. I'll go at once." But the old doctor was anything but humble as he stalked toward the surgery door. "May I make just one query before I leave you?"

"I doubt it."

"A dozen people have told me that a full-scale filibuster would land here tomorrow. A few dared to hint that you were behind it."

"Would any filibuster land here otherwise?"

"Liberty moves in strange ways to free the people."

Adam Leigh's stare was unwinking. "That'll do nicely as an exit line, Dr. Tyler."

"I thought as much myself. Good evening, sir."

Michael, still scrubbing in the door of the lean-to, kept his own face impassive as Leigh stumped over to the oil lamp and lit a fresh cigar. There had been rumors of a filibuster for months now—of expeditions, organized at all points of the compass to take over this smugglers' heaven and put smuggling on a strict business footing. Some, as Hilary had intimated, had even considered the filibuster as a prelude to an outright revolution in northern Florida to free the peninsula from Spain. Watching Leigh's saddle-brown face come alive in the glow of lamp and cheroot, he accepted the planter's boast completely—if that calm statement of fact could be called a boast.

"Do you want *me* to ask questions, Mr. Leigh? Or should I be a good listener?"

"There's very little to tell, Doctor. I merely thought we should talk alone. What I have to say will be important to your future."

"The fact that Dr. Tyler and myself are now the only physicians in Fernandina?"

"Precisely. I've established you in a twinkling—by a *coup d'état,* so to speak. Unfortunately, there was no time to inform you in advance. I learned the news myself only this morning, an hour after my return from Havana."

"The news that Marsden had accepted your price?"

"You might put it that way. At least it's the first part of the story. I've always wanted someone in Fernandina I could trust. Emil

Marsden *could* have been that man. But Emil Marsden is really Emil Toller, an Austrian wanted in Vienna for crimes against the Empire. Like many others, he decamped to America with a new name to seek a quick fortune. A truculent man, whose only gods were gold and fear. He could never be loyal to me, Dr. Stone."

"As you hope I'll be loyal?"

"Once again your precision is admirable. Marsden, as I've said, had ambitions in too many quarters. He'd already failed me as an estate doctor. I could never trust him to represent me in Fernandina now. So my agents in Charleston applied the only pressures that mean anything to the Marsdens of this world. I appealed to his greed by paying him a handsome price for his practice here. I chilled his Austrian heart by promising to turn him over to his ambassador in Havana if he showed his face in the Floridas again."

"Stop me if I'm wrong, but was Marsden about to filibuster his way into Fernandina and take over Amelia Island?"

"Not Marsden himself. Marsden was only the advance agent for a syndicate that plans to do just that."

"A syndicate headed by yourself, I gather."

"By no means," said Leigh blandly. "I will admit I'm a heavy stockholder in the enterprise. I must have my finger in the pie, though I expect the dough to fall."

"It isn't like you to speak in metaphor."

"True. You must forgive me the flight of poetry, but I'm feeling rather well tonight. It always diverts me to watch my fellow humans overplay their hands. I can assure you that certain gentlemen in Charleston and Savannah will live to regret this enterprise."

The planter came back from his private musings with the air of a man who has been caught thinking aloud. "The facts, as always, are simple enough. Certain mercantile interests in the States have decided to take over Amelia in their own interest. They've found their man in the person of one Gregor MacGregor, a Scot who's done his share of freebooting in the South. Ostensibly, he's coming here tomorrow to liberate yet another colony from the dead hand of Spain."

"*Tomorrow,* did you say?"

"With the morning tide, if the wind holds northeast. They're coming by the Inland Passage, I gather. A flagship and three sloops

—quite an armada. General MacGregor is bringing his lady, so he can hardly expect bloodshed."

"You mean the Spanish garrison won't resist?"

"I've just come from Fort San Carlos. Morales is quaking behind his cannon. He expects a fleet of men-o'-war to blow him to bits—and a thousand picked boarders to cut up the remains. You've doctored that miserable crew he calls a garrison. How long will they stand up under gunfire?"

"Most of them should have been pensioned long ago—if the Spanish Crown grants pensions."

"The scourings of the Caribbean," said Leigh. "Fernandina can manage without them."

"Does that mean you're in favor of the filibuster?"

"I paid five thousand dollars into MacGregor's treasury at Charleston. Morales has another thousand to make sure he'll strike his colors. Does that sound as though I'm in earnest?"

"Yet you just said the expedition would fail."

"Let them. I'm playing a lone game here. What's more, no one can count my cards."

"I think I'm beginning to understand. You contribute to this filibuster because you must—yet you hope it will fail."

"I *know* it will fail. I've met MacGregor. Once in Havana, and again in Nassau. A peacock who wears a dress uniform like an operatic tenor. Have you ever seen a South American general in full epaulets?"

"If the man's a charlatan, why was he chosen?"

"Because he has an honest heart under that peacock coat. Because he looks like a leader. Lastly, and most important, because he holds letters of marque from three revolutionary governments." Leigh considered the picture gloomily. "It's an imposing front for any adventurer. My guess is that the Spanish-American citizens of our region will accept him with open arms."

"Perhaps he'll succeed in spite of you."

"Perhaps. An honest belief in your own omnipotence, plus a dashing carriage, can work wonders."

Leigh had been pacing the surgery restlessly for some time. He paused now in the lean-to door and surveyed his own stubby person in the glass with obvious distaste. "The fact remains that Mac-

Gregor's army is anything but a crusade of high-hearted liberators. Most of the rank and file are rednecks from the Carolina piedmont or sailors who jumped ship in Charleston and Savannah. The officers, so-called, are gentlemen of fortune, or second sons decamping from bad debts."

"Isn't that true of most revolutionaries?"

"I concede the point again. But there can't be more than sixty troops aboard that armada I just mentioned. If our invading general expects to gather recruits here, he's a greater romantic than I expected. It's one thing to live in the midst of a revolution and enjoy it; most folk in this neighborhood have developed a knack for that. It's quite another to join that revolution and lose money."

"Precisely what are MacGregor's plans?"

"First, the conquest of Amelia Island. As I said, that's already as good as accomplished, with a coward in Fort San Carlos. Next, a proclamation to the countryside to join him in revolt—which will be received with cheers, and no other response whatever. MacGregor's schedule calls for a march on St. Augustine before the autumn rains. Even he must know that that's out of the question without a far larger force."

"Why wasn't it provided?"

"For two reasons. A full-scale invasion from the United States could hardly be explained in Madrid. As it stands, this whole affair has been covered up admirably. When it's over, most outside observers will think it quite spontaneous. Its origin will be ascribed to regions already in revolt against the Spanish Crown. The second reason is more mundane. Those estimable merchants in America who hope to make a fortune in land grants if the filibuster succeeds were all a bit niggardly when it came to putting cash on the barrelhead. For that reason alone MacGregor is doomed. A true revolutionary can never spare the dollars when the fur is flying. By August he'll be living on forage and making enemies everywhere. By September he'll be in full retreat."

"Yet you invest six thousand dollars in the enterprise."

"Yes, Doctor. The price I paid for establishing you in Marsden's shoes—and Marsden's fine house on the Prado."

"I know I should be flattered. Will you forgive me if I'm suspicious instead?"

"When you took over my pens, I promised to make you the first doctor in Florida. This is my way of performing."

"In a Florida overrun by revolution?"

"MacGregor will go. Others will follow him here, when the garrison is eliminated. Outright pirates, and worse. Eventually the American Army will be forced to move in from St. Marys. It will be the prelude to annexation—and law and order."

"Of which you're thoroughly in favor?"

"A respectable merchant is always in favor of order."

"American law prohibits blackbirding."

"But not the breeding and culture of existing stock. Give me another year, and I'll make that my full-scale business without another raw black from the Coast."

During all his harangue Adam Leigh had not ceased his pacing. He paused for a moment now and tossed up both hands, the gesture of a man who has outlined a blameless future. Michael studied the planter with wary eyes. The pattern of Leigh's planning was quite obvious now, though he still waited for Leigh to put his own contribution into words.

"Let me see how well I understand you. You expect this coming year to be a critical one in your enterprise. You need a man in Fernandina who'll keep you au courant. A man who can live with a foot in both camps, as it were—without exciting suspicion——"

"Continue, Doctor. You are stating my case much more succinctly than I."

"Wouldn't someone like Aravello be a better choice?"

"Aravello is only another Marsden, with a Latin manner. I'd trust him no farther than his moneybags."

"Whereas you'd trust me to the limit?"

"I'm asking you to do nothing dishonorable. Only to take your rightful place as the first doctor of Fernandina. To inform me how well MacGregor's brand of law and order is taking hold."

"And when you see he's weak enough, you'll inform the governor in St. Augustine?"

"I'm protecting my interests with an agent in the enemy's camp. What's so odd in that?"

"Did it occur to you that I might refuse the honor?"

"Not for a moment."

"Or that I might be one agent you can't cajole—or bribe?"

"I expected this reaction, Dr. Stone. May I say it's the best proof of your value to me?"

"I don't know this MacGregor. He may be the greatest lump of bombast living—or the greatest menace to Florida. But I won't be a spy in his camp for you or for anyone."

Leigh took out his morocco case and extracted another cigar. His manner was serene and completely unhurried. "Let us not forget the Castillo in St. Augustine, Doctor—and its oubliette."

"Perhaps it's time I called that threat."

"As you like. There are two of my best men outside that door. I've only to raise my voice, and they'll be happy to beat you insensible. Does the prospect tempt you?"

"You need me too badly for that, Leigh."

"I'll concede that, for the sake of argument. But I've assigned two other men to the hulk where you've been making your home. Ostensibly, they are sleeping on deck as a guard—in case your wife should waken in the night and grow alarmed at your absence. But they are just as ready to take *her* to the Castillo—shall I say as a hostage in your stead?"

Michael held the planter's eyes for a furious instant before he turned aside. Pacing to the surgery window, he saw that a pearl-gray dawn had already begun to break over the Amelia. There was the *Resolve* riding serenely at her mooring buoy—with the familiar plume of smoke amidships, as Dimity prepared an early breakfast against his hoped-for return. There, a bit farther offshore, was the sleek silhouette of Leigh's own *Hirondelle*. The sloop danced at her anchor chain like a restless seagull, eager to be away. Curiously enough, he thought of Sir Forrest Leigh (tossing now in a hot bunk aboard the sloop as he came out of his opiate and felt the demons of pain riot in his broken bones). Somehow it was easier to pity that adipose wreck—and to wonder if the risk he had taken was justified.

In that flash he admitted that Dimity was in no danger though Leigh's threat had been genuine enough. Once again he knew that he was accepting the planter's dictum in advance—even as he dickered to the end.

"Suppose we make a bargain?"

"I seldom bargain, Doctor."

"This time you've no choice. If you paid six thousand dollars to install me here, you must think I'm worth the price. Let's say I'll continue my practice—in the frontier palace you've purchased for me. Let's say that MacGregor permits me to visit the Point as before."

"He'll give you a permit. Why do you suppose I'm staying on until he lands?"

"Very well. I'll visit your pens: I'll fulfill my personal contract to you. If you care to ask me any questions about Fernandina, I'll answer them fully. But I'll do no spying, as the word is understood. And if there's real violence here, take my wife to St. Marys before I return to my patients."

"We understand each other perfectly, Doctor. Why have we argued?"

"Can you pretend this is all you want of me?"

"But of course. Can't you see that you'll be twice as valuable if your observations are made in the open?"

The planter thrust out a square, deep-tanned hand. Once more Michael found himself striking palms with an enemy who had turned into a friend by an alchemy all his own.

"And now, Mr. Leigh——?"

"And now, Doctor, you've just time to do a bit of housemoving before the invasion. You'll find Marsden's place in order for your bride. My men saw to that overnight."

Michael could not suppress a faint smile as he drew out his battered watch. "It's not quite seven. Can you name the hour of the attack?"

Leigh's wooden-idol stare was unchanged. "My guess is they're lying offshore now, waiting for the light. You can expect a landing by ten o'clock. Perhaps sooner."

"Then we'd best be on our way. Not that it will take us long to move. We can carry everything we own from the *Resolve,* with Tola to help."

The planter considered that point gravely. "From here on your wife will be one of the first ladies of Fernandina. Will she enjoy the role?"

Michael said, just as gravely, "My wife enjoys everything, if I'm there to share it. Will you breakfast with us aboard the *Resolve,* and let me prove my point?"

"You've proved it now," said Leigh. "I'm proud to have you here as my—shall I say, as my *observer?*"

"I won't object to that word. And you'd still do well to stop at the *Resolve* for coffee. Like myself, she won't quite believe you're real."

"In that case, I accept with pleasure. But I can stay only a moment. I must confer with Farrar."

You mean to be free of the town when the filibuster starts, thought Michael. He glanced at the Long Wharf and the steep flight of stairs that led down from the bluff. As he had expected, Leigh's men had vanished as quietly as shadows, now that the sun was up. Fernandina would be occupied in the traditional style, by an unknown invader. Only a few of Marsden's ex-bullies would mutter in their beards.

Aloud, he said only, "Of course. You'll want to go aboard the *Hirondelle* and see to your son. He'll be asking for you by now."

"My son never asks for me when he's in pain. It's *you* he'll be bellowing for, Doctor. That's why I sent old Tyler out with the stretcher."

"Answer one more question, and we'll go. Do you ever have time for strictly human feelings?"

Leigh said, patiently enough, "I've already explained my future. It's built around my grandson, whom I'm now expecting from England. My son is outside that pattern entirely. Why should I pretend an affection I don't feel?"

The planter went down the stair without waiting for a reply. Michael locked the surgery door and followed soberly. On the top step he paused for a final look. It was full daylight now. Pale sunlight covered the river with its patina. In that glow the hulk of the *Resolve* (and the sprightly silhouette of the *Hirondelle*) seemed to float in a self-contained mirage.

The plume of Dimity's galley fire arched over the water like a beckoning finger. He walked toward it soberly, conscious that a chapter of his life had ended almost before it could begin.

Thanks to Adam Leigh, the tempo of his existence would be faster now—and far less predictable. Despite his brave words in the surgery, he wondered if he, or Dimity, would tread this new measure with the same lighthearted ease.

V

Dimity waltzed across the black lake of parquet: light as a moth and just as daring, she moved into the lemon blaze of light at the two tall jalousies and flung them wide.

Morning burst in from the Prado, filling Dr. Marsden's living room with its radiance. In that flash the house came alive for them both. With no effort at all, Michael found, he could seat himself at the wide rosewood secretaire and pretend to go over his accounts, just as Dimity plumped into the Queen Anne chair by the fire screen and took up an imaginary embroidery frame. They had explored the house from basement to attic now, and her delight had all but melted his apprehension. He could even forget the strange stillness outside the windows, as she laughed aloud for the sheer wifely joy of possession.

"It's *enormous,* Mike. And it's all ours. I still can't believe it."

"That's why I brought Leigh to breakfast. I hoped he'd convince you."

"He likes you, Mike. I could see that straight off."

"Adam Leigh doesn't like anyone, strictly speaking. He simply picks men, and trusts them. I'm not too flattered at that trust."

"But he's made you, Mike. Overnight, you're an important man in Fernandina."

"At a price."

"Do you think it's too much to pay? We'll run away this morning." She glanced out across the square. "Everyone else is doing that, now the rumors are spreading."

"I think we can sit out this invasion in safety."

"You see? You trust Adam Leigh too—just as he trusts you. Why shouldn't you help him here, if you can?"

"Be honest, Dimity. Is Leigh the sort of man you'd enjoy helping? Weren't you repelled from the start?"

"I'll be really honest, Mike. I was too happy to think, once I found you wouldn't have to fight Marsden."

Dimity curled her small person deeper in the wing chair. "Do you realize that I was stealing oranges from his grove only a month ago? Now I'm sitting in his house, and it's all mine. Don't make me ask questions today. It's too much fun just being here." Her face clouded as Michael took a quick step to the sill of a french window. "Of course if you want to cut and run I'm still your girl. You know that."

Michael spoke with his back to the room. "I intend to stay on. The town can't be without a doctor." He was glad that she had accepted their change in fortune so lightly. Dimity, it seemed, was one of those rare females who can take life as it comes—without spoiling its simple pleasures by analysis. "Would it surprise you if I said I'm sorry for Marsden—sight unseen?"

"Don't be. The man was a pig."

"He left a handsome sty."

"It'll be even nicer when I'm done with it," said Dimity contentedly. "Do you suppose I could have a servant?"

"You should have had one long ago."

"Felippa will send me a Seminole girl. I'll let no one cook for you but me."

"Naturally," he said—and let his last doubts vanish as she stole across the room to him, alert as a kitten who knows it is time to be petted. Stroking her hair and staring down at the empty square, he marveled again at woman's knack of homemaking, even on the edge of chaos.

"When does the war start, Mike?"

"Any moment now—if I can trust Leigh's timetable."

"Are we the only audience?"

"So it appears from this window."

There was sober truth in his words. Standing side by side on the shallow iron balcony of the living room, they seemed the only living souls in the village. The sandy parade ground of the Prado spread before them, empty as the moon. On all sides the houses were shuttered and silent. Fernandina, in the glare of mid-morning, seemed to huddle behind drawn blinds while it waited for the first boom of MacGregor's cannon.

"Leigh's rumor mongers have done a first-rate job," he said.

"I heard that six hundred people crossed to the mainland last night."

Michael nodded abstractedly, with his eyes on Fort San Carlos—and the banner of empire. Above the terreplein the flag of Spain still made a brave show in the breeze: the imperial lions, rampant on their golden field, seemed to breathe defiance at invaders. As he looked, a sentry in a dirty, sun-faded uniform appeared at a gun port, spat into the empty square, and resumed his patrol of the ramparts. Morales, the gossips said, had already decamped. When the filibusters landed, they would find the town wide open and undefended. The very guns of Fort San Carlos would explode in the gunners' faces, if they dared to fire the time-frayed fuses.

"A citizens' committee should call on the colonel at the fort," he said abruptly, hardly aware that he had spoken his thoughts aloud. If Leigh had actually paid the commander to give up without a fight, there would be little point in such a visit. Yet Michael felt himself consumed with a strange curiosity as the hour of decision neared. With his own eyes he had watched Doña Morales wheeze down the Long Wharf and tumble panting into the lugger that would take her to St. Augustine. The Amelia had been white with sails then, as the inhabitants of the island fled to other sanctuaries in the back country—a wholesale departure before a threat that had not yet materialized.

"Fernandina has been invaded by other freebooters. Back in 1811 it was even the capital of a republic—while the republic lasted. Why can't they take this business in their stride?"

"Mr. Leigh's guards told me that there were at least a thousand pirates ready to land today," said Dimity, with a flicker of a grin.

"And you believed him?"

"Not for a minute. Even if it was true, I knew you'd find some way to outlast it."

Michael ran an arm around his wife's waist and drew her close "A true companion for a condottiere?"

"Don't call yourself names, if I can't translate."

"Old Hilary said I'd turn into one if I stayed on here. I'm beginning to believe him now."

"But what does it mean, Mike?"

"A soldier who works for hire, and doesn't ask questions of his prince——" He broke off as a voice hailed him from the square. It was Tola, ambushed in the shade of a China tree that grew at a corner of Marsden's land—as though the Minorcan had hesitated to show himself in the vast emptiness of the parade ground itself.

"The invaders have been sighted, jefe. They are entering the harbor now with all sails spread."

Dimity had already started to vault from balcony to street; Michael anchored her firmly with an arm at her waist.

"Let me go, Mike! I wouldn't miss this for worlds."

"The garrison may resist, after all."

"They wouldn't dare. You said yourself that Morales——"

He dragged her inside and motioned to Tola to follow them. "We'll have a better view from our own captain's walk. Don't forget we're householders now. We must preserve our diginity." He led her, still protesting, to the stair and chuckled as he watched her scurry up, with her skirts bunched at her knees.

As one of the town's chief smugglers, Marsden had made his observation platform accessible enough. It was only necessary to take the stairway to the attic, where a sturdy ladder led up to a trapdoor and the neatly fenced walk that sat astride the ridgepole of the house itself. Dimity had popped up into the eyrie before Michael and Tola could follow her. When Michael reached her side, she was leaning far out from the precariously low railing and staring into the blue vastness of the harbor to the north.

"There isn't a sail on the Amelia."

"Look to the south, señora," said Tola. "You will see that they passed the town in the night. Now they return with the wind and the tide behind them."

At first view of MacGregor's armada, Michael just escaped laughing aloud. Dwarfed by distance, the little fleet seemed no more menacing than a child's flotilla caught in the shallows of the marsh. Even the flagship, a schooner with an improvised gun deck, seemed an unwieldy tub in miniature. The smaller vessels —cat-rigged sloops, a few longboats with jury sails—were mere matchsticks in that endless sweep of blue.

Tola spoke hoarsely at his elbow. "As you see, they beach their troops in the marshes. They will attack from the south."

"How many have they beached?"

"Along the water front, they say at least two thousand."

Michael shook off that echo of nightmare and stared down at

the town itself. At first glance Fernandina seemed tight-shuttered as ever—but he saw that the town was not quite deserted, after all. Perhaps a hundred citizens lined the bluff, shading their eyes against the cobalt blaze of the Amelia as they exchanged rumors and waited for the first blast of doom. Warehouse roofs were thick with heads. The rigging of the ships at the wharves were busy with seamen making sail. Even as he watched, Michael saw two fat merchantmen slip their cables and stand away for the protection of the first American channel buoy a scant half-hour's sail to the north.

"Surely there's a telescope in that crowd. Can't they see that such a fleet couldn't carry more than seventy men, at the outside?"

"Señor Canova has said as much," said Tola. "Señor Aravello is of a different mind. He says that this fleet is but a promise of what will come, if Fernandina resists. And Señor Aravello has more voices on his side."

Dimity spoke without turning aside from the pattern of war in the making. "Couldn't you tell them the truth, Mike? They'd listen to you."

"A doctor should be neutral at a time like this. Small as it is, that flagship could do considerable damage, if the fort surrenders."

He turned to Morales's bastion as he spoke. There was no sign of life on the ramparts, though the flag of Spain still whipped in the breeze. He tried hard to picture fifty valiant (if somewhat moldy) soldiers of the Crown, bunched at their gun mounts as they waited for MacGregor's flagship to swim within range. And then he laughed, despite himself, as the comandante burst into view—not in the fort, but in the doorway of his own imposing residence across the Prado.

Morales had a satinwood box under each arm—bulky receptacles that could contain nothing but the family silver. A brace of slaves followed in his wake, tottering under the weight of Morales's personal luggage. The comandante kept his eyes straight ahead as he stamped through the dust of the Prado. Even at that height, Michael could see that his heavily frogged dress uniform was soaked in sweat.

He watched the putative master of Fernandina scurry into the shadow of his fort with shoulders slumped and tongue all but lolling. Here, in perfect miniature, was the symbol of Spain's crumbling power in the New World: A fat soul panting with nameless terror at the first threat. Fat wrists in dirty sleeves, fumbling among orders that had lost their meaning long ago. To complete the picture, a purse, bulging with Leigh's bribe and all but visible under the tarnished gilt of that tunic. Morales kicked twice at the sagging gate of his bastion. At the second assault of his boot a panel opened grudgingly: the comandante vanished like a rat in its burrow.

"Señor Canova has a following, of sorts," said Tola. "What if he mans the blockhouses at the south gate?"

"Aravello will make sure he doesn't."

"Can't we go to the water front, Mike?" cried Dimity. "I want to hear what people are saying."

"Stay where you are, or you'll miss the capitulation. It's my guess it's coming any moment now."

Even as he spoke there was a dull, discouraged boom from the fort, as one of the ancient cannon ventured a belated warning. A cloud of smoke rose from the gun port and whipped away in the fresh breeze. Michael saw instantly that the round shot had plumped into the harbor, ridiculously short of its mark, though MacGregor's armed flagship was well within range. The smaller vessels had scurried into hiding among the marsh grass to the south, to complete the landings. Already there were whorls of dust along the island road as the invaders marched recklessly toward Fernandina's stockade. Another gun barked an old-fashioned warning at this presumption. This time the solid iron projectile kicked a spout of sand from a clump of palmettos a scant hundred yards beyond the town gate.

"Token resistance," said Michael. "Even a fat rat can't strike his flag at once."

As he spoke, the schooner belched its first broadside. Maneuvered to within easy range of the fort, this volley was much more effective, though hardly as dangerous as it might have been—had the invader's flagship been intent on real destruction. Two of the shots crashed into the foundations, sending up a puff of splintered palmetto and tabby stone. One, angled high, sailed over the terreplein itself, and—missing the flagpole by inches—bounced crazily into the Prado. Michael watched it burrow its way, like a giant's bowling ball, until it vanished among the weeds of a vacant lot.

There was no answering retort from the bastion: the schooner, turning clumsily on her heel to bring her other gun deck into position, withheld her second volley. As though the signal had been agreed on from the beginning, the flag of Spain dipped with almost indecent haste. A gunner had already leaped to the ramparts, to wave a ragged white sheet on a bayonet point.

"The sack of Fernandina," said Michael, with his watch open on his palm. "Playing time, five minutes exactly. We can go down now, Dimity. Apparently the next curtain will rise at the town gate."

The prediction had begun to come true before they could gain the street. A confused murmur of voices drifted across the Prado. There was the sound of shuffling feet in sand as the watchers on the bluff streamed through the rutted streets to catch their first glimpse of the invading army. There was no sign of life within the fort. The soldier who had waved the flag of surrender had merely upended his musket and vanished from the ramparts. MacGregor's flagship had come about on an easy tack and was coasting along the shore, her guns still trained on the terreplein. If the travesty of battle had ended, so had the temper of the populace. Michael heard more than one jeer thrown at the silent fort as he took Dimity's arm and joined the living stream.

"*Ladrones!* Dogs and sons of dogs!"

"What more did you expect of Morales?"

"No wonder he doesn't show his face!"

Aravello fell into step beside Michael and Dimity as they crossed the corner of the Prado. The Spaniard's smile was an odd contrast to the lowering faces about him—a cynic's grin that did not belong on that boyish face.

"So we change masters, Señor Médico? Can you bear the thought?"

"You seem to be bearing up admirably."

"And why not? I have assurance that my business will continue to prosper. This MacGregor is no rascal: he wants a busy town as much as I."

"You'll pay for his protection."

"Never mind. Better to pay that sort of tribute than to divide with Marsden."

Michael shrugged off that facile wisdom. Despite the frowns about him, he could hardly doubt that Aravello had summed up the feelings of Fernandina at the moment.

"Obviously you had no choice," he said.

"Obviously, Doctor. A thousand invaders, armed with the best American muskets—such a force is irresistible. Each man a giant, with a green plume in his hat and a flag with a green cross at the column's head. MacGregor himself has been tested by fire in South America—a true revolutionary. His adjutant is a veteran of the Yankee revolution."

"You're well informed, señor."

"My Savannah connections are excellent. MacGregor did most of his recruiting there: his officers come from Charleston. Take my word, these fanatics will follow him anywhere. Why shouldn't they burst our gates without a fight?"

"Why not, indeed?"

Aravello darted on, with a baker's dozen of his henchmen packing him in a tight square. Glancing over the growing crowd, Michael saw that it was composed largely of Aravello men, though a few of the faces were strange to him. The rest of that small, milling mob was made up of water-front idlers from the moored ships—most of them the worse for rum, despite the early hour.

He recognized few householders: at first glance, it seemed that Don Xavier Canova was the only propertied man who had dared to remain in town—and Don Xavier was haranguing the crowd in vain, a patriarch without an audience. It was Aravello's boot that kicked up the great crossbar on the town gate—Aravello's shout that brought a white flag into his hand and a ragged cheer from his followers, augmented now by the girls from Ladies Street. Gaudily handsome in their mantillas, smiling boldly from kohl-darkened eyes, these robust young females blended perfectly with the moment. Dr. Michael Stone (the only gentleman present with a wife on his arm) withdrew a little from the melee, and tried hard to preserve his air of detachment.

"It's like a fiesta," said Dimity. "All it needs is music."

The shrill of a bugle outside picked up her words like a theater cue. When the gate swung open under the nudge of a dozen eager shoulders, Fernandina's invaders were drawn up at parade rest on the burned-over scrub beyond. Once again Michael just escaped laughing as he viewed the difference between romance and reality.

Seen in its entirety, in the pitiless glare of noon, MacGregor's army was anything but terrifying. Perhaps half a hundred strong, wilted by the sun, smeared to the armpits with marsh water, this crew of ragged boys and tatterdemalion oldsters made no pretense at military order. Poverty-pinched shanks peered through more than one pair of homespun pantaloons; the green plumes in every hat were no more than sprigs of dog fennel plucked from the swamp. Michael noted instantly that several of the conquerors were almost too drunk to stand. Drunk or sober, they were all staring at the open gate as though they could not wait for the looting to begin.

And then his roving eye picked out the leader, and the derisive laughter died in his throat.

Gregor MacGregor stood a little apart from his rank and file—a magnificent figure with arms folded on a barrel chest, an outsized Napoleon brooding on his latest conquest. The uniform he wore was as impressive as the man's own towering figure: a sky-blue coat with enormous white revers, it was belted with a vast flowing sash. The left breast was heavy with medals; the sword at the waist was a bright lighting in the sun. The fine curly head (crowned with a Scotch tartan) was fit to be stamped on a medal. Michael drew in his breath; at his side he heard Dimity's gasp of joy.

"Didn't I tell you it was as good as a play, Mike?"

"Grand opera, you mean. Doesn't he seem about to burst into an aria?"

MacGregor did not stir as Aravello walked out to the road with his flag of truce. The parley, if it could be called that, was entrusted to a beetle-browed adjutant whose threadbare uniform more than balanced the general's pomp. No one stirred in the tight-packed throng at the gate as Aravello conversed with this shopworn martinet: every eye was still fixed on the resplendent commander as the Spaniard returned, as jauntily as ever.

"The general prefers to enter Fernandina on horseback. A white one, if possible. Run to the smithy, Enrique; see if my gelding is saddled."

A boy darted to obey the order. Don Xavier's voice struggled to be heard above the rising hubbub.

"Does this fellow come in peace?"

"He has given his solemn word that none of us will be harmed. You are to go to your homes at once, and await his proclamation. There must be no loiterers on the street in the meantime—and no sign of violence."

"What of the garrison?"

"Morales has struck his colors. General MacGregor respects the soldier's code. There will be no more fighting, and no reprisals. Morales and his effectives will march back to St. Augustine unarmed. The general's proclamation will declare North Florida liberated forever from Spain."

A ragged cheer went up, drowning Don Xavier's sputter. Michael, still holding Dimity firmly on the outskirts of the crowd, smiled at Fernandina's willingness to accept this change of rule. The skeleton yoke of Spain had rested lightly enough on the town. He wondered if the new masters would be an improvement.

The crowd parted as Enrique came back from the blacksmith's on the run, leading a massive white gelding by the bridle. Watching the glittering uniform swing into the saddle, blinking at the gleam of the sword it flourished, Michael found that he could laugh again, after all.

"Close ranks—maaaaarch!"

MacGregor had a parade-ground bellow to match his bulk. His army still slumped at the shoulders, and its eye had lost none of its weasel hunger. But there were no stragglers as it marched into Fernandina to the wheeze of a fife and drum.

Turning into a back street with Dimity, skirting the Prado to to gain their house again, Michael wondered why he had accepted this usurper so completely—and knew the answer in advance.

"He looks like an empire builder," he said. "It's a pleasure to watch him in action. So great a pleasure, that I wouldn't have stopped him if I could."

Dimity chuckled at his side. "You're right there, Mike. I never saw such handsome sideburns."

"Still, it's a strange thing about empire builders. Most of them look like starved clerks—or monkeys in search of a jungle. Don't tell me you'd have turned on the street to stare at Julius Caesar or Napoleon."

"I think this one's honest, in spite of his looks," said Dimity. "Don't ask me why. And I feel that he'll keep that army in hand —in spite of *their* looks. So don't think you have to stay with me, Mike, if you want to get back to the surgery."

"Aren't you afraid of anything?"

"I lived through a lot to find you. Why shouldn't I live through a revolution, and cook your dinner when it's over?"

He looked down at her snapping blue eyes. As always, Dimity had summed up in a sentence. He would not spoil her pleasure by voicing his own vague fears. He would not tell her that Gregor MacGregor (a pawn of forces he could not even name) was marked for extinction even before he accepted the town's surrender. A bright chip in the maelstrom of history, MacGregor only accented the violence of the whirlpool.

Aloud, Michael said only, "You're quite right, of course. Revolutions may come and go. It's girls like you who keep us alive between."

"And doctors like you, Mike."

A bugle shrilled in the Prado. They ignored its challenge as they walked toward their new home—a pair of leading citizens who had come to stay.

VI

"September 4, 1817: See General MacGregor, at 4 P.M., to discuss the situation on Amelia Island and the threat of the 'Spaniards of the Main.' "

Michael hesitated above this final entry in his journal—and teetered in the armchair before his rosewood secretaire. The desk (like the handsome room in which he sat) had once been the property of a Dr. Emil Marsden, ex-scoundrel of Vienna; today, it was the undeniable property of Dr. Michael Stone, successful doctor of Fernandina, a nimble practitioner who managed to be both a pillar of conservatism and an excellent friend of the usurper.

The pen still hesitated as Michael asked himself if he should cancel the reminder he had written a week ago. He had expected history to move faster than this easy-driving quill, but this was the first time it had overtaken him since he had begun his journal. It was incredible that he had not been settled in this house forever, noting the progress of Fernandina's fortunes and his own. Viewed in retrospect, it was even more incredible that this summer, which had started so explosively, should have reached this September date at so tranquil a tempo.

He dipped his pen and wrote quickly, without pausing to think:

"The above appointment was canceled abruptly when General MacGregor and staff sailed from Fernandina with this morning's tide, leaving the affairs of the island in the hands of the General's backer, Jared Irwin, a *politico* from New York City, New York. . . ."

Set down in neat black ink, the fact of MacGregor's flight looked dull enough. There was no hint of the honest Scotsman's railing at destiny as the long Florida summer moved toward its end. No picture of the sublime indifference of Fernandina to its conqueror —when the town discovered that MacGregor's force had more bombast than brawn, that these hungry raiders were adept at pilfering on nearby farms, yet fearful indeed of the unknown threat of the Castillo to the south. Worst of all, there was no feel of MacGregor himself in those words—the filibuster's warm humanity, his insistence on the rightness of his cause, his certainty that all Florida would rally about him, now that he had planted his banner on the Amelia.

Dimity's estimate had been quite accurate: MacGregor was an honest zealot, according to his lights. The fact that his force had melted to half its strength, that most of the rank and file had drifted into smuggling with Aravello, had not dimmed his optimism. It was only yesterday (when Jared Irwin's brig had dropped anchor in the roadstead, bringing a demand for prize money in place of re-enforcements) that MacGregor's spirit had broken at last. Michael's quill danced on with the record:

"No one in Fernandina seems to know precisely how or when MacGregor vanished. But his lady and her effects were gone from the house he had commandeered on the Prado; his staff decamped with him, to the last man. His flag with the green cross still flies above Fort San Carlos, but Irwin and his crew have already come ashore to take over that shaky citadel—and prepare for reprisals from the mainland, which cannot be long in coming now.

"Irwin, it seems, merely hopes to repel the Spanish attempt to re-establish military control here: his only purpose, so far as one can gather at this writing, is to hold Amelia Island as a base for privateering. . . . Irwin, in short, represents the next step in the island's degradation. Though I have yet to see him in the flesh, it is apparent that he brings no torch of liberty from his wealthy backers in the North.

"Ave atque vale, Gregor MacGregor. It is unfortunate that you must pass into Florida history as an overweight bluejay whose proclamations are better than your campaigning. I have talked with you too often to escape the conviction that you are a true revolutionary who believed your speeches to the last adjective.

"Today the American man-of-war *Saranac* sailed into the estuary from Point Peter, tacked for a half-hour under the guns of the fort, and returned to American waters. Does this mean that these United States have had enough of lawlessness across her border and will annex the island at last? MacGregor hoped so until the end. . . ."

He heard the invader's bellow once again, the heavy swish of his kilts as he paced the terreplein of Fort San Carlos and shook his fist at a mainland whose gray-green immensity had so far ignored his presence. Even in that gaudy tartan, Gregor MacGregor was nothing less than magnificent—a baffled lion that had expected to stalk over all Florida with a conqueror's stride. Now he was cooped on an island with a handful of hungry jackals behind him, a town oblivious of his presence, a surrounding wilderness that mocked him with emptiness.

"Why doesn't Coppinger come out of Augustine?"

"Perhaps he's waiting for you to invest the Castillo."

"Damn it, man, I cannot invest another country farmhouse without men and guns." The general's burr, combined with the general's choler, threatened to choke him for a moment. "A fortress that defied Oglethorpe? I would need a thousand men to take it."

"Morales was told you'd beached a thousand men back in June—and surrendered. Perhaps you could deceive Coppinger as well."

"Coppinger is a fighting Irishman, Michael. And he doesn't bribe." MacGregor had shaken his fist once again at the mainland. "He has no right to insult me by ignoring my presence."

"This corner of the Floridas has been without real government since the British left. Coppinger knows that Spain's days on the peninsula are numbered."

"I still say it's insulting that he won't come out and fight. I'm an honest man, with an honest purpose. Look me in the eye and deny it."

"I've never doubted you, General."

"Then tell your friend Leigh I'm pining for battle. *He* has the governor's ear. Tell him I'd prefer annihilation to patrolling this sand bar——"

Michael remembered how MacGregor's voice had cracked on that. For a long time the general had merely stumped his lonely lookout, letting his kilts whip in the hot land breeze, lost in Scotch melancholy. . . .

It had been difficult to break that silence, but Michael had ventured it at last. "Perhaps the authorities at St. Augustine are afraid to join battle on the States' doorstep. After all, it would only call attention to our current anarchy."

"That was my purpose from the beginning. Believe me, I've prayed for intervention."

"I believe you, General."

"It's what Florida needs to open the land to settlement. While the Spaniards remain, Florida will be a wilderness—even if their authority is only a shadow. Why can't they see that in Washington?"

"America has just fought a costly and ill-advised war with England. She won't risk another."

"Spain is no longer a threat to the future of this hemisphere. I've proved that myself, in Venezuela; I proved it once again on this very ground. I'd march on Augustine tomorrow if I could hope that the troops at Point Peter would move into the void—and govern it. But I can see now that they've their orders——"

MacGregor shook his fist again at the sun-bitten vista of scrub palmetto. Despite his height and his splendid sideburns, he looked oddly like a spoiled child who has suffered his first defeat—and cannot quite understand the suffering.

"I'll tell you a small secret, Michael. If I'd known what this country was like, I'd never have set foot on it. D'you realize it could swallow us both—and this whole thieving town—without even noticing we were here?"

"It will grow civilized someday. Americans will see to that."

"Sometimes I have my doubts."

"But you just said that intervention was what the Floridas needed."

"Perhaps Washington is too busy elsewhere. The British may come back—or even the French. The land is wide open to any conqueror who desires it—and has the will to grasp his desire."

"And the army, General. Don't forget the army."

"My backers in the north have forgotten I need one. Why should I sit here—and pray for a miracle that won't come?"

There had been many such talks; most of them had ended in the same vein. As a leading citizen of Amelia Island, Michael had had the conqueror's ear from the start. MacGregor, a man hungry for friends among his subjects, had been only too willing to pour out his troubles to anyone. As willing, thought Michael, as MacGregor's steward had been to fill the dons' glasses at his master's receptions. MacGregor and his plumply handsome Spanish bride had entertained the Fernandinans incessantly; the general, one gathered, enjoyed a quadrille as much as a burst of rhetoric. It was unfortunate that the soirées should taper off as the summer advanced and the conqueror's purse grew leaner; that they should cease abruptly when word came that Governor Coppinger had massed an invading force on the mainland and expected to descend on the island the moment fresh ordnance arrived from Havana.

For once reality had all but matched the rumors. On his last trip to Leigh's plantation Michael had learned that more than five hundred troops (most of them picked militia) were encamped in the scrub a half day's march from Amelia and would cross to the island itself when the marshes were dry. He had returned to Fernandina, determined to warn MacGregor of this threat. Leigh, who had felt sure that the Scotsman would capitulate without a struggle, had offered no objection to the warning. It was evident that MacGregor's own spies had earned their fees. Equally evident that MacGregor himself had planned to decamp for some time.

Now, the man on horseback was only a memory, a tall ghost that had cantered to the door of Fort San Carlos and demanded surrender in the name of . . . Michael frowned as he tried to recall the tenor of that first bombast.

Jared Irwin (who sat like a dusty spider in that same fort and waited for Coppinger to strike) had issued no proclamation since his arrival. But there was no doubting Irwin's purpose or his tenacity—though the man himself remained less than a shadow. The armed brig that rode grimly at anchor in mid-river was better than a dozen promises of abundance and peace.

Michael stirred uneasily at his rosewood desk and weighed his diary in his hands. The bulky book was filled with these random jottings—memory aids, for the most part, as well as footnotes to history in the making. There would be no more footnotes today: he had lingered long enough, with a practice waiting. Hilary, of course, would take care of this morning's cases; this was the morning he must board the *Hirondelle* for his weekly trip to Punta Blanca.

A bell tinkled in the hall outside, and he heard the pad of Ulee's feet as the Seminole girl ran up the back stairs with his wife's morning tea. It still amused him to think of Dimity, at ease in their great double bed upstairs, waking contentedly in the late morning and ringing for her breakfast as any lady should. It pleased him still more to realize how well she had assumed that role—and how much she enjoyed its solemn play-acting.

From now on, of course, Dimity could hardly appear in society, as Fernandina understood that word. Great with his child and proud of the ungainly burden she was bearing, she would keep to her bedroom and the sun-weary garden outside until she was delivered. He had tried a dozen times to persuade her to cross the sound to St. Marys—at least until the threat of Coppinger's assault on the island was resolved. But Dimity—a vivandière who had found her niche at last—had refused to budge, even as she laughed off the threat to her own doughty person.

"Every lady on Sevilla Street has decamped since the first news came up from Augustine. Now that MacGregor's gone, you'll be the only wife in town."

"They'll be back soon enough—mad as blazes with themselves for being such cowards. Remember how sheepish they all were this July, when they came over in a body to attend the general's first levee?"

"There'll be a real fight this time. Perhaps a pitched battle. Outside the city walls—or outside this door."

"Then I'll go aboard the *Resolve* and wait it out."

"What if Coppinger bombards the town?"

"Answer me this, Mike: will *you* be leaving the island if it's attacked?"

"Naturally not; I'll be needed as never before."

"Then I'll be needed too. I'm a first-class nurse now, thanks to you."

"You can't nurse in that condition. No respectable woman would."

"I can and will, if I'm really needed. And don't keep reminding me that I'm respectable. It makes me feel old. With this figure, I know I look every bit of twenty-five, and I'm not yet twenty."

The argument had ended, as most of their discussions did, in kisses and carefree laughter. . . . Weighing his diary in his hands a second time, riffling the pages at random, he wondered if he had any right to be so carefree. So assured, in mind and heart, that this tranquil happiness would endure forever, no matter who ruled from Fort San Carlos.

An entry caught his eye, and he read it through, feeling the quick tears start behind his lids as the picture came alive again:

"*August 18, 1817:* Returned early today from Punta Blanca—and the usual battle between cleanliness, godliness, and Raoul Ledoux's laziness. Found Dimity curled in my own armchair, reading as though she'd read all her life! Such fruit does devotion bring, when it's joined to a quick brain and a real wish to better one's state. . . . It was Shakespeare's *Sonnets,* of all books: she quoted *How like a winter has your absence been!* in my teeth. A strange poem to be reading in the depth of Florida's dog days, with the sand of the Prado hot enough to bake eggs and MacGregor's flag drooping like discouraged sparrow grass on its stalk. And yet, I'd never heard the Bard rendered more beautifully. Is it because this girl of mine is all mine—and no one else's? Is it because I'm a proud Pygmalion who has made my Galatea into a wife any doctor would be proud of?"

She could cipher now as well as read: she was proud as a child of her neat rows of figures in the old account book they had found in one of Marsden's cupboards. Now that she could read like a parrot (and store away what she read like a frisky squirrel) he would teach her to go beyond writing her name and such notes as the one he uncovered in his diary now:

Dere Mik:

I hav gun to walk awile on the Seewall. Pleese do not skold, the young un hardlee shows when I ware this pinnyfor. Beesids, you sed that walkeing was gud for all Muthers-to-bee.

Dimity Parker Stone

If such delights as these were deserved, if his happiness at the quick unfolding of her mind was truly earned, it was equally obvious that he must guard what was his. Like every householder in Fernandina this summer, he had taken what precautions he could: Tola (with a brace of pistols in his belt and a loaded musket behind his chair) was always in attendance in the lower hall in Michael's absence; Willi, the Seminole aide who was his gift from Aravello, had been re-enforced by another native from the back country—a member of Hospetarkee Emathla's tribe, who had come into the garden one morning, placed his blanket roll in the shade of the arbor at the kitchen door, and taken up residence thereafter. Answering only to the name of Gator (which, Michael gathered, was a diminutive for the reptile that inhabited the chocolate-dark reaches of the Okefenokee), the newcomer had explained his presence in pidgin Spanish, and taken a welcome for granted.

"The jefe sends me—to the jefe of Fernandina."

"To General MacGregor?"

"To you, Señor Médico. To thank you for the salvation of his son. To serve here as you may wish."

Willi and Gator lived in the garden now as amiably as a pair of nimble watchdogs who could show their teeth in a twinkling, if need arose. With this trio to guard his hearth, Michael had gone to his surgery with a free mind. Felippa, to his astonishment, had appeared (as usual without a summons) when he departed on his inspection trips to Leigh's pens or accompanied old Hilary in a back country call. If it was a comfort to know that Dimity was as safe as any woman could be in Fernandina, it was a greater comfort to find her waiting for his return—rosy with sleep in the gold-swan gondola of their bed or conning the books he had bought her in a basket chair in their latticed patio.

This morning it was easy to tell himself that he was right to let her stay on in Fernandina, regardless of the plans Coppinger might be hatching on the mainland. To insist that Fernandina's only doctor would be immune to flying bullets even if the battle ended on the Prado. He could even smile at that romantic sophistry—and face the real stumbling block to Dimity's departure, which was Dimity herself.

"I'll never leave you, Mike. Not so long as you need me. And I'm sure you need me now."

"Enough to have some regard for your safety, my dear. Tola will sail you over to St. Marys this afternoon."

"It's nice to be needed, Mike."

"Haven't you heard a word I've been saying?"

"So nice that I won't mind dodging a few bullets."

Of course he should have been firmer. He repeated that conviction now as he stared down solemnly at the fat diary between his palms. Here was abundant evidence that Florida's summer of '17, which had moved at such a happy tempo for Dr. Michael Stone and bride, had been anything but tranquil. A record of looting on remote farms, of large-scale pilfering on the plantations of Amelia itself; a list of reprisals from embattled pioneers, who had staged wolf Iliads of their own among the palmettos to drive MacGregor's bullies back to the Fernandina stockade. . . . Now, at long last, the real reprisal was gathering on the mainland like a delayed thunderstorm. What right had he to take Dimity's loyalty for granted, to insist they would both come through unharmed?

If Marian Leigh were breakfasting upstairs in that gold-swan bed, would he have permitted her to linger?

He avoided the question deliberately as he opened the diary at random. Staring for a blind moment at the page under his hand, he realized that the book had opened here of its own accord. Certainly he had brooded on this entry long enough to know it by heart:

"July 3, 1817: Sir Forrest Leigh, Knight-Commander, Major in His Majesty's Life Guards Green, died this afternoon in his bed at Punta Blanca of gangrene, the aftermath of a bonesetting operation undertaken by me five days previously. Just, as always, his father has absolved me from all blame. Word has gone forward to his widow, whose departure from England was delayed by bad weather, and who will, presumably, remain in that country indefinitely, thanks to the troubled political state of the Floridas. . . ."

He remembered how his pen had raced through that absolution, and how he had stared at the finished paragraph, realizing that he was thinking of the widow rather than the man who had died from the ministrations of his knife.

The thought of Marian (how she would receive the news, what action she would take) had been vivid, even then—far more vivid than his memory of the dying man, the dark pulsing of gas gangrene, the odor of death that had clung to Sir Forrest from the third day of the bone-setting. At that time he had put down the case as hopeless, though he had done what he could to ease the Waterloo veteran's last hours. . . .

"You did right, Doctor. Don't reproach yourself. I'm going to walk again. You'll see if I don't."

"Quiet, now; just try to move as little as possible. If you'll drink this, it will help you to sleep."

"But I don't want to sleep. I want to lie here and think of the hunters I'll be breaking in another fortnight."

Sir Forrest's voice had had the bright color of his delirium even then. The following day he had slipped into a coma, though he continued to mutter brokenly of the prodigies he would perform afield. Old Hilary had been at his bedside when he thrashed away his life. Michael himself, operating one of MacGregor's officers on the messroom table at the fort, had reached Punta Blanca in time for the funeral.

Adam Leigh (correct in black linen, his cheroot unlighted for once) had explained that early funeral tersely enough:

"Flesh spoils quickly in this climate, Doctor. Will you say a few words at the graveside?"

Michael had repeated what he could remember of the burial service he had heard a score of times at sea as the first spadefuls of sun-dry earth had thudded on Sir Forrest's coffin. Mozo and Dominique, stripped to the waist in the glare of mid-afternoon, had sweated at their work; Leigh, his cold eyes veiled, had merely bowed his head beside the grave. . . . When it was over, Michael searched his heart for an appropriate emotion, and found only a ghost of the old pity that was a leftover from his first visit to Punta Blanca.

Leigh had said, "He's well out of it, poor devil! Is that what you're thinking, Doctor?"

"I'm thinking I should have listened to Dr. Tyler and amputated."

"He'd have ridden again, peg leg and all—and taken another header. Don't reproach yourself—you had no other choice."

"Will you explain that to his widow—or shall I?"

"Leave the letters to me, Doctor. I'm good at letters."

And better at judging men, thought Michael. It's quite like you to put me at my ease (and in my place) with a few curt words.

Aloud he said only, "It won't be an easy letter."

"Why not? She didn't love my son. No more did I. In my way, I tried to be sorry for him, and botched the try. Your thought was appropriate, Doctor—he's well out of it. I'm glad now for just one thing." Leigh lighted his cigar with deliberation as they walked out of the family graveyard by the water's edge. "When Marian returned with the boy, I'd made up my mind to announce that he would be my heir, not Forrest. At least I've spared him that."

"Perhaps he was spared more than we know. He died thinking I'd patched his bad leg." Michael hesitated on that thought. "He must have been out of his head from the fall. I found no concussion, but——"

"It's my opinion he was out of his head for some time," said

Leigh. "Another reason why I stood dry-eyed at the grave. Do you consider me a monster for that?"

"A consistent one, at least."

Leigh had blown a long plume of smoke into the branches of the live oak that arched their path to the house. As always, he seemed to expel a gathering rage with that long, easy breath. Michael would never know if the rage had been generated by his last remark, or the obscure workings of a fate that had robbed this patriarch of his last branch. But the planter's voice was almost gentle when he spoke again.

"I don't care for half-alive stock—in my house or out of it. I'd be a hypocrite if I pretended to take pride in that wreck we've just buried. Or mourned his passing." Leigh stared at Michael with his owl-eyed calm unshaken. "Which labels me a monster in your book, Doctor. Make the most of it. I don't mind."

"A seeker after perfection, Mr. Leigh. Granted, you lose some human values in the search, but——"

"Complete the thought, sir. I've failed as a father. Through no fault of mine—or Forrest's. It wasn't *his* fault that he was born without brains, or ambitions; that his creator put in stubbornness instead of courage. So be it. Forrest is dead—long live Forrest Leigh the Second!"

Yes, it had been as simple as that to bury the hero of Waterloo. To walk back to Leigh's office at the great manor house and drink a cold toddy while he checked the bills of lading from the *Dos Amigos,* fresh from Charleston with foodstuffs for the pens. Already the tempo of Punta Blanca had resumed, as though Sir Forrest Leigh had never been. And yet, try as he might, Michael could not hate Adam Leigh for an attitude that was obviously sincere. If Leigh had failed as a parent, he would be a brilliant success as a grandfather.

Repeating that conviction now, he locked away his diary at last and walked on tiptoe into the hot stillness of Fernandina's early morning. Usually, when he was sure that Dimity was awake upstairs, he stopped for a final word before hastening down the street to the stairs and the Long Wharf. Today (knowing what awaited him at that same wharf) he left his house quickly, without a backward glance.

At the pitch of the stairway he paused to draw a deep breath and stared across the harbor with all the tension of a man whose fate was in the balance. For the tenth time that morning he told himself that it was ridiculous to be concerned over a routine visit to Punta Blanca. But he could not restrain the wild leap of his heart when he saw the *Hirondelle* dance among the harbor shipping, as daintily as her name, and set her course for José Aravello's stringpiece.

Only yesterday his heart had leaped as wildly, when he had learned that Lady Marian Leigh had ignored the storm signals hanging over Florida and returned to Punta Blanca with her son and heir.

VII

Plump as a sleek black plum and howling as lustily as a young wildcat, the two-day-old infant lay between Adam Leigh's palms.

Watching the planter heft the child one more time before he returned it to its mother's breast, noting the warm gleam of possession in the planter's eye, Dr. Michael Stone checked the ledger in his hand and moved on to the second bed in the nursing room with a small inward sigh. It was a routine he had repeated many times with Leigh, as they examined the newborn infants together and estimated their chances of survival. He could never quite down the shock of Leigh's casual acceptance of this increase in his stock in trade.

"Twenty-one whelps so far this month, and not a single death." The planter just escaped rubbing his hands as they walked out together. "September was always our worst season for childbed fever: last year we lost more than half our get and nearly as many mothers. How d'you account for the change, Stone? It can't all be luck."

"Last year you delivered the infants in the compounds and made no effort to segregate the mothers afterward."

"You can't blame Marsden in that department. I saw to it myself that every mother was left alone and allowed a full month of rest before she went back to the fields. There were double rations for that cabin and a tot of rum for each man who fathered twins."

"Fair enough. But we were speaking of puerperal fever and its cause. I'd be called a fool in England for saying this, but I'm convinced that the doctor himself introduces the trouble at the time of delivery."

"I don't follow."

"I don't quite follow myself. But in London it was a common practice for medical students to combine dissecting with their obstetrics. I myself have delivered infants in the evening after working all day on a cadaver. Perhaps I was too finicky for my place, but I always took time to wash between the dissecting room and the labor ward. Most of my colleagues weren't that fastidious. More than half their patients died. I didn't lose a case. Perhaps it proves nothing, but I've followed that practice religiously ever since. So do Fulton and Ledoux, as you've observed. Not even you are permitted in this building until you've washed your hands and left your field boots outside the door."

Michael paused at the turn of the path to look back at the makeshift hospital Leigh had built at his orders. High-stilted to keep out roving livestock, wide-windowed, and fitted with a broad gallery that faced the sea, it could accommodate a hundred slaves without danger of crowding. Michael had fitted one wing as a dispensary and surgery. It was here that the two resident doctors slept when on duty, here that minor ailments were diagnosed and treated. The nursing room, which held a score of extra beds, was a separate structure, connected to the main building by a gallery that also housed a crude delivery room. Argue as he might, Michael could not persuade Leigh to send the women to the hospital before their pregnancies were at term. But the overseers had instructions to summon a doctor if labor pains began in the field. If the pains were authentic, the mothers-to-be were brought under the hospital roof for their actual delivery. It was some weeks now since Ledoux or Fulton had galloped across the plantation to tie off a cord in the shade of a palmetto. . . .

"Will you admit now that it was worth all it cost?"

Leigh snorted a grudging affirmative as they followed the path to the workshops—and the invisible line that divided plantation proper from the manor-house grounds. "I haven't disputed that for a moment. My cattle deserve the best of care; just don't coddle them—that's all I ask."

It had been a relief to Michael to find the planter waiting, to plunge into this long tour of inspection from the moment he stepped ashore at the plantation dock. Now that it was time for the usual pre-dinner scrubbing, the change from work clothes to white linen, he could almost regret that the crowded day was ending.

So far, it had been easy enough to keep his mind away from the inevitable meeting with Marian. Now (with the manor house filling the western horizon like a vast white mirage that beckoned him to explore its delights) he could not down the conviction that he was walking into a crisis whose end he could not see. Walking in gladly, with the resigned air of a man who has struggled too long with a riddle—and insists he must solve it fully before he knows peace again.

At the gate they were joined by Roger Farrar, with the two resident doctors in tow. As always, Michael found himself studying these two worthies as Leigh scrawled his signature on the daybooks the head overseer offered for his inspection. Ledoux, he observed, was still the model *émigré,* self-contained in exile as only a Frenchman can be, handsome in a worn-medallion fashion, and smirking faintly at the follies of man. Ledoux would carry that smirk to his grave—even if he followed his plan to retire (after a fixed sum had accumulated on Leigh's ledgers) to a chalet above his beloved Grenoble. Fulton, the ex-Quaker, the full-blooded satyr who still battled in solitude with his conscience (and still pocketed Leigh's liberal wage without a qualm), would go back to the city of his fathers in time—and atone for this unholy traffic in his own fashion. . . .

Both men were first-class doctors, in their way—needing only the driving force of a will stronger than their own, the lowering presence of an Adam Leigh to keep them fit. Michael, who knew just how far each man could be driven, had used their skills wisely this summer—working long hours at tasks he might have left to them when he saw that Leigh was pushing them beyond their powers. Today, he knew, he could count on their help in an emergency, if not on their devotion. Devotion, he gathered, was something that not even Leigh could buy.

As usual, the group broke apart at the garden gate after this short interchange. As estate doctor, Michael was a familiar of the manor house beyond. Without words (with no overt resentment) his assistants were restricted to the plantation, with separate quarters in the overseers' stockade. Such leaves as they enjoyed were spent in the overseers' company at Fernandina or St. Augustine. Even Roger Farrar had never set foot in the manor house, save to report in Leigh's private sanctum. Tonight, Michael found, he could watch the trio disappear among the work sheds with a small twinge of regret. Adam Leigh's caste system had its drawbacks. If he, too, had been forbidden to cross the sill of this garden gate, he might have crushed the questions that waited now on the threshold of his mind —the burning questions that had waited so long and might have died, quite painlessly, had Marian Leigh remained in a world remote from his own. . . .

"It isn't like you to brood, Doctor."

Michael scowled lightly as he came back to what Adam Leigh was saying. "I was thinking of my wife—and cursing myself for leaving her in Fernandina. There may be trouble while I'm away."

"I can ease your mind on that score, at least. Coppinger is determined to storm Fernandina eventually. But I'm positive he'll give this new usurper time to retire peacefully."

Michael hesitated, with one foot on the steps that led up to the colonnade. He knew that Leigh was waiting patiently for his report; from the beginning, they had fallen into the convention of making this exchange of information quite informal—precisely as Michael had warned MacGregor of the terrors in store for him when he returned from a visit to the Point. Now, as he leaned wearily against one of the great soaring columns of the portico, he found himself speaking a thought aloud rather than relaying facts:

"Irwin will fight. So far, I'm not sure if he's a pirate, an American *politico*—or a little of both. Nothing could be more piratical than the vessel he chose to arrive in."

"The Morgiana," said Leigh in the same conversational tone. "A brig flying the flag of Buenos Aires, and bearing eighteen guns. Accompanied by the privateer *St. Joseph,* bearing ten guns, and the armed schooner *Jupiter*. Counting their crews, there aren't more than a hundred fighting men in Fernandina—and perhaps a dozen of MacGregor's poorer officers."

"Your information tallies with mine. How did you secure it?"

"Coppinger has his own spies in Fernandina, of course. It never does harm to check figures with an authority. Will you present my respects to Irwin—and advise the scoundrel that he'll be cut down without mercy if he insists on lingering?"

"Irwin has ignored me so far."

"The fellow is no fool: he must know by now that you have a foot in both camps. The fact that he let you sail down to visit me is proof of that."

"No one on this coast would dare detain the *Hirondelle*."

Leigh accepted the compliment with a stony stare. "Or my estate doctor. True enough. He'll know I'm not boasting when I say that Coppinger outnumbers him five to one."

"Most of the Spanish companies are Negro."

"They'll fight, nonetheless—better than sailors who have jumped ship."

"Stop me if I'm wrong, but are you trying to provoke Irwin, so he'll be sure to resist?"

"Remember, I'm Coppinger's deputy."

"You are no one's deputy but your own, Mr. Leigh," said Michael. "This is Punta Blanca—and you're the law here. God help any poor mortal who dares to question that fact—in uniform or out."

Once again he waited for the detonation that did not come. Adam Leigh's voice had never been gentler.

"Sometimes, Dr. Stone, you understand me too well for comfort."

"You pride yourself on speaking the truth. Why does it trouble you to find the same trait in a janizary?"

"Janizary? The word is strange to me."

"A trusted member of the palace guard. Sworn to defend the empire to the death."

"May I take that oath at its face value?"

"You may indeed."

On that note they walked through the tall, fanlighted doorway, which swung open at their approach, with a house slave cringing at each of the two brass knobs. Adam Leigh paused on the first landing of the stair well and let his eyes linger on the gleaming emptiness of the hallway. This time, his voice took on a mocking, almost silky tone—as though he were playing the role of Sun King to the hilt and enjoyed every syllable.

"The dinner bell will ring in an hour, Doctor. Perhaps I should say that I'll be unable to join you."

"It's still daylight—and a flat sea. I could return by open water to Fernandina."

"I've already spoken for the *Hirondelle*. The governor's adjutant is waiting now, to take me down to Augustine."

Michael kept his voice as steady as his eye. "In that case, I'll be happy to dine with the overseers. Ledoux and I can check the dispensary."

"Lady Marian is expecting you. Surely you won't disappoint her?"

The master of Punta Blanca and his estate doctor faced each other on the stair. Even as the duel of glances continued, Michael found that he was taking in details with grim precision—the glint of gold on a picture frame high up in the sunshot dimness, the ivory perfection of the stair well itself, that seemed to spiral away into space with no visible support, no real reason for being. . . . When he spoke at last, he knew that his voice was as calm as the resolve that had built steadily in his brain all through this long afternoon.

"Who am I to disappoint your chatelaine? If Lady Marian is alone tonight, I'm only too happy to keep her company."

"Perhaps I should say that she's unaware of your presence, Doctor. And unaware of the emergency that calls me down to St. Augustine."

You've planned this perfectly, thought Michael. Aloud he said only, "I've hardly had time to hear of her return from England."

"She arrived only yesterday, from Charleston. Fortunately the *Dos Amigos* was outfitting at that port. So she had an easy voyage."

Michael hoped that his smile was as knife-thin as Leigh's. The *Dos Amigos,* he thought, is hardly the transport to mention at this moment.

"Did she bring your grandson too?"

"Naturally. Lady Marian is an intrepid voyager. I'd written, advising her to remain in England until the political pattern of the Floridas had time to shape itself. She answered my advice by appearing in person—with her son."

"And your heir?"

"And my heir. He's sleeping in his nursery now, at the eastern end of your hall. Would you care to look in on him, when you've changed?"

Michael drew a deep breath. "As a doctor—or a godparent?"

"As a doctor, of course." Adam Leigh's voice was only mildly reproving. "His godparents have been chosen long ago—two noble lords as dull as their arms."

"Is the child ailing?"

"To my knowledge, he's in the best of health. Still, he's one of your patients now. It will do no harm to verify a grandfather's diagnosis."

They stamped upstairs without another word, and exchanged bows in the corridor that led to Michael's quarters. As always, Guillaume was waiting in the doorway, with his Gallic welcome burnished.

"Le douche, M. le Docteur?"

"Le douche, parbleu! L'averse, je te prie!"

He needed floods of cold water—a whole Niagara, in fact—to cool the sudden antic pulsing of his blood. Even as he slipped his arms into the long white linen coat that was his evening uniform on these visits to the Point, he could not be sure of its genesis. Accepting a boutonniere from the valet's reverent fingers, admiring the snug fit of his waistcoat in the glass, he did not know if his pulses throbbed at Adam Leigh's challenge or at the prospect of the head-on collision that must surely come, now that he would face Marian Leigh across her table. Alone, save for their collective conscience and the hot invitation of the night outside. Alone, with a hundred unanswered questions that must find tongue at last. . . .

This, of course, was rank heresy; he would put the temptation aside at once. He nodded to Guillaume, and the valet, with the quick intuition of his calling, left the room as quietly as a shadow. Facing himself one more time in the cheval glass, Michael repeated his credo aloud: *I am a happily married man,* he assured himself, even as his spirit revolted at the necessity for such assurance. *I am fortunate beyond my deserts. Curiosity is another emotion than love. If I satisfy that curiosity tonight, I'll ask pardon of no one. If I pay off a few scores in the process, I'll only prove that I'm human, after my long forbearance. Above all else, if the old fox is testing me, I'll show that I can outsmart him. . . .* Holding that ethic before him like a knight-errant's buckler, he stalked into the hall, turned east, and knocked firmly on the door at the end of that vast and silent corridor. When silence answered him, he turned the knob and entered—remembering to walk softly just in time.

He had expected Marian and the same coifed Negress who had attended her on the *Dos Amigos*. He had expected a jungle of lace and a cherub nestled like a contented silkworm in the white depths Actually, the nursery was Spartan in its scrubbed bareness. He saw the netting on the window, the narrow nurse's bed at right angles to the bassinet, before he saw the child itself.

Forrest Leigh the Second was curled in deep slumber—a ruddy, dark-haired boy who already seemed too large for his wicker cradle Michael stood silent above him, noting the strong plane of the forehead, the barrel of the chest that promised deep strength to come. Even as his mind catalogued facts, it fumbled for an appropriate emotion. He had expected the tug of a mystic bond, a feeling of instant kinship. But there was no bond here so far: this was merely another healthy infant, sleeping in a stranger's bed. . . .

"He celebrates his first birthday next week, Doctor. Already he has two teeth and walks like a man. Can an indulgent grandfather supply other particulars?"

Michael turned slowly to the tall-backed chair in the corner. Adam Leigh had not stirred as he spoke, only the craggy line of his jaw and the inevitable cheroot (unlighted now, in deference to the young) showed against the damask.

"May I say that he's his mother's image?"

"You may indeed. A handsomer lad was never born in the old world—or in this."

The infant opened his eyes and crowed happily with his tranquil wakening. The eyes were a laughing hazel, completing the picture. Michael turned away abruptly as Marian looked up at him out of her boy's sleepy lids. This was more than he had bargained for. The warm rush of tenderness that overwhelmed him did not quite betray its origin. He knew it was in control when he turned back to the room. Adam Leigh had cradled the child in his arms. He was smiling down at it with fierce grandfatherly pride.

"Each man must have his weakness, Doctor. As you see, I've found mine at last."

Michael stared at the tableau in silence, and wondered at the red throb of rage in his brain. He had prepared himself for this moment as carefully as any man could; he had told himself that his part in producing this healthy mite was too casual to involve his emotions. Now, confronted with the child itself, he needed all his will to keep his fingers from Leigh's throat. There was no logic in this fury: no reason under heaven why the planter should not rejoice in the grandson that was his by every legal right. Yet Michael felt the will to destroy build its dark whirlpool within him, until it threatened to hurl him into action.

Why should he hate Leigh for this brief flash of affection—framed, as always, in the absolute power that was Leigh's own essence?

The answer came just in time, as he stood behind the chair and flexed his muscles for the leap that would send the planter spinning, even as he snatched the child from his arms. Leigh had mated him with Marian as casually as he would mate a prime field hand with a Gold Coast princess: he had already accepted that fact. He had not bargained for the gleam of possession in Leigh's eye—the selfsame gleam he had noted in those eyes an hour ago, when the planter had cradled a newborn black infant in his arms and crooned the tyrant's lullaby of ownership.

"Is it too hard to bear, Doctor?"

The soft question was his salvation—and Leigh's. Michael crossed the room in three long strides and stared through the white mist of netting at the window.

"The fact that you must own everything you touch? I've known that long ago—and learned to bear it nicely."

"I don't own you, Doctor. Or this boy's mother. That's why I felt we should have this little chat now—before I sail down to Augustine."

"I've just reaffirmed my loyalty to your empire. Lady Marian hardly needs to state hers. She's given you visible proof."

"As it happens, I've no doubts about Lady Marian." Leigh's smile was almost benign now. "Incidentally, she's at the family graveyard now, decorating her husband's mound with laurel, as befits a model widow. Usually she can hardly bear to leave the child's room; the nurse has had a sinecure."

"I can believe that."

"A model widow, Doctor—and a model mother. But she's also a free agent since her husband's death. If she wished to leave Punta Blanca in the near future—with you, or another man—who am I to prevent her?"

"Who, indeed?"

"If that's a challenge, I'll accept it. As I say, I trust my daughter-in-law's good sense completely. Her marriage contract stipulates that her child is to be raised in Florida, under my direct care. If she decided to leave with you, she'd leave penniless and alone."

"Aren't you forgetting that I'm established in Fernandina, with a wife of my own?"

"I'm hoping that *you* won't forget it, Dr. Stone. Stronger men than you have forgotten, when passion submerged their judgment."

"Thank you for underestimating me."

"I seldom underestimate the men I trust. In your case, the problem is peculiar. You've a stubborn conviction that I'm an evil old man who has used you quite shamelessly. The devil, in a rather grim reincarnation."

"I've thought nothing of the kind. You're ruthless, not evil. You're as normal as greed itself."

"Precisely. You believe that men should be born without greed. With pure souls, and hearts brimming with pity. In short, that men should help one another. Naturally, that prescription includes infants in the clutches of an ogre and all ladies in distress."

"Can you quarrel with such a credo?"

"Only if it includes me among your ogres, and inscribes Lady Marian's name on your buckler. I can assure you that she's ideally happy here. Perhaps you'll find her a bit subdued this evening. No matter. *That,* my dear idealist, is only decent grief at her husband's passing. With the new year, she'll shed her mourning and be my chatelaine, precisely as I'd planned. Yes, and see to it that her son inherits the life for which he was intended."

"Have I questioned that?"

"I'm afraid your heart questions it at this moment. Just as your eyes question my right to hold my grandson in my arms."

Michael bowed—and knew that he had found his aplomb with that flourish. "I am sorry if my eyes betray me. A janizary should be more discreet."

"I don't care for that kind of discretion. If you think Lady Marian is unhappy here, why not ask her?"

"Do I have your permission?"

"And my blessing. As I say, I must leave in another moment. I shan't return from Augustine before morning. In my absence, Lady Marian is absolute mistress in this house. Ask her what you like. I'll abide by her answers."

Michael kept his poise with an effort. "When I came here today, I expected that I'd be tested."

"You'll be testing yourself, Doctor. Believe me, my daughter-in-law will come through with flying colors."

"Suppose I've no questions to ask her?"

"Don't play the shrinking dreamer who would keep his dream inviolate. You're much too healthy for that, and much too curious. I'll go further, Doctor: you'll never rest until you've found why Lady Marian made this bargain with the Leighs."

"You've told me why."

"And you believe me, to a point. You still can't believe that she could enter such a bargain with her eyes open, and have no regrets thereafter. Being a romantic with a positive urge, you insist that she needs your help, now that she has no legal tie to the Point."

"Do you enjoy this mind reading, Mr. Leigh? Is it an indulgence after hours?"

"Nothing is more vital to me at this moment than your peace of mind. I'm trusting Marian Leigh to set you right, once and for all."

"Have you arranged this interview between you?"

"At the moment, as I told you, she does not even know you are on the estate. But she does know that a meeting is inevitable. When she returns from her husband's grave——" Leigh made the barest of pauses here and brushed back a damp curl from the child's face. Forrest Leigh the Second, who had dropped asleep again, stirred contentedly.

"When she returns from that ritual," said Leigh, "she will be informed that you are dining here tonight, as her only guest. Don't look so troubled—I'm positive that she'll see you, and keep your wineglass filled. From that point the evening is in her hands—and yours. Could any proposition be fairer?"

"Suppose I persuade her to give all this up, and find a new life elsewhere?"

"Try it, Doctor. Make love to her, if you think it'll help your cause. I've every confidence that she'll handle the situation adequately."

Michael ventured a smile. "In other words, I'm repulsed before I begin."

"Prove I'm wrong, if you can. Persuade her to abduct the child and flee to America." Leigh placed the sleeping infant in the bassinet with gentle hands. "I've the legal right to stop you there, but I won't. *Tonight,* Dr. Stone, Punta Blanca is open to your assault—and you may fire at will. May I wish you luck?"

Michael did not stir as the planter moved toward the nursery door. "You don't mean that, of course."

"Luck with your problems, sir. Ours, as I've intimated, are well settled. After tonight, I'm convinced that you'll return to your resolute little bride in Fernandina a wiser man. As you observe, I'm staking a great deal on that conviction."

The planter stalked down the hall on that without a backward glance. Michael held his ground, with one hand on the wicker cover of the bassinet. Looking back on the moment, he knew that he had swayed under that final challenge—enough to shake the cradle and send Forrest Leigh the Second into a thin wailing.

The child was in his arms, now, though he had no memory of lifting it from the mattress. Soothing it mechanically, he found that he had pressed a kiss against that peach-bloom cheek. Pacing the floor like a father in a lampoon, he knew that his eyes were darting wildly—to find an escape for himself and his own.

The vague bulk of a nurse loomed in the doorway as he restored the sleeping infant to its cradle. He stood for a moment more at its side. This is no real part of me, he told himself, with no special conviction. My future is in Fernandina. With my wife, and a child yet unborn.

"Is the child ailing, Doctor?"

The nurse's face was unreal as flat black fruit, framed by a bandana turban that resembled a sunset gone berserk. He stared at her moodily, as though he were seeing her for the first time. Much later he would remember that this was Aunt Queen, a house slave he had seen a dozen times.

"The child is in perfect health. Where is the mother?"

"Waiting for you, Doctor. In the big drawing room. Will you go to her now?"

"I will indeed."

VIII

An hour later (a ritualistic hour that had followed his expectations to the letter) he was still facing her across the great golden épergne in the dining hall, still waiting for her mask to drop.

"More wine for the doctor, Jaime."

"Thank you, I've had enough." Enough wine, and more than enough fencing. Enough gossip of London and its literary lions. Of Shakespeare at the Haymarket, and the zarzuelas at the Teatro Inglaterra in Havana. Of Charleston gardens, heavy with cape jasmine and snobbery. Of a new poet named Shelley and a horse named Lightning that won the emeralds you are wearing (and did you wear those emeralds, and that wine-red velvet, when you laid flowers on your husband's grave?). Of the grateful peace of these Florida acres, so soothing after a London season. Of a governor's ball in St. Augustine which a widow had no choice but to decline. . . .

Jaime and Dominique, deft as a brace of silken cats, had already begun to serve the dessert, a pineapple blazing in brandy. He smiled at his hostess across the épergne and wondered why she was no more actual than that vast golden mirror, no nearer than the pyramids of tropic fruit that rose between them.

"Perhaps I should leave you to your cigar, Doctor?"

As always in that endless meal, the well-poised voice had filled the silence and mastered it—before silence could take on a meaning of its own. He found himself forcing the attack at last, holding her eye for a long moment before he answered:

"You're fatigued, Lady Marian?"

"Certainly not. I've never felt more rested. I'll be at my embroidery frame in the salon."

"I'll go in with you, if I may."

They rose together as the platoon of dark servitors whipped back from the table, leaving them alone in the circle of candlelight. Michael's wineglass was in his hand: he lifted it against the light, enjoying the ruby gleam of the claret as much as the question that hung between them.

"A toast before we go. To the seigneur of Punta Blanca."

Marian Leigh lifted her own glass, and he noted the steadiness of her hand, as though she were well schooled in the American custom of matching drinks at table, regardless of sex. In that same glance he saw a faint tinge of color at her cheek and hoped that it did not come from the wine.

"I'll drink to that gladly, Doctor."

"A remarkable man, no matter what your viewpoint."

"A man it's an education to know," she said gravely, and touched glasses with Michael across the golden épergne.

"I'll endorse that from the heart."

They drank slowly, holding each other's eyes. He felt a little of his tension melt in the wine, even before he could offer his arm. The servants fell back still farther, backs rigid against the wall panels, their faces gleaming in the half-light like moons in eclipse. For the first time that evening he was near enough to speak without being overheard. He seized the advantage instantly.

"A remarkable man indeed, Lady Marian. Why do you suppose he's left us alone?"

He watched her chin lift proudly, felt her eyes dwell on him with a lingering appraisal he remembered all to well. "I expected that question. Somehow, I didn't expect it so soon."

"Let's say my eagerness has overstepped my caution."

"Isn't *eagerness* a large word, when you consider your position here?"

"What is my position here? I'd give a great deal to know."

"You're our estate doctor—no more, no less. An important post, I'll grant you. It hardly gives you the status of a family member."

A house slave bowed in the tall double door that gave from dining hall to salon. Marian moved easily across the ice-smooth parquet with a hand still on Michael's arm. He held her eyes and smiled inwardly as he found no echo of rebuke there.

"Believe me I'm more than merely curious."

"You've no right to be—more than that."

Again her whisper was easy, with no hint of anger. She studied him for a moment—gravely, unsmilingly. Then, with a vast billowing of her velvet gown, she settled in the love seat. The panniers of the dress covered the seat completely. Michael held his ground, knowing that a single flick of his hand would make room on the cushions beside her. A house slave had already sprung forward with an octagonal coffee table inlaid with the arms of Spain—and sprang back again, to flatten in the doorway as Jaime entered pontifically with a vast coffee service. Dominique minced in his wake with a liqueur tray almost as magnificent.

"May I venture a conjecture?"

"With my permission—or without it?"

"Without it, naturally. I think you are one of the few people that Adam Leigh trusts completely. I think he's proving that trust tonight——"

He let the rest go as Jaime stalked into earshot of whispers. Leaning on the back of the love seat, watching the dance of Marian's hands as she checked the contents of the trays, he admired the perfection of her withdrawal once more. She seemed oblivious of his presence now, unaware of the fact that he was devouring her with his eyes—the cream-white shoulders, magnolia-smooth in the scalloped immensity of her *grande tenue,* the generous curve of breast glowing in the deep V of the bodice. Perfume, faint as a remembered caress, teased his senses. He found that he must give ground after all, before memory could make him a slave again. Seated on a leather pouf a safe yard's distance from the love seat, he felt safer—and far more certain of his next move.

"Sugar or clear, Doctor?"

"Clear, please."

He had accustomed himself to the after-dinner ritual of coffee at Punta Blanca. He could even smile when Dominique came forward by rote and opened a slender wooden bottle that contained Adam Leigh's best armagnac brandy.

"And chartreuse tonight, just for variety."

"I can recommend the curaçao too," said Marian.

"Curaçao, then—if you'll join me."

"I'll pour, Jaime. That will be all."

The slaves marched out with all the high solemnity of acolytes. Watching the tall doors sigh shut behind them, Michael felt his resolve harden into a familiar pattern. This was his moment, after all: he had planned it too long to yield an inch.

"Was that last remark addressed to me as well?"

"On the contrary. You say that Father Leigh trusts me completely. Now that I'm alone with our estate doctor, I hope I'll be worthy of the trust."

"Must we go on like this?"

"I'm afraid I don't follow——"

"As you see, we *are* quite alone. It's a chance we may never have again. Can't you tell me why you're here?"

"Isn't that self-evident?"

He turned away quickly, exulting at the tremor in her voice—and afraid she might notice the triumph in his eyes.

"You're quite right, of course. As you say, you owe me nothing."

"I was lying, Michael. I owe you everything."

She had said it quite calmly. So calmly, in fact, that he turned back to her hesitantly, as though he had not quite grasped her meaning.

"You said——?"

"Only that it's high time we were honest."

He settled deeper in the yielding leather of the pouf and stared at her with sagging jaw. Marian Leigh returned the stare with her wide-eyed calm unshaken.

"Ask me what you like. I'll try to answer truthfully."

"There's nothing to ask really," he said, forcing a tone that matched her sudden burst of candor. Now that he had recovered from the first shock, he knew he could play this game as well as she.

"This isn't a game," said Marian Leigh. And went on quickly, before he could break in: "Just don't—force me too hard. Or too fast. You see I haven't been honest with anyone. Not for a long time." She breathed deeply and seemed to grow more confident. "It's just that I—don't want you to hate me any more."

"I don't hate you, Marian. I've never hated you."

"That's the first time you've used my name," she said.

"You just used mine for the first time. If you insist on candor——"

"I do, Michael. From the beginning."

"You might begin by explaining your—shall I say, your familiarity?"

Her eyes dropped on that at long last. He watched her strong, slender hands as they moved a cup on the coffee table. "Don't be offended, Michael, whatever I say. I'm sure to begin this badly."

"Remember, I'm the family doctor," he said. "Perhaps I understand my patient better than she suspects."

"You don't understand me at all so far. And you did hate me that day you left the ship at the Boca. I can remember your eyes, when you glared up from the longboat——"

"I can remember the joke you used as a farewell," he said—shocked at the sudden hoarseness in his voice, shocked still more by the burning intensity of the picture her words had created.

"Don't you see, Michael? I had to be coarse that afternoon. I had to be as brutal as a woman could be. Just as I had to pretend you had no—no Christian name. That way, I could make myself forget you were a person when we——"

He got up on that and strode toward her—pulled up just in time and stalked over to the mantel, where he stood for a long moment, beating his fist softly on a chair back. Much later he would remember how he had stared up at the great oil painting. How the painting had stared back at him just as blankly—a suet-colored face drowned in a vast periwig, the eyes pouched in hillocks of fat like the eyes of a Christmas porker. For the moment he was conscious only of the silence behind him—a stillness that pleaded eloquently for tolerance.

Marian spoke at last. "I warned you that it wouldn't be easy."

"And I repeat: I understand perfectly."

"The facts, Michael. Not the motives. You know that we met aboard the *Dos Amigos* for a purpose—a purpose I could hardly divulge at the time."

"You needn't apologize." He continued to face the painted ancestor above the mantel. "At the time, I said I enjoyed our—meeting. I won't withdraw the statement."

"How much has Father Leigh told you?"

He blazed at her in earnest then. "Why do you call that devil Father Leigh? Why didn't you break free of him—and of this—when you knew?"

"When I knew what made him rich?"

"Consider the question withdrawn." Despite his outburst, he had not dared to face her. "It's as needless as your own. If you know him at all, you must realize he's told me everything. As calmly as though you were a——"

"A black girl in the quarters?"

"Thank you for finishing the sentence."

"Is that what really hurts you, Michael? Or do you hate him because he used you too?"

He did not answer her at once. When he found his voice, it sounded oddly distant, even to his own ears. As though he were thinking aloud—and wondered, a little, at the sudden clarity of his thoughts.

"Your mask was so perfect. I still don't see why you dropped it."

"I've thought about you a great deal, Michael. Ever since I knew I'd be here permanently." Again she drew a deep breath. "Ever since I knew that the—the child I'd hoped for was a reality."

"Why should you waste a thought on me? I'd played my part."

"I'd heard what you'd accomplished at the Boca. I knew what you could do here, if you became the estate doctor. I realized that you were a good man, Michael Stone. A humane man. I'm sorry if I realized it too late."

"So you thought——"

"Admit we didn't make much attempt to—to get acquainted aboard the *Dos Amigos*."

"Would you have been happier if you'd learned I was a rakehell?"

"Why did you come back to me, Michael?"

He turned to her at last, startled by the question. Knowing his answer in advance, he wondered if he would have the courage to utter it.

"You'd escaped Adam Leigh," she said. "And all he stood for. You could have taken this—this girl you married to the States, or back to England. Instead, you walked deliberately into our stronghold. *You came back to me, Michael.* Can you deny it?"

"No, Marian."

"Then tell me why."

"I wanted to understand you—and what you'd done to me. I knew I'd never rest until——"

"Until you could sit beside me, and talk like this. Quite frankly, without shame. But we still aren't frank with each other. I'm excusing my—my conduct with a puritan's reasons. *You're* pretending that I'm only a monstrous problem in evil."

"Tell it your way," he said. "I'll try not to spoil the story."

"You know most of my story now. I married Forrest Leigh to save my father—and my father's Irish acres. I believe that's still a respectable reason for marriage. The fact that there was no love on either side didn't seem important at the time: our need was too great. Besides, I wanted to escape my family and all it stood for. Most of all, I wanted a child."

"So far, no one is blaming you."

"I knew enough of the marriage contract to understand that a child was important to—to the future of my union. And Forrest was handsome, and bearable enough. Only another woman would understand this, but—I didn't resent that part of our relationship. In time I even learned to pity him a little. I pitied him still more after Waterloo."

Michael broke in quickly, despite himself. Remembering the quick flash of tenderness that had passed between Marian and her husband on his first visit to the Point, he could believe every word she had spoken.

"How much did you know of the Leighs when you married?"

"Only that it was a respected name in Scotland. Naturally, our lawyers investigated their assets carefully. I was told merely that they were colonial planters, with great riches in the Floridas."

"You knew better when you boarded the *Dos Amigos.*"

"True. I'd also made a bargain, which I intended to keep. And I wanted a child more than ever. Something outside myself that I could believe in. Someone whose future I could fight for."

"And an excuse to be the queen of all this?"

"I was afraid you wouldn't understand. Do you think it wrong of me to want a child so badly? As a doctor, you must know that no woman is fulfilled without one."

"True enough. But the means to that end——?"

He saw that she was smiling, and choked his rage just in time. Marian's voice had a faraway music in its heart, as though she were speaking from a plane he could never reach.

"I knew my position was secure here, once I provided the estate with an heir. Father Leigh was determined to be just that to me: we were *en rapport* from the start. Call him the devil if you must; he has a hard earth wisdom of his own. He never questioned my need: he was proud of me when I agreed to go aboard the *Dos Amigos*"—she was really smiling now—"when I promised to seduce you as expertly as I could."

"May I compliment you once more on your skill?"

"Now you're fencing again, Michael. Using word play—when this is our last chance to be fair to each other."

"Have it your way, then. My pride was hurt. I daresay it'll never mend completely."

"It'll mend before you leave this room—if you will hear me out!"

"My apologies. I won't interrupt again."

"I wanted a child, Michael, more than I wanted anything. So much, that I thought I could forget its father. I was young then—and proud—and certain of my destiny. I know now that it would be impossible to forget you no matter what comes between us. I'll never be whole again until you've forgiven me."

Once more he stared at her wordlessly, as though he had not heard aright. He remembered the imperious lift of her head as she waved good-by from the deck of the *Dos Amigos*—the cool courtesy she had offered him on his first visit here—the *femme du monde* ripostes across the epergne an hour ago. He contrasted these bitter pictures with the girl who stood before him now with downcast eyes—and could not help wondering if his victory was genuine. But there was no mistaking the completeness of her surrender—or the quick sob in her throat when she spoke again:

"Some women can play a part all their lives, and enjoy every moment. I thought I was such a woman, until you took me in your arms."

"Go on," he said hoarsely. "I promised not to interrupt."

"I'd planned to take a part here, for my son's sake—and play it brilliantly. As you've observed, I'm doing just that. Father Leigh will have no regrets."

"For God's sake, don't call him Father Leigh!"

"I'm afraid I must, Michael. I owe him that much while I'm living here."

"Can't you see that he's bought you, and the boy, just as he tried to buy me?"

"Most women are bought, one way or another. It's a fate we'll be a long time outliving."

"I'll take you out of here tonight if you like. He wouldn't dare to stop me."

"And the boy?"

"The boy too, of course. D'you think I'd let him become the master of *this?*"

"I'm afraid we've no choice there. Under Spanish law, this estate is deeded to my son—and vice versa. My contract of marriage is just as definite. It states that his grandfather is to have absolute charge of his education until he comes of age—and absolute custody."

"Damn the contract, then. Once you're in Charleston, you can laugh at his claims."

Marian's voice took on a patient, tired calm. "Aunt Queen stays with him day and night. She's the best nurse in the world—and the best watchdog. I needn't tell you that Mozo guards the boy by day and sleeps outside the nursery door."

"Why did you return here at all? You might have defied Leigh in England."

"I've answered that question, Michael. I had to see you again."

She lifted her eyes on that, and he saw they were moist with pleading; the hand she gave him was deathly cold, but it clung to his as though she would never let him go. "I believe you," he said slowly. "Don't ask me why, but—I believe you."

"You know why, Michael. You had to see me too. You had to convince yourself that I was—what I seemed to be."

"And now that you've proved me wrong?"

"Say that you forgive me."

"I forgive you."

His voice was only a whisper, but it seemed to satisfy her; the hand within his own began to glow with a faint warmth. Her wide hazel eyes, alight with purpose now, met his unspoken question proudly.

"Even if I stay on here, Michael?"

"You can't help staying here," he said. "I can see that now." He forced himself to break free of her tight, hot fingers; he crossed the room again and yet again, quartering Adam Leigh's immaculate rich carpets in long strides, as though he could walk off the frustration that all but choked him.

"If I could break these walls for you, I would."

"But it's his now, Michael. The boy's. I must stay to make sure of that."

"Slavepens and all?"

"We'll open those pens someday. You'll help in that opening. Until then, it's our world, and our time. We can't fight our century, Michael."

"You're still right," he said. "Women usually are in these matters. It's men who are born romantics."

"We needn't submit to it, either," she whispered.

"What would you have me do?"

It was a cry of pain, wrenched from his heart. Marian answered it without words as she turned to him with surrender in her eyes and held out her arms. A thousand times in Africa, in heat-drugged, sleepless midnights, he had planned to take her thus—to bruise her lips one last time, then fling her aside in triumph. Tonight, as he kissed her mouth tenderly, he knew that his triumph was bitter as ashes. Then his arms closed about her in earnest; their mouths met and mingled for a heart-bursting eternity, and he knew that he had never been away; that he would never escape her now—and had no wish to escape.

When Marian spoke at last, her cheek was against his shoulder, her eyes veiled. He knew that she was crying: he could not be sure that they were happy tears.

"I'm really forgiven now. Is that what your kiss meant, Michael?"

"There's nothing to forgive you for."

"Only this, my dear: I've belonged to you from the beginning—and I couldn't give myself. I've wanted you ever since I watched you go ashore in Africa. I'll go on wanting you until I die." She stirred in his arms as though she would leave them—then clung to him with all her strength. "And now it's *you,* Michael, who won't give yourself. If that's my punishment, don't say it's deserved."

"I promised not to interrupt long ago," he said—and watched her break free. Her chin was high, her step firm as she went to the bellpull; only the wild throb of her breasts betrayed her.

"One thing more, Michael, before the servants come. I've had lovers in the past. In London before I married Forrest. I enjoyed them, as they enjoyed me." She held up her hand for silence as he tried to speak. "None of that is important now. If they made me a more expert bedfellow, I'm glad. Yes, my darling, glad that I could make your voyage to Africa a bit more exciting."

"Don't, Marian."

"There's been no one since," she said, with that same fierce emphasis. "No one at all. Even if Forrest could have been—well, a husband to me, I wouldn't——" She let her voice sink to a whisper that was vibrant with meaning. "I'd have killed him if he'd touched me, do you understand that? I belong to you completely. I love you completely and forever. If you want me again, I'm yours—on your terms." Her voice turned formal instantly as the double doors swung wide. "Does that settle our account, Dr. Stone—once and for all?"

"Don't, Marian!"

"It's said, Michael. And I won't take back a word." Her whisper had been as intense as his. The glaze of polite interest on her face was lacquer smooth as Jaime marched into the room to take the coffee service. "Just remember, the offer stands."

"I'm afraid I'll be engaged elsewhere, Lady Marian."

"Of course, if you really mean that——"

"It's a subject I can't discuss."

"And quite right too." She was talking with easy brightness now, for the black major-domo's ears. "As Fernandina's doctor, you must be busy beyond belief. Too busy to devote much time to us."

"I'm afraid you have stated the case admirably. Even with Dr. Hilary to assist, there's more work than I can handle."

"So we'll be seeing less and less of you as time goes on?"

"With Mr. Leigh's permission. After all, I've a contract to keep his slaves healthy——" He paused on that and stared down moodily at Jaime's shining bald pate, as the aged butler bent to lift the heavy silver coffee tray. "From the detention pens to this house itself. It's a large order."

"You've managed admirably."

"Now that our hospital is functioning, I should be able to turn most of the detail over to the resident doctors." He heard his voice continue this calm recital and wondered if it was as empty as it seemed. "Eventually, I should be able to supervise through them—with only an occasional visit."

"But you'll settle in Fernandina?"

"Only until I can afford to buy land in the interior. At Cowford, I think. On the St. Johns—when the King's Highway crosses from Augustine."

"So you mean to grow up with the land, Doctor, like any pioneer?"

"The Floridas will be part of the United States, then. I think I can turn into an American with very little effort."

"Father Leigh will sell you slaves at cost," she said—and there was a light mockery in her tone as she watched Jaime vanish with the tray.

"By that time, I hope, my account with your father-in-law will be settled in full."

"You'll turn planter as well as doctor at Cowford?"

"A quarter section, perhaps, if I can buy title to a Spanish land grant. Like most rootless Englishmen, I've always wanted land of my own. As an American-to-be, I understand it's a necessity."

"That means cotton, Doctor. You can't have cotton without slaves."

"I plan to farm with freedmen."

"Must we discuss your agricultural future, Michael? We're quite alone."

"I find it a fairly safe subject," he said. "Isn't that why you summoned your butler—to give us both a chance to—find our way back to the lives we've chosen?"

"Take your revenge, if you insist. I know you've earned it."

She had spoken quite steadily. He found he could match her, word for word. "It isn't a question of revenge: I'm merely trying to be clear-headed about—about us both. I'm married to a girl much finer than I deserve. I'm happy in that marriage——"

"You were happy in my arms just now," said Marian.

"That was our good-by kiss. My proof to you, and to myself, that there's nothing to forgive. No reason why we should hate each other. You've cast your lot with this." His gesture included the perfect Georgian symmetry of the drawing room, the gold-crusted ancestor above the mantel, the black world that slept without. "You'll buy and sell this human cattle when Leigh is gone. You'll teach your—your boy to be a sharp trader——"

"I said we'd open the pens someday, with you to help us."

"Humanity will break those locks before the thought would cross Leigh's mind—or yours."

Her eyes blazed in earnest on that, but her poise was unshaken as she rose from the chair to face him. "So you've joined us both in your mind."

"I'm not blaming you. Money and power are important to a widow with a son to raise. But don't ask me to pity your loneliness. Or to console it, when the seigneur is away. I've a life of my own to lead, and a wilderness of my own to tame. May I wish you good night, Lady Marian?"

She had taken the words without flinching: now she stared at him blankly for an instant, as though her mind refused to accept the meaning of his formal bow. "That's a sterling defense, Michael. And I'm sure you mean every word. Of course you know in your heart that it's nonsense."

"May I wish you good night?"

"You'll go on wanting me, no matter what you put between us. You tried to escape me before, and failed—when you thought I'd forgotten you. When your only motive in finding me again was simple, all-male revenge. Can you deny that I was the magnet that held you in Florida?"

"I'll admit that much, freely."

"Then how can you deny your need tonight?"

"I've done that long ago," he said. "That's why I'm wishing you good night. I trust you'll sleep better than I."

"But I won't sleep at all, Michael. I've never slept while you've been under this roof."

"A friend of mine once told me that I had a New England conscience," said Michael. "Don't tell me you share the same burden. You'll find it awkward baggage in the life you've chosen."

"Just as you say, Michael. Good night."

He knew that he had won his point: the husky ghost of tears in her voice told him more than words. Yet even now, he did not quite dare to face her. "Perhaps we've both said too much, Marian. Perhaps that's what your satanic father-in-law hoped for, when he threw us together."

"Look at me, Michael. Don't go like this."

"I'm afraid that's a risk I can't quite take."

"Look at me, darling! Don't hate me for demanding something I can never really have."

Her voice broke in tears, and he turned to her with that wild yielding, and clung to her one more time. Their bodies rocked in another kiss that seemed to have no ending; her lips opened under his, as though she would draw his very breath into the center of her being; stung by the same compulsion, he let his fingers close at the low V of her gown. But he broke free in time, before he could husk her body from that clinging wine velvet. Breaking from her arms, turning his back on all her remembered sweetness, he stumbled like a drunken man in his flight to the door.

"Good night, Lady Marian!"

Then he reminded himself that he could scarcely venture into the hall beyond—not in this breathless disarray, this case of blind staggers. Pausing with one hand still on the doorknob, he smoothed his tousled hair (her fingers had had their will while she held his mouth on hers) and settled his neckcloth. Only then did he dare to glance in her direction. Marian half leaned, half lay across the love seat—and he noted with satisfaction that her breathing was quite as stormy as his own; that her cheeks flamed like battle flags under the dark tumbled mass of her hair. Her deep-cut bodice, its lacings ripped, now exposed all of one firm young breast—a breast that glowed like living ivory in the candlelight, the flesh lifted proudly in that wine-velvet frame, the nipple taut as the boss on an Amazon's shield.

"Good night, Dr. Stone. I'm glad we understand each other."

He left her on that, giving her the luxury of the final word. In the hall he closed the door carefully behind him and leaned against it for a moment while he fumbled in his case for a cigar. It would hardly do for her slaves to find her thus, until she had had a chance to repair his marauding. The room behind him seemed quiet as the tomb of love. If she wept at his brutal desertion, he could catch no echo of her tears. Crossing the wide circle of the stair well at last and squaring his shoulders at the thought of tomorrow, he knew that Marian Leigh could hardly hate him as he hated himself.

A house slave leaped forward with a lighted lamp and marched up the noble curve of stair to light the guest to his bed. The slave paused on the landing and blinked sleepily as the doctor turned into the eastern corridor.

"Your room is this way, Señor Médico."

"I will go for a moment to the nursery."

At the nursery door Michael pulled up to curse himself one more time. Obviously it was too late to retreat now: Mozo (twice as large as life in his white burnous and twice as threatening) had already taken shape in the thick shadows that clotted the corridor.

"Señor Leigh feared the child might be ailing. I will make sure that he sleeps soundly."

"As you will, Doctor." But Mozo waited stolidly in the open door—and the slave held the lamp high to mark Michael's progress across the moonlit carpet within.

He saw instantly that the room was unchanged. Aunt Queen, relaxed like a tired watchdog on the nurse's bed, slept deeply. In the wicker cradle the child's tranquil breathing made an absurd obbligato to the woman's snores. Michael took the lamp and held it nearer to the bassinet, letting the muted glow creep up the child's body until only the tousled head lay in the penumbra. He stared at his son for a long moment without speaking—and told himself, for the last time, that it was absurd to claim this small bit of humanity as his belonging.

Adam Leigh had marked his putative grandson as his own from the moment of his conception. Now that he had stared into the deeps of the mother's soul, now that he had tested her fierce loyalty to her own flesh, Michael knew that she too would side with Adam till the end. Forrest Leigh the Second would grow into his name with each passing year. Young monarch of all he surveyed, backed by a grandfather's wisdom and a grandfather's hard American dollars, he would become another of those small but potent kings that were burrowing in the fringe of the American democracy and enlarging their empire with each crisis of the American politic. . . . So much was certain, as he stared down at the sleeping child and timed each tender inhalation with his own sad heartbeat.

Life in this new world, Michael pursued, was still in a state of healthy chaos; a better world might still evolve, if the Adam Leighs could be stopped in their tracks. His particular Nemesis (and he saw clearly now that Leigh was precisely that) had proved a clever sultan, assuring his empire's continuity by a stratagem as old as empire. Feeling Mozo above him, looking down at the competent bulk of the nurse in the truckle bed, Michael could see the pattern of his son's future forming, as clear-cut as Mozo's monstrous shadow on the wall: The tutors for his fledgling years, the golden wall that Grandfather's millions would build between Forrest Leigh the Second and the world. . . . Michael amended that estimate instantly: old Adam was far too thorough a grandfather to let young Forrest degenerate into a rich man's heir, with no brain of his own.

He moved the calendar ahead a quarter century, with all the ease of a parent who is surrendering his rights in advance. He saw young Forrest—a potentate at twenty-five, knowing that his orders would be obeyed without question—lounging on the portico of this same flamboyant mansion, reporting on the day's get from the pens. Old Adam, at seventy-odd, would be in full possession of his faculties and brimming over with sage advice for his successor. Ruthless, confident, and filled with the same hard wisdom, young Forrest would listen and nod—and offer a few facts of his own that would bring a chuckle to his grandsire's lips. Thanks to environment, an active mind, and a feeling for the main chance in history, young Forrest would be that grandsire's image.

Unstirring at the boy's bedside, tasting the bitter dregs of prophecy, Michael reviewed the stories of Adam Leigh that were current in Fernandina. Punta Blanca (so ran the legend) was only the focal point of Leigh's empire. With smaller stations nested in bayous along the coast, with plantations dotting the banks of the St. Marys, Adam kept his finger on each black pulse in his kingdom, even as he counted each drop of black sweat that was shed in his behalf. . . . Breeding more than he bought as history moved forward to choke off his supply of raw cattle, training his get by ever more rigorous standards, Leigh would keep pace with the growing demand in the States—and make sure that his offering represented the cream of the market.

Who but a wide-eyed romantic would assume, even for a moment, that the boy in the cradle would spurn this ready-made gold when he came to man's estate? Even as old Adam, he would rove his empire—on horseback and under sail—to make sure that it prospered. Sweating in the cotton rows with his own field hands, he would drive them to greater prodigies. He would train the nimble in gin and forge; checking his breeding pens each spring, he would plow the wenches of his choice (like a wise seigneur) and count his offspring by the hundreds. . . .

Michael studied the silhouette of Mozo on the facing wall. Like the other Mozambique blacks on the estate, the giant Negro had been brought round the Cape, at enormous expense, to receive his training at the Boca. As an alert guard, Mozo had few peers. Still, it would be simple enough to stab him now: the emergency scalpel in Michael's coat sleeve would make a perfect weapon. With Mozo dead on the carpet, he could smother Aunt Queen as she slept. He could take the boy to Marian, force her to decamp with him, and reach Fernandina with the morning tide. The plan died in the back of his brain, as he reminded himself that Marian's stake here was no less than her son's. If she left Punta Blanca, she would leave willingly—or not at all.

"The boy sleeps like a happy puppy, Señor Médico. Did you fear for his health?"

"Not now, Mozo. Good night."

"Buenas noches, Señor Mike. May you sleep as well as he."

Taking the lamp from the slave's hand and waving the houseboy aside, Michael retraced his steps until he stood on the landing again. The estate was silent now, wrapped in midnight like a cloak. He had felt the pressure of these silences before, in other great houses, when only the mastiffs prowling under the moon and the occasional creak of a warped molding betray the fact that this is indeed an abode of the living and not a ghostly silhouette against the sky. Michael breathed deep of the quiet before he ascended the stair to his own bedroom, resisting the impulse to slam the door as he stood in the dim silver bath of moonlight streaming through the pillars of the portico. Though he still swayed a little (the vertigo of that visit downstairs, joined to the thoughts he had beaten down at his son's bedside, would be a long time dying), he was remarkably calm. Shedding his coat and waistcoat, stripping his shirt from his back and flinging the sodden mass into the first convenient corner, he found that he could think clearly now—after a fashion.

The moonlight winked on the great tidal estuary that fanned out into marshland at the foot of Leigh's formal garden. The spars of a ship lifted gaunt antennae against the stars. . . . For the time being he could pretend that he was in Fernandina again, standing at the grimy window of Dr. Hilary's surgery and looking across the harbor at the bulk of the *Resolve* (a thriving hospital now, packed to the last cabin with paying cases and famous for its cures). He could even pretend that this was his bedroom on the Prado—that he had only to turn to find Dimity sleeping in the swan-boat bed and stirring happily to make room for her lord and master, when he chose to retire at last, after another harried day.

Only a few hours ago he had been certain that this was his destiny. Returning now to the muted ivory-and-gold luxury of his bedchamber (the fine muslin nightshirt that Guillaume had spread on the silk counterpane, the water carafe beside the brandy bottle at his bedside), he told himself again that reality still awaited him in Fernandina, that this was only a treacherous mirage. Leigh, as always, had been distressingly right. Measuring the loyalties of Dr. Michael Stone to the inch, the planter had been sure of his man and his reaction. Knowing Dimity and the life that Dimity had made for him, there was but one choice possible.

And yet, even as his mind clung to this safeguard, he felt his whole being tingle to the memory of Marian's kisses, the warm promise her body had offered at every point of contact. And he knew beyond a doubt, as his mind slid dizzily down into the warm cave of memory, that her kisses had been the greatest reality he had ever known.

"It's more than the body, Michael. More than the thralldom of the flesh. We were made for each other. All else is a pale pretense of living. . . ."

"I'm happy in my marriage. Can't you see that?"

"Not as you were happy just now—in my arms."

"Dimity needs me as you've never needed anyone. Dimity is carrying our child."

He pulled back from the unspoken dialogue as though Marian stood beside him in the room. Thank God he had held back that final argument as he had fought downstairs for this breathing spell.

A breathing spell from her thralldom. Was it no more than that, really? He faced the great, tall rectangle of moonlight with arms akimbo and renewed his marriage vows with all the fervor he could muster. True, he had yielded to the tug of memory tonight, on more than one front, in this age-old battle of the sexes. And it was quite as self-evident that Marian, in the first pulse beat of his ardor, had shown a capacity for yielding that could more than match his own. . . . The fact remained that he had broken free (to gain the sanctuary of his bedchamber) before the tide of passion had overwhelmed him completely.

He shot the bolt on his hall door and found he could chuckle at that needless precaution, even as he stripped to the skin and went to stand just inside the window to seek out what breath of air was stirring across the tidal reach. Save for the hour, he would have tugged at the bell rope and summoned his room slaves; a quarter hour under the cold-water shower would have soothed the lingering fever in his blood, made sleep more than a remote wish somewhere this side of a cotton wool dawn.

He paused with a hand on his bellpull, smiling at his own forbearance. The house slaves (with Guillaume to shepherd them in the upstairs regions and old Jaime to mutter half-forgotten Mozambique curses in the formal rooms downstairs) were a pampered lot, as the word was understood at the Point. Selected relentlessly from the top of the breed, trained no less relentlessly in the processing sheds, each man and wench was a bred-in-bone servant before he put his first cautious foot on the service stairs.

Only a confirmed romantic would hesitate to summon such an automaton at midnight, if he wished a cold plunge, a nightcap—or a half-hour's dalliance on a counterpane as a prelude to serious slumber.

His fingers closed on the bottle at his bedside. He drank deep, without waiting to measure his drink in a glass, letting the brandy build its own tempting lullaby in his bloodstream. One tug on the bell rope and Guillaume would come on the run. Guillaume could have a black girl in the room in three minutes. He would ask for Concha first, the sleek, dark upstairs maid who rolled her eyes so enticingly when she brought in his morning tea. Or perhaps Imola, that coffee-colored houri six months out of Africa, should be his first choice. Imola, whose mother had once been a princess—whose father (and Ledoux swore to the truth of this cross-breeding) was a Tuscan prince who had fallen on evil days.

He drank again, more deeply—choking on the brandy as he whipped his thwarted passion toward this new and enthralling image. Imola's body had all the pure beauty of sculpture in the classic manner. Was this a heritage of her Italian forebears, or did that opulent perfection stem from older and darker kings? Would ancestry matter, when he held this golden goddess in his arms and drowned his fever in surcease that could be had for the asking?

Pacing the room again, and drinking as he paced, he knew that he would not touch the bell rope tonight—or any night. Concha and Imola (and the myriad black virgins who slept in the sand-floored pens) were safe from the attentions of their estate doctor—clinical or otherwise. Now that he was locked securely away from Adam Leigh's world, he would simply drink himself into oblivion. Tomorrow was time enough to plot a new life with Dimity—an existence that would exclude the chatelaine of Punta Blanca firmly.

He went to the window again and stood with one foot on the gallery that crossed the upper portico. Staring down blankly into the reaches of the harbor, he found his eyes focusing on the ship that lay at anchor. Obviously it was the *Dos Amigos,* the old supply vessel that served the Boca: Leigh had no other ship so large, now that he had sold his fleet of slavers. Thanks to the white radiance of the moon, he could see her lines clearly. There was the cabin, just under the high poop deck, that had been his prison once. There, nested snugly amidships, was the white-painted deckhouse, where the heir-apparent to Leigh's empire had been conceived. . . . Remembering that moment, he knew that his heart was thudding like a jungle drum. Remembering (and admitting, from the depths of his being, that he could never put down the memory), he faced the truth.

He had loved Marian Leigh from the first—loved her wildly and completely. Tonight he had found that she matched his love, and his need: tonight he must slake his thirst for her or go quite mad. . . . Tomorrow would be time enough to make his peace with Dimity.

Willing that consummation in every fiber, claiming her in his heart even before he could seek her out, he was hardly surprised to find her standing before him, an ardent wraith that had taken form in the bath of moonlight at the window frame. Instinct caught the breath in his throat and forced him back a pace, until he was standing just within the room, surrendering the wide rectangle of the french window to a ghost that was not a ghost. But his voice was quite calm as he greeted her. Calm, and a bit solemn too, as befits a man who has stood up to his fate at last and admitted its inevitability.

"I'd forgotten that connecting gallery."

"I thought you'd remember it in time," she said, in a tone as balanced as his own. "On the other hand, there's that New England conscience to consider."

"Don't talk, Marian. We've hurt each other enough."

"You'll be less hurt tomorrow, when you remember that it was I who came to you."

"Not another word, darling!"

"Not another word," she whispered.

The robe she wore was moon-colored, save for a gold-crusted border. It gave a rich, silken whisper (like an overtone of Marian's last words) as it slipped from her shoulders to the floor. She had stalked him thus, for the first time, in the deckhouse of the *Dos Amigos*. He waited now, letting her stalk him once again—knowing that he had waited a lifetime for this moment and could afford to yield the first attack.

Closing his eyes against this warm white phantom that was not a phantom, he knew that she was remembering that first moment as vividly as he. Lips tender as moth wings on his cheek, fingers that touched and withdrew as swiftly, breasts that lifted in a quick savage thrust of their own to brush his flesh with glowing points. . . . She was gone when he opened his eyes wide, but he needed no words to find her. The moonlight patterned his approach as he bent above her, there in the pale wide desert of his bed. Before the kiss had ended, her body had surrendered completely—claiming him in that surrender, in a shared rhythm that had no ending.

IX

The *Hirondelle* leaned with the wind, skirting the shore of Amelia with a few scant yards to spare. Michael relaxed against the starboard gunwale, knowing that the water was deepest here, thanks to the scour of the ebb. It was enough, for now, to pick out landmarks in the slowly lifting mist: a gaunt file of cabbage palms, rising from the cotton wool to shake their frowsy heads at the sunrise; the bald pate of McClure's Hill, dominating the scrub to the south of Fernandina itself. . . .

An eternity ago he had sat atop that same hill and looked down at Fernandina for the first time. In that interval he had found a wife and the deepest affection he had ever known. He had stumbled wide-eyed on an older love, a love that could engulf him in a twinkling and wipe out the last of his scruples. . . . But he would not think of that pitfall now. He had put love behind him, along with a night of shared ecstasy, of broken, hopeless planning that led nowhere. He would make no plans in this cotton-wool dawn. He would not even ask himself for an attitude when he faced Dimity again.

It was enough, for now, to doze like an unrepentant tomcat on the deck of the *Hirondelle*. To listen to Roger Farrar's easy drone, as the head overseer called directions to the helmsman.

"Harrison's Landing is around the next bend, Doctor."

"I'm aware of that."

"Coppinger's forces have been camped there since yesterday. But we'll give 'em a hail to be sure."

"And stop a few bullets?"

"This is the best-known sail on the Amelia River. Besides, I'm a go-between today. No one's firing on us—not even Irwin."

The overseer's fist, banging on his bedroom door a scant two hours ago, had shaken him from the deepest slumber he had ever known. He had stirred resentfully for a moment, as his mind refused to identify the sound; his mouth, like a sleepy lover in this black hour before dawn, had sought Marian's lips and found them, as their bodies met and clung. . . . She had rested quietly there while he dressed; she had left him at the last possible moment, just before he unlocked his door. His lids drooped as he placed her again in the dim frame of the french window; the night outside had boiled with fog and blackness, but her body had glowed like alabaster against that dun backdrop as she swooped to retrieve her robe. . . .

"You'll come again, Michael?"

"You know I'll come again."

Hers had been the barest of whispers, and he had answered it in kind. The fog had swallowed her as she walked out to the airy gallery. If she had come to him like a living phantom, she had left in the same guise, to vanish without a sound.

"Sleep all you like, Doctor. I'm sorry if I woke you too soon, but I had my orders."

He came back to the present and the overseer's easy voice with no sense of transition. "Don't apologize, Farrar. It isn't every day that you can sail between two battle lines without a scratch."

There was a full-throated bellow from the shore, and Michael raised on one elbow to locate it. At first glance, the lookout's homespun uniform seemed to blend with the dusty green-brown of the scrub that lined the riverbank. Then, as the fist holding the musket raised in greeting, the vague silhouette in the palmettos became a man, complete with broad-brimmed sombrero, whiskers, and snaggle-toothed grin. A faint whiff of wood smoke assailed Michael's nostrils, along with the odor of broiling bacon, the stirrings of a camp preparing for a new day. . . . In that instant the *Hirondelle's* bowsprit all but grazed the bank. Farrar raised his hand, palm out, and swept it down slowly, with the index finger leveled north.

The guard returned the gesture, his grin broadening. As the sloop cut away for mid-channel, Michael looked back quickly, but the man had already merged with the palmettos.

"As simple as that, Doctor," said Farrar. "My signal means that I'm to go direct to Irwin and advise him to surrender. Our man's response means that he'll take the message to Walters, who commands the militia for Coppinger. Walters is a good moccasin boy: he enjoys a shooting scrape as well as the next man. But he'll give Irwin until noon to evacuate Fernandina."

"No war is that simple. Not even this one."

"It can be, with Adam Leigh sitting between the two camps. I've told you how he met Coppinger's commander last night at Fort George. A whole company of Cuban regulars crossed to the island last night in the dark. If you had a telescope, you could see them dragging their cannon up McClure's Hill."

"Does Walters command this force as well?"

"Unfortunately no. The leader is this fellow we saw at Fort George. A strutting jay named Cervantes—though you'd never mistake him for Don Quixote. If you ask me, *there's* a Spaniard who'll never tilt with windmills—or fight if he can avoid it."

"Yet he's moved in ahead of Walters."

"To a parade-ground position behind the hill. Thanks to my message, Walters will fan out down the road and invest the town head-on. Aided by a few gunboats, if you can call them that, from St. Augustine. The idea being that a little first-class cannon fire will give Irwin an excuse to strike his colors. *Then,* of course, our Colonel Cervantes will deploy, move up to join the militia, and accept the surrender."

Farrar mopped his brow and looked resentfully at Michael, who still sprawled against the starboard gunwale of the *Hirondelle,* lost in thought. "You might show a bit more concern. After all, a battle is a battle—no matter how long it lasts."

"Somehow, with almost five hundred men closing in on Fernandina, I can't believe that Irwin will fight. MacGregor, yes: he was born to die on his shield. But not a New York *politico.*"

"It isn't that. You just weren't interested. Don't be so blasé, Doctor."

Michael glanced at Farrar sharply, but the overseer had already turned to shout an order at the helmsman. I must shake off this trance, he told himself: as the only surgeon in Fernandina, I'll have my busiest day ahead, come what may. . . . Perhaps a first-class battle is just the antidote I need. At least I can put off facing Dimity—and asking myself what's become of our marriage.

Aloud, he said only, "I've been shelled before, you know. Arab dhows tried to storm the Boca more than once when I was in residence. And I was in Spain with Wellington, as a contract surgeon."

"Coppinger fought over the Peninsula too," said Farrar. "Leigh tells me that he's burning to lead this party himself. If *he* were on McClure's hill this morning, instead of that Havana colonel, I'd have no doubts."

"Why does he remain in Augustine?"

"Spanish protocol again. As governor of the Floridas, he's in supreme command of the military. But he's forbidden to lead an army in the field. Another reason for the delays. If you ask me, Irwin has dug into that town with teeth and toenails. He'll have to be blasted out; even politicos don't always blast easily."

Michael shook off the worst of his inertia and glanced into the widening tidal estuary that had opened ahead. Already he could sense the bustle of shipping in the Amelia: as always, the chandlers below the Fernandina bluff were taking invasion in their stride.

"When I left yesterday, there were a half-dozen privateers anchored in echelon beside Irwin's brig. Won't they make it rather hot for our invaders?"

"The bluff will snub off most of their range," said Farrar. "And Walters isn't *our* captain, Doctor—if I may make so bold. Remember, we're only Spanish citizens by proxy: that makes us strictly neutral."

"Which gives you the right to bear surrender terms from St. Augustine?"

"Exactly. And the right to sail away with a whole skin if they're refused." Farrar stared thoughtfully over the tidal reach ahead. "Dr. Hilary has rigged a white flag on your hulk—to warn the gunners that she's a hospital ship."

Michael followed the overseer's pointing finger. The sight of the *Resolve,* bouncing gently at her mooring with a tablecloth at her splintered forepeak, stabbed him back to complete reality. Automatically his mind checked over the sick list aboard: the three dengue cases that were mending so nicely in that bracing river air; the fracture that had escaped gangrene by a miracle; the lung case that was curing slowly on the sun deck and would surely die if it was brought ashore, even for a day. . . .

"Leigh could have warned us that this was coming. We could have towed the ship to St. Marys."

"The Americans would never permit a pesthouse inside their quarantine, even if it's afloat."

"The *Resolve* is a convalescent home," said Michael hotly. "I've yet to lose a case I've taken aboard."

"I wouldn't try explaining that in America," said Farrar. "Rely on that white flag—it's safer."

They both fell silent on that as the *Hirondelle* skimmed among the first of the harbor shipping with all the easy grace of her namesake. A full-rigged ship, with her whitewashed gunports gaping, and an officer in each ratline, was tacking heavily upstream and leaning on her starboard scuppers to give the *Resolve a* wide berth to leeward. Michael scowled at the candy-stripe flag at her mizzen. The vessel's finicking maneuver and the concerted glare of those officer-manned telescopes had driven Farrar's point home neatly enough.

"The American brig, *Saranac,*" said the overseer. "Shall we cut across her bows, and give the skipper what-for?"

"Land me at the Long Wharf. If there's a war to be fought, it'll need surgeons. I can serve as well from this side."

He had expected great changes under the bluff. The sleepy morning stir along the wharf was strictly as he remembered it when he set foot on José Aravello's stringpiece, dodged under the bowsprit shrouds of a moored barkentine, and made his way toward the shed that housed his surgery. Stevedores were loading a squat merchantman that flew the British flag and cursing the muggy weather with no more than their usual gusto. From the open doors of the Silver Dollar a few sleepy roisterers, unaware that it was now morning, were arguing, just as gloomily, over a final nightcap.

He hesitated at the swinging door and wondered if he needed a bracer of his own, but that craven thought perished on the threshold. Dr. Hilary Tyler, as befitted an elder colleague, would drink enough for two today. Since he could not bring Dimity an unencumbered heart, he would face her with a clear head—and hope for inspiration before he betrayed himself.

At the steps that led up to the surgery he paused to check the town above. The houses that lined the bluff stared back at him with a hundred shuttered eyes: evidently the news of the Spanish landings on Amelia had spread during his absence. There was no other sign that today might be a milestone in Fernandina's history. On the ramparts of Fort San Carlos the green-crossed flag still whipped smartly in the offshore breeze; a uniformed guard at sentry-go paraded with his customary shamble, paused to curse an unseen comrade in the court below, and continued his lonely prowl.

Michael turned to sweep the harbor one more time and counted seven ships anchored at intervals about the *Morgiana's* mooring buoy. Irwin's own ship was stripped for action, her ten-pounders winking in the sun that had just climbed above the bluff. The other privateers (bright-painted birds of prey, their colors as polyglot as their flags) all but blended with the other shipping at anchor offshore. Only an experienced eye would have marked the masks that concealed their gunports, the neat boxes that housed the swivel guns amidships. Obviously there were many such eyes aboard the *Saranac;* and yet, that American visitor had already taken the wind on her quarter and was coasting north to her own waters. If the United States intended to interfere in the affairs of Fernandina, it seemed unlikely that intervention would come today. Fernandina would fight this battle alone.

Glancing up the steep side of the bluff, Michael was in time to see Roger Farrar top the stairs and vanish down Sevilla Street in the direction of the Prado. Perhaps his visit would be effective after all: Irwin would certainly respect the report of Adam Leigh's minion. Dr. Michael Stone might well have accompanied Farrar on the first leg of that errand—and turned in at his own door to see how his wife was faring. Instead, he squared his shoulders and entered the surgery at last—admitting that he was postponing his meeting with Dimity and hating himself for the admission.

This morning the surgery was luminous with early sunlight

gleaming on neatly scrubbed instruments, geometric patterns of splints, piles of freshly rolled bandages. Ulee, the Seminole kitchen helper, sat facing Tola across the big work table, cutting compresses under his watchful eye; Gator, the brand-new bodyguard, squatted on his heels at Tola's feet, to put the last touches on a traction box. Dimity herself, comfortable in a padded armchair at the table's head, smiled up at her husband's astonishment and offered him her lips without a word.

"Come right in, Mike. You're just in time for the war."

"What on earth——?"

Dimity kissed him again: her lips were warm and trusting—and laughing a little, as she indicated the handiwork on the table.

"You said I could be your nurse, if trouble came. Dr. Hilary thought we'd best be prepared."

"You've enough splints here for an army."

"We may need them. Already there are fourteen wounded in the shed downstairs." Dimity's lips were unsmiling now; she put a hand on Michael's arm, as though she would ask forgiveness in advance for bad news. "We needed you here last night, darling—but we managed."

He walked to the window while he fumbled for an inward calm to match his manner. In a way, what distressed him most was that outward ease, and Dimity's acceptance. Try as he might, he could feel no sense of betrayal, now he was actually in her presence—no need to explain that he could never be the same husband again. That a ghost stood between them now, a compelling phantom that no charm could exorcise. . . . He brushed these imponderables aside as he faced her again. Thanks to the crisis that hung over Fernandina, his own crisis could wait awhile.

"Where did you produce fourteen wounded?"

"There was a skirmish outside the walls, Mike. Dr. Hilary can describe it better than I."

"Where is he now?"

"Downstairs—if he's back from his early calls."

Here was an easy escape, but Michael rejected it firmly. Instead, he sat beside his wife and folded her hand between his own.

"Of course you did your share of nursing."

"All yesterday, and a fair part of the night."

"You don't look tired."

"I'm not tired in the least. Felippa spelled me after midnight. I'm spelling her at noon."

"You'll do nothing of the kind. The *Hirondelle* is at the wharf with a full crew aboard. I'm ordering them to take you to St. Marys—now."

"Haven't we been over this before, dear?" Her smile had come back to counterpoint his level gravity. "Haven't I explained where I belong?"

His eyes lingered on her. He kissed her with real feeling, letting tenderness invade his spirit with its own peculiar balm.

In a loose smock, her pregnancy was hardly noticeable as she sat bolt upright in the armchair to accept his kiss with pride. This morning she could have passed for an excited, not-too-tired child who has been permitted to sit up for a great event—and insists on waiting out the delay. Her flushed, unpretty face had a quiet attraction of its own, as though she were hoarding her happiness against the curious prodding of the world. . . . This is my girl, he told himself; this is the waif who gave me shelter, my hostage to the future. Come what may, she'll never know that my love belongs elsewhere.

Aloud, he said only, "You're stubborn as a back-country mule, my sweet. I should beat you oftener."

"You can't beat me for a while. I'm in the family way."

He looked 'round the busy circle in the surgery, who returned his stare with the grins of privileged friends. "Dimity! Remember your manners."

"Remember yours; you threatened me first."

"Very well. A lady with child has no business nursing wounded men."

"But this lady enjoys it. And she'll promise not to overdo. Moderate exercise is good for the prospective mother. You said as much yourself, when we took those long walks on the beach."

"I came here with Farrar; *he* came direct from Leigh. Coppinger is sending gunboats from Augustine. They'll shell the town if it resists."

"We'll work from this surgery, Mike. And it's part of the Long Wharf. You know they won't drop a shot near José Aravello's warehouses. No matter which side wins. They're much too valuable."

Michael threw up his hands. "Tola could take you aboard by force."

"You won't send me away, Mike. You're going to need me today—really and truly. I feel it in my bones."

He felt his eyes mist under her steady, trusting look. He kissed her again, with a brusqueness he did not feel. "Just for that, I'm going down to Hilary. Don't leave her, Tola. I may change my mind."

As he had expected, the shed that had always served as an overflow to their floating hospital was crowded with truckle beds and filled with the groans of wounded men. Willi squatted in the entrance, fanning away the worst of the flies; Dr. Hilary Tyler, his beard an uncombed wilderness in the sunlight that cut in from the wharf, was lashing a splint in place as Michael paused beside him. To his surprise he saw that the older doctor was cold sober and intent on his work: it was a bit of good fortune he had not dared to hope for today.

Felippa stirred in the gloomy depths of the shed and came up with a chair. Michael thanked her with a quick smile, but the witch's eyes were veiled as she hurried on to the next bed.

"Take this, Hilary. You need rest more than I. Let me finish with that splint."

The old doctor subsided gratefully and fumbled in the pocket of his bloodstained ulster for the inevitable wicker flask. "Join me in an eye opener, my boy? I'd say you could stand one too."

"Thank you, no." Michael kept his attention on the wound, a simple fracture of the tibia, which Hilary had swabbed and set with unusual skill. It's the smell of powder that brings out his best, he thought. I'll bed him down for the present and take him to the field when the fight is really joined. . . .

"You're looking at our worst case," said Tyler. "I needed laudanum to set that bone. But he'll be out of shock when he wakens."

"Don't tell me you set this bone in the scrub?"

"They brought him in by litter. The others walked their wounds in to me, and sucked at their bottles while I probed."

Hilary blinked owlishly across the hunched figure in the cot and yielded to the luxury of a massive yawn. "But of course you haven't heard how it happened. Irwin sent out skirmishers to pin down the location of Walters' camp. Instead, they visited the first empty plantation house on the route, and broke open the still."

Michael sniffed the close air of the shed, and nodded his understanding. Most of the wounded, he saw, were still deep in the blissful coma of drunkeness. The few who had emerged from alcohol-drugged sleep stared at him with torpid eyes and sighed out their pain as the numbing effect of the spirits dwindled from their nerve ends.

"Drunk as billy goats and roaring for a fight," said Hilary. "It didn't help when Walters marked their position and closed in. Shooting from the scrub, and dropping their targets like squirrels. Nine dead for the Spanish militia to bury before their officers could whip them into some kind of retreat." He yawned again and drank deep from the bottle in his fist. "Do you mind if I sample the same potion, now you're here? Believe me, it made our work easier yesterday."

"Drink all you like, so long as you're on your feet by afternoon. I'll check these cases in the meantime and plan some kind of field hospital."

"D'you think Irwin will fight, after this fiasco?"

"Judging by the way his privateers are deployed in the Amelia, he means to make some kind of stand. Farrar's at the fort now, offering him a chance to surrender with honor. My guess is that it's only a gesture on Coppinger's part. The Spaniards are on the island in force. Obviously they're itching to throw everything they have at Fernandina—and smoke out the last monkey."

Dr. Hilary Tyler drank once again and considered this pronouncement gravely. "I've just come from the stockade. Irwin has fifty men at the gate and another fifty in the blockhouses. Every cannon in the fort is trained on the approaches. As you say, that little fleet of allies is ready to rake the enemy's flank if they dare to show their faces." The old man's nostrils dilated, for all the world like a cavalry charger that scents the battlefield. "On the other hand, the Spaniards outnumber us ten to one."

"Four to one, perhaps. Remember *I've* checked the muster roll with Farrar."

"Have it your way. Four to one is a figure to give most heroes pause—especially if the bulk of your effectives is composed of riff-raff who'd rather loot than fight. Is it true that they're moving artillery to McClure's Hill?"

"Irwin can answer that now, if he has a telescope in his sentry tower."

Hilary shrugged eloquently—and bounced to his feet with the gesture, swaying from a vertigo that was half weariness, half Jamaica rum. "Medical men, as you should know, are only wasting time when they debate military strategy. A good battle surgeon catches forty winks when he can—as *I* have every intention of doing."

"Take your rest, Doctor. You've earned it."

"Call me at noon," said Dr. Hilary Tyler. "Call me sooner, if I'm needed."

He lurched into the blinding sunlight of the Long Wharf, bowed solemnly to his successor, and vanished in the blot of shadow that now covered the stairs to the surgery. Michael was still smiling at that exit when he felt Felippa's presence at his elbow. He turned quickly, trying to keep that smile intact, and conscious that he had failed in advance.

Felippa said only, "The wounded rest quietly, Inglés. Most of them are too drunk to know they are hurt. It is a good time to check Dr. Hilary's work."

They made the rounds on that solemn note, pausing briefly at each bed to lift or change a dressing, testing pulse and forehead for signs of fever. For the most part, the older doctor had done an admirable emergency job. As he had indicated, nearly all the cases were bullet wounds, with the splint case the only serious casualty. Here and there Michael noted torn tissue where Dr. Tyler's forthright probe had been a shade too abrupt in filching the deadly lead pellet from arm and thigh and buttock. At this early date there was not a single laceration that showed the storm warning of gangrene in the making.

"They will scream when they have slept off the rum," said Felippa. "They will curse the day that they left their Georgia farmland to seek easy riches. But most of them will live to plunder once again."

Michael met her eye directly now. Felippa was an old friend: he could speak his mind in her presence with no regrets. "Thank God Dr. Hilary was sober last night. I'll say no more."

"Dr. Hilary is always sober when he is really needed. As you see, he goes now to wallow with his bottle for a while. But he will be waiting at the stockade this afternoon, when you go out to save your first wounded."

"So there's to be a battle after all. Is that your prophecy?"

"The time has moved beyond prophecy, Señor Médico. This new usurper must fight for what he had stolen here, or go back to New York a beggar. I am told New York is a great city—the greatest in America. Cities do not welcome beggars."

Felippa's hooded eyes stared down at the bloody dressing in her hands. She dropped the cloth in a basin with the air of an aristocrat spurning dross. "Look in the man's mind, Doctor. He will fight today, and pray that a stroke of luck will turn the scales in his favor. Tomorrow, if he is still in Fernandina, he will sell the port to the highest bidder."

Michael, washing his hands just inside the door, accepted a clean towel from Willi and faced the witch as casually as he could. Felippa had prophesied before, and he had learned to respect those prophecies. Instinct told him to let her go in peace even as a perverse demon urged his tongue into its next indiscretion.

"The filibusters will fight the Spaniards today. We're agreed on that. Who will win the victory?"

"The filibusters, through no fault of theirs. The Spaniards will skulk back to the main like frightened dogs."

"When they outnumber this garrison four to one?"

"I have spoken, Inglés. Do not question me further. Look in your heart for the next answer. You will find it there, clean and shining."

It was Michael's turn to step into the blaze of sunlight. Even as he lifted his face to those burning rays, he felt the chill sting his fingertips and burn like ice at his spine. Felippa stood calmly in the doorway with her long, dark hands folded beneath her apron, as though she was daring him to speak again.

"So you read my questions in advance?"

"It is not difficult, Doctor. Like me, you know that it is dangerous to remain in Fernandina today. But you know also that no power under heaven will drive your wife from your side. Few men are blessed with that sort of loyalty. Accept it gladly; do not question it."

"She's in the surgery now. Tola will take her to St. Marys, if I give the word."

"She would only return to you when Tola's back is turned. Such loyalty will win its own reward."

"So she'll come out of this business unharmed?"

Felippa's lips curved in a smile. "Do you trust me that far?"

"Wait, please. I didn't mean to ask. I'm not sure I want an answer. I love her too much for that."

"You cannot love her as she loves you. No man could."

"I know how fortunate I am, Felippa; I've known from the beginning. Grant me that, at least."

The witch's eyes drew him back to the door and held him there, as though they could pin him to the frame. "I will grant you more, Doctor. Much more. You are a good man. I have known *that* too from the first. Dimity is fortunate to have you. There are few enough like you in this world."

"Shall I prove my goodness by going to Irwin and volunteering as a surgeon?"

Felippa just escaped smiling. "You have raised a question. Now you avoid the answer. You wish to feel sure that your wife will escape today's fighting. You wish to prove to yourself that your sin last night will be without retribution."

"I think you've said enough."

"More than enough. If I told you that I can read the dead lust in your eyes, you would call me mad. If I say that you will go to this woman again and yet again, you will hate me for reading your innermost heart. Be content, Inglés; I shall put no curse upon you." Again the witch just missed smiling. "I said you were a good man—not a perfect one. Man was born to lust after many women. It is a law no wife can change."

"No one must know." He drew back, aghast at the ease of that confessional. "What right have you to accuse me? You can prove nothing."

"Only that your feeling for your wife is unchanged. Today, like all good men who are fresh from sinning, you feel unworthv. Do your work, Doctor, and keep your own counsel. The feeling will pass. No man can call himself a sinner forever. In time you will tell yourself that devotion atones for most sins."

"If you breathe a word of this to her——!"

But Felippa did not flinch as he let both hands fasten on her shoulders. "Wives who know too much are seldom happy. It is the first lesson a wife must learn. Would I teach her differently?"

"Go to her, Felippa. Persuade her to cross to St. Marys until these troubles are over. Until *I* can"—he hesitated on the next words, then forced them out in a low whisper—"until I can make peace with myself."

"You will make that peace with time, Doctor. And you must not reproach yourself for today. She stays of her own free will. Her will can be as strong as yours. Stronger, if need be."

"Stay with her then. Make sure she keeps to this wharf. The main fight will surely be at the gates—beyond the town."

"I will do my best, Doctor. But I make no promises. There will be many wounded, and she is a good nurse. She will go where she is needed."

Again Michael glanced up at the stair that led to the surgery. Debating the advisability of putting Dimity aboard the *Hirondelle* by force, he abandoned that course once and for all. A small voice (was it that New England conscience on the prowl again?) whispered that it was a too-easy solution. Once Dimity was in St. Marys, it might be logic to *keep* her there. To cover his later meetings with Marian with the husband's oldest subterfuge. . . .

"Very well, Felippa. Let her stay, if that's her desire. Just keep her safe."

"She will not die today," said the witch evenly. "She will live and cleave to you as long as you need her."

"Is that a prophecy too?"

"Call it what you like, Inglés. You will understand the words with time."

He walked into the sunlight again, without quite daring to face her. When he looked back, Felippa had vanished into their impromptu hospital. He shook off the enigma of her final words and waved to Roger Farrar, who was descending the steps from the bluff, three at a time.

The overseer's face was blank as they met in the shadow of a warehouse, where the Long Wharf joined the land. "You're wanted at the fort, Doctor. You and your scalpels, and all the nurses you can drum up."

"So Irwin means to fight?"

"I warned him of the odds; he says he knows them as well as I. Apparently he's willing to gamble—and hold that brig of his in reserve. Take my word for this much: he'll cut and run if things get really hot."

"And let them gut the town in the meantime?"

"He feels he can hold the stockade and enfilade any attack from the blockhouses and the fort. Those guns in the river will stop an attack from the beach. Of course Cervantes can pitch shot into the town from the hill, but Irwin doesn't give a tinker's damn for that sort of damage."

Michael let his eye stray to the wharf where the *Hirondelle* (already making sail at Farrar's appearance) danced impatiently at her moorings. "Perhaps I should take my scalpels downriver to Walters' camp."

"You'll find that Walters has struck camp long ago. His men are thick as ants in the scrub just beyond the town gates, waiting orders to board the stockade."

"Are you betting on the result?"

The overseer pushed back his broad-brimmed hat and offered Michael a dour grin. "Doctors shouldn't bet on wars. Doctors are supposed to save lives and not take sides."

"I'll put a hundred pesos on Irwin's nose, just the same."

"Done," said Farrar, striking palms. "I'll collect on your next visit. Now will you get up to the portcullis before Irwin sends a provost guard?"

Michael climbed the crazily angled stair that led from water front to town, forcing his steps to a tempo that fitted the dignity of Fernandina's chief doctor. At the top, where the stairway ended a rickety wooden platform to Sevilla Street, he paused to glance down at the stringpiece of the wharf. He was just in time to see the *Hirondelle* (a lithe swallow again, now that she was under way) tack saucily under the guns of the *Morgiana,* spin on her heel, and set the first leg of her course to Punta Blanca. And he felt his spirits drop, as though he had deliberately severed a link that bound him to Marian. . . .

MacGregor's green cross still whipped in the breeze as he forced his mind back to the realities of the present and followed the rutted street to the Prado. Fernandina was a ghost town today, the last house bolted to the eaves, the streets empty of even a foraging cat; Fernandina, wise in the ways of filibusters, had crossed once again to the main to sit out the battle. He walked through that silence with his eyes withdrawn, deep in his own self-doubting. At the ancient wooden portcullis of the fort he ignored the guard's salute and stalked into the courtyard with his scowl unchanged—his nose wrinkling against the reek of ancient sweat that seemed to soak the tabby-stone walls, rubbed smooth by generations of itching uniforms.

Today, he saw, the complete uniform was conspicuous by its absence: Irwin's ragged army (or such units as were yawning their way from messroom to open air) seemed as polyglot as their strange attire. Before he could gain the stair to the commandant's office, he counted a dozen moth-eaten British officers' coats and as many light-blue tunics of the United States in the same advanced state of disrepair. One hulking mulatto was buttoned to the gills in a resplendent blood-red dress coat that could have come only from Haiti; another wore nothing at all but tights, hip boots, and a pair of crossed bandoliers that supported two dragging cutlasses. The latter, Michael gathered, was an orderly of sorts. He put an elbow in the fellow's ribs when he tried to bar his path.

"Out of my way! Your general sent for me."

"The general is on the ramparts, Doctor. May I show you the stair?"

"I know the way by heart." But he followed the clanking cutlasses nonetheless, if only for the sake of protocol, across the sandy courtyard with its discouraged mat of Bermuda grass making an idiot's circle around the flagpole; through a dizzy, latrine-reeking underpass, and up the well-worn ladder that tilted to a distant patch of blue and the benison of fresh sea air.

He heard the clink of the general's spurs before he could glimpse the general's spindly booted legs as they stumped the terreplein. Generals in Fernandina—whether they represented the Spanish

Crown or an American syndicate—had a fondness for the terreplein of Fort San Carlos and the clean sweep of bay and wave-harried dunes. (MacGregor had phrased it perfectly: a man could plan his battles with a clearer head when he had the sky at his back and his nostrils free of the rabble stink below.)

General Irwin did not speak at all for a long moment. Stumping to the watchtower and back, fixing a rather tarnished telescope to his eye at each turn in his restless prowling, the general seemed a poor figure of a man, even in this ratty setting. Any one of his officers was a more heroic figure, despite the unshaven jowls and the reek of rum that hung about them. And yet Irwin's authority was evident when he barked a belated greeting. The man might resemble a clerk rather than the commander of a hard-pressed garrison; his aura might suggest the countinghouse rather than the battleground. But there was no mistaking his dogged courage as he fixed Michael with pale fisheyes and barked his question a second time.

"Dr. Michael Stone, General. If you can use me——"

"Do I look the sort of fool who'd refuse a surgeon's help today?"

"I wasn't aware of the disposition of your staff. For all I knew, you brought surgeons aboard your——" Michael hesitated on the word. *Vessel* seemed a bit weasel-mouthed at the moment. *Privateer* was certainly too forthright.

"Pirate's the word, sir," said General Irwin with the same bilious glare. "And it's quite true I shipped a brace of sawbones in Charleston. One of them went ashore in Savannah and was never heard of since. The other's behind bars now for striking an officer." Irwin favored his staff with that same bilious contempt. His staff withdrew to the last man and gathered in a resentful knot at the sentry tower, with a half-dozen telescopes trained on the Amelia. "Perhaps he was wiser than I knew, Doctor. As you see, my officers are busy hating me, because I won't sell out."

"How much did Farrar offer you?" It was the last question Michael had meant to ask, but he was obscurely relieved, now he had given it voice.

Irwin took the jab without blinking. "Four thousand American dollars, Dr. Stone. Half on the barrelhead and the rest when the Spanish flag rises on that staff. Of course I laughed in his face. Aury will pay me twice that amount, and a percentage to boot, if I can deliver this island on Monday."

"You mean Luis Aury, General?"

Michael's voice stuttered on the name despite his inward calm. If Irwin had taken over in MacGregor's absence, the proceeding still held a shade of legality. Aury, as every resident of Fernandina knew, was a bare-faced pirate who had lost his last foothold in the Caribbean a year ago and had roamed without a base since that date, cutting down what prizes he could on the open sea.

"Does my frankness shock you, Dr. Stone? As you'll observe, it's poor weather for manners."

Michael fitted the proffered telescope to his eye and swept the horizon to the south. What he saw brought a gasp to his lips. To the naked eye, the palmetto wastes of Amelia Island were empty as the moon and drowsing in midday heat haze. Under the glass, he could see a dozen antlike columns of men moving into battle line among the scrub oaks a mile to the south; the pall that hung above the powder-dry savannah there to the west was not mist, but a whirlwind of dust raised by a hard-pressed ammunition train in the act of wallowing from marsh to higher ground. On McClure's Hill the iron snouts of at least five mortars were tilted into the blazing sky like the beaks of lazy birds. There was no sign of gunners as yet, but another fan-shaped cone of dust, hanging above the hill like a miragelike extension of its actual contour, advertised the stir of infantry on the far slope.

"May I commend your courage, sir?"

"You may indeed," said Irwin—and snatched back the telescope. "I won't call your attention to my navy. You can see *that* without a lens. Or to the intrepid gunners who are shivering in the sunlight down below. Or would you prefer to count heads on the ramparts? I refer to the stockade at the town gate, Doctor, where we must withstand the first blow. Of course most of my staff will cling to these stone walls and supervise my artillery."

Michael snatched the telescope in turn and studied the stockade in detail. As he remembered, it was stoutly built of palmetto logs and capable of withstanding any punishment, save cannon at point-blank range. At the distance, the motley crew that manned the gun ports and loopholes seemed formidable enough—dozing like good soldiers up to the last possible moment or drawing murderous beads on the squadron of vultures that circled prophetically over the burnt-out ground beyond.

"I'll set up my field unit in the blockhouse, if there's room."

"Suppose we beat them off and move out to cut their retreat?"

"I'll have three male nurses and an assistant. All of us are accustomed to working under fire. If your army moves, we'll move with the army."

General Irwin accepted the hyperbole with the same peevish alacrity. "Tell me one thing before we go down the line. Why did Leigh's overseer come here today with that offer?"

"I happen to be Adam Leigh's estate doctor in my spare moments. He seldom discusses his politics in my hearing."

"The question was rhetorical, Doctor. I've had the answer up my sleeve from the beginning. Adam Leigh is a large-scale pirate who wants no other pirate on his doorstep. We all know he financed MacGregor because he thought that Scotch woolgatherer would create a republic of sorts here—and make it stick long enough to cover Leigh's own skulduggery—or should I say his shipments of black gold across the border? Jared Irwin and Luis Aury are birds of another stripe—and he'd pay dearly to keep this corner of the Floridas as his own."

"Do you plan to threaten him later?"

"I plan to exist on Amelia. Isn't that enough for now?"

"More than enough," said Michael, still sweeping the terrain with the general's verdigris-colored telescope.

"Look to the south, Doctor. Far south, beyond that spur of land tufted with cabbage palms. Can you make out the topsails of a vessel moving into position in the channel?"

"Perfectly. Is that the beginning of your bombardment?"

"Spoken like an amateur tactician, sir. I've the best gunners in the Caribbean aboard that brig. Watch the harbor now; you'll see that three others are quitting my main echelon, to make the fire continuous. I shall begin it in just sixty seconds, like a good pirate. A full three hours before the expiration of my truce."

"You'll have the militia in town before noon."

"Never mind those militia. I've spies in their camp, and I've counted noses. Without that Cuban company behind the hill, they'll never board the stockade. And the Cubans won't move until it's too late. I'm not contenting myself with pitching cannon balls into the scrub, Doctor. I'm beaching half my army behind Walters' flank—and cutting down that ammunition train before the mud dries on the drivers' boots."

Michael studied Jared Irwin with a new respect—and tempered that judgment instantly. Irwin's low-voiced confidence was vitiated by his bantam strut, the nearsighted glare that swept the scrub without seeing it at all. A map soldier who can speak by the book, thought Michael. A graduate clerk who's learned to cut throats with a pen—and blusters now because he's restless in the open air. That cherry-red blister of sunburn on his forehead tells more than all his talk of strategy.

A cannon boomed dully in the misty estuary, followed by a whole muffled salvo. Michael grinned behind the telescope as General Irwin shied away from the sound. The glass picked out the plumes of cannon smoke, like the floating feathers of some prehistoric bird—snared for a moment in the nest of cabbage palms that masked the privateers' station, then drifting away in the heat haze. Irwin took back his authority with his telescope and watched the smoke lift in a second salvo. The antlike scurry of men, far down the sandy road, vanished into the scrub as though it had never been; Irwin chuckled deeply, as the god who had decreed that scramble for cover.

"Give me an hour, Doctor; they'll come out of those thickets in droves with their hands in the air."

"So you mean to fight them *outside* the stockade?"

"Naturally. I must take the offensive, or I'm lost."

"May I wish you luck before I go?"

"Don't. I'm still not sure which side you're on."

"Does that matter—since I *am* a doctor?"

"Not too much, I suppose." Irwin bowed from the waist and lapsed into a Spanish that was both florid and inaccurate. "Go with God."

"Go with God, General."

But Irwin stopped Michael, with one foot on the ladder that

descended to the court. "We haven't agreed on terms. Naturally, I'll pay you your full contract rate."

"The Duke paid me twenty pounds a day on the Peninsula."

"Today's battle will be worthy of Wellington. Twenty pounds till midnight, then?"

"I'd prefer a hundred American dollars. In gold."

"Why do we bargain?" said Jared Irwin. "You have only to name your terms."

Michael could not quite suppress the next question. "What if the battle goes against you? How do I know I'll be paid?"

"Come, Doctor. Can you doubt the language of those cannon in the Amelia?"

Michael laughed aloud. "I'll take your generalship on credit. In the meantime, *mucha suerte!* Do you know enough Spanish to translate that?"

"More than enough," said Irwin—and resumed his pacing.

Michael held his ground and studied his man at leisure. Deep in the strategy of the coming battle, Jared Irwin had forgotten him long ago. Stumping the length of the terreplein, glaring alternately at the sullen knot of officers and the sweep of palmettos at his feet, he was a grotesque Napoleon—a Napoleon who was not without a vitality all his own. A weasel emperor, more than willing to gamble with an untried force, in a land he was invading for the first time. Michael shook his head, as he recalled how Irwin's prototype had achieved world-shaking results in a setting not too dissimilar.

Another salvo rumbled dully across the scrub as the privateers, tossing round shot from the harbor, forced the advancing militia to scatter once again. McClure's Hill answered the defiance at long last. As a man in a dream, Michael watched the roof of a house in Fernandina splinter under the blow of a giant's fist, watched the quick tongue of flame lick from chimney to rooftree as a forgotten chunk of fire leaped into life under that iron impact. . . .

He went down the stair soberly enough, forcing himself to run a little as he burst from the portcullis into the full glare of the Prado. Another round shot whined overhead, as insistently as a banshee bound on an unknown errand. He watched the tabby stone pulverize in a gray-white cloud above the gateway he had just quitted. Jared Irwin barked an order from the ramparts overhead; there was a mighty thud of feet on the terreplein, the screech of ropes in pulleys as the landward-facing guns swiveled into position to reply to this insult from without.

Michael did not wait for the answering salvo from Fort San Carlos. He was running in earnest now, shocked to the depths of his being by the image that had just formed behind his eyelids as they had closed under the impact of the near-miss. Marian, naked and shining as a pagan's dream of heaven. Marian, with her arms held out to his approach. . . . A man on the brink of eternity had no right to such flaming images. He banished them sternly as he ran down the stair to reassure a wife who needed no reassurance—a wife who would survive this day, and worse, if he could close his heart to this subtle invasion.

X

Hours later, wriggling forward like a weary snake behind Irwin's skirmish line, pausing to be sure of Dr. Hilary's labored breathing in his wake, he was alive again and glorying in a *raison d'être* that banished thought for a while.

Ahead—but not too close for comfort—he could hear the rapid staccato of small sticks breaking. A sound that meant war the world over—in this case, rifle fire from Walters's stubbornly resisting militia. To the left, where the scrub rose on a slight incline to merge with the seaward-facing dunes along the beach, he could hear a devil's slashing among the palmettos and the mingled cursing of men locked in a stubborn contest for the higher ground beyond. It had been like this since noon, when Irwin had burst from the shelter of the Fernandina stockade to drive back Walters's skirmish line. It had continued, with small wolf flurries in hammock and savannah, as ground was lost and won again—and Dr. Michael Stone, as befitted a good contract surgeon, had fumbled in bloody earth to save what lives he could.

He rose to hands and knees now, then bent double in a quick scurry to the shelter of the palmetto clump ahead. Dr. Hilary Tyler, heavy as a Saint Bernard deep in cockleburs, heaved up at the same moment and moved in Michael's steps. Together they knelt beside the wounded man, who thrashed in his sand wallow, as despairingly as a fish that has leaped into the wrong element and knows it will never breathe again.

"Straight through the throat," said the older doctor. "It's a wonder he's breathing at all."

Michael confirmed the diagnosis as he knelt beside a casualty that was already beyond help. The sailor, sprawled in his death agony in that sandy hollow, was little more than a boy—and, like a child too far from home, he fixed these strangers with beseeching eyes to beg for succor that had come too late. A musket ball, piercing his throat from ear to ear, had ruptured the carotid artery long ago. Michael probed mechanically for a point of contact, knowing in advance that such a wound was beyond the surgeon's fingers. The ruptured larynx wheezed with the death rattle as the boy's body gave one last despairing heave, then lay still at last.

"Someone's calling in the next clump."

"Stay where you are, Hilary. It's my turn to stick up my head."

Michael inched forward, nursing the last scrap of cover as he answered the bellow from the palmetto screen ahead. Without looking back, he knew that Dr. Hilary Tyler was squirming in his wake, as always. Like a war horse scenting battle, the older doctor had more than pulled his weight today.

A bugle shrilled from the slope of McClure's Hill, but Michael did not even glance up from his snakelike progress through the palmettos. Bugles had shrilled all through that afternoon, while the Spanish guns on the summit dueled with Fort San Carlos, joining their thunder to the quarrel in the harbor, as the ships from St. Augustine moved up to dispute with the privateers. Working under that broiling sun, his whole being concentrated on spurting artery and broken limb, he had learned to ignore such martial echoes. . . .

"Easy does it," said Dr. Hilary Tyler, and scampered into a hollow among the palmettos with all the grace of a homing goat. "Here's our boy—in fact, there's two of 'em."

The first case, Michael saw instantly, was the bellower—a sallow-faced young officer from Irwin's ship, nursing a fractured arm and screaming his agony to the indifferent sky. The second case was a more serious matter—another boy, naked save for tattered nankeen pantaloons, wallowing in a bath of blood that still pumped in a bright red fountain from his thigh.

"The femoral artery," said Hilary Tyler. "Will you take it, Michael?"

"If I may. Tell that second mate to stop howling. He'll live to fight again."

Hilary Tyler scampered to the officer's side and whipped a splint from the haversack on his shoulder. Michael did not even turn to watch his companion soothe the wounded man into a position that would permit a quick setting of the bone. The old doctor had performed a dozen such emergencies today and sent the casualties back to the stockade on their own legs. Michael's own case, thrashing rapidly into the coma that precedes death, called for instant attention if he was to be saved at all.

It was a simple matter to slash away the blood-soaked sailor's trousers, to expose the jagged bullet tear below. Enlarging the wound with a long scalpel cut, Michael had already whipped a tourniquet high about the leg; twisting it now with all his strength, he watched the pump of blood falter and die in the wide exploratory incision his free hand was making. Two-handed surgery had saved lives before, when he worked at the Boca. His fingers moved swiftly now, following a routine he could have practiced in the dark.

The boy was still strong enough to writhe in protest at the cruel bite of the tourniquet. Michael soothed his body in the sandy wallow even as he dragged him to a less exposed point. The sharp-pointed tenaculum forcep came into his hand with no waste motion: he had gone into the fight with that invaluable instrument slung at his neck by a lanyard. Already he could see the pale stalk of the artery pulsing faintly in the depths of the wound; the forcep closed and held, lifting the vessel into plain view. Michael slipped the loop of a ligature into place, lifting the handle of the tenaculum with that gesture so that he could clench it between his teeth—a trick he had learned in his first ship surgery, when he had been forced to operate without an assistant.

With both hands free, he tightened the knot, letting the whipcord stream free. Another knot was placed for insurance on the far side of the forcep; the vessel dropped back into its bed as the steel jaws released their bite. He released the tourniquet gradually and sponged away the superficial bleeding: the femoral artery, cinched in its double knot, had been closed with only minutes to spare, but he was sure that his patient had a fair chance at life.

Strapping a temporary dressing across the wound, his whistle already at his lips to summon his nearest litter-bearers, Michael noticed the quiet for the first time. The bugle, shrilling once again from the slope of the hill, cut through that stillness like a brassy knife. It was a soothing stillness—heat-drugged as any Florida afternoon in September, but wrapped in a peculiar hush all its own. At that moment he felt himself happily apart from the battle, happily alone with his thoughts—and, for the first time, willing to face up to those thoughts directly.

Hilary had gone back through the palmettos to guide his casualty to the road: the faint swish of those dusty fronds was the only sound that reached him besides the breathing of the unconscious boy whose head rested on his knee. He whistled again, and let the quiet enclose him completely. It was evident now that the battle had moved on to another, as yet unknown, plane. Perhaps they were parleying now on McClure's Hill. Or feeling out each other's position before the next burst of firing, the hand-to-hand extermination in the tangle of cedar and bay grape that masked the northern approaches to the hill. (Battles, regardless of their dimensions, ebbed and flowed at no set tempo, despite the neat bursts of flame that etched the heroic canvases, and the poet's pentameters.)

The explanation was logical enough—though it hardly accounted for the sudden end of cannonading from both fort and river. Michael whistled again for his bearers and settled back tranquilly when he heard Tola's distant halloo. In another moment this boy would be whisked safely down the trail to Fernandina—another item for the beds that now overflowed from their hospital in Aravello's shed and spread in a great white fan across the Long Wharf itself. There were the less seriously wounded, writhing feebly beneath their sheets; the lung cases, gasping for water; the three amputees (he had saved them with Hilary's help) deep in the coma of morphine, shaded from the sun by the grass mattings that his litter bearers had spread between the bowsprits of two moored vessels. Dimity would be moving among those beds like a ministering angel as the blazing afternoon waned at last, with Ulee and Felippa to assist her. Side by side with his wife in these endless visits of mercy, Señora Aravello and Madame Chica, the only other women who had lingered in Fernandina after the start of the cannonading, would help to save lives. . . .

Michael leaned back comfortably against the sandy bank and checked what he could see of Fernandina through the screen of pines. Streets were burning now, down their entire length—including the Calle de las Damas, fired by a direct hit from McClure's Hill a scant half hour after Madame Chica had evacuated her young ladies to the mainland. He could mark the splintered sentry tower on the fort itself, the gaping roof of a house here and there that he recognized, where the fire had not spread. From where he sat he could not tell if his own house had escaped injury. Somehow it did not matter greatly, now that Dimity was safe below the bluff.

Nothing mattered (when you came down to cases) but the integrity of that small person's love—and his own resolve to keep their marriage inviolate. Nothing that had happened last night could shake the firmness of that resolve. If his love belonged elsewhere, if he yearned for Marian Leigh as he had never yearned for food, drink, or immortality, he could keep that yearning from Dimity. Or so he reasoned now, at the tag end of this weary day. A brain that had battled death with all its skill and won a fair share of the battles could turn back to life again (and Dimity, he insisted stoutly, was the essence of his life no less than Marian). A body tired from eight hours in sun and palmetto could go home to its legal counterpart—hoping to be faithful for a time, at least. . . .

Tola and Willi tumbled into the hollow with a bloodstained leather stretcher. Dr. Hilary followed on their heels, incoherent with news.

" 'Twas a glorious victory, my boy. Why aren't you up on that hill, cheering?"

The old doctor's tone was noticeably blurred; Michael remembered the half-gallon jug he had brought into the scrub, ostensibly to brace the wounded against a bullet probe.

"The war's moved on, Hilary. We'd best move with it."

"I'm telling you I just met Irwin's own adjutant on the road. The war's over."

As though to emphasize his words, Dr. Hilary leaped boldly to the top of the little rise that, only a few moments ago, had screened them from Spanish bullets. Michael made a quick dive for his colleague's legs, but Dr. Hilary eluded him nimbly as he rose to his full height and surveyed at the open ground to the south.

"Look out there, if you won't believe me. Those woods are empty as Eden. So's the road beyond, and the hill itself. Spain's in full retreat and the island's ours. Or will be by morning, when they've covered their crossing to the main——"

Michael hesitated for another moment as he turned a veteran's ear to the quiet woods ahead. It seemed incredible that Walters's militia—which had peppered their advance so briskly all through the afternoon—had yielded that broken ground without a struggle. Yet there was no denying the emptiness that bounced Dr. Hilary's shout back to them in a mocking echo. . . .

"Put a white flag on that stick. Whether you're right or wrong, we've got to finish our job."

"You'll find no more wounded, Doctor. The accursed enemy is licking his own bruises as he withdraws. Irwin, like a wise conqueror, sent a cease-fire order to ships and fort. So long as he holds the road, and the hill, they've no choice but retreat."

"What makes you so sure he's on the hill?"

"The Spanish gunners deserted their mortars a half hour ago. You can see for yourself, when we reach the highroad."

Again Dr. Hilary skipped boldly from thicket to open ground and stalked into the wide, rutted road without so much as a sidelong glance. Michael, holding his breath gingerly for the shot that did not come, followed him with the truce flag held high—a device that had saved his life more than once today, when he had moved forward to operate in enemy terrain.

"Of course you can't tell me why."

"I've a perfect picture of the battle," said Dr. Hilary indignantly, "Like many greater generals, Irwin owes today's triumph to a combination of luck and gall."

"Granted. But why should the Spaniards retreat, when they outnumber him?"

"Point one, their ammunition reserve was cut off and captured in the savannah an hour after the action began. Point two, they counted much too heavily on that battery they'd planted atop McClure's Hill. Granted, it commanded the town: they could pulverize the houses at will. But their shot could do no more than raise a cloud of oyster dust on the fort: they couldn't call the range on the wharves beneath the bluff without dropping death on their own wounded——" Hilary paused to catch his breath and chuckled. "You were wise to bring in wounded from both camps and let it be known that the lot was taken to The Long Wharf."

"Never mind *my* higher strategy. I was only thinking of Dimity. Why didn't Cervantes take the town by storm the moment the truce was ended? He had more than enough men to go over the stockade and pen Irwin in the fort."

"You can't storm a stockade without ammunition."

"A hundred first-class boarders could have broken into Fernandina this afternoon, with nothing but cutlasses and courage."

Dr. Hilary squatted pontifically in the grateful shade of an oleander bush on the first steep slope of the hill. Dead ahead, where the scrub oak jungle widened into pinywoods, Michael noted a strip of fought-over ground—one of a dozen small battlefields that had been contested when Irwin sallied forth from his fortress. Lost and won and lost again, it was tumbled thick with bodies. He counted twenty inert cloth bundles, sprawled in the ungraceful abandon of death. Most of the casualties were militia, he noted absently, though a few wore the nondescript sailor garb that marked the victors. Here and there (where they had been spied out and blasted from cover with accurate musket fire) a soldier of the Royal Cuban Guards lay spread-eagled in the coarse grass. Despite their scarlet tunics and magnificent gaitered shanks, these effectives of His Catholic Majesty's looked no less dead than their enemies.

"You've yet to explain the retreat."

Dr. Hilary took up his story with no indication that the thread had been broken. "Cutlasses and courage might have won the day —if there'd been a driving will behind them. Unfortunately, the command was entrusted to the wrong man—in this case, a colonel fresh from Madrid. My guess is that he was burning with resentment that he should be assigned a Negro company. To say nothing of a filibuster as his first antagonist."

"Then it was Cervantes who sounded retreat?"

"Who else could call off Walters' militia when they were picking off our boys like squirrels?"

Dr. Hilary scowled at the open ground ahead and sucked at his rum bottle. "Irwin's adjutant gave me the picture—and I don't doubt the truth of this part. Cervantes was suffering from a soldier's most vexing disease all during today's action. Dysentery, in its most malignant form. Nothing under heaven can so distort a man's judgment—or sap his heroism. . . . Try to see our Spanish nemesis, fighting his first battle from the palmettos, as it were. Hearing Walters' guns snapping all day, to say nothing of those ships in the river. Hating the whole pack of moccasin boys for their daring. Knowing he was in absolute command—and doing nothing."

Michael settled on a fallen cedar well within the screen of oleander and bay grape. "If you insist on an audience, Doctor——"

"I'm only trying to part the murky curtains of war for you, Michael." Dr. Hilary looked faintly hurt as he took another prodigious pull on his bottle. "I'm trying to put you in the fine varnished boots of that brand-new warrior."

"Heaven forbid!"

"Come out of the scrub for your first real look-see. You've lost your pickets on this side of the hill. Another half dozen have gone up in a twist of sand and perdition when one of your mortars exploded. Capturing that hill *was* a brilliant stroke, but what comes next? With a full company of fighting men, you could turn the battle's scales in a twinkling—if you could tell north from south. Of course you're too proud to call on Walters for advice. And you're far too well trained to advance blindly—as Irwin did."

"So a double handful of pirates drive Cervantes into retreat?"

"Don't blame the cutthroats, Doctor; blame Irwin's bad marksmanship. All day long his gunners were trying to find the range of McClure's Hill. Incredible as it sounds, they hadn't even scouted Cervantes' exact position: they were merely trying to silence those mortars. Eventually enough of their round shot went over the hill, smack into the Cubanos' bivouac. Like so." Dr. Hilary spread his hands, puncturing the sand with agile fingers. "We'll never know who panicked first—the troops or their commander. The fact remains, they've skedaddled. Stick out your head, boy: you'll see MacGregor's cross is flying from the hilltop."

Michael cursed mildly as his colleague stalked into the open, set his straw sombrero at a saucy angle, and began to stump up the hill. Dr. Hilary Tyler's gait was a bit unsteady for such steep climbing, but he had all the sang-froid of a man on a casual promenade. Again Michael waited for a shot that did not come. Perhaps he was ultracautious to skulk here in the bay grape while his older colleague outdistanced him. The green-crossed flag, fluttering on a sapling at the brow of the hill, would certainly indicate that the slope had been cleared of enemy long ago. Only a cautious veteran (and he was anything but that) would insist that there was something sinister in this emptiness. That death still lurked here—waiting to strike one more time, now that the armies had moved on.

He found he was following the older man, as loyalty overcame caution at last. Skirting the tumbled windrow of the dead, he plunged for the next spot of cover as he shouted for Dr. Hilary to do likewise. The shot came at that precise moment, just as he had expected: the faint finger of smoke rose from the palmetto clump ahead; gaitered legs scurried for the next ambush. Michael let out his breath in a whoop of relief when he saw that the bullet had missed Dr. Hilary's head by inches, to splinter harmlessly against a tree. With that shout of warning, he burst into the open in a belated effort to outflank the lone sniper and disarm him between rounds.

Running with his shoulders hunched, zigzagging among the clumps of wire grass lest he draw a bullet of his own, he saw Dr. Hilary's profile, as calmly as a duelist on a chosen ground—saw him whip a pistol from his coattails and take careful aim. The bark of the pistol and the crash of the musket smote his ears like a single report. Hilary, it seemed, had fired a split second ahead of the man in ambush. Michael pulled up with another shout of relief as the sniper, twisting like a gold-and-scarlet top in his nest of palmettos, sprawled face down a scant hundred feet from the old doctor's smoking barrel.

"Between the eyes," said his colleague. "I had no choice." As he spoke, he collapsed in turn, with a black-browed scowl. The long-nosed pistol, plummeting from one nerveless hand, stood upright in the sand. Dr. Hilary, sliding down a pine bole by inches, managed to keep his own face from the sand with a great effort. Using the tree as a chair back, he grinned up at Michael with his humor intact.

"You were right, my boy. We should have scouted our ground

more carefully. Even money says that's the last Cubano on McClure's Hill."

Michael was already on his knees beside the wounded man. "Where did he hit you?"

"Through the chest. In and out. Can't you hear my broken bellows?"

The shirt ripped under the knife. Michael's hands moved automatically now. He had checked several such wounds today, and watched death creep into the congested lungs as the casualty fought for breath. An in-and-out wound stood a chance of recovery, despite the double puncture, if he could stop the bubbling suction at once.

"Only a field surgeon could make such a good self-diagnosis," he said. "Of course it's a wonder you aren't dead now." He had spoken deliberately to sustain Hilary's spirits; the old doctor's grin was his reward.

"Be honest, my boy. How many chest wounds have you saved in your time?"

"Never mind my record. I'm going to save this one."

"The therapy's simple, of course." Dr. Hilary's voice seemed to come from a distance now; his pale lips shaped the words with care. "Seal off wound—or wounds. Stop hemorrhage and air leak. Patient takes over—from there."

"You're going to take over beautifully." Michael was following routine to the letter: double linen pads, at the entry and exit points of the bullet, had stopped the flow of blood for the moment. From this point the patient's needs were simple: absolute quiet and heated blankets to lessen the impending shock. Above all, it was necessary to hold both dressings firm, to make sure that there was no leakage from within or without. With cloture insured, there was a fair chance that the pressure of air within the lungs themselves would stop internal bleeding.

Checking over these imponderables as he worked, Michael felt the old man sag under his hands and eased him into a more comfortable position on the sand. Hilary's lapse into unconsciousness would simplify his task in a way. He blasted on his whistle, repeating the signal at intervals as he planned his next moves—and knowing in advance that there was little likelihood of that signal being answered. Tola and Willi would have reached Fernandina by now. Hearing that the battle had ended in a full retreat of the enemy, they would assume that Michael had followed in their footsteps.

He faced this fact as calmly as he could, and spread his coat under Dr. Hilary's body even as he tossed the other's coat across his legs and chest to conserve what warmth he could. Thanks to the pitiless beat of sunlight on that hillside during the long day, the sand made a warm enough bed: it would retain its heat for some time, now that the day had begun to wane in earnest. If he moved fast—and thought faster—he might still improvise a victory of his own.

The first problem was the anchoring of the double compress—a formidable one without the new adhesive tape he had used in England. He lashed the dressings in place as best he could, whipping a triple length of linen around Hilary's chest and shoulders and knotting it as tightly as he dared. A faint bubbling tortured his ears, but he forced himself to ignore that small leakage. Just above his head, in the pine bole, he found his first substitute for the field technique he had planned—a steady ooze of resin from the wood, where the sniper's bullet had lifted splinters a moment ago. Rubbing a linen square over this laceration in the tree bark, he soon had a sticky, uneven lump of resin, enough to fashion a plaster of sorts, if he could spread it smoothly on the cloth.

He dared to leave Hilary for a moment while he foraged among the dead for a tinderbox. A few pine splinters were all he needed to begin his fire; oozing with that same glutinous sap he had gathered on the cloth, they lighted as readily as wax tapers. He fed the blaze carefully, concentrating it for heat, rotating the cloth above it patiently until the lump of resin melted and spread, like stubborn glue.

Hilary's pulse was thready now, but by no means hopeless; the breathing was fast and not too congested. The leak under the temporary compress was definite, however—air and blood bubbled crimson under the lashed-down linen. With the plaster ready for his hand, he cut the lashings away and kept the wounds closed by pressure for a moment. Timing his motions to Hilary's breathing, he lifted each pad for an instant to study the pouting edges of the bullet holes; so far as he could see, the surface wounds were clean;

there was no indication that the arteries between the ribs had been injured by the bullet's passing.

A single slash of his knife divided the plaster neatly. He slapped a section over each of the bullet holes, smoothing the edges to the skin as carefully as a grocer tamping stickers to his windowpane. He held his own breath as he drew back and listened for the telltale hiss that would show an imperfect cloture; this time, the wounds were sealed completely. The surgeon's job was finished when he lashed two wide linen pads across the bullet holes and wound Hilary's chest and shoulders with all the bandages in his kit, until the old doctor resembled a freshly swathed mummy from collar to breastbone.

His improvision was not quite ended. This time he returned to the dead without shame, to rob them of a dozen coats and as many ulsters. The former, neatly rolled, served as pillows and mattress for the patient; the latter, spread in concentric layers, would give ample protection against the dews that fell in these latitudes after sundown.

So far he had worked smoothly, without pausing to take thought. It was only when he gathered a bundle of dead branches to build a first-rate fire—and noted that only the dregs of sunset lingered above the marshes to the west—that he realized he would make a perfect sitting target if another Spaniard still lingered on the hill. But he shrugged off that possibility as he knelt to listen to Hilary's tranquil breathing. It was a chance he must take, if he expected to leave the scrub before morning; his litter bearers would never find him without a beacon to guide their search.

His battered hunting watch told him that more than two hours had passed since Tola and Willi had carried their last casualty to the blockhouse. It had been almost eight hours since he had had time for his last fleeting visit to the hospital that had mushroomed from his surgery to the planks of the wharf. There were a dozen cases there that demanded his immediate care—amputations whose surgery would need to be revised after the quick patchwork job in the field, fractures to be checked, lung cases like Hilary's that needed attendance urgently. . . . Yet he could not risk leaving the old doctor for more than a moment—and could think of no other way to advertise his presence in this fast-graying wilderness.

He wandered down the slope for an instant, hunting through the huddled dead for an unfired pistol or musket; all the bodies he examined had apparently collapsed on their last ounce of powder. Staring down at a dark, quiet body at his feet (and wondering why he was not more afraid in this grisly company), he realized that such a search was useless, even if he could have fired a rifle shot to announce his need for help. Fernandina had heard too many rifle shots today. Mending its broken walls and dousing the last of its fires, the town would lurk behind closed shutters tonight and pray that the battle of Amelia was really over.

The Cubano's dark face began to gleam with a strange radiance. Michael looked about him and saw that the same glow was reflected on the sandy slope of the hillside, on the cartridge belts of the dead, on his own battle-weary hands. Turning to the source, he was just in time to see the moon thrust up from the Atlantic and show its copper-red disk at the summit of the hill.

For an instant the abandoned mortars stood out gauntly against that huge radiant wafer; then, as the moon bounced free of earthly landmarks (as jauntily as a giant's balloon that had suddenly escaped his grip), the whole flat sea of palmetto came alive and danced a silver rhythm under the breeze that always swept Amelia at dusk, regardless of the season. Listening to that metallic whisper, he felt a strange peace descend upon him. A peace that was part of that bath of moonlight, part of the tired conviction that he had done his work well.

Dr. Hilary moaned faintly; and Michael settled to the sand beside him. Automatically he measured a dose of laudanum in a tin cup from his haversack and poured the soothing drug between the old man's lips. God willing, Dr. Hilary would sleep off the worst of his pain tonight—and waken tomorrow in his own bed, with a better than even chance of surviving a bout of lung fever.

He settled deeper in his warm bed of sand, yielding a little to his bone-deep weariness. The moon was well up now: he could see the Fernandina stockade clearly through the gaps in the pines. There was the road, a wide, pale ribbon in the palmetto sea, laid down neatly from the stockade gate. Tola and Willi, or another brace of litter bearers, would be searching for him any moment now:

he had only to keep his eyelids open and make sure that the red star of his fire continued to glow brightly on the hillside.

Piling another armful of pine knots on the small cheerful blaze, he returned to his patient's side. Dr. Hilary was wrapped in the languor of morphia now as snugly as he was tucked in that cocoon of purloined Spanish uniforms. Michael settled easily at his side, and smiled when he noted two figures far down the road from town. They were still too far away to identify, though he was positive they were moving toward the hill. He could afford to rest now and wait for them to seek him out. He could even risk dropping into a light doze as he admitted how tired he really was. To watch the road through half-closed lids, to dream that his troubles were washed away at last, in the sweat of battle.

The warm earth soothed him into a kind of waking dream. He had earned his right to this land today—to call himself a pioneer in its future. Surely there was some solution to his personal future, even if he had the bad fortune to owe his love to one woman, his devotion to another. . . . He could see the two searchers clearly now as they breasted a slight rise in the road and paused to look anxiously to right and left before they proceeded. He would shout his whereabouts in another moment—when they had topped the next rise and had begun to skirt the hill itself.

His head lolled in the sand; he slept in earnest for a moment, then wakened with a small start of panic. And he smiled drowsily at that irrational fear. Resting in his bed of sand, he knew that he was drawing fresh sustenance from the earth with every passing moment. Like the Greek warrior of the legend, he had fallen only to rise again.

He heard his name called, somewhere in that moonlit palmetto plain, and half rose to his elbow to shout an answer. Yes, he could go back to Dimity now with a clean heart, a high resolve. He had only to whistle for his stretcher-bearers and be on his way.

"Mike!"

It was a cry of agony, stabbing like a hot iron at his heart. It wrenched him to his feet instantly and sent him stumbling down the hillside. Still half awake, he felt his memory somersault backward to a hot afternoon among those same jack pines—when Dimity Parker had come stumbling down a marshy creek bed in search of him. When he had met her at the water's edge, a second before death had struck her like a coiled spring. . . .

"Where are you, Mike?"

With that cry, the two figures came into plain view at the slight rise in the road. He would have known Dimity instantly, even without that wild, wailing question—known that the tall, spare figure at her side was Felippa. And, as his tired mind spun wide awake, he knew just as surely that Dimity was at the end of her strength—that she must reel in that rutted sand and fall like an ungainly sack, just before Felippa's arm could save her.

He guessed the reason for her collapse long before he could kneel beside her: the surgeon's eyes diagnosed instantly, even as the husband's numbed senses recoiled from her next scream, the spreading dark stain in the moonlight. . . .

Felippa said only, "She thought you were dead in the scrub, Inglés. She would let no one else find you."

"Help me, you fool!" In that shout he regained his perspective again: he was a doctor now, with a life to save. "Can't you see what's happened?"

But Felippa was already on her knees beside Dimity. They worked swiftly then, dark hands as deft as white there in the bath of moonlight.

"I feared this would happen," said Felippa. "I feared she would work beyond her strength today. But she said she must find you."

"You should have kept her in Fernandina! Couldn't you see that——"

"You should have sent her to St. Marys." Felippa's tone was infinitely patient.

"You know she wouldn't leave me."

"That is also true. She would not leave you in life: she wished to lie beside you in death. In a moment she will find her reason for living."

Michael drew back a little and met the witch's eyes above Dimity's inert body. He tried to speak again, but no words came.

"Tonight she has lost her child," said Felippa. "She will survive that loss. She will be your wife again as long as you need her. What man could ask for more?"

Again they worked without words—lifting Dimity gently between them, carrying her up the hillside to a softer patch of earth. Felippa spread her dark cloak deftly as Michael lowered the unconscious girl to the impromptu resting place.

"You're right, Felippa. She'll survive this miscarriage. But does it mean that she's too frail to bear a child in the future?"

"Answer your own question, Señor Médico," said the witch. "You are the doctor, not I."

Michael looked away. At the moment he could not bring his eyes down to his wife's face, though Dimity could not see the agony there. The child might well have been a bond between them, a common interest that no outside force could destroy. He put aside that thought quickly. No bond was needed now to keep him at Dimity's side.

But Felippa lifted a detaining hand as he tried to speak again. "She will bear your child again, Inglés—if you wish a child by her."

"How can you question that wish?"

The witch's eyes seemed to pierce his brain, but there was an understanding in their depths. "Even though your heart is given elsewhere?"

"Even so, Felippa. If it's what she wants."

"Men have become fathers before without love, and their issue has prospered. Men have found contentment when happiness was impossible."

"But I love Dimity. I'll always love her!"

"Tell yourself that often. You will believe it in time."

Felippa turned as she spoke and moved up the hillside with long, sure strides. Her bare feet were soundless among the palmettos; she seemed to float among them, a tattered silhouette lacking only a broomstick. When she spoke again, her voice seemed to come from far away.

"I will sit by Dr. Hilary until the bearers come. They have seen your fire from the stockade; they will not be long."

But his voice held her on the slope a moment more. "She must never know, Felippa. I'd never forgive myself if she guessed that I——"

"Do not ask for miracles."

"Why should she know?"

"So long as Adam Leigh lives, you must go to the Point to doctor his slaves. You will meet this woman again. The woman you cannot help loving." Felippa's voice was the barest whisper, though her silhouette was sharp against the moon. "The woman you should have had, Señor Médico——"

Dimity stirred in his arms, and he held up a warning hand. But Felippa had vanished among the jack pines when he looked again. . . . Dimity moaned faintly, and he saw that her lips had shaped his name. Michael cradled her head against his shoulder and leaned back until his face was bathed in moonlight. He wanted his wife to see his face when she opened her eyes again. From that moment he wanted her to believe that he had returned to her in every way.

V

The "River of May"

Cowford, at the warm ending of the winter's day, suited its name to the last crude corral, the last of the short row of cabins that straggled along the high bank of the St. Johns. Standing at the rail of his sloop as that smartly fitted vessel gained way on the wide reach of the river, Michael waved to the tubby Spanish lawyer who still stood beside his skiff on the water's edge. Señor Eduardo Hoyo y San Martin lifted a rolled parchment in symbolic answer—the duplicate of the Spanish land grant that Dr. Michael Stone of Fernandina had signed only a few moments ago, under the flowering poinciana on the bank.

"Hasta mañana, amigo!"

"Hasta mañana, Señor Médico! Buena cosecha!"

A good harvest. That too was in the Spanish tradition: Don Eduardo would have belied his ancestry had he wished the new landowner a lesser bounty. A good harvest before the ink was dry on the document that made Dr. Stone proprietor of five hundred acres on the St. Johns. Florida's most recent man of property watched the lawyer from St. Augustine as that dignitary lowered himself into the stern sheets of his rowboat and signaled grandly to the slave at the oars. The skiff danced across the St. Johns, pointing its bow to the southern bank of the broad tidal river, where horse and escort awaited Don Eduardo for the thirty-mile ride to the Spanish capital.

The sloop, running sweetly toward the sea with a sundog in her teeth and the last stitch of canvas belling, had already dropped the tiny settlement on the north bank far astern. So far astern, in fact, that the handful of weathered cabins had begun to merge with the encroaching scrub.

Tola shouted a warning from the wheel as the sloop came about; Willi, smartly fitted with white ducks and a glazed boater, ran forward to handle the flying jib. Michael leaned at his own taffrail for a moment to watch his crew handle the trim little vessel that was yet to bear a name. Like the purchase he had just consummated on the riverbank, the sloop was a visible proof of prosperity. This afternoon he could pause to take pride in such proofs: land, transport, the burgeoning fortune he had been prudent enough to deposit in London until the political future of the Floridas assumed a definite pattern.

He could even insist that he was part of that pattern now. A Floridian for all time—planning, like all its forward-looking citizens, for annexation to the American Union. A solid family man who would soon be settling on his own broad acres. With the wife of his choice beside him, and children-to-be tumbling in play on the doorstep. . . . The picture faded painlessly. He folded the Spanish land grant into his wallet and walked 'round the corner of the snug afterhouse to sit awhile with Dr. Hilary Tyler.

This afternoon Dr. Hilary basked like an aged tomcat in his canvas chair, his eyes closed against the river glare, his shirt open to the life-giving sun. Sheltered from the wind by the shoulder of the deckhouse, his little corner made an ideal solarium. This too had been part of Michael's therapy when he had invited his colleague to sail down with him from Fernandina to the St. Johns. His wound had healed weeks ago, after a negligible bout of lung fever. Looking for the bullet scar now, Michael could scarcely find the small depression in the snow-white mat that covered the old surgeon's chest.

"Don't let me disturb your dream, Doctor."

Hilary Tyler opened a benign eye and beamed at Michael through his whiskers. "I was dreaming of you, Doctor. Or should I say *Squire,* now that you're one of the landed gentry?"

"I'm afraid we don't allow such titles in America. Was the dream pleasant?"

"Very. In fact, you weren't a squire at all. You were the mayor of a city in the making. Owner of a lumber mill, a whole county of turpentine woods, and six of the busiest docks in all Florida. Spoken of for governor when our territory becomes a state."

"Does all this happen at Cowford?"

"At Cowford, my boy. Of course it's changed its name to something more dignified."

"Thanks for your optimism. But I'm more than content to be a modest river planter when I'm not doctoring."

"You'll be that too, of course. But your plantation will be miles up the St. Johns. Look at that land grant again, Michael. Then look at the map. Can't you see you've bought five hundred acres on a crossroads—to say nothing of the finest river port on this whole coast?"

Michael shaded his eyes to look back at Cowford, but the straggling group of cabins had vanished long ago in the golden haze. The vast surface of the St. Johns (blue as the sea in this wide tidal reach, chocolate-dark at its heart) riffled with whitecaps in the making as the breeze freshened. The flat pine barrens on the northern bank, the haunt of nesting pelicans, seemed untroubled by a single ax blade, and empty as the day the Spaniards came. And yet it was not too hard to give Dr. Hilary's dream the shape of reality.

It was natural that the old King's Highway should cross the river where it narrowed at the so-called Cowford—natural too that a far-seeing man should picture a thriving city, with deep-water docks, along the wide tidal reach just beyond. A glance at the map showed that Cowford was also an inevitable nexus for the permanent highways that must eventually open the peninsula to commerce from the north and west. A man with river acres in his pocket might see the time when the newfangled steamboat hooted at his doorstep, when that equally newfangled monster, the railroad, roared through his backyard. . . . Dr. Michael Stone emerged from that Utopian vision with a chuckle. A hard-pressed surgeon (whose own life needed spadework before it could call its foundation secure) had no right to harbor such chimeras, however briefly.

"So I've bought my share of metropolis. Is that it?"

"Why shouldn't this land have cities someday? It's rich enough."

Dr. Hilary's gesture included the whole horizon; his finger leveled at the hazy spot where the St. Johns narrowed. "Today the Spanish *vaquero* swims his cattle from bank to bank for sale at the Georgia border. Precisely as his grandfather did before him—when and if there wasn't an Indian war, or an American army on the border. Spain has squatted in this land for centuries, like a mangy watchdog—and growled at all comers. No one's impressed by those growls any more: the whole world knows that Florida's wide open to settlement. All that remains is to get the watchdog out of a land he doesn't want."

"What about a government to enforce a few laws?"

"That will develop naturally, when the right men come south with the flag—and join the men who are here." Hilary grinned widely through his whiskers. "I hope your ears are burning, boy. You needn't deny you're one of them."

"I'm an Englishman, Doctor. So are you. Can you explain why we're both so eager to move under the American flag?"

"We aren't moving an inch, Michael. The flag is coming to us. And don't pretend you're English now—if you ever were. You've belonged to the world from the start, just as you belong to Florida now."

"And to Dimity."

"And to Dimity. It's a good settlement."

"Speaking for yourself, Dr. Tyler, where do *you* belong? Or isn't that British passport in order these days?"

"A shrewd guess, Doctor. A renegade Englishman is happy anywhere but in England. Why shouldn't I bask in your shadow—and call myself a citizen again?"

Michael grinned in turn, and stepped out of the path of sunlight. "Right now I'm baking the last of that cough out of your chest. Why do you suppose I recommended this sea voyage?"

"You wanted an expert along when you closed for your land," said Dr. Hilary, unperturbed. "I may be a renegade, but I can smell prime acres in the dark. Yes, and predict just what they'll be worth to a man's grandchildren."

"Your prediction is accepted. I'll file it tonight in my diary."

They both fell silent for a moment, with their eyes on the shifting shore line. Tola leaned on the wheel and shouted again to Willi. Watching the bowsprit swing under the compulsion of those strong brown hands, Michael saw a wide arc of sea open where pine barrens had been an instant before. A gull cried in the clean blue stillness and wheeled to plummet down on an invisible prey in their wake. The sloop, straining like an eager racer at her pole, danced away from the brown confines of the land, coasting the white water of a sand bar in her quest for the open Atlantic.

Hilary said easily enough, "I'd have settled for a trip down to Augustine, and a visit with my old friend Coppinger. Your money has been in the Spanish treasury for weeks now, while we dickered for the best acreage; I could have closed the deed in the Plaza over a glass of Fundador."

"As your physician, Doctor, I've prohibited brandy until the new year."

"Come off it, Michael. You know what I'm saying. This is Dimity's future as well as yours. Why couldn't you bring *her* along to see her new home? She's as well as she'll ever be."

"I wanted to surprise her. And I wanted to be sure the land was mine. I couldn't believe it, somehow, until the deed was signed."

"But she's known for some time that you were buying land at Cowford."

"She doesn't know that I'm planning to raise a rooftree there in the spring."

"Look at me, boy. Are you still fretting about Dimity's health? Believe me, she's recovered completely from that—shall I say that miscarriage on the battlefield?"

"If you insist, Hilary."

"I'm afraid I do. You've been brooding too much about that occurrence. A misadventure, I might add, which is all too common among expectant mothers everywhere."

"I'm aware of that too. And I'm still of the opinion that Dimity should conserve her strength."

Dr. Hilary Tyler studied his younger colleague carefully. "We're quite alone, boy. If you've what the French call an *arrière-pensée,* spit it out."

"I've no doubt that Dimity's recovery from her miscarriage is complete. Dr. Gaines has vouched for that as well as you."

Dr. Gaines was Hilary's new friend at Point Peter—an army doctor who had joined the St. Marys garrison a month ago and called frequently at Fernandina for consultations. Michael still remembered how he had paced the living room of his fine house on the Prado while the two doctors had consulted on the landing—for all the world like a brand-new bridegroom whose fate might hang on those bearded lips. Of course their verdict had only confirmed his own. Dimity, three months after her collapse on the slope of McClure's Hill, was as well as she would ever be.

Hilary Tyler spread his hands. "You agreed with me before I called Gaines over. It would be most unwise for Dimity to have another child in the near future—assuming that she could bring a child to term."

"Isn't that reason enough for keeping her quiet now?" Michael's voice had rasped like a rusty lock as he ground out the words. He frowned over the question, wishing he had kept it to himself.

"Be sensible, boy. Dimity is one of the most carefree girls God ever made. But she can't help remembering the—the fact you just raised. Anything that will divert her mind——"

"Why should she blame herself? The fault was mine, not hers!"

"It was no one's fault, Michael," said the old doctor. "It merely happens that you loved each other too much for caution. Set your mind at rest. She'll recover in time. You'll still have strong sons to farm those acres—if you insist on playing the patriarch in your old age."

"I'm afraid I do—eventually."

"Then bring her down here on your next visit. Show her where you've planned to build your manor house. Where you'll moor your sloop. What'll you'll name the tub?"

"I've named her now," said Michael.

In that breath, he found that he had put aside his malaise. He could step over the low roof of the afterhouse and take the wheel from Tola's hands without betraying the residue of sadness that still clung to his mind. The subtle shading that would color every thought, until he could forget the taut silhouette of Dimity against the moonlight—the slow agony of her collapse as he stumbled toward her, knowing that he would be too late to help. . . . That he would always be too late to help Dimity Stone as she deserved to be helped.

But such thoughts were his to fight alone in that corner of his mind he shared with no one. It was enough, for now, to take the wheel from Tola—to shout once again to Willi as he set the new course. To hold the sloop steady with the full thrust of the wind at his back and let the bowsprit rake the southern bank of the river at a spot where pine barrens merged with seaward-facing dunes.

"Mark that mound of earth, Hilary—on the rise of ground. Can you name it?"

"Naturally," said the older doctor, with a proper show of indignation. "It's the ruins of Ribault's fort. You've a keen eye, Michael. It's almost gone back to scrub."

"Fort Caroline?"

"History should mark that spot with a thumbprint at least," said Dr. Hilary. "The mound you see today was dug by hands that have been dust for two and a half centuries."

But Michael's eyes were riveted on the crumbling hillock now. Raised as it was on a slope above the riverbank, the memory of Fort Caroline (it was too slight in that gray-green sweep of palmetto to call itself a ruin) was no more than a gentle swelling in the landscape. Yet, as Hilary had remarked, history might well have paused, if only to inscribe a footnote. For this was the site of Jean Ribault's fort—Ribault, who had dared to dispute Spain's sovereignty in this land, however briefly. The Huguenot leader who had planted the flag of France on this riverbank. Who had dared to name the river itself and claim its shores for his sovereign. . . .

Michael held his course until the sloop's bowsprit seemed to impale itself in the dense marsh grass that fringed the bank. When he spoke at last, his voice was hushed, as befits a man who glances back at a century whose blood lust surpasses his own.

"The St. Johns is a name that never suited this stream," he said. "Ribault was its first real explorer. What did *he* call it, Hilary?"

"La Fleuve de Mai," said Hilary Tyler.

"The *River of May*. Can you think of a better name for this sloop—since it's soon to bring Dimity and me to the home we'll share forever?"

II

That same morning he was still at the wheel (save for a brief interval at dinner, when Tola had taken the early watch). The *River of May* still danced before a following wind, setting her course north by northeast, with an infinity of ink-dark ocean before her.

Her skipper, letting his own thoughts blow clean in that fresh offshore breeze, held his course with one eye on the binnacle, the other on the constellations that spun away from his plunging bowsprit, only to re-form dead ahead as the sloop coasted over the next wave. The skipper's mind was far away—and far less tranquil than his manner would indicate. The skipper had cultivated that manner for a long time now. He assumed it by instinct, even when he stood alone at his wheel in the last black half hour before the sunrise.

Willi dozed in the forward scupper, his shoulder lashed firmly to the foremast, his bare toes braced on the port gunwale as the sloop raced on, logging the miles like a casual dolphin with a destination all her own. Michael had been steering by instinct for hours now and counting the miles on the same log. He had come about shortly after midnight, to beat his way inshore on a long tack, until he heard the boom of breakers and marked the wink of a beacon at the tip of Punta Blanca. It made as good a landfall as any—and excuse enough to tack sharply and spin away to sea again. Now that he had put the threat of land behind him for a while, it seemed a shame to waken Willi for another change of course. He would keep his bowsprit east by northeast until the rising sun warned him that it was time to beat into the estuary of the Amelia.

Even with the singing wind in the cordage, he could hear Hilary Tyler's snores from the after house, a sound that was neatly counterpointed by Tola's basso profundo breathing just inside the cabin door. It was good to know that these two friends trusted his seamanship completely: they had not even protested when he suggested that they spend the night on the open Atlantic, rather than risk anchoring in one of the coastal bayous. With that easy breeze and a sky clear as a blue-black bowl there had been little risk involved. Of course it had been hard to explain his reason for passing Adam Leigh's estuary in the fading light and the friendly wink of that beacon. . . .

Hilary had said only, "I can sleep at sea as well as any man. Still, I don't see why we shouldn't break our trip at the Point. Ever since noon my mouth has been set for a glass of Leigh's madeira."

"There's madeira in the cabin. You may have just one glass with your biscuit. After that fish chowder Tola made at Cowford, it will do you good to fast a bit."

"You're in command aboard this vessel, my boy. I never argue with the captain at sea."

It had been as simple as that to enforce his will. If Hilary had wondered at his refusal to dock at Punta Blanca, he had given no sign. . . . Now, with miles of wind-harried sea between himself and Marian Leigh, Michael could wonder a little at his own panic. After all, it had been three months since they had met face to face; though he had called regularly at the Point in his role of estate doctor, he had not set foot in the house itself since that night of double surrender. He had made that silent vow to Dimity and kept it to the letter. Did he fear a lapse, even now, if he dared to enter Marian's orbit again?

Watching the sea's rim gray over with the first faint promise of sunrise, he knew the answer to his question in advance. And he put the helm hard over as he called down the deck to Willi—knowing that he could solve no problem by turning his back on its challenge.

Hilary had been right, of course. He should have taken Dimity on this trip to the St. Johns, proved his devotion once again by letting her see her future home with her own eyes. Was he hoping against hope that that future (which he had planned to the last detail as grimly as a general digging moats between himself and the enemy) was not irrevocable after all?

He had bought the *River of May* to protect that future. With a crew of his own, it had been a simple matter to sail up to Leigh's wharf in the mid-morning, complete his chores among the pens, and depart at the day's end. He had followed that routine with each visit to the estate, conferring with Leigh, when necessary, on the right side of the invisible line that separated land and manor house. So far it had been easy enough to explain his new schedule: an ailing wife had demanded his early return to Fernandina. Now that Dimity was no longer ailing, he would have a new excuse—the need to visit his property on the St. Johns, to superintend the building of his own modest estate there. Adam Leigh would be the first to understand such a reason; he could hardly complain, so long as Michael fulfilled his duties. As for Leigh's daughter-in-law—well, he had simply broken his promise to return to her again and yet again. His failure to cross the line explained itself. If

Marian Leigh had failed to grasp its import, she was more stupid than he imagined.

He had glimpsed her just once in this three-month interval—at the day's end, spurring a great dark gelding down the damp sands of the point, where sea and beach leveled into a hard-packed tidal flat ideal for galloping. She was riding astride, like a man, with her dark hair unbound—and driving the gelding through the shallows as though she meant to turn seaward at any moment like some barbaric Europa. He had stood at his own wheel that afternoon, nursing a long tack that took the sloop into the ground swell a mere two hundred yards offshore. If she had recognized him, she had given no hint of it. He had kept his eyes on his ticklish task, knowing that a second's relaxation could capsize him in the trough of the waves, but he had guessed, even then, that Marian Leigh had chosen that ride deliberately.

He had come about in another moment and raced seaward again under a full suit of sails, thankful that the swing of his boom had blanked out the beach and the lone rider. When he dared to look again, the dunes were only a white pencil mark against the sky. But he could still mark her presence there, reined in atop the highest dune, a knife-thin statue filled with its own defiance even at that distance. And he knew (without a shadow of conceit, with no effort to still the hungry thud of his pulse) that she would continue to watch until its peak dropped down the northern horizon.

So much for Marian. So much for a need that matched his own.

He had turned his back on that need to dedicate himself to Dimity. With luck and a sturdy conscience, he would hold his precarious ground and consolidate his gain. Perhaps the flame would die out eventually. As a planter at Cowford, with strong sons to work beside him, he might even translate the pale contentment he had planned to a stronger emotion.

Strange that he had needed a whole night alone at his wheel to thrash out that simple hope. Stranger still, that he should continue to avoid Marian Leigh, when he had renounced her long ago. He would tell her as much on his next trip to the Point; he would explain why he could never deceive his wife for a moment, much less desert her.

His fist struck the binnacle, as though a burst of violence could drive his resolve home. He smiled up wanly as a hot arrow of sunlight touched his canvas like an omen. There, dead to starboard, were the low hills of Amelia Island blazing with their familiar gold. There, on its high bluff, was Fernandina, tranquil as ever in its aura of ill-gotten riches. There (he would mark the rooftree in another moment, the white, spidery tracery of the captain's walk) was the mansion of Dr. Michael Stone, the town's richest doctor. There, presumably asleep in her swan-boat bed, was the wife the doctor had chosen above all others—the wife he would cherish forever. . . .

He held that image firm in the foreground of his mind as he fetched Cumberland Sound on the next long tack and turned on his course to make his first real landfall. Across the blue-green glass of the sea the Georgia coast was crystal-clear in the morning light. He could see the inevitable American gunboats anchored in the shadow of their base at Point Peter, count the businesslike gunports, all but hear the summons of the morning mess bugle. . . . As always, he resisted the impulse to hold his next tack, to cross into American waters. Rumors had flown thickly on the Fernandina water front these past weeks, insisting that intervention could be expected hourly. But Aury's row of corsairs seemed eternal as sin, and just as confident of their permanence, as he took the wind on his other quarter and beat up the estuary of the Amelia.

Here, then, was the lawless world of the privateer, ruled by the privateer's own guns, though it was separated by no more than a few miles of open sound from the vastly more powerful gunboats of the Union. Michael had long ceased to wonder why the Americans permitted Aury to bring in prizes under their own cannon, when a mere show of strength could have sent the pirate sprawling on his knees—or skedaddling for deep water. So, for that matter, had the permanent natives of Fernandina—who (Michael noted wryly) had lost no time in returning to their blasted homes when they saw they could do business under Aury's banner. . . . He took another tack to set his course for the Long Wharf and saw that selfsame banner, whipping bravely in the morning breeze. The gaudy colors, the still gaudier arms of the infant republic of Mexico—the cause that Aury championed at the moment.

Already he could count the pirates anchored prudently in mid-channel where they could slip their cables at a moment's notice, if need arose. Most of the South American flags were familiar to him now, to say nothing of the ships themselves. In the past ten weeks he had climbed most of those Jacobs ladders with his surgical case slung at his shoulder, to go about his trade. The brethren of the coast, it seemed, were dedicated to short but merry lives: if the surgeon could prolong those lives with a few well-aimed slashes of the knife, so much the better. . . .

The *River of May* (a slender virgin gliding warily among these roués) skirted the mooring buoy of Aury's own brigantine, with a safe two yards to spare. The window of Aury's cabin was still closed against the fresh breath of morning—an indication that the present ruler of Fernandina had slept late after a night devoted to the twin gods of Bacchus and Priapus. Michael smiled tolerantly—and felt a bit ashamed at his tolerance. At least Aury did not make the mistake of sleeping ashore these days. Fernandina was used to strange rulers now, but the pirate had enemies by the score, most of whom had sworn to divide his heart for breakfast.

The Long Wharf, now. Warp the sloop's nose into the stringpiece and run forward to help Willi with the jib as the gaffboom slotted home. Tola was already padding down the afterdeck to stow the running gear and make sure that the chocks were down along the gunwale. Dr. Hilary Tyler, he noted, still snored like a contented calliope, oblivious of the rich sunshine that now flooded the afterhouse.

"Will you go to the señora, *jefe?*"

"At once—if there are no cases in the surgery. Tell Dr. Hilary to breakfast at the Silver Dollar when he wakens. I'll join him when I can."

Michael was already standing on the stringpiece. With a last look to make sure that the sloop was moored snugly, he ran down the dock, affecting a lightness he did not feel. Always, at the end of these short homing voyages, he had made himself run lightly. Just as he forced a smile to his lips—and raised his eyes to the crazy stair that climbed the bluff, on the chance that Dimity might be stirring early. . . .

Today the street above the dock was empty in the early morning. Only the water front stirred with a wide, yawning life of its own as the endless loadings resumed along the quays. He breathed deep of the familiar spicy odors—and recoiled by instinct when an even more familiar stench assailed his nostrils. There was no mistaking the tapered lines of the slaver as she warped into her berth at the Sugar Wharf, a scant hundred yards beyond his surgery windows. Mounting the steps to the bluff, Michael permitted himself the luxury of a black-browed frown. Slavers were commonplace in Fernandina, true enough, but it was seldom that a blackbirder came into port without scrubbing down offshore. Only last week he had heard rumors of a load of blacks, beached at a fire-gutted plantation dock a mile south of town, and knocked down to wildcat traders on the spot. How long would it be before Aury permitted such sales to be held in the Prado, on Dr. Stone's own doorstep?

He went up the steps three at a time and crossed Sevilla Street with the same long-legged stride. Fernandina slept behind its shutters, shut away from last evening's damps. He stared blankly at the empty-eyed ruins at the corner of the Prado, the grotesquely preserved cabin that lacked only a roof—the only visible proofs that the town had suffered bombardment a few months ago.

His own house, untouched in its garden of palm and bougainvillea, welcomed him gravely, though its heavily curtained windows stared back at him as blankly as any on the square. He burst in as always, making his entrance hearty—and a trifle anxious. So far, Dimity had never failed to meet him in the hallway—a tranquil sprite, hugging her knees on the deep carpet. At the worst, she had always called down to him from the floor above as she stirred drowsily in the swan-boat bed.

Today the empty hallway gave back the echo of his homecoming. He took the stair in a bound—and stared back at his reflection in the vast gilt mirror that filled one bedroom wall.

"Dimity!"

The room spoke of her recent presence eloquently enough. A tumbled mass of lace, where she had stepped out of the nightgown he had ordered from Havana. A faint trace of scent in the air—the equally expensive perfume he had bought from Paris, via Charleston, to grace the *grande tenue* she had promised to wear in his honor at the next Governor's Ball in Augustine. He smiled wanly as he pictured that scene: Dimity, in a vast, many-panniered evening gown, cut to the wishbone and prodigal of ruching, parading in that oversized mirror like a dove preening before the sacrifice. . . .

"Dimity!"

But it was Ulee, the Seminole maid, who came in on noiseless bare soles to offer the master her best smile.

"The señora goes walking, jefe."

"Alone?"

"Gator is with her." Ulee looked faintly surprised at Michael's bark. "Who would harm the doctor's wife?"

"Who indeed?"

He had not meant to sound bitter, but Ulee had said more than she knew. Fernandina was a brawling, lawless town—now, more than ever, it was unsafe for a lady to show her face on the streets, even by daylight. But the doctor's lady was immune, thanks to the doctor's connections on the water front. Aury, and Aury's bullies, owed the doctor too much to harm his wife even with a look.

Ulee was pointing to the marble-topped chiffonier; Ulee's eyes were lowered modestly under the master's glare. "She left a note. You will understand, when you read."

But Michael had already broken the wafer on the sheet of letter paper, folded meticulously against the pincushion. Dimity's flowing script was beyond reproach. Dimity's message, as always, left something to be desired in the grammar, though the sentiment was evident in each word:

DERE MIKE:

I codent sleap, so I thot Id sit on deLeon's nose, and watch you sale in. Dont worry coze of me, if you have bisiness. I love you

yore wife

DIM.

He was out of the house and raising the dust of the Prado with free-striding boots before he would admit there was moisture in his eyes. He had known before this that Dimity scanned the horizon for his return from the Point; more than once his glass had picked her out on the widow's walk as she followed the sloop's last long turn into the Amelia. But she had always pretended a vast unconcern when he joined her, a teasing lack of interest that covered those vigils neatly. Today was her first real admission that her whole life hung on his return.

De Leon's Nose was a limestone outcrop below the Fernandina bluff, on the ocean side, where the headland crumbled into dunes and boiling surf. Named after the discoverer of the peninsula, the rugged point of land did bear a faint resemblance to its namesake organ—a giant's proboscis all but masked in the green whiskers of beach grass and yucca. No one could verify the legend that Ponce de Leon himself had set foot on this beach some three centuries in the past; it was said that Oglethorpe, not Ponce, had carved his initials in the limestone on one of the British raids in Florida. Michael had sat here often in the past weeks, with his eyes on the open sea and his thoughts far away. It was natural that Dimity should choose the same vantage point to await her first glimpse of the *River of May*. . . .

Now, tramping through the palmettos where the last cabins of Fernandina thinned away among the dunes, Michael felt that the omen was good after all. Not that he had real news for her. She had guessed for some time that he was about to close the deed for those Cowford acres; she had known that he would build their first true home there, that they would put down their first real roots beside the St. Johns. But there was real emotion in his voice when he topped the highest dune and called her name. *This is my final dedication,* the voice of reason whispered. *Once we've talked about Cowford—and the roof-raising I've planned for the spring—there'll be no turning back, ever.*

He pulled up short on the top of the dune, coasting a few steps down the seaward slope, as his eyes searched the point for some sign of Dimity. There was Gator, right enough—impassive as ever in his homespun trousers, his bare toes splayed in the sand, his copper-corded arms folded on his chest. Michael let the hard throb of his unspoken fear ease back to normal. So long as the Seminole was guarding Dimity, she had nothing to fear.

"She watched you come about to enter the harbor, jefe. It was a sight that gave her great happiness. Then she went walking on the beach alone."

"Why didn't you follow her? You know it isn't safe to——"

"Look south, Señor Médico. Where the damp sand widens beyond the wreck. You will see your wife, wading in the shallows——"

Michael ran down the dune before Gator could quite finish, waving as he ran, and shouting Dimity's name again into the teeth of the fresh offshore breeze. She was wandering aimlessly among the timbers of the wreck—half hidden, even now, in that grotesque skeleton, like an intrepid mayfly that has ventured into the cairn of some prehistoric god. With each panting step, she was more real—and more desirable. Already, he noted, she was wearing a costume he remembered all too well—wide-bottomed sailor trousers and a gay-striped sailor's jacket that exposed her brown limbs at knee and elbow. And he remembered that he was her husband just in time, lifting a scolding finger before he took her in his arms.

"What did Dona Xavier say when you walked past her door in *that?*"

Dimity returned his kiss with interest and settled in the curve of his arm as they moved lazily on at the meeting place of sea and shore. "If you must know, I wished her a very good morning, and she didn't turn a hair. What's more, I was still wearing this——"

"Under a skirt, I hope?"

"Under that bleached muslin you bought me in Havana. Of course I left it on the nearest bush when we were safely out of town." She looked up at him in earnest then—and her eyes were wide and unashamed of the love that burned like clear flame in their depths. "You didn't have to come, Mike."

"Couldn't I come out to the Nose if I felt in the mood?"

"You must have a dozen cases waiting at the surgery. You always do, when you come back from Leigh's."

He looked at her narrowly, but he saw instantly that it was a simple statement without overtones. "If you must know, they're stacked on the stair like cordwood."

"Then I mustn't detain you. In fact, I refuse to keep you another moment. Ulee has made a shrimp pilaff for lunch, if you're interested."

"I'm extremely interested—since my breakfast was a sea biscuit and cold coffee."

"Come home at once, Mike. You know I love to feed you."

But he had already pulled her into the shadow of a dune for a long kiss—and released her only when he felt her shoulders tremble. There were stars in the eyes she lifted to him now. He rejoiced in their luster for a moment before he plunged on.

"Sorry—my news won't keep."

"What about your patients?"

"Hilary will see to my patients. Remember, they're his patients too."

"But, Mike—you always said that Dr. Hilary——"

"Not another word about my colleague. Suppose I announced that I'm selling my practice to him this spring?"

"You wouldn't dare."

"I would indeed. He's steadied wonderfully after he lived down that wound." He watched the cloud pass over her face at that reference to the battle and plunged on hastily. "In fact, I'm sure I can surrender Fernandina to him without a twinge of conscience. What's more, Dr. Hilary agrees with me."

Dimity danced out of the curve of his arm and ran hip-deep in the green-curdled shallows. He followed her instantly, careless of the damage to his boots, and pulled her back to the shore line for another kiss. It had been a sufficient antidote in the past, when she had refused to follow the trend of an argument.

"Don't pretend to be stupid, my dear. Surely you can see that a Fernandina practice will suit Dr. Hilary perfectly, come spring."

"And the American Army?"

"Precisely. You followed me perfectly."

"I'm not sure I *want* to follow you, Mike."

"Not even to the St. Johns—and an estate all your own?"

The stars still glowed in her eyes like a tangible reward. Her voice was husky when she spoke at last. "So you've bought the land, Michael?"

"I've done more than buy. Masons are riding down the King's Road from Augustine this moment to lay our foundation stones. Lumber is coming from Savannah on the Seaboard Company's next schooner. I'm raising my own roof this May, or knowing the reason why." He pulled her close with the words. They swayed together for a long moment there at the sea's edge.

"Why are you crying, Dimity? It's what we planned from the first."

But she had already broken away without a word, to dance through the shallows like Ariel himself—pausing to snatch a great rope of seaweed from a dying wave and garlanding herself as she scampered on, eluding his pursuit with light-footed ease.

"Rosemary, Mike—that's for remembrance. Hamlet, Act Five. Or is it Act Four? Anyhow, Ophelia's mad scene. . . . Don't tell me I haven't studied hard while you're away."

"Is this a time to quote Ophelia?"

"A perfect time, darling. Remember, she went mad and drowned herself for love."

He stared at her for a quiet interval, puzzled by the laughing cadence of her words, not by their import. "Did you have similar plans—assuming that my sail hadn't shown today—or the day after?"

"Of course not, Mike. Why are you so serious all at once?"

She had waded deeper as she spoke. Now she turned to face him, with the sun and spindrift behind her. The seaweed rope still hung about her shoulders in a wet garland. She tossed it aside, letting the next wave diamond her hair with spray as she stood hip-deep in the backwash. He saw that she was laughing at him when he took her firmly by the hand and led her back to the dry slope of a dune. He could not be sure if the tears in her eyes were a by-product of that laughter.

"I'm glad it means this much to you," she said, and settled contentedly in the sand with her head in his lap.

"Are you sure you weren't joking?"

"Not quite sure, Mike." He saw the tears in her eyes were real enough. Her fingers crept inside his coat sleeve and anchored hard just above the elbow—as though she needed that assurance of his reality. "Maybe I wouldn't drown myself straight off. Maybe I'd even pretend to go on living for a while."

"I think you've said enough, Dimity."

But she went on as though she had not heard; there was a dreamy remoteness in her tone that did not belong to the Dimity he knew so well. "You think I'm still playing Ophelia—and I don't blame you. This is something I couldn't explain to anyone. Not even to myself. It's just that I'm more than a *part* of you—I'm *one*. So much one that I can't divide myself and think of going on—if I lost you. Or if you didn't want me any more."

"You'll never lose me. I'll never stop wanting you."

"As you did that first night?"

"As I did that first night."

He could see that his avowal had satisfied her completely. The hypocrite in his soul might grimace behind his mask; he was glad that he could make the romantic gesture convincing.

"Will you be sorry to leave Fernandina, Mike?"

"Not in the least. From now on I mean to grow up with the country as best I can."

"You'll still be a doctor?"

"The back country needs doctors too, and Cowford will be a town soon enough. An American town. Somehow, I can't think of this smugglers' heaven as part of America. Not as it is today, at any rate."

"Fernandina will be respectable again, when those gunboats move over from Point Peter."

"Respectable, and quiet, and forgotten," said Michael. He stroked his wife's hair and smiled down at her. "*We* were part of its history when it was still the harlot of Florida. We'd never endure the anticlimax."

"We could learn to be respectable too, Mike, if we really put our minds to it."

"I'd much rather learn on the St. Johns. With a wilderness before me and a town I'd helped to start on its way. Of course if you insist on being the wife of a prosperous city doctor——"

"You know I was always a country girl at heart. I can't wait to leave, Mike. Really I can't. When can I see the land you've bought?"

"The moment I've cleared ground for the house and put in the tabby stone."

"Will we close the house here?"

He frowned lightly and kissed the tip of her nose. "Adam Leigh acquired this house when he set me up in practice. He may keep it."

Dimity's hand had not left his arm. He felt the fingers tighten now. "Will Mr. Leigh mind if you leave Fernandina?"

"Why should he mind? Cowford is even closer to his slavepens. I can ride over on horseback for my weekly visit."

He felt her fingers ease their pressure and smiled inwardly. God guard you, he thought: you *want* me to keep my connection with Adam Leigh. You haven't even guessed what that connection might have cost us. What it may cost us, even now, if I don't keep my head. . . .

Aloud he said only, "We can afford to do without Leigh whenever we like. I'm merely filling a contract, after all."

"How long must it run?"

"Another year perhaps." How could he explain that Leigh had put no time limit on his services? That he might be Leigh's slave forever (in the worst sense of that word) so long as Marian lived at the Point?

"I'm glad to hear that, Michael," said Dimity. "Lord forgive me, I thought you needed Leigh's money—the same as everyone in Fernandina."

"Haven't you any idea how rich a man you married?"

"I never could picture money. You know that."

"Wait until you see the house I'm building you. And the furniture you're bringing down from Charleston." He smoothed the hair from her temples (it was still gleaming with sea spray) and smiled into her wide eyes. "You're a woman of property, Mrs. Stone—a frontier matriarch in the making. Can't you grasp that much?"

"I know I'm rich, Mike. Richer than I deserve." This time it was she who lifted her lips to his. "There's just one thing you've forgotten. Where will we live while the house is building?"

"You can live aboard the hulk with Felippa if you like. I'll clear the patients in the next few weeks. Dr. Hilary can handle the rest easily."

"Couldn't we camp out at Cowford—and help the builders?"

"We could—but no wife of mine needs to be that rugged a pioneer."

"I've slept in tents in my time," said Dimity. "I wouldn't mind another, with you beside me."

"Don't cast me in such a heroic mold, please. I'll visit Cowford often while the house is building—but I'll moor the sloop in the river and live aboard. Naturally you'll come whenever you like—until it's time to go to Charleston."

"Did you say *Charleston?*"

"When it's time to buy our furniture. Haven't you heard a word I've said?"

"You'll have to come with me, I'd be afraid to go alone."

"Mrs. Michael Stone can go anywhere. You'll have a maid, and Tola can double as your coachman." He chuckled at her frown as he let the picture build. "My bankers would meet you at the dock——"

She clung to him for a long time without speaking. He felt the wild throbbing of her heart and smiled as it settled into a steady, confident beat. "I'll try to—live up to that trust, Mike. How soon would you want me to"—she hesitated for the proper phrase—"to outfit our home?"

"We should have the last nail in by late summer."

"And you'll live aboard the sloop and work on the land while you're waiting?"

Michael nodded slowly. He knew that she was hoping he would ask that she join him in ground-breaking, but he was remembering the advice of Dr. Clement Gaines—late of the finest surgery in Vienna, now a practicing physician in the uniform of the United States Army. Dr. Gaines, who had crossed from St. Marys to consult with Dr. Hilary Tyler, had insisted that Dimity would be herself in time. He had insisted, no less solemnly, that rest and quiet were indicated for the near future.

"You may come and watch as often as you like. But you must get back your strength in between."

"I never felt stronger than today."

He kissed her one more time as he lifted her to her feet, cradling her in his arms a moment more, as though she were a child. "Be stubborn with your husband if you must. You can't fight another doctor's advice."

"Very well, Mike. No tents, if you say so. But I won't live in Fernandina when you aren't at the Long Wharf. I'll live in St. Marys."

He stared at her, remembering their long argument over just such a move when Fernandina had been threatened with invasion. "Can I believe my ears?"

"Dr. Gaines has a wife, you know. She's opened a house just outside the army post. I'll stay with them, if you like. And I'll follow his treatments to the letter."

"You're a model after all. I was beginning to doubt my discipline, but——"

"Not such a model," said Dimity. "Wait till I'm really well again."

He let her go on that note and climbed the dune only when she had darted down the far side. Pausing on the crest, he watched her vanish briefly in a yucca thicket and emerge with proper decorum in a long-skirted walking dress, her chin at an angle suitable to a matron in the making. Every line of her small person was radiant with pride—in her husband, in the future he had promised her, in the love he had offered so freely.

Dr. Michael Stone waited patiently until his wife's confident feet had found the path that snaked through the beach grass to the Fernandina bluff. Then he followed her—making his stride deliberate, knowing that she would slow her own pace until he overtook her at the Prado.

Like all dedications, it had not been without its panicky moments; on the whole, he insisted, it had gone off triumphantly. If Dimity realized that his heart was elsewhere, she had given no sign. Watching her sweep her skirts through the palmettos, judging the tilt of her head with an expert's eye, he repeated the wisdom of the French philosopher in the barest of whispers: "Speech was given to man to conceal his thoughts."

Thanks to that sly alchemy, Dimity seemed as happy as any wife since marriage was invented. With luck and an alert brain he would keep that happiness inviolate.

III

Don Sebastian Castro—who was also Dr. Castro, and a first-rate surgeon when sober—bowed courteously as Michael stepped up to the improvised operating table in the ship's cabin. Aury's flagship bobbed gently in the suck of the outgoing tide—a prophetic rhythm, as though the brigantine, like the rest of Aury's fleet, was only too eager to be about its business, far outside the confines of the Amelia estuary. Aury himself (seated in the embrasure of the stern window like a compact idol and watching the visiting doctor with Argus eyes) seemed a world removed from the surgeons' whispered consultation. But Michael knew that the pirate's eyes and ears had missed nothing from the start.

The girl on the table stirred under his hands, moaning a little as his fingers outlined the danger point. He watched her knees draw up in a muscular spasm that was, in itself, a confirmation of his first diagnosis. He kept the thought to himself, waiting for Castro to speak as he continued to delimit the spot where the knife would go in—if he dared a surgical exploration. So far he had not quite risked looking at his patient's pain-racked face. All Fernandina knew that Aury's girl was beautiful. The fact that Fernandina's surgeon had been called to the flagship and entrusted with Doña Felicia's desperate illness was only routine, after all.

"The pains began yesterday, Dr. Stone." Don Sebastian Castro, as befitted the surgeon of a first-rate privateer, spoke with the Hapsburg lisp, whistling his diphthongs with an ardor worthy of the Escorial. "Last night I administered opium—and a cataplasm to the back. Doña Felicia has had no relief so far."

"Was there nausea?"

"A little. The pains have continued to be spasmodic in character—with no evidence of fever."

"Did you attempt any other medication?"

"A little jalap this morning. I hesitated to administer the bark."

The girl moaned in earnest. Michael lifted his hands from the taut muscles of the abdomen as he felt Luis Aury's eyes bore into his back. He took refuge in his own fluent Spanish, omitting the lisp.

"Where does it pain most, señora?"

Almond-white hands closed above his own. Full, pouting lips (they were bloodless now, though he remembered their pomegranate red when she had smiled at Aury's last levee) gasped as he outlined the danger point one more time—a rounded swelling just above the pelvic bone.

"The mass has been in evidence from the beginning," said Castro.

Michael's fingers tested the tumor in detail. The muscles were tense above it, and Doña Felicia winced again as his fingers dug deeper, but there was no real tenderness in this area, and the muscles themselves were soft. The knife could save her—if he dared to use the knife.

"Am I *enceinte,* Doctor?"

He smiled at the too-lovely girl on the table as reassuringly as he could. "My examination would say otherwise. You are sure that you wish me to operate?"

"If it will cure me, yes." The liquid eyes met his question steadily. Doña Felicia, so the rumor ran in Fernandina, had scaled a convent wall to elope with her pirate. Today's decision had taken courage of another sort.

"Perhaps *I* may say a word, Doctor?"

They turned in unison as Aury himself stalked up to the table, black-browed and stocky—and handsome as a gipsy tenor. Swarthy French to his fingertips, a bandit from another century, Luis Aury was not at his best today. The red veins in his small slitted eyes were evidence of a sleepless night—Michael (like all Fernandina) knew that it had not been his mistress's illness that caused the pirate to lose sleep.

"Why is it necessary to operate at all?"

Michael curbed his irritation. "I was given carte blanche when I came aboard, monsieur. The lady herself is willing. As you see, we've prepared the table; already she is under a heavy opiate." Doña Felicia, who had nodded a drowsy affirmative, held out her hand to Aury. There was something touching in the way the Frenchman bent to kiss the long, pale fingers one by one.

"So I am the rude captain, Felicia, who breaks your tryst with death?"

"Don't mention death, Luis. Not with two doctors at my side. It is hardly polite."

"Perhaps we should talk for a moment on deck," said Castro.

"Someone must stay with Felicia!"

"Observe her, Comandante. She sleeps like a child as she awaits the healing knife."

Aury stared hard at Castro, then marched out of the cabin. The two surgeons followed him wordlessly, pausing by common consent in the shadow of the deckhouse while the new master of Fernandina (a king whose days were clearly numbered) stumped his rail and glared at the harbor.

Once again Michael noted the strange hush ashore. Every wharf was black with heads today, but it was a quiet crowd, watching the row of anchored privateers like a contented audience that knows the show must soon begin. The flag of Mexico still whipped bravely above the sentry tower of Fort San Carlos; its gaudy magnificence was echoed in another banner at Aury's own forepeak. But Fernandina knew that Aury's last note to the Point Peter had been a capitulation, pure and simple. Boxed in the Amelia estuary, with a small American arsenal covering all exits, the pirate could only strut a little now, to save his face. Precisely as a hog-fat ambassador was strutting in Washington, as he dictated a memorandum to his sovereign in Madrid, explaining that the Americans would occupy Amelia Island solely as a favor to that busy monarch. An occupation in the interest of both countries—ending the reign of the filibusters, holding the golden island in trust for Spain. . . .

So much for history in the making. Michael stared hard at Aury's broad back—the shoulders of a butcher who could masquerade as a gypsy lover when he chose as adroitly as he could pose as a liberator. If MacGregor had been an honest sheep dog in uniform, Irwin a cold-hearted man of business, Luis Aury would be operatic till the end. In a way it was appropriate that Dr. Michael Stone should minister to this rascal in the last moments of his stay—or, rather, to the rascal's mistress.

Aury spoke without turning, his eyes still brooding on the gaudy flag above the fort. "I have told you that my time is limited, Doctor."

Michael dared to smile. "As you see, my sloop is at the Long Wharf. When you make sail, she has orders to do likewise. I'm due at Punta Blanca this noon for an important conference with Adam Leigh."

"To report my departure, perhaps?"

"Go to the Silver Dollar bar, monsieur. They are offering three to one that you'll raise anchor with the tide."

"Can you finish this operation by then?"

"If you'll permit me to proceed at once."

"You insist that it is essential?"

"Dr. Castro agrees with my prognosis. It is a tumor of the left ovary. If the patient is to live, it must be excised."

"Put your thoughts in French, Dr. Stone."

"L'ovaire à gauche," said Michael. "It is twisted on its stalk and enlarged beyond enduring. With its blood supply cut off it will degenerate—mortify—and, eventually, cause death."

"Is this a common ailment?"

"Common enough, I'm afraid. Thousands of women have died because of such enlargements. Few surgeons are willing to risk an ovariotomy."

Michael glanced at Castro as he spoke, but the Spanish surgeon's face was bland as his own. To his knowledge, ovariotomy had never been performed in the New World, though he had assisted at such an operation in Vienna, and again at the side of his old mentor, Dr. Holly, in the latter's London surgery. Surgeons the world over still considered the abdomen as *terra incognita* so far as their scalpels were concerned. Bleeding, mustard pastes, and the mumbo jumbo of the pharmacopoeia were the standard refuges of the profession, when questing fingers detected a cyst in the Fallopian region, or a still more dreaded enlargement of the uterus itself.

Castro said only, "It *is* a risk, Comandante. But you are a man who lives by risk."

"Would you take her ashore for the operation?"

Michael said patiently, "As you have seen, we're prepared to operate now—in the cabin."

"You'd let her sail with me?"

"Dr. Castro would be responsible for her convalescence. As a sailor, you know that wounds heal better on shipboard."

"I am aware of that, Doctor." Aury's black-browed frown was intact. "What I object to principally is your willingness to use my ship as a surgery."

"We merely made ready, Comandante," said Castro with the same benign calm. Evidently he was inured to the captain's temper. "If you wish, the operation can be abandoned even now."

"With Doña Felicia under an opiate?"

"It will do her no harm to sleep for a while—and the drug will ease her pain."

Someone was shouting Aury's name from the Long Wharf. Michael saw that it was José Aravello himself, who had ridden down the quayside on horseback and was waving an envelope as he rode. The pirate turned toward the ladder that dropped down the ship's side to his waiting gig. With that movement his shoulders sagged visibly, as though he had read the letter Aravello brandished in advance.

"Operate and be damned, gentlemen. But you'd best be quick, Dr. Stone—or you'll find yourself at sea."

Castro offered Michael a silken shrug as the pirate vanished overside. "You will not believe this, Doctor, but he adores the doxy. He is afraid you will kill her."

"And you?"

The Spaniard's eyes gleamed. "It would be an honor to assist at an ovariotomy. Even if I do not believe such an operation is possible."

"May I convince you to the contrary?"

"Your fame has preceded you, Dr. Stone. You say this operation can succeed, with luck and boldness. I accept that chance."

"Remember, you'll bear the brunt if I'm wrong."

"Aury will curse me, and bury the girl with honors. And find himself another, when we dock at Havana. Shall we begin?"

Michael stripped off his shirt and flexed his muscles in the warm sunlight. "You've ordered boiling water and two men to hold the patient?"

Castro smiled thinly. "All is in readiness, Dr. Stone. I waited only for the comandante's departure."

Michael echoed the other's grin as his eyes followed Aury's progress across the harbor. Aravello already stood at the dock's end, with the letter extended across the narrowing strip of water. The crowd packed along the stringpiece watched the pirate as one man—and seemed to sigh in unison as Aury stood up boldly in the gig and broke the seal.

Like those watchers ashore, Michael could guess the letter's contents well enough. Aravello had acted as unofficial go-between for the American forces since the first exchange of notes had informed the pirate that his days here were numbered. It was common knowledge in the town that Aury had promised to depart without bloodshed—if the price was right.

Castro had matched Michael's stripping. Now, as the younger surgeon dipped his hands and arms in a basin of hot water proffered by a cabin boy, he duplicated the action—with the air of a man performing a rite he does not quite approve. "As you observe, the final terms are in the comandante's hands. He will curse them awhile, of course. He will step ashore, to argue with Señor Aravello—if only for the sake of form. Then he will take his fleet out of these waters forever. Perhaps within the hour. We must move fast."

"Do you know the final terms?"

"Your Mr. Leigh is paying him two thousand gold dollars to be about his business. Aury has asked the government in Washington to match the sum. This morning the Americans are landing three hundred marines below McClure's Hill as their answer. The comandante is only now learning that America does not pay tribute."

Michael nodded soberly. He had heard rumors of Leigh's bribe and was still puzzled by the planter's action. Leigh had all but financed MacGregor's expedition a few months ago; now he was paying through the nose to clear away the very incubus he had fastened on Fernandina. Perhaps that too was part of the man's stategy; enough anarchy to cover his tracks . . . a firm quietus to that same element, when filibuster degenerated into outright freebooter. He spoke the thought aloud as he dried his hands on a mass of cotton waste.

"Perhaps we're to have a taste of government here, after all."

"Put that another way, Doctor. Say you've seen your last corsair at anchor in Fernandina, as of today. And your last slaver——"

"Where does that leave Adam Leigh?"

"Like all wise men, Adam Leigh knows better than to swim against the tide. You have seen how he grew rich when there was no law—like a sultan in the wilderness. Now that the Americans are bringing law to this corner of the Floridas, he joins their side—or appears to. But he has made his own world at Punta Blanca: he is above the law. Piracy is no longer fashionable in these waters. The blackbirders will be swept from the seas in time. But the Adam Leighs go on forever, Doctor. And they grow richer, no matter what flag they fly."

Michael glanced sharply at Castro, but the ship surgeon's face was still bland as cream. "May I endorse that statement completely?"

"Thank you, Dr. Stone. I was afraid you would call me a cynic. Are you ready to operate?"

"As ready as I'll ever be."

They went into Aury's cabin together. Michael saw at a glance that Castro knew his business. Table and floor had been scrubbed clean; the table was covered with a wadded cotton spread that would ease the inevitable thrashings of the patient. The two brawny seamen who stood with folded arms at either end of the cabin had obviously assisted Castro a hundred times: lynx-eyed and wrapped in a kind of surly reserve, they stared down dispassionately at the lovely flesh that awaited the doctor's knife. Stripped of her last garment and lashed to the table at knees and elbows, Doña Felicia was deep in morphia; in the jeweled light that fell through the high stern windows of the brigantine, her body had a muted glow of its own, like living ivory. Michael stepped up to the table and tested the girl's strong young heartbeat. Marking the line of the incision he had planned, he felt his mind recoil from the task ahead. This body was created for the act of love; it deserved midnight ardor, not the slash of steel.

Even as the thought crossed his mind, he opened his hand across the table, letting Castro slap a scalpel into the palm. The brace of seamen moved forward as one man, to spread their fingers at the girl's shoulder and thighs, anchoring her to the table in those four hairy vises. He found that he had made his first long incision without conscious thought. The girl screamed under the heavy opiate—a wail of pain that deepened as the knife moved into the fascia, separating the muscular layers from umbilicus to pelvic bone. Already the screams were strangely muted in his ears, as his iron wall of concentration, so carefully fashioned over the years, dropped between him and the world.

Castro followed him easily in the deepening wound, to control the bleeding firmly. Retractors came into his hand, enlarging the operative area and holding the muscles firmly parted as he tented the thin, transparent membrane of the peritoneum. So far his surgery had gone by the book, with all the precision of a printed schedule of anatomy. His mind stayed just behind his fast-moving fingers, clocking each small milestone of the operation, comparing it with the diagrams he had pored over long ago in his first classes in dissection. Beyond this point (and he knew that Castro had sensed the fact across the table) they must venture into all-but-unknown territory. He tented the peritoneum with a forceps and paused to draw breath as he noted the precision of his entry point. The ovarian tumor lay just beneath those small steel jaws. Even as he lifted the membrane, he could feel the tension beneath.

Castro slapped a fresh scalpel in his hand and bent above the wound, his black eyes snapping with the excitement of this climactic moment.

"Will you enter the cavity at this point, Doctor? Or is it dangerous to cut just above the swelling?"

"Only if the tumor is hemorrhagic."

He watched his hands move with no conscious message from his brain, saw the blade nick the membrane and incise cautiously. Castro's hand moved behind his own, holding the small opening as wide as the incision would allow. Complete access was as yet impossible, but the tumor itself sprang into view instantly in all its gleaming whiteness—an evil globe that seemed distended to the bursting point, iridescent as some monstrous grape nested in the healthy red coil of intestinal wall. Michael felt his heart turn over with relief. Despite its forbidding hue, the tumor was apparently benign; there was a yielding softness in its surface, despite its unhealthy distension, that suggested it was filled with fluid.

"Shall we enlarge the opening, Doctor?"

Michael shook his head. He had decided on his routine from this point on, before Castro could phrase the question. Even with a deeper gash in the peritoneum, complete access to the pedicle of the tumor seemed impossible until the distension was relieved.

"I'm perforating—and draining off the fluid."

"What if there's a hemorrhage?"

"It's a risk we must take, I'm afraid. All my experience would indicate that we can drain without danger."

He hoped that his voice did not betray his trepidation. It was quite true that he had opened a score of cadavers (on Holly's table in London) to expose an identical cause of death. It had been a simple matter, then, to lance the offending swelling—to deliver the collapsed remnant from the incision, and amputate from its stalk in a few easy strokes. In those classes in anatomy the textbooks were always right, the tumors inflated with a harmless fluid that drained away as simply as water from a punctured canteen. Or solid as the rock crabs they vaguely resembled, spreading their mushrooming claws into the remote depths of the cavity—malignant killers all, born of some evil growth he could not name.

The tumor that threatened Doña Felicia's life was not of this genre. Yet he could not be sure that a single touch of the scalpel would not undo his whole approach—exploding the girl's lifeblood into the wound, beginning a hemorrhage that would be beyond repair.

"Why do you wait?" said Castro.

"Pray for her, Doctor. She'll need your prayers."

The knife moved as Michael spoke, jabbing deep in the tumor's wall. A geyser of blood would have spelled failure for the operation; the fluid which jetted from the rent was bright yellow, not red. His fingers darted deep in the wound, closing a forceps about the tumor itself, delivering it bit by bit as the pressure eased with this pulsing drainage. In a matter of moments the pulsing dwindled; he allowed himself the luxury of a deep breath as he delivered the whole collapsed sac into the open.

There was still resistance to his pull; he inserted his index finger in the wound and swept it about the base of the sac to localize the cause. There was the attachment, precisely as he had placed it in his mind's eye. He pressed his thumb down to bring it into view and revealed a stalklike structure as large as the thumb itself.

"Observe the attachment, Dr. Castro. Twisted about the Fallopian tube, as I predicted. Will you tie off while I excise?"

Castro knotted the heavy whipcord deftly, and placed a second tie just above the waiting knife. Two sharp strokes completed the ovariotomy neatly enough. The organ itself, along with the growth that had caused its strange degeneration, dropped to the waiting basin. Michael cross-sectioned them both with the scalpel, testing the tissue for any hint of the thready fibrous growth that spelled carcinoma in the making. Castro, with a stack of linen pads beside the wound, had controlled the last of the bleeding in the meantime. Now he moved closer, to stare at the neatly bisected ovary. Michael permitted himself a small smile as he noted the surgeon's dilated pupils.

"Would you care to close the incision, Doctor?"

The Spaniard flushed with pleasure as Michael stepped back from the table. The man's fingers were just as deft as they whipped in the sutures and drew the needles through skin and muscle. Michael watched narrowly, glad that he could approve the older man's technique. Doña Felicia would be in excellent hands for her convalescence. With a smooth voyage to Cuba, she might even walk ashore when the brigantine dropped anchor in Havana.

Castro tied the last knot and stepped back from the table in turn.

"The operation is finished, Doctor. I hope you remembered to time it. I must confess I was far too nervous."

Michael consulted his battered hunter and stared incredulously at the hour hand. "Seventy-one minutes, I'm afraid. And I'd hoped we established a record."

"Time moves fast when the concentration is absolute. And we did make history. Never mind the records."

Michael lifted Doña Felicia's wrist and found that the pulse was a trifle fast, but strong and regular. The opiate had worn thin, and she stirred drowsily now under the seamen's hands. But he knew that she had lost little ground because of the operation. With youth on her side, she had every chance for recovery.

"Would you call it a success, Doctor?"

"A complete success, thank you."

The wall that had enclosed his mind was lifting slowly now. He was conscious of externals one by one: the heavy breathing of the larger of the two seamen (who still clung doggedly to the girl's shoulders), the bright jeweled sun at the high stern windows, Doña Felicia's warm-ivory nakedness. He watched the sailors draw away from the table at Castro's curt gesture of dismissal. He smiled in earnest as the older surgeon took a boat cloak from a cabinet and swathed the patient in its folds.

"They'll bring blankets in a moment. I'll enter the event in the ship's log, of course. It's unfortunate that we can't give the story to the American press. They'd be delighted to print it in Savannah and Charleston."

Michael came back to externals completely as he felt the cabin floor cant gently beneath his feet. "How long have we been under way?"

"Long enough to round the point, I'd say. I hope your sloop is still in our wake. This is a fast ship when she's in the clear."

"Is Aury aboard?"

"Obviously, Dr. Stone. A flagship would hardly sail without its admiral. Even the flagship of a pirate fleet."

Michael caught the new note of deference in Castro's voice and turned to the cause. Aury himself was standing in the cabin door. Over his shoulder Michael caught a glimpse of dancing blue water whipped by a following breeze. A white mountain of canvas filled the sky for an instant as one of the brigantine's companion vessels raced into view, her last jib spread to keep pace with the leader—and vanished abruptly as she heeled on her starboard scuppers to sail closer to the wind.

"Finished just in time, Dr. Stone? Or should I say a trifle too late?"

"See for yourself, monsieur."

Aury went quickly to the table and lifted one of Doña Felicia's hands to his lips. Watching his man narrowly, Michael could not doubt that the gesture was genuine: there was real concern in the rapid hiss of French that passed between the pirate and Castro. A sixth sense made him hold his ground until the Frenchman spoke to him again, though every instinct urged him to the deck.

"It seems you're a genius, Dr. Stone. Castro tells me that the girl's recovery is all but assured."

"The operation was an unqualified success. I can say that much."

"You've doubts as to her recovery?"

"Very few, if she convalesces at sea. If you'll follow Castro's instruction to the letter——"

"Why shouldn't I follow *your* instructions, Doctor? After today's display, I've every confidence in your ability."

"If you'll forgive me, I've an appointment at Punta Blanca."

"With Adam Leigh. I remember that appointment perfectly. At this point I've little love for Adam Leigh."

"Surely he paid you well to leave Fernandina."

Aury took the question with a thin-lipped sneer. He laid Doña Felicia's hand gently on the table and strode across the room to stand eye to eye with Michael. "Only an hour ago Aravello told me the price was halved. He added that marines were marching on the town's gate. That I had the choice of departing with my gun ports closed or losing my fleet—and sailing to Savannah in irons."

"An ignominious end for a revolutionist, monsieur. I'm glad you chose otherwise." Even at this moment Michael could pause to wonder at his own easy tone.

"I've also chosen to keep Leigh's surgeon awhile, since I can't have his gold."

"I'm not Leigh's surgeon, Aury. I'm a free agent."

"No man who takes Leigh's gold is a free agent."

"Where's my sloop? I ordered her to follow you if you put to sea."

Aury stood across the cabin door with arms akimbo. His thin-lipped smile had broadened to a vulpine grin. Despite that animal grimace, the man's swarthy good looks were unimpaired. Michael took in that pagan handsomeness one more time—the Panlike perfection of the lean, tanned profile, the magnificent waxed mustachios, the gold ring that glittered at an earlobe. Suddenly he saw Luis Aury more as symbol than man: the epitome of the evil aura that had hung above Amelia Island for so long.

Aury spoke with studied calm. "A smartly rigged sloop called the *River of May* is hanging on our wake as best she can." It was insolence that went beyond hate, a cold sense of authority that could ignore the person addressed. "She's dropping behind fast, now we're breaking out our sail."

"Be good enough to hail her and shorten sail. I must go back at once."

"You go with me to Havana, Dr. Stone. After that we shall see.

Perhaps I'll keep you permanently, as Castro's assistant." His jaw snapped shut on the rest with the precision of a pistol shot. Michael's fist, swung from the floor, had landed flush on that bony target.

Aury swayed for an instant; the handsome dark eyes stared blankly, as though they could not credit what they saw. Michael took full advantage of that incredulity to set himself for the next and final blow. This time he struck with his right fist, with every ounce behind it. Aury took the blow at the joining of neck and jaw and lifted his own fists a split second too late. Michael stepped back calmly as the pirate's clenched hands relaxed. The pirate's knees had already buckled; he pitched forward now and fell face down on the cabin floor, a swarthy Lucifer who had had his day.

Michael spoke to no one in particular. "I've wanted to do that for a long time. Not just to Luis Aury. To all he stands for."

"One moment, Doctor, if you please!"

He whirled with his fists raised, and dropped them when he saw that Castro was balancing a scalpel in his palm.

"Very well, Doctor. I'll surrender. But it was worth it."

The pirate moaned feebly on the carpet between them and strove to lift his head from the floor. Castro skipped over his prostrate employer as nimbly as a schoolboy on a lark—pausing en route to bang a brutally accurate heel against Aury's head just behind one ear.

"Do not be confused by the scalpel, Dr. Stone. It was your second line of defense, in case your fists failed. Stay where you are for a moment—make sure our comandante is unconscious." He went through the door as he spoke, changing his skip and jump to an easy stroll as he vanished aft. Michael knelt beside the pirate and saw at once that Castro's kick had been delivered precisely. Smashing against Aury's skull just above the motor area of the brain, it had rendered the pirate *hors de combat* for the time being.

The Spanish surgeon stood in the door again when he looked up—the picture of nonchalance now, with an unlighted cigar between his teeth. He handed Michael a second roll of Havana as the younger doctor stepped out to the deck.

"Stroll, Doctor—do not run. As you see, our taffrail is only a few steps aft." Castro's voice was a careful whisper as he rolled the cigar between his smiling lips. "Do not mind the helmsman—his whole mind belongs to the course he is steering. As I hoped, the crew is still aloft, breaking out the last of our sail."

"Why did you help me?"

"I belong here, Doctor. Your place is *there*." The Spaniard's florid gesture took in the wave-pounded sandspit that ended Amelia Island to the north—and the whole vast sweep of marshland and pinywoods that bounded the far horizon. "Do not concern yourself with Aury. When he sits up again, he will remember he was a fool to think he could pluck a hostage from America."

They stood at the taffrail now. Michael stared down dazedly at the white dance of the wake, a pale arrow that seemed to pierce the blue ocean floor. The brigantine, he noted, was the apex of a long wedge of shipping, straining toward the open sea with every jib and skysail belled to take the wind. Already the pale-gold contours of the land had begun to blur a little at the edges, to merge with the clean blue of the Atlantic. For a moment he saw no sign of his sloop and felt his heart plummet. Then he choked a shout of exultation as the *River of May* whisked smartly 'round the stern of the next vessel in the wedge and cut boldly into the brigantine's wake again, a scant hundred yards astern.

Castro said, quietly enough, "I can give no orders, Doctor. Besides, there is no time to lower a gig. You must go overside and swim to your freedom."

Michael leaned out from the rail. He saw that the *River of May*, running wildly before the wind, was barely clinging to the heels of the larger vessel, that Tola, handling her with all his skill, could not avoid losing way in that freshening breeze, as compared to the forward surge of the brigantine.

"Now, Dr. Castro?"

The Spaniard pressed his hand warmly. "Now will be your only chance. Go with God, Americano!"

Michael plunged in a long, raking dive as the brigantine's stern dipped in a swell. His body struck the wave at its crest and flailed down the far slope. In that flash he remembered another blind plunge he had taken not too long ago—from another ship's rail, from the threat of another bondage. Then, he had dived into an inky sea with no real hope and no future worthy of the name. Today, he knew that he was free with the first sturdy stroke—and his future (save for a bit of unfinished business at Adam Leigh's) was serene as any man could hope for.

For an instant it seemed that the plunging bowsprit of his sloop would spit him like a roasting fowl. He heard Tola's grunt as the Minorcan leaned hard on the wheel; the cutwater missed his head with a safe yard to spare. He let the gunwale race by and trod water easily while he waited for the *River of May* to come about and pick up its skipper. Already the dark wedge of privateers, beating their final retreat from Fernandina, was a vanishing threat in the blue. . . .

There was the sloop again, leaning easily on the wind as she worked back across her course. He swam toward her with long, unhurried strokes, enjoying the bright sting of the open sea, almost unwilling to climb to his own deck again. Yet he caught the tossed painter on Willi's first try and swarmed aboard—with all the nonchalance of a man accustomed to swim a mile offshore. Standing beside his wheel, he shook his fist at Aury's sail, and felt his heart sing with an explosion of righteous anger.

Tola's voice brought him back to realities, not too painfully. "There is blood on your knuckles, jefe."

He smiled down at his bruised fist and rejoiced in the sting of pain. "So there is. I don't regret it for a moment."

The Minorcan, keeping his eyes on his sail, held the sloop steady on the first landward tack. "Willi is bringing you dry clothes, Señor Mike. It is cold in the wind."

"I hadn't noticed."

"As you see, we set our course for the Amelia. Do we go to Adam Leigh by that channel—or the open sea?"

"Take the inland route. I want a look at the water front in Fernandina."

Tola's agile toes let out a guy rope, heeling the *River of May* on her beam ends, but holding the tack with two iron hands. "With this wind, we could dock at St. Marys in an hour."

"Why St. Marys?"

"Surely you remember how Gator and I spent yesterday?"

Michael buried his face in a towel. Drying himself vigorously, he could take time to reproach himself before he answered Tola. It was quite true that Minorcan and Seminole had spent most of last week aboard the *Resolve*—tidying the empty cabins as they transferred the patients aboard to the Long Wharf and Dr. Hilary's care, readying the afterhouse against Dimity's return. It had been her plea that she be allowed to return to her old home aboard the hulk, now that Michael had boarded up the house on the Prado and surrendered the bulk of his Fernandina practice to Dr. Hilary. Michael, in turn, had promised to bring her back from St. Marys the moment the American occupation of Fernandina was a thing accomplished.

"We'll do it this way, Tola. Take me first to the Point—I'm late now for my inspection tour. Leave me there for the night." He buried his face again in the towel and ordered the image of Marian Leigh back to its prison in his memory.

"For the night, jefe? You have not stayed the night at Punta Blanca for many months."

"I'll make an exception this time. You can still dock at the Long Wharf before sundown. Report to Dr. Hilary and make sure the occupation is a success. If the town seems quiet, you may cross to St. Marys this time tomorrow and bring my wife over." He knew that his voice was completely calm. Tola could have no inkling of his inner turmoil as he faced the unfinished business ahead.

"Tomorrow then, jefe. If the town is quiet." The sloop came about on her next tack. The Minorcan smiled at his master as they ducked to avoid the boom. "Do you have a message for the señora?"

"Tell my wife this: that she's to help me with the house from now on. That we're to plan every detail together." He knew that his voice was trembling, but he knew that it was sincere to the last syllable. "Tell her that I'm going with her to Charleston in another month to buy the furniture. Tell her that I'll expect fish chowder when I return tomorrow."

"And a drum steak, Señor Mike," said Tola. "I will take the fish myself, on the way to St. Marys."

They smiled at each other, then—two old friends who could

leave the rest unsaid. Michael plunged into the shirt that Willi offered from the cockpit and stood on the coaming of the deckhouse, sweeping the harbor while he dressed. Aury's flotilla was not even a threat now, a smudge that seemed to melt into the blue as he watched. A lone slaver, slinking after its master like a jackal that fears the daylight, was the only visible sail. Thanks to the offshore breeze, the blackbirder had taken its own stink into the open Atlantic. Michael wondered if he had breathed that strange exhalation for the last time. If he could put the memory behind him, now and forever. And then, remembering the unfinished business that awaited him, he faced away from that romantic hope—for the time, at least.

The *River of May* came about to take the wind on her port quarter. With that spin of the boom, Michael found he was facing the Fernandina water front again. Already he could make out landmarks: the warehouses of the Long Wharf, ship's berths that already seemed empty, now that the last slaver had slipped her cable. The town on the bluff looked quiet too, and strangely serene. The candy-striped flag that whipped from the sentry tower of Fort San Carlos was a part of that brand-new peace—and an assurance that it would continue. As the sloop spun closer on her long push down the Amelia, he counted the twenty stars of union in the blue field. It was a good augury for his future—and Dimity's.

With no sense of volition, Dr. Michael Stone found that he had come smartly to attention on the deckhouse coaming—that he was saluting the new flag that whipped so bravely in the clean-washed morning.

IV

Roger Farrar stood with crossed arms a safe distance from the doorway of the isolation hut. Despite that discreet ten feet of sun-bitten sand, the head overseer of Punta Blanca had not removed the heavy cotton mouth mask he had worn since he led Michael down the path through the dunes. Michael himself, swathed in an identical mask, rose slowly from the detailed examination he had just made. He stared down for another instant at the black corpse sprawled on the litter bed—at the hideous blotches that all but covered face and body, at the drum-tight distention of the abdomen, at the mushroom swelling of the groins. Too often in the past he had made this same diagnosis—in a setting not too different from today's.

"The plague?"

"The plague, Roger—in its most virulent form." His voice, muffled in the cotton, had sounded almost sepulchral. He backed from the hut as he ripped the mask aside—damning his superstitious caution even as he fought down the fear that this same Black Death might spring at his throat.

Farrar stripped off his own mask as they climbed the shoulder of the dune. Michael smiled wanly as he watched the overseer take his first real breath in the clean sea air. "When did he die?"

"Last night. He was sprawled on the floor as you saw him when I came with his supper bowl."

"You should have sent for me at once."

"Why, Doc? He's dead, isn't he?"

"You're sure no one's gone near this hut since you brought him here?"

"Sure as shooting. Fact is, anyone but me who came down that path *would* be shot. You know it's guarded night and day."

"From all visitors, including rats?"

Roger Farrar frowned his bewilderment. "So you think that rats can spread the Black Death?"

"It's a thought worth pondering. Leigh always rat-proofs his ships when he carries human freight. You know what we've spent to clear the Point of rodents."

The overseer chuckled grimly. "If a rat came visiting, he'd have to carry his own provisions. I think we're safe enough."

"So do I, since he's been isolated from the start. Still, we've no choice but to burn the hut. To the ground—and at once."

"I hoped you'd say that. Lafe and Paddy are standing by now in the barn with a bucket of turpentine. God knows I'd never get anyone to handle the body for burial."

"The body itself must be soaked in turpentine. Can you persuade either of those rednecks to enter the hut?"

"Not unless I put a gun at their backs. Don't make me do that, Doc. They're mad enough now, missing their Christmas leave."

"Give me the turpentine, Roger. I'll pretend it's part of my job."

Ten minutes later, with the isolation hut soaked in turpentine and pyramiding in flames from floor to palm thatch, Michael felt he could wash his hands of the incident. The hut had been burned down before, here in its nest of dunes—once when a pox had threatened the pens and the cases had been confined beyond the threat of incubation, again when a fever case had turned out to be not the dreaded *coup de barre,* but a simple case of dengue. Burnt and rebuilt as needed, its faded palm thatch had always loomed among the white hillocks like a phantom tent. . . . Michael glanced back just once as he followed the path to the hospital proper. He had cause to remember the picture later: Roger Farrar, impassive as a snuff-brown mummy as he chewed a straw atop the highest dune; the two lanky rednecks, armed with brooms to beat down any spreading fire, scowling at their task like hardly animate statues. At the time he was conscious only of the faint golden sheen of the sand, and how well it served as a background to the roaring blaze.

He had avoided touching the body in the hut, but he scrubbed vigorously nonetheless in the hospital anteroom, flung his work-soiled clothing into the pot of boiling water that always stood in the small courtyard just outside, and went into the dispensary that also served him as an office. Here he donned the traditional white linen he would wear when he paid his respects at the manor house. The afternoon shadows were lengthening when he opened his record book and inscribed the particulars of the death:

"REX. Angola Black. Two hundred pounds, age *circa* twenty years. Certified a prime hand by the skipper of the *Nantucket Belle,* from whom he was purchased, off Punta Blanca, December 22nd, 1817. . . ."

He copied the facts in a meticulous hand from the bill of sale at his elbow. It seemed a needless rite, now that Rex had been reduced to a pile of ashes; in a way, it seemed a desecration to write off that name in a ledger before the ashes could cool. But Leigh had always insisted on complete records.

"Since Rex was suffering from ophthalmia after his long confinement on shipboard, sailors from the *Nantucket Belle* delivered him direct to the isolation hut, where he was held for observation for the time being. As was our custom, there was no contact between Rex and our beach guards, or between the guards and the sailors from the slaver, who rowed back to their vessel at once, boarding her as she put out to sea. . . ."

He considered that point for a moment with his quill suspended above the page. The meticulous routine at the Point, which recognized the danger of contagion when fresh blacks were brought ashore, had paid a handsome dividend.

Thanks to that routine, Rex had been segregated completely from the moment he set foot in Florida: the slavers themselves had been subjected to the same rigorous rule during their brief sojourn on the beach. Had Rex been delivered to the first detention pen, he might well have spread disease among the other newly arrived blacks, held under observation in that stockade over the past fortnight. Fortunately, the fear of the highly contagious ophthalmia (that disease of darkness that afflicted so many newly shipped blacks after their month-long confinement in the stinking holds) had banished him to solitary confinement.

"So far as I could ascertain, there was no suspicion of plague when Rex was put ashore. The disease struck the Negro, as it so often does, suddenly and without warning. Thanks to his absolute quarantine, and the total lack of contact, it is my considered opinion that the infection was confined to the isolation hut itself, where it has now been scotched by fire."

Michael tossed down his pen and listened to the quiet that surrounded him. For once the hospital was nearly empty—so nearly empty, in fact, that brief Christmas holidays had been granted to both Fulton and Ledoux. The two resident doctors had gone down to St. Augustine the day before, along with a good half of Leigh's private army. Michael considered that fact soberly as he closed the ledger. Forty-odd rednecks, with Roger Farrar to whip them into line, were sufficient to police the estate—if the pens were quiet.

Farrar would surely have needed a larger force, if a threat of bubonic plague had spread through the pens. He snapped to his feet, startled by the sudden wild wailing that had just swept down the high-stilted hospital veranda—and laughed aloud at that burst of nerves. As always, the veranda (with its long file of mattings to shut out the glare) had made a perfect wind tunnel for the inevitable sea breeze that came up with afternoon.

He had sat in this pine-box office a hundred times, listening to that same wailing sea wind as he pored over Leigh's ledgers—turning to light a candle spill as the last light faded, hardly lifting his eyes as the threnody of the sea breeze merged with the deeper threnody from the pens themselves. . . . It would be bad tonight, he reflected, even if the news of the plague victim had not spread: tonight was a full moon, and the moon magic brought frenzies all its own to those captive hearts.

Tonight he would steel his thoughts against that threnody of despair: he would ignore its wordless appeal, now that he was hearing it for the last time. . . .

Rehearsing the words he would speak to Adam Leigh, he found that he had gone out briskly to the hospital steps. Standing in the shade of the veranda mattings, watching the black coil of smoke spiral up from the dunes, he felt the inevitability of this moment press down on his senses once again—as though all his life had been a preparation for the last hard battle with Leigh, for the good-by he would speak to Marian. When he saw the planter himself stalk down the path (dusty as one of his own field hands, but indomitable in his weariness), he found he could cast off his last doubt, like an outworn cloak.

"Sorry if I'm late, Doctor. But we couldn't risk opening all the pens today. Even so, we needed whips to lock them in."

"You'll always need whips, won't you?"

If the abrupt question had jarred his aplomb, Adam Leigh gave no sign. "I'm glad to see you burned the isolation hut. It was the only way to be sure."

"And stockades—and branding irons."

"Are we conversing, Doctor, or are you addressing an unseen audience from your hospital steps?"

Michael stepped down to the path. "I'm telling you I've had enough—or trying hard——"

"Don't try, Doctor. I believe every word."

"The American flag is flying over Fernandina tonight. This morning *I* was called an American for the first time. I'm taking both facts as omens and offering you my resignation."

Leigh's level glance had not wavered: he continued to stare at Michael as though he had not heard, though it was obvious that his brain had closed instantly on the words.

"So you think my days are numbered, Doctor? You're leaving me while there's still time?"

"On the contrary. I think you're as indestructible as Beelzebub—if you'll permit the comparison."

"The compliment is accepted."

"Probably you'll outlive me. Probably you'll prosper, while I'm still carving my own small corner on the St. Johns. But I'm living my own life from this day on. I'm making my own fortune, with no help from you. When I'm strong enough, I'll begin to fight you in earnest. You, and every breeder in the south." Michael drew a great angry breath, as the words shattered against Adam Leigh's silence. "As you say, it's a fight that'll outlast our lifetimes. So we can't join battle too soon."

"True enough, Doctor."

"Is that all you can say? Why don't you call your guards and lock me up?"

"With two thousand slaves milling in their stockades, I'll need all my guards tonight."

"Why not pen me with the others? That's where I belong, in your book."

"Once more you underestimate me. Slaving is my business. I don't deny that. Nor can you deny that most men were born to slavery, if you'll keep an open mind."

Adam Leigh considered his credo for a moment and found it good; his voice was oddly gentle as he faced Michael again; only the feral whisper of his whip, as he flicked the sand between his dusty field boots, betrayed his emotion. "Some men, of course, are born too weak to rule—and too stubborn to submit to the lash. Such men are useless to me. I must kill them—or dismiss them. Precisely as I'm dismissing you, Dr. Stone. Or, should I say, accepting your resignation as of now?"

Michael felt the next words choke in his throat. He could not doubt the evidence of his ears: the wintry smile that tensed Leigh's lips was proof enough that the planter meant what he said.

"Perhaps I came here to dismiss you, Doctor. Have you thought of that?"

"It's hard to believe."

"I'm aware of that. I'm also aware of the fact that I've spoiled your urge to be a knight-errant once again. Will you accept my apologies?"

"May I ask why I'm dismissed?"

"Haven't you stated the reason? We're enemies. We'll always be enemies."

"We were enemies when you forced me into your service. But you made good use of me."

"Precisely. My use for you has ended. I shall make out nicely with your two assistants from now on. You've taught them all you know; you've built me the finest breeding farm since the Pharaohs. Let that be your monument, Dr. Stone. Go in peace."

"Is that your only reason?"

"Precisely. Call it a divine coincidence, if you like—that my need for you should end just as your hate for me has reached the bursting point."

"Is that your only reason?"

Adam Leigh's stare was still bright as twin dagger points. "Of course it isn't, Dr. Stone. Go up to the house. Let my daughter-in-law complete the picture."

Their eyes held on that, as though they could break each other's armor with hate alone. Then Michael turned away without a word and strode down the path to the manor house. He remembered not to run, just in time: a man does not run when he goes to resolve his fate—especially when he has planned the resolution well in advance.

Much later he would remember how strangely empty the great apron of lawn had seemed that afternoon and how ominously quiet in its emptiness. He would remember that Mozo's white burnous, an inevitable sight on the portico in this final hour of the day, was nowhere to be seen; that the tall stair well echoed emptily to his boots as he charged up the steps, looking in vain for Guillaume; that Marian's luggage, standing beside her door in a neglected mountain, all but tripped him as he vaulted over and swept her into his arms. All that mattered, for the moment, was the sweet eternity of her kiss; the fact that she was standing in her window frame, watching the lawn below as though she had waited for him forever. The fact that her first words, clear as doom itself, only echoed the certainty in his heart. . . .

"I'm leaving tomorrow, Michael. On the *Dos Amigos*. I'm taking the boy back to London."

"I know, my dear." He held her at arm's length, doing his best to match the wise finality of her smile. What he had said was quite true: he had always known that she would save that smile for their parting.

"I promised to come back—when he felt I should. I promised never to see you after today. He knows I'll keep that promise. It's the best bargain I could make."

"I know that too."

"He said he'd let you go—if I'd do the same."

"Can we let each other go—ever?"

"I think we can, Michael. You see, I've learned a great deal these past few weeks. About you—and about myself." Again she lifted her face to his, to offer him the barrier of that smile. "If I've made that boast before, it will bear repeating. This time I really mean it. I think I've—suffered enough to mean it."

He found that he was speaking as though he had not heard—as though his voice could shut out Marian's own hard-won wisdom. "I wanted to come back to you. Again and again. It wasn't easy to stay away."

"But you managed it, Michael. Just as I'll manage now."

"When did you—reach this decision?"

"When I heard you were building on the Cowford. The river is only an hour's ride across the barrens. How could we have kept apart—even for a day? How long would *he* have permitted us——?" She gestured unhappily at the great apron of lawn below her window, at the threat of Adam Leigh that still lay, like an invisible shadow, across its satin-green immensity. Michael led her gently away from the window, obscurely glad that she had not called the planter by name.

"He knows, of course—about the night we——?"

"He's guessed enough. I can see now that he left us together—expecting just that to happen." Her eyes held his steadily, without shame. "Naturally he knew I'd never let it happen again—once I'd thought things out."

"What was there to think out—beside the fact we're in love, and will always be in love?"

"Our boy's future, for one. Your wife's, for another."

"You knew I'd go back to my wife. Just as I knew you'd never leave the boy."

"It will make the going easier if I'm in England." She took an impulsive step toward him and searched his face for affirmation. When he took her in his arms again, when he covered her face and her breast with his pleading kisses, she seemed to yield to his pleading completely. And yet, even as she returned his embrace, even as she gave back those kisses with flaming interest, he knew that this too was only a part of her farewell.

"You understand me. You've admitted it's the only way, even if you won't say the words aloud."

"Where will you go? How will you live?"

Again she offered that maddening, perfect smile. "Have you forgotten that I'm a rich widow, with a son to educate? Surely I can carry out that duty in London."

"Does Leigh admit that much?"

"Freely. I won't return to torment you, Michael. Not until it's safe to return." She looked away on that, and the iron calm she had imposed on her voice just escaped crumbling. "Don't be troubled: I'll stay clear of Punta Blanca until you're so firmly married you wouldn't dream of—straying from your duty."

"I came to tell you that *I* was leaving," he said, and the dead timbre of his voice all but matched her own. "You didn't give me time to speak. Somehow, I thought you'd fight to—to hold me. I'm not too flattered by your—common sense."

"You'll thank me in time," she said, and left his arms at last, to go to the gallery outside the tall french window. He held his ground, permitting her to establish the symbolism of that slow, sure withdrawal.

For a long moment (and it was an oddly tender moment, despite the vast echoing emptiness within his mind and heart) he made no attempt to speak. Instead, he treasured her silhouette against the flamingo-bright sunset—storing each item in his memory against the long loneliness ahead. Marian, with her eyes on the shadowed sweep of bayou, made no attempt to break the silence Their last argument, for all its violence, was already over.

"Shall we say good-by, then?" he demanded at last.

"I think we've already done so, Michael."

"Just like that?"

"Just like that. Isn't it simpler?"

"May I kiss you just once before I go?" He had failed to keep the bitterness from his voice: he let it emerge now, full strength. "As your ex-lover, I won't abuse the privilege."

She had turned as he spoke, but she was staring across the lawn now, her voice strangled in a soundless cry. He saw her eyes go blank with terror as they took in a threat he could not see within the bedroom—and grasped the reason for that terror when a devil's harp string twanged out there in the crepuscular stillness.

The gull-feathered shaft had already quivered home, a scant six inches above her head. His muscles exploded into action as he marked the arrow's flight and realized that the archer must have stood somewhere on the open lawn. He was on the gallery now, sweeping Marian out of that line of fire, ambushing them both behind the great fluted pillars of the portico. With that lunge, he heard the musket roar, heard a thin, keening scream that told him it was safe to look. But he held back a moment more, to make sure the girl in his arms had not fainted. To cling to her one more time —and wonder if this gull-feathered shaft was fate in another form.

"He was aiming at me, Michael—I *saw* him!"

"Don't try to talk, dear." He reached above their heads and wrenched the arrow from the wood. "It's a Seminole, all right. Probably some marauding stray. Apparently he was just stopped in his tracks."

A bellow from the lawn underlined his words. Recognizing the voice of Jack Poore, Leigh's stocky field boss, Michael thrust out a cautious head.

Poore stood astride the Indian, who lay spreadeagled on the lawn like a giant doll in snow-white buckskins. Poore's musket, still lying in the crook of one arm, smoked in triumphant aftermath.

"Stopped him dead, Doc. Anyone hurt up there?"

"How did he get this far?"

"Get down to the beach—you'll have your answer. Leigh's howling for you now."

There was no mistaking the urgency in the overseer's tone. Michael knew that it had reached Marian when he heard the rush of her feet on the gallery. Without turning, he knew that she had run down the hall to the nursery, and knew, just as surely, that the nursery would be empty. He followed her wildly, feeling his own heart stop on that knowledge. But Marian was already swaying in the doorway when he reached her, with the child safe in her arms. He felt his throbbing breath ease a trifle when he saw her steady, watched her chin rise defiantly as she held the heir to Punta Blanca closer. Only her eyes betrayed the nameless fear they both were sharing.

"How did it happen, Michael?"

"I still don't understand."

"Why is the house empty? Where's Queen? This is the first time she's left his side for a moment."

"You'd better stay here, and lock the door. I'll send Poore up to guard you."

"No! I'm coming too!"

She ran down the stair with him, matching him stride for stride, ignoring his protests. And even as she ran, she held the child gently, preserving his slumber by some miraculous balance of her own.

"Didn't you hear? I'm wanted on the beach."

"I've got to know what happened."

"Poore will tell you, Marian. Stay where you are."

The overseer was waiting on the portico, as he had hoped; Michael saw instantly that he had had his orders from Leigh.

"You're to stay right here, ma'am. I'm to cover the house until the doc reports back."

"In God's name, Poore, *what's happened?*"

But the overseer only jerked a thumb eastward, even as he restrained Marian with a competent hand. "See for yourself, Doc. It's still happening—fast."

He could smell the smoke as he ran, though the fresh sea wind had shifted to the north now, and most of the billowing cloud was obscured by the tall east wing of the manor house. He could hear the sickening crescendo of the flames, peppered by gunshots. Above and beyond that barrier he heard the sound that had haunted his nightmares for years—the animal mouthings of black men in agony, the hoarse gasp of humanity struggling to break its bonds and trembling on the brink of success.

Later, he knew that his mind had never paused to sort that threat into its proper parts. He knew that he had merely crossed the truck garden at a panting run, circled the gin to avoid a red volcano of sparks as the rooftree crashed, and plunged into the dunes with his hair burning, as he hurdled a palmetto clump that had just geysered into flame. At first glance the whole estate seemed to be burning, from the tip of the Point itself to the green fire lane of the vegetable garden. There, at last, was the circle of dunes that boxed the isolation hut—the feeble genesis of this holocaust, though the blaze had moved beyond its starting point long ago. There, just outside the circle of ashes, lay the two estate guards, tomahawked into bloody rag piles. There, on the summit of the tallest dune, was Roger Farrar—his body still hunched in an attitude of frozen surprise, an arrow haft deep in his back.

Michael came down the slope of the dune, banishing the last of his horror in a great shout of rage. Adam Leigh answered the shout quite calmly. The planter, who sat halfway down the slope with his back to the dead overseer, was in the act of loading the brace of pistols that swung by lanyards from either shoulder. His eyes were fixed, calmly enough, on the two dead Indians tumbled on the flat a scant fifty feet away.

"Will you make sure Roger's beyond hope? As you see, I've been rather busy since you resigned."

V

The arrowhead (a white quartz wedge filed to needlepoint sharpness) had exploded from the overseer's chest and snapped off short in the sand. Michael weighed it in his hand as he came down the dune and squatted on his heels beside Adam Leigh. It seemed an absurd moment to pause for thought, when every instinct urged him to flight, but the planter's calm was infectious, even in this ring of death.

"Roger was killed at point-blank range. Someone crept over the dune and drove this arrow through his back."

Leigh indicated the nearer of the two sprawled red bodies. "There's your man, Doctor. I stopped him with a bullet, just as he —and his friend—were finishing off our two fire watchers. It's my opinion Roger never knew what hit him."

"Are you sure there aren't more?"

"Just one. He broke free and ran for his life when Poore and I surprised him here. Poore has accounted for him by now, I trust."

The planter listened in silence as Michael spoke of the third Indian's death outside the portico; the planter's eyes, concentrated on the priming of his pistols, lifted briefly to survey the wall of smoke that rose between them and the pens. Gunshots still burst out at intervals behind that barrier—followed by wild bursts of shouting that could have come from black throats, or white. . . .

"For three interlopers, they made their mark. You'll agree to that, won't you, Doctor?"

"How can you be sure there are only three?"

"Poore found their dugout canoe hidden in the marsh—a few minutes after he'd locked the last pen. Apparently they'd waited there in hiding all through the day—and slipped out when they saw a chance to snatch at this fire and spread it." Leigh smiled bitterly. "In another moment we'd have nipped that in the bud. It was the third devil who carried the torch to the cotton—and the storage bin. As you'll observe, the shifting wind did the rest."

"There could still be other dugouts."

"True enough, Doctor. But this was a hunting canoe. Not a war party. My opinion is that Hospetarkee Emathla is waiting now, across the tidal reach—hoping at least one survivor would return. He's much too wise to risk a full-scale raid without some report. Thanks to Poore and me, that report won't be made."

Hospetarkee Emathla. Michael remembered the proud figure in his surgery door, the wink of light on the ceremonial breastplate of beaten silver, the eyes that had studied him from the aloof height that separates chieftain and interloper. And yet, Hospetarkee had offered him the time-honored salute of peace. Hospetarkee had sent Gator to Fernandina, to be the doctor's servant. . . .

"How can you name the raiders?"

"Hospetarkee Emathla has raided me before, Doctor. A slave here and there, in the pinywoods. Just as they take shoats from back-country farms. You might call it a sort of tribute." Adam Leigh sighted a pistol at an imaginary target. "So far, he's never dared to send his braves this far. But he's always hated me for buying land he considers his own hunting ground. Twenty years ago the Seminoles had saltpans on the Point; to them, it's still sacred ground, and we're still the intruders."

The planter's voice was still calm beyond belief as he sat on the shoulder of the dune and watched a fortune go up in smoke. A professor of history, lecturing a backward student on the habits of the red man (and stressing the Indian's strange refusal to surrender his land to others), could hardly have spoken with more deliberation. Michael bounced to his feet at last, in a tardy effort to break through that bland shield.

"Surely there's something we can do down there!"

"Patience. As you see, the fire is quite beyond control. There's no way under heaven to get through. If you wish to be useful, send up a prayer to your special deity. Ask that the flames spend themselves before they reach the pens."

"I'm afraid the pens are burning now."

"So am I, Doctor. We'll know when the smoke clears."

"Does it mean nothing to you that over two thousand souls may be perishing down there now?"

"*Twenty* souls at the most, my friend, if you'll concede that red neck estate hands have souls. The rest are cattle; we'll replace them in time. Grieve for my bank balance, if you must—it'll stand the strain."

"If you ask me, the rednecks are fighting for their lives. The cattle seem to be winning." Michael stared at the wall of smoke. In that interval it seemed to have risen even higher. "Surely there are more than twenty guards on the estate. Farrar said that he'd kept over forty in the blockhouse after the holiday leaves."

"If you'd stood on this dune a half hour ago, Doctor, you'd have watched at least half our guards decamp. The patrol boat was jammed to the gunwales." Again Leigh sighted his pistol at an invisible, and well-hated, target. "They put off from the Point just as the fire closed in. The others cursed them from the beach—and went back to their guns. I saw it all quite clearly; it wasn't a pretty sight."

The planter broke the sentence in the middle and rose squarely to his feet to level a finger at the coiling screen of smoke. Michael stared through the brief rent in that hideous, red-gray wall. He saw the watch tower of the nearest stockade, teetering on its palmetto base as fire gnawed relentlessly at the logs. He saw the trapped guard, swaying on his perch with a clubbed musket in his fists, watched the man lose his balance and fall into a black, shrieking void—a hollow among twisted logs that was suddenly alive with hands. Before the smoke could blot out that vignette completely, Michael had an indelible picture: black fingers, closing a dozen traps on hair and groin, black arms cinching neck and waist like jungle lianas, as they drew this captive white flesh to earth.

"That too was not a pretty sight," said Leigh. "Can you blame the others for leaving when they could?"

"Surely the patrol boat can beat back into the bayou."

"I doubt if there's a first-class seaman aboard. I'm sure there's no room for extra passengers. Even if they had some thought of rescuing us—which I doubt most of all. No, Doctor, the most that we can hope for is that they'll reach Augustine by morning. With the best of luck, Coppinger could hardly land a rescue force before tomorrow afternoon——" Again Leigh did not complete the sentence. He merely settled comfortably, with his back to the dune, and watched the fire do its work.

Michael watched the fire too with eyes that made no effort to match the planter's basilisk stare. Already he could see that the holocaust had taken on a pattern: beginning at the cotton warehouse, leaping wildly from gin to forge to storehouse, it had closed the neck of the Point long ago. Now, moving southward and eastward under the compulsion of the sea wind, it had blanketed the scrub and marsh that fringed the Point's southern rim. In that fast-moving wall of flame the guards' blockhouse had been an early casualty: he could mark the glowing shell of that bastion as the flames moved on. The guards, scuttling for their lives through the scrub, had evidently taken what shelter they could find—and had fired across the tops of the pens even as they fled. Michael could picture that flight all too clearly: the rabbit scuttle of mean men who feel death's tongue licking at their heels and realize, too late, what it means to lose the whip hand in a twinkling.

There had been no more shooting for some time. Voices still boomed through the smoke screen, but these too had taken on a different tempo: a hoarse, deep-bass rumble that seemed to gain in depth—and in confidence—with each passing moment. Somewhere (he did not dare to guess its origin) a cow skin drum had begun to talk its secret language. Across the Point a second drum answered in a rumbling *brio* of its own. . . .

Adam Leigh said as quietly as ever, "I paid them well to take these risks. Don't feel too sorry for them now."

"Will you permit me to be sorry for your cattle, as you call them?"

"If you insist, Doctor. But why pity them now—when they're about to make a break for freedom? Didn't you always insist they should be free?"

"Can you understand the language of those drums?"

Leigh stared at the thinning wall of smoke and shook his head. "They've never been allowed a secret language here. Or a system of signals. Whenever we heard a drum before, we smashed it with a whip handle—and marked the offender, so he wouldn't try again."

"Speaking purely as a breeder, do you think that was wise?"

"I'm afraid I don't follow you, Doctor."

"When a man keeps slaves, it's well to know their secret language."

"When a man keeps slaves, he builds his pens strong and trains his guards. If I've failed in that, I'll pay for my neglect—and do better tomorrow."

"God may not grant you a second try. Would you like to know what that drum is saying?"

"Don't tell me you can translate drumbeats, Stone!"

"Those happen to be two Angola tribesmen talking to each other across the Point. Apparently they're in different pens." Michael turned his ear toward the farther drum, beating the rhythm with a palm flat on the shoulder of the dune. "We had an Angola houseboy at the Boca. He taught me the alphabet in a few weeks—if you can call it an alphabet."

"Never mind your houseboy. What are they saying?"

"Both palisades are down. One was eaten out by fire; the other was smashed by the blacks themselves, after they'd torn their guard apart." Michael watched Leigh closely, waiting for the other to flinch. "Would you like the details of that—dismemberment?"

"Never mind the details, either. Are they planning to break free?"

"That's the pathetic part. They aren't quite sure."

Adam Leigh broke at last, with a growling burst of words that were half-sneer, half-snarl. "For God's sake, man, stop talking riddles. When are they coming through that smoke? How can we stop them from coming?"

"You're their master, Leigh. Go down to meet them with a whip in your fist. Order them back to their darkness. They may prefer it."

The planter's cold eyes opened to that thought. Michael could see that he was considering the measure seriously. "I've always respected you," he said slowly. "Even when my hate was at its peak, I couldn't help admire your strength. A man who can face defeat—and refuse to admit that the word exists—is a hard man to kill. But you're marked for death, if you don't give up this prison now. If you don't stand aside now the door has burst open——" Michael paused on that and stared at the planter, wondering if his jeremiad had pierced the man's skin—or his steel-bright ego.

Leigh said only, "If they're hesitating, there's still hope. It's a bare half hour to dusk. Perhaps they'll cling to their pens and wait."

"For what? Tomorrow, and Coppinger's militia?"

"Why not? Where can they go, now that they're free? Into the scrub to starve?"

"Don't you see that that's your greatest crime? Enslaving other men is bad enough. But you've put a blight on their will to be free, to escape you. Is there anything more tragic than a man at an open prison door—afraid to use his freedom?"

But Leigh had recovered his self-control long since. When he broke in on Michael now, his voice was hard with purpose—the authority of the man who has always given orders, who cannot believe for a moment that his orders will be ignored.

"What do the drums say now?"

"They've stopped talking," said Michael. *"That's* a battle call. Where's your ear?"

They both fell silent for a moment as the roll of taut cowhide built to a savage crescendo. The smoke had thinned to a ragged curtain now. It was still too soon to see beyond the gutted walls of the storage barns or to assay the degree of damage to the stockades.

"How long before they'll answer it?"

"I couldn't say, Leigh. How well have you molded them to the yoke?" But even as he spoke, Michael leaned forward sharply. The smoke had cleared to a mere haze to the northeast, opening a vista of the far reaches of the Point, as though a tattered curtain had been drawn aside. Black ants were stirring by the hundreds in the first detention pen—a sluggish malaise, as yet, though it was building by the moment. The drums increased in frenzy. From nowhere, it seemed, a dozen steel points flashed in the last rays of the declining sun.

"Evidently they had other secrets from you," said Michael. "Can you deny that those are pike points? Or that they mean to use them?"

"We'll hold them back," said Leigh.

"You and I?"

"Add Poore to the army. The house slaves can fire muskets. I've trained them myself."

"There isn't a slave indoors. They slipped away at the first sign of trouble. Didn't you know they would?"

Leigh did not turn a hair. "I might have expected that. We'll still stand at the wall, and shoot across the truck garden. We've no other choice."

"Three men against thousands?"

"There are sixty-three loopholes in that wall, and a rack for extra rifles at each loophole. It was planned deliberately as a reserve line for just such a time. Why shouldn't we arm ourselves and wait? As I say, they may be afraid to venture off the Point. If they do, we can drive them back."

"I'll leave that miracle to you and Poore. I'm rescuing Marian and the boy while there's time."

"I'd send Marian away if I could, Doctor. If there was a safe place to send her—and some means to get her there."

"Surely there's a sailboat at the dock."

"You aren't your usual observant self, Stone. Didn't you see there wasn't so much as a skiff moored at my dock when you came in this morning? Only the patrol boat, anchored off the blockhouse?"

"Don't tell me Hospetarkee robbed you of your boats?"

"It was my notion, Doctor. I sent every skiff on the plantation, and every catboat, to Augustine for repairs. In the *Dos Amigos*. Otherwise, I was sure my guards would take French leave over Christmas." Leigh shrugged off the fact with his same baffling calm. "I'll admit now that it was a mistake. I should have kept the *Hirondelle* moored at least."

"Why not take the Indians' dugout? We're only four—or five, with the boy."

"I'd prefer to defend my land, Doctor."

"Where's the dugout now?"

"Poore had orders to bring it to the dock. To make a show of it in the bayou, in case we're being watched from the far shore—which I'm sure we are."

"So you still believe that Hospetarkee's war canoes are skulking in the marsh grass?"

"What else can I think, after this visit? By mooring that dugout at the dock, I've told him that his raid was stopped in time. Now I must stay where I am, and play the deception out. If he saw us board the canoe and try to slip away, he'd know we were beaten—and be on us like a flash."

"Isn't it still worth the chance?"

"No, Doctor. I've told you I prefer to fight. The decision is final."

"So is my decision to save Marian—and my son."

"He's not your son, he's my grandson. I will decide how to save him—not you."

Michael let his rage explode at last—and gloried in the release of energy. His fist closed on Leigh's shirt front; with all his strength he wrenched the planter to his feet, to send a fist crashing into the man's incredulous stare. Leigh sprawled against the dune with that stare intact—as though that smashing blow had failed to dent the superb armor of his conceit. Leigh's two fists, closing on the pistols that hung at each hip, fixed Michael in his tracks.

"You can't hurt me, Stone. Or change me. Haven't you learned that much even now?"

"I'm taking Marian out of this."

"You're going to the wall, and taking your place at a loophole."

Michael took a quick step forward just as the pistol at Leigh's right side burst into flame. Reeling with the reflex, sure that he was hit, he dropped to knee and elbow on the sand; only then did he hear the hoarse animal cough behind him. He turned in time to see the hulking black body crumple and go down. The Negro—naked as some ebony Adam, his wool flame-singed, his vast white eyes rolling in death—coughed again as blood filled his throat and lungs. Flat on the slope of the dune, he made a final effort to crawl toward them, like a broken snake—gave a last convulsive shudder, then lay still.

Leigh said quietly enough, "He was the first. Give them a few minutes to stop howling, and they'll begin to pop out of that smoke by the dozens. We must fall back, Doctor."

Michael looked at him steadily as he got slowly to his feet, a move which the planter paralleled with the same dead calm. "I've thought for some time that you were mad. Now I'm sure of it."

"Will you come with me now, and discuss my madness later? Or must I remind you that this second pistol is still loaded?"

Michael shrugged and went over the landward side of the dune without looking back. Leigh stayed doggedly on his heels. The unfired pistol was a very real threat between them, all but brushing Michael's back as they dodged among the smoking ruins of the gin and took the path to the truck garden. Thanks to the steady north wind, the holocaust had burned itself out just short of that broad green fire lane; there was even the half-ruined shoulder of a barn to screen them as they broke into a run by common consent.

"Here," said Leigh, and vaulted a white-washed tabby-stone wall that cut the garden like a rule, a ghostly line of demarcation in the quick Florida twilight. Instantly the gun barrel thrust forth from a narrow loophole, ordering Michael to follow in a curt language of its own.

He did not need that inducement now. Stretched at full length on the lawn, putting an eye to his own loophole, he looked at the blackened ruins they had just quit and tried to measure the doom that must descend on them all before the night was out. He did not protest when Jack Poore, alert as an ungainly grasshopper on the vast emptiness of the lawn, thrust an English army musket into his hand and indicated a neat rack of its fellows, loaded and waiting beside the loophole. He did not dare to risk a glance at the manor house, serene against the dying sunset.

For the time being it was enough to guard the approach to that sanctuary. He shifted his weight on one elbow and sighted down the long barrel of the musket—quiet as a stone in the gathering night, calm as Adam Leigh himself, who lay at the next loophole, a solid, dark silhouette that seemed to merge with the earth. Watching the ruin of Leigh's estate for a threat that did not come, hearing the frenetic rise and fall of the drums, he found that he had ceased to think at all.

Yes, it was enough to know that his child and the woman he loved were safe for now in the white sepulcher behind him. He shifted his weight again and drew a careful bead on a quick-moving target—holding his fire just in time when he saw that it was only a whorl of ashes between two dunes and not another hulking black shadow. Beyond, as pen queried pen in the dusk, the drums rose to a crescendo—and died abruptly, as though a giant's hand had risen to still their beating. An invisible conductor, signaling the end to this overture to death—and giving no cue for the *danse macabre* to follow.

VI

An hour later the quiet was still absolute.

There had been breaks, of course: quick flurries of gunfire from each of the loopholes to drive shadows back to their web of darkness. High-pitched howls among the dunes, as a bullet spatted home. Then the quiet again—soothing at first, an indication that the slaves' abortive attempt to fumble their way across the truck garden had stopped dead. Gelid with a mounting tension of its own, as the mind probed its cause. . . . Night was pitch-black now above the dunes, and the gutted silhouettes of barns and workhouses. He needed no sixth sense to feel the shadows massing there, to hear the whisper of bare feet on sand, the slow gathering of mob courage, as the blacks prepared for their final rush.

I must act in a moment more, he told himself, or it will be too late.

Already the row of gun barrels had taken on a special sheen in the rack at his elbow, reminding him that the moon was about to rise beyond the circle of humpbacked sand hills to the east. He glanced at Adam Leigh, stubbornly on guard at his loophole. They had exchanged no words since their vigil began. Leigh had barked just one order as the last light faded, and Michael and Poore had obeyed that order without question, leaving their posts for a moment to carry the dead Seminole from lawn to dock, where they tossed him into the suck of the outgoing tide. A careless routine to impress the eyes that must be watching from the marsh grass on the far bank—a casual proof that the estate, well garrisoned and firmly entrenched, had already beaten down its black rebellion.

Michael had marked the dugout then, bobbing easily at its painter in an empty berth at the dock's side. His eye had sought Poore's for an instant, and he knew that the overseer had caught his unspoken question. But they had returned to the lawn and their posts, with Leigh's cold stare like a spell upon them.

"Take your places, gentlemen. Lady Marian herself will bring our supper in the servants' absence. I hope you're honored."

Leigh's voice had been tranquil in the gathering dusk. There had been no hint of fear in his manner as they settled to their vigil, no sign from Marian that her life, as well as theirs, hung in the balance. She had emerged from the house as regally as a queen at her own garden party—a queen who lost none of her dignity when compelled to serve her guests from a silver butler's tray. They had taken their food in silence as she knelt at their sides to offer it. Michael had felt the words choke in his throat as he tried to speak to her. With Leigh's eyes upon him, he could only press her hand quickly as she moved on. It was the planter who asked the questions, and Marian who answered, with matching aplomb.

"You've brought the boy downstairs?"

"I've made his bed in the foyer, just inside the main door. It—seemed the safest place."

"He's sleeping soundly?"

"Soundly. I was afraid he'd miss Aunt Queen, but he thinks it rather a lark to sleep downstairs."

"What about candle spills?"

"I've brought a dozen from the kitchen. Shall I begin lighting the rooms now?"

"By all means. The house must be lighted as usual. *That* should give our friends pause—on both sides."

It had been as simple as that, and as cold-blooded. If Marian was troubled at this mad play-acting, she kept her thoughts veiled. She had hardly glanced at Michael as she returned to the house, her bearing regal as ever, her eyes straight ahead. On the portico she had paused for an instant, a white shadow against the soaring white of the great pillars, and examined the grounds coolly—a chatelaine who surveys her holdings and finds them good. A moment later the windows began to glow with light as she moved from room to room with candle spills. Leigh's stratagem was apparent at once: to a watching eye among the dunes the house would have seemed alive with people, and contemptuous of any threat.

All this had happened a good hour ago, with the slow-paced tempo of nightmare made real. He turned to look at the house and saw that Marian was standing in the lighted doorway; his eye moved back to Leigh, still immobile at the next loophole. The sheen on the gun barrels had deepened, though there was no more than a hint of moonrise to the east. *A moment more,* he told himself, *and I'll be too late.*

There was no other course to follow. The attack would come with the moon; he was confident of that much, remembering the eerie compulsion of that planet in Africa. Most of these tribesmen mated by moonlight, consecrated their young to war, bowed to their gods; it was thought good fortune to be born under those pale rays, good fortune to die in battle while the moon was shining. Once the attack was launched in force, it must prove irresistible. Leigh's entire army could never have stemmed that tide, once it began its remorseless flow across the Point.

He looked one more time at the planter, and weighed his chances, even as his finger closed about the trigger of his English army musket. A quick sideways roll, a swiveling of that gun barrel would blow out Leigh's brains; a quick rush to the portico would give him time to snatch the boy from his bed inside the door; a word to Marian would force her to follow him, once the child was in his arms. . . . There was no other way to save his own, no other exit from the hell that would engulf them all with moonrise. A man's life could hardly tip the balance of that cold logic—especially when the man was mad.

He closed his mind to logic and tensed his muscles for the ordeal. His right elbow dropped from loophole to ground; his body rolled with that motion as the gun barrel swerved. But it was Marian's shoulder that came into the sights, not Leigh's head. Marian, who had crossed the lawn like a white shadow while be brooded and gained the wall in one last lithe stride. Marian, whose body was no less tense than his own as she thrust the long barrel of a dueling pistol against the planter's ear. Marian, whose voice was cool as spring water as she spoke her first quiet order.

"Get up. We've waited long enough."

She drew back a little as she spoke, giving Leigh room to rise. Michael saw his face clearly, pale as a worn coin in the first promise of moonlight, distorted by an incredulity that left even Adam Leigh wordless. Mind and spirit seemed to break in unison as his hands fell from the rifle barrel. *He pinned his life on her loyalty,* thought Michael swiftly. *Now she's turned against him, in his last defiance of fate.* And he knew it was this bitter discovery that brought Leigh to his feet, rather than the fear of the muzzle that teased his ear.

Marian said evenly, "We're going to the canoe. All of us. It's our last chance."

No one spoke as they moved across the lawn in a tight knot. With no surprise, Michael saw that Poore had fallen into step on Leigh's left—that the overseer's musket, like his own, was trained on the planter's head. Leigh himself marched like a man in a dream, as though he was hardly conscious of the deadly steel triangle that pointed his steps inexorably, from wall to driveway, from driveway to the oystershell path that led to the water's edge.

"Get the boy, Marian. I'll handle this now."

Michael heard the voice bark the order and realized it was his own. He had no clear memory of Marian's rush to the portico. The air was full of an unearthly thunder now, and the roar of many voices, but he could not orient the sound. Nothing mattered but the blessed ring of their heels on the planking of the dock, the still more blessed certainty that Marian was beside him again, with the child in her arms. . . .

On the dock, he dared to look back, and regretted the impulse instantly. The moon was up now, though it was little more than a blood-red globe on the horizon's rim. The inchoate mass that had erupted from dunes and gutted barns was still only a silhouette against that red background, a cloud that threatened for an instant to blot out the moon itself. Then, as the orb swam clear of earth (and changed to silver in its passing), the mass took on form and meaning.

He watched it engulf the truck garden as though that wide green lane had never been; he saw it flow over the wall with hardly a pause and erupt on the lawn like some monstrous flow from the earth's heart. And he knew now that the thunder he had heard was man-made, the slap of palms on cowhide. Guided by that thunder, and transcending it, the deep-throated growl of a thousand voices lusted for victims. Black feet on the portico, black fists crashing through door and window, black arms writhing like serpents as a severed head was lifted high on a pitchfork, to be joined by another and yet another.

Michael stared at those bobbing, moon-silvered heads, and knew that they were mementos of the afternoon's battle with the estate guards. He felt the flesh prickle at the base of his skull, as he thought of his own escape.

"We would have died there too. Now we'll die in the river. Is it a better choice?"

Leigh had spoken in a kind of hoarse animal croak. Michael stared dazedly at the planter, as though a stranger had spoken in their midst. He heard Poore draw breath to speak, and understood that the overseer's throat was dry as his own: only a weird rattle escaped in lieu of words. . . . Again it was Marian who took command. Marian, who thrust one hard fist at Leigh's back and sent him stumbling down the dock.

"It's still worth the chance. What are we waiting for?"

Leigh settled in the bow of the dugout with all the stiff agility of a marionette. Poore snatched a paddle and dropped into place behind him, rocking the unwieldy canoe with his bulk. Michael found that he had taken the stern paddle with no sense of transition, that he was steadying the heavy craft now with one hand on the dock as Marian took her own place just behind the overseer. She turned for an instant to whip a shawl from her shoulders and wrapped the sleeping boy in that improvised blanket.

Clearing the shore with long, sure strokes, matching his paddling with Poore's, Michael found sudden release—and a surge of meaningless hope. The bayou was millpond smooth now that the gnawing north wind had died. A strong current ran toward the open sea, where the tidal estuary turned sharply to meet the Atlantic. As Leigh had said, they had no choice but to drive for this narrow channel, between the flanking walls of mud flat and tide-flooded marsh grass. If Hospetarkee Emathla had chosen this nest for his war canoes (and there was no other vantage point that commanded the dock of Punta Blanca) they must come within arrow shot in another moment. . . .

Behind them the air was hideous with curses in a dozen tongues, as the baffled slaves engulfed the last foot of lawn and waded hip-deep in the bayou to mark the dugout's flight. Ahead, the spreading wall of marsh grass, a deep, sick green even by moonlight, offered its formidable barrier. With each straining stroke, the dugout swam closer to freedom. Already Michael could see the dog-leg kink in the channel that opened to the wide tidal reach beyond the Point and the freedom of the sea. He closed his eyes against that glimpse, driving his paddle with all his strength to match Poore's strokes. When he looked again, he understood the meaning of the overseer's gasp, of Adam Leigh's cackling laughter.

The great war canoe (thirty feet from beaked prow to the sweep at its stern) slipped from its nest of marsh grass as calmly as a ghost that knows its rendezvous in advance. A second canoe (bristling like the first with egret-plumed braves, but noisy with the cacophony of a dozen plucked bowstrings) glided, just as precisely from its ambush on the far bank. Poore threw his paddle aside and buried his face in his arms. Michael put his own paddle into a quick reverse spin, stopping the dugout dead. The sweeps of the two huge craft paralleled that motion, holding them steady in mid-channel, boxing the dugout in dead water as the two beaked prows nuzzled each other.

The voice of Hospetarkee Emathla boomed from the first canoe. Michael recognized it instantly. There was no mistaking that vibrant bass—or the hiss of the sense-bearer's Spanish.

"It is you, Señor Médico?"

"Greetings, Hospetarkee Emathla. May we go in peace?"

"A moment, first."

Michael drew a deep breath and held a rein on his hope. The Seminole's voice was gentle: there was no mistaking its note of friendliness, so far as the doctor from Fernandina was concerned. Just as there was no avoiding the whisper (as well timed as a battery of savage violin strings, fresh-tuned to concert pitch) as arrows fitted to a score of bowstrings there in the facing war canoes.

"There is a woman in your canoe," said Hospetarkee. "A woman with a sleeping babe in her arms. Will you name her, Señor Médico?"

Michael answered instantly, knowing that their lives balanced on the thin reed of his assurance.

"The woman is my wife. The child is ours."

"You have a wife in Fernandina."

"There are many wives in the chief's house. Does he deny me the same right?"

The war canoes rocked with laughter. Michael stared down the burst of levity, the paddle blades raised to him in salute. The child, wakened by the gust of mirth, stirred at last in Marian's arms and whimpered faintly. He watched her still the whimper, saw her wrap the boy more closely in the shawl and place him carefully on the dugout's splintered floor. Her chin lifted as she completed the soothing act; her eyes blazed at the feathered Seminole with enough heat to wilt the feathers in his turban. She spoke in a furious burst of Castilian, throwing the words straight at Hospetarkee, leaving translation to the sense-bearer.

"The doctor is my husband. He has been my husband from the beginning. Let us go in peace!"

"A moment more, señora. Who is the man at the bow paddle?"

A new voice spoke from the other canoe. With a start, Michael recognized Toby, who had been headman of Leigh's turpentine gang before he vanished into the scrub some months ago. Tonight, this black Hercules wore a feathered turban as resplendent as the chief's; his buckskins and the silver half-moons on his chest gleamed bravely in the moonlight. His voice too had a resonance to match Hospetarkee's when he leveled a dark fist at Poore.

"El sobrestante, Hospetarkee! The field overseer whose lash drove me to you."

"Arriba, perro!"

The huddled figure in the canoe did not stir. Toby shouted the command in English.

"On your feet, dog!"

No one stirred in the dugout as Jack Poore rose like a drunken man with his hands locked in prayer. Twenty bowstrings twanged a veto to that supplication as the chief's hand flailed downward. Poore shrieked just once as he staggered under the smashing impact of as many arrow points. Crisscrossed as they were in arms, neck and body, the gull-feathered shafts made a grotesque caricature of the overseer's massive frame. When he tumbled headfirst into the bayou, he resembled a white porcupine in search of its burrow.

"And the man in the bow?"

"Must I name him, jefe?"

"Stand up, Adam Leigh!"

The planter rose instantly with folded arms and stood rock-firm in the bow with his feet spread wide and his eyes fixed on his executioners. Leaning hard on the paddle to balance the dugout, Michael could not suppress his admiration for a courage that surpassed the man's fanatic pride. There was no break in Leigh's voice as he addressed the Seminole leader.

"You will pay for this a thousand times, Hospetarkee. You will live to see your people go down in the dust. You will march at their head when they are banished beyond the sea——"

The rest was lost, as the second canoe swam closer. Toby's Gargantuan arms reached casually across the gunwale and snatched the planter aboard as easily as a trainer lifts a dog by the scruff. Leigh made no resistance. His eyes were closed now; his face was its own death mask as the war canoe glided from channel to shore. From the water's edge the slaves, packed by the hundreds in the shallows, raised a baying chorus of welcome.

"Do not hide your face, Señor Médico," said Hospetarkee. "We forgive it freely in your woman: this is not a sight for woman's eyes. You are a man who has borne many things; you can bear this as well."

"What will they do to him?" It was a whispered thought rather than a question, but the Seminole answered instantly.

"That is their pleasure, not ours. For our part, we offer him as an expiation. To Outina, the god who remembers all things and forgives no evil. Least of all, the profaning of our sacred earth."

The canoe was scraping the wharf now. Michael kept his eyes riveted there and prayed it would end quickly. He did not see Toby toss Leigh overside, for the ex-headman was obscured, for the moment, by the rhythmic backs of the other paddlers as they spun their blades in reverse and backed the canoe into the channel. When he dared to focus on the planter again, Michael saw that Adam Leigh stood alone on the stringpiece—still rock-firm in the moonlight, still glaring at encroaching doom as though he dared the first dark hand to brush his flesh.

Adam Leigh's slaves moved in from all sides—through the shallows, along the dock itself. The planks complained beneath their weight; a crosspiece snapped between two pilings, pushing the whole structure down and down, until it seemed to flatten into the ooze of the bayou. Leigh still stood erect on the stringpiece, daring the black ring to close. Michael knew that the leather bludgeon in his fist was not a whip, but the planter's own belt, which he had wrenched from his waist in a last assertion of authority. . . .

He watched the leather hiss down in the moonlight, saw it rise and fall and fall again as Adam Leigh marked his last pattern on the dark shoulders that closed in with such terrible patience. Then he went down among the milling bodies. The whip rose again and was lost forever in that black whirlpool.

"Go in peace, Señor Médico," said Hospetarkee Emathla.

VII

He watched her walk down the King's Wharf in St. Augustine with the child in her arms; he did not even raise his hand in farewell when she turned to look back at the *River of May* and the sloop's bone-weary skipper. Instead, he stood immobile at the taffrail as Willi and Tola cast off from the dock and spun the vessel into the Matanzas. It's better so, he told himself, fighting a weariness of mind that went far deeper than his tired flesh. Better to let her go ashore alone, as she wished. Better by far to let her go quietly, with no promises—and no offers of a help she doesn't need. . . .

"I've met the governor a hundred times, Michael. He'll see me in a moment, when he hears the news. Reprisal is his task, not yours."

"Let me see you to the Castillo at least."

"You must take the story to Fernandina yourself, my dear. I won't have your wife worried for a moment."

"But, Marian——!"

"You've suffered enough because of me. This is the end of your suffering."

"This is only the beginning."

He had spoken those words a scant half hour ago, when they had stood on the sloop's deck together, with Anastasia on their port quarter and the tranquil old town coming alive in the sunrise dead ahead. Marian had understood his meaning instantly; her fingers, closing on his hand and clinging for a moment, had ended the argument without words.

There had been no words for last night's horror: they had still been dazed by its impact when Tola (cruising easily in the fresh dawn breeze off Nassau Sound) had hailed their drifting dugout and sailed toward them at the sloop's smartest pace. . . . Fumbling in his memory now, Michael found he could bring back those moonlit hours only in snatches. It seemed that they had paddled forever, like puppets jerked by the same string. Paddled far offshore, for the most part, as though the empty beach still swarmed with enemies. . . .

Now, as the sloop cleared the last of the anchored vessels in the Matanzas, he watched Marian go down the King's Wharf and knew he would remember the moment forever. The proud lift of her shoulders that made light of weariness; the glint of early sunlight on the hair that tumbled like black glass at her shoulders; the scurry of a young officer's smartly booted feet in the dust of the plaza as she paused to accept his salute; the officer's outright run as he took in her first words and dashed into the cobbled street beyond to hail a carriage. . . .

Michael saw it all, quite calmly, in diminishing perspective, as though he were watching Marian vanish through the wrong end of a telescope. He watched her step into the carriage, knew she would roll over the drawbridge of the Castillo in a few more moments. That too was part of the pattern of their farewell. Reprisals, as she said, were the business of the governor. Dr. Michael Stone could leave such business in those capable hands and proceed about his own.

Brooding on the problems of Governor Coppinger (so simple beside his own), he found that the sloop was almost abreast of the Castillo now. San Marcos brooded like a gray archangel today, a serene bastion circled with moats, dominating the town it had protected so long from its artificial hill. He stared tiredly at the lions of Spain, defiant as ever on the flag that floated above the northern tower, and remembered the candy-stripe flag with its twenty brave stars that floated above another sentry box, not too far to the north. For no reason he could name, the comparison lifted his spirits, however slightly. He smiled wanly at his own forepeak, where Tola had prudently hoisted a smaller Spanish flag for their visit, and saw that the Minorcan was dipping that ensign decorously as the *River of May* slipped by San Marcos on her way to the open sea.

"Have you an American ensign in your locker?"

"Of course, Señor Mike. I will break it out this evening, when we sail up the Amelia."

"Break it out at once! We're American from now on."

He took the wheel as Tola scampered to obey the order. He had not meant to shout, somehow the act of shouting had eased his sleep-hungry nerves. It was good to give the sloop her head, to let her heel dangerously in the wind as the flag of the Union broke out smartly at her peak, defying the dwindling gray bulk of the Castillo.

"I didn't intend to bellow, Tola. Will you forgive me?"

"But of course, jefe. You have endured a great deal. Will you give me back the wheel and sleep awhile?"

The canvas chair, lashed down in the snug corner of the deckhouse, invited him to repose in the sun. He settled gratefully, admiring the gnarled wisdom of the Minorcan's hands as he eased the sloop into the Atlantic ground swell and pointed her bowsprit due north. A day's hard sailing lay ahead, if they meant to fetch Fernandina before dusk, but Michael knew that he could trust that task to the saddle-brown man at the wheel. It was good to yield to that knowledge completely—to close his eyes against the dancing cobalt light. . . . Dimity was waiting aboard the *Resolve*. Dimity and her happiness would close his horizon from tomorrow on. Yes, it was good to put the past behind him (its horror and its ecstasy alike) and plan for Dimity with all his mind.

"You're sure my wife is aboard the hulk?"

"I took her there myself, Señor Mike. Yesterday afternoon—when I had made sure the town was quiet." Tola smiled down at Michael from the steersman's post. "It was earlier than your orders, I know, but I could not help sailing to St. Marys with your news."

"You're forgiven in advance."

"It is well that I came south by moonlight. You had been afloat a long time when I picked you up."

"Your timetable was perfect. Was that my wife's idea as well?"

Tola smiled in earnest. "She insisted that I go for you at once. She wished to be alone on the hulk. To prepare for your return. For the next journey to Cowford."

Michael nodded and closed his eyes in earnest. Thinking of Dimity's happy bustle aboard the *Resolve,* he felt his relaxation deepen. The hulk had been their first home; it was oddly fitting that they should return to it now, however briefly. There would be time enough later to explain that he had given up his plan of settling at Cowford. . . .

He could feel his tired body easing down into slumber now and courted that oblivion as an addict might fumble for a drug. For the moment his mind seemed detached from weariness and racing at top speed. A squirrel in its cage, whirling in the same desperate round. Storing the last picture of Marian, her final words. . . . Coppinger has received her by now, he thought. The Castillo is humming with orders as the soldiers of the Crown prepare to repossess her land. Adam Leigh is dead, but Leigh's acres are inviolate, to say nothing of such slaves as they can round up in the scrub. Adam

Leigh did well by Spain in his lifetime. Spain's governor will now return the compliment in the name of Leigh's heir.

"Of course I'll return to the Point, Michael. The moment it's safe to return. I must salvage what I can, for the boy's sake."

"You're quite right. There are at least thirty house slaves in hiding—to name just one item. They'll come out of the scrub in time; someone must feed them."

Someone must decide about the *Dos Amigos,* when the supply ship returns from Savannah. Someone must dispose of the *Hirondelle* and the cotton on the King's Wharf, and the Spanish bonds that are filed in Leigh's name in the St. Augustine treasury. Someone must give Leigh's body a Christian burial—if his slaves haven't cut him up for medicine. . . . He had left those thoughts unsaid when he watched Marian go down the wharf. They returned to plague him now as he dropped into slumber at last.

The dream pounced instantly, a great black beast that had lurked under the surface of his mind. He sat on the portico of the manor house again—a pale wraith who had no business there, a watcher whose very presence was ignored, though he missed nothing. Marian Leigh sat on the lower step with her child on her lap. She was flanked by brilliantly uniformed soldiers—he saw at a glance that they were picked men from a royal regiment. Each soldier held a whip in his hand; the long leather coils were restless on the flagstones of the portico. In the background a voice called names that were mere tag ends from the heart of darkness. A giant's hammer (or was it an African war drum?) throbbed in maddening rhythm to counterpoint the voice. . . .

The slaves crossed the lawn before the portico in an endless file. Hands shackled, heads bowed, they took the soldiers' lashings one by one. Marching without protest through the blood-red light, they did not flinch from the whips; they did not even cry out when the branding iron seared their flesh just before they shuffled away into that vast outer darkness.

Marian (and his thoughts never left her) accepted the lashings and the branding with averted eyes. But she offered no protest when the child leaped from her lap and snatched up a whip in his turn. No one seemed in the least startled when the son of Michael Stone cut his first red ribbon in cringing flesh. His father, powerless as a ghost, watched the boy grow and grow, until he was taller than the tallest soldier on the portico. The whip hand, with a man's corded muscles behind it, was crashing down in earnest now. The boy who was no longer a boy laughed aloud as the blood spattered his boot tops—and screamed with laughter when he reversed the whip and sank the leaded butt deep in a man's skull. . . .

The images faded and he slept deeply for a while. They returned, in other guises, to remind him of the depth of his surrender, and he cried out in slumber, insisting that such things could not be. Once he half wakened with Tola's hand on his shoulder and Tola's anxious face above him. He was too tired to shake off the hand as he fumbled his way to sleep again, though he hoped that Tola's presence had restored some sense of reality to his brain. . . . The hope was justified: he did not dream again. He merely sank deep in the cotton wool of exhaustion.

The sun was past the zenith when he wakened. Willi stood at the wheel, handling the sloop with care as Tola called soundings from the bow. Michael bounced to his feet instantly when he saw that they were skirting the shore just outside the surf.

"Why aren't we on our course?"

Tola spoke guardedly, with his eye on the sounding lead. "We are on our course now, jefe. In another moment we pass Punta Blanca. Will you take your glass to the shrouds?"

"Why didn't you waken me sooner?"

"There is still time for a view, Señor Mike. Though it would seem that the smoke above the dunes answers our questions in advance."

Michael nodded a solemn agreement as he stood high in the bowsprit shrouds and trained a telescope on the beach to the north. At first glance the scrub behind it seemed empty of life: only the hideous smoke pillar was alive in that desolation. And then he marked the dance of black silhouettes among the dunes, the wink of steel in the sunlight as the slaves (milling among the ruins, still uncertain of their next move) wandered aimlessly from beach to looted manor house. He could not see the house itself, thanks to the cedar windbreaks. He was glad that his eyes were spared that much.

Tola said quietly enough, "It is a judgment from heaven. Do not mourn the loss, Señor Mike."

"Someone must corral them—and care for them. They'll never fend for themselves."

"Coppinger will be master of the Point tomorrow," said Tola. "Those who linger will be locked in another stockade. The house slaves will come back to their mistress. Leave the rest to Hospetarkee Emathla. The Seminoles too need slaves."

Again Michael nodded his agreement, with his glass still trained on the Point. The Seminole nation had always welcomed runaways. In the unexplored fastnesses of the peninsula (deep in a hundred jungle hammocks, a hundred lush savannahs) the fugitive Negro could be sure of asylum. It was true that he must exchange one bondage for another; even the untutored black knew that the Seminole's bond was lighter. Hundreds of ex-slaves had worked their way to freedom under the Indian rule, to perfect equality. Some, like Toby, had married the daughters of their former masters, had sat at the chief's council fire. . . .

"The nation can hardly absorb that many blacks."

"Those whose hate is deepest will go to the Apalachicola," said Tola. "There is a Negro fort there, garrisoned by escaped slaves. Some say there will be a Negro kingdom in time. Even those will not be allowed to starve. Hospetarkee will give homes to the others."

"All of them will be fugitives. Coppinger is duty bound to track them down."

"The estate of Adam Leigh will enter its demand, Señor Mike. The lists will be filed in Augustine. Already the names of such runaways are legion. Hospetarkee Emathla and his brother chiefs are savages by our lights. But they understand the needs of runaways."

Michael stepped down to the deck and closed his telescope. Accepting the Minorcan's logic, he found that he could almost condone that mass hegira from stockade to wilderness. Above all, he could be glad that what came after was the problem of a Spanish governor—a dilemma that a governor could be excused for tabling indefinitely. The bondsmen had simply burst their shackles—and the scrub had swallowed them. He stared hard at the sweep of pine barrens as the sloop quartered away from the shore. The smudge that marked the ruin of Punta Blanca had begun to dwindle into the marsh mist that rose in these tidal bayous at the end of day; already the scrub seemed ready to close over Adam Leigh's empire as though it had never been.

"A judgment from heaven, indeed."

"Perdone, Señor Médico?"

"I was quoting your wisdom in your teeth, Tola. If you'll take the wheel from Willi, I think I'll sleep in earnest. Can we still fetch the Amelia by dusk?"

"Easily, jefe. As you see, the wind is freshening."

"Then I surrender my command."

Michael stumbled down the cabin stair on that and settled in one of the facing wall bunks in the deckhouse. After that reconnaissance, he knew that his sleep would be dreamless.

The afternoon was far advanced when he wakened again. Without even glancing at the port, he knew that they were in the Amelia estuary; without asking why, he sensed that he must go on deck at once. Groping his way to the rail with a brain still heavy with sleep, he took in the familiar shore line—welcoming each landmark as an old friend. There was Fort San Carlos once again—looking a bit like a pepperbox, now he had glimpsed the great Castillo to the south. There was the flag of the Union, stiff as a knight's pennon in the wind, its peppermint-candy stripes a slash of color against a gray rainy sky. There was the well-remembered silhouette of José Aravello's Long Wharf—its warehouses curiously silent today, its slips all but empty. . . .

He wondered how José's smuggling would prosper under the watchful eyes of American gunboats. If José and the rest of Fernandina would relish a season of honesty, after their raffish years. Most of all, he wondered how Dr. Michael Stone and wife would manage when they had turned their backs on Fernandina and the Floridas.

His brain was still heavy with too much sleep, with the leftover of last night's terror. His heart (too empty, at the moment, to ache for Marian, though the ache would return soon enough) was back in its familiar rhythm and stronger with every beat. Dimity's happiness was his life's work now. He could never risk that happiness by lingering in Florida, by pretending to farm on the St. Johns when Marian Leigh was only a half day's ride away.

Even if she turned over the Point to overseers, she must remain in St. Augustine to protect the boy's interest. Her farewell had been final this morning, but she would forget that finality with time. . . . For Dimity's sake, he could not make his future a thing of stolen ecstasy, of secret rendezvous. For the boy's sake, he must leave Marian Leigh in peace. For his own sake, he would put the ocean between them and go back to the past. To his English heritage. To Dr. Felix Holly's surgery in London and easy wealth.

Perhaps he would tell Dimity of his decision tonight. He stared hard at the tall peak of Aravello's warehouse, which still masked the open harbor beyond, and the buoy where the *Resolve* was moored. Though the hulk was still hidden from his eyes, he could see her clearly enough—cleaning a fish for his supper in the tiny galley and humming as she worked. Dimity would have been ideally happy at Cowford. But then it was one of Dimity's best points that she could be happy anywhere. There were a dozen reasons he could offer for his change of mind, and all of them were plausible: the danger of frontier life (illustrated so tellingly only a few hours ago at Punta Blanca); a flaw in the title of his land grant; a sudden loss of fortune, balanced by a munificent offer from his aged guardian in England. . . .

The sloop rounded the Long Wharf, and the harbor opened before him at last—steel-gray under the rising wind and white with rain squalls at the horizon line. For a moment he stared blankly at the spot where the hulk had tugged so long at her mooring; the white buoy bounced crazily in the pull of the tide, but there was no sign of the *Resolve*.

"Did you shift her mooring, Tola?"

"Look to starboard, jefe!" The Minorcan's voice was quite as hoarse as his own. "The hulk has broken her cable, it seems."

He saw Dimity then for the first time. She was standing on the high deck of the *Resolve* with both fists anchored to the rail, as though it cost her an effort to stand. Even at the distance he could see she was wearing the torn blue wrapper she had worn at their first meeting. Her hair was wild in the wind and she seemed careless of the fact that the hulk was drifting in the tide and settling rapidly at the bow. Her whole being was concentrated in her eyes. He could not see clearly for the sudden tears that blinded him, but even now he knew that she was watching him as though she could never leave off watching. Measuring the fast-closing distance between hulk and sloop—and waiting, quite calmly, for the hulk to sink before he could leap aboard.

"She has opened the sea cocks, Señor Mike!"

"Can we reach her in time?"

"I think so, if the wind holds." Tola's knuckles were white on the spokes of the wheel. "Why did she slip the cable just as we turned the wharf?"

"Never mind that now. Break out the spinnaker, Willi!"

The sloop heeled wildly as the flying jib belled in the tearing wind. In that instant Michael was sure they would turn turtle in mid-channel. Then Tola wrenched the bowsprit up and sent the *River of May* booming after the *Resolve,* with every ounce of the wind behind their sails. The hulk was sinking fast now, but the sloop was coming faster. Spread-eagled above the bowsprit, Michael shouted to Dimity just before she vanished from the rail. . . . He saw her face clearly then and knew that the kiss she blew him was light as spindrift, that the smile on her lips did not belong to this world.

He heard the quick patter of her feet on the deck as the bowsprit ground against the hulk's weathered planking. In that flash he was over the rail, running as he had never run before in a last heart-bursting effort to turn her from her purpose. Water was roaring into the hold below his feet; the forward scuppers were awash when he just missed cornering her behind the capstan. His fist closed in the tattered skirt of her wrapper just as she eluded him. He never knew whether it was the wind that whipped the blue cotton garment across his eyes or Dimity's flung arm. But he knew that she had spurned life with that gesture, even before she vanished into the gray sea without a splash.

It had happened too fast for thought. Spray stung his eyes as he groped his way to the rail with the cotton wrapper still tangled at his arm. He saw her instantly, her yellow hair streaming in the tide, her slender arms driving for the open Atlantic. He shouted to her one more time, though he knew that she was beyond hearing now. Plunging from the hulk's broken rail, shedding his clothes as he struck the water, he thrashed desperately in her wake.

She had boasted often that she could outswim him when she chose. Today she made good her boast. When she sounded at last, he was a good fifty feet away and fighting for air with bursting lungs. When he reached the spot where the sea had swallowed her, he plunged despairingly, knowing she could still elude him at will.

Almost instantly his fingers closed in her hair. His heart was hammering when he burst to the surface again and drew her gently toward the looming gunwale of the sloop. And then, as his hand touched her breast, he knew there was no further need for haste. That Dimity Parker Stone had quit this world as naked as she entered it, and quite according to plan.

VIII

"Bosquebello," said Hilary Tyler. "The beautiful wood. Naturally it sounds better in Spanish."

The old doctor stood with bared head under the canopy of the live oak, his words, a mere tentative in the silence, drifted away in the warm, sunny morning. The old doctor's hand closed on the shoulder of his younger colleague. For a moment more they stared down at the new grave, as though they were seeing it for the first time. The small, compact rectangle of earth, framed neatly in its coquina wall, was already beginning to shine with new green, as nature moved in to soften the first harsh contour of death.

"Bosquebello," said Dr. Hilary. "She'll rest quietly here, Michael. How often must I tell you that?"

Michael tried to speak, but no words came. When he found his voice at last, it was calm enough. "I wanted to take her away. I would have told her that night."

"You know why she wouldn't wait for you. Gaines told you why."

"You and Gaines had no right to hold back that secret."

"We gave her our word, Michael. I've explained that too. She wanted to spare you."

"Does that make me hate myself less? I shouldn't have left her for a moment."

Again the familiar silence fell between them. Dr. Hilary Tyler dropped his hand to his side and walked a few paces along the shell path that wound between the graves. "You brought her here a fortnight ago. She won't want you to linger at her side forever—even if it *is* a lovely wood. That wasn't Dimity's way."

"You'd better go, Hilary. I know you've a dozen calls in town."

"I've brought my wagon," said the old doctor. "I'll wait a few moments, if you change your mind."

Michael raised his head at last, and stared at his friend as though he had not heard. Dr. Hilary shrugged again and walked slowly on through the shadow pattern of the new oak leaves. At the cemetery gate he paused to nod at a dark-cloaked figure who waited just outside. Michael, who had watched him go with indifferent eyes, did not stir as Felippa moved down the path and stood facing him across Dimity's grave.

"Why did you come?"

"To wish you well, Inglés. Though I have no right to enter consecrated ground."

"You loved her too, Felippa. That gives you every right. You know I wanted you—at the funeral."

"I mourned for her in my own way," said the witch. "I set a time for my grieving. It is not good to grieve forever."

"So Dr. Hilary tells me. For the present, I prefer to—to remain at her side."

"You have heard the reason for her death." Felippa spoke slowly, as though she did not relish the words. "I could have told you it was coming when you married her. That she could not hope to live beyond the year. But I thought she deserved a man for a while. A man like you——"

"Do you know what you're saying?"

"Have I ever spoken falsely?"

"How can you be sure she was dying? I'd planned to take her to England with me. London doctors might have saved her."

"You yourself are a doctor. You know that is only a delusion." Felippa paused, with her eyes on the greening mound. "*She* knew that she must leave you. She knew it long before she lost her child. She—gave me a letter to prove her knowledge. A letter to you, her husband."

Michael Stone stared at the witch for a space, as though he had not heard aright. Then he held out his hand for the square of paper folded in Felippa's shawl.

"Why did you wait a fortnight to deliver this?"

"She wanted it so. She said it was fitting that you grieve a while. She hoped the letter would end your grieving once and for all."

But Michael had already snatched the folded paper. Felippa watched gravely as he read. When he had finished at last, she moved to his side of the grave and stroked his cheek gently. The dark fingers should have seemed grotesque against his cheek, but Michael's hand closed above them in silent thanks.

"She could have told me this sooner."

"And hurt you all the more?"

"I could have endured the hurt—and cared for her until the end."

"She was not born to die in bed, Inglés. Read me the words again."

Michael opened the folded sheet. He read slowly, feeling the page blur. But he spoke the words clearly enough. Already they were part of his enduring memory.

It was a short letter, heartbreaking in its clarity. Read aloud, without the grotesquerie of Dimity's spelling, the words took on added poignance:

"'Felippa will bring you this, two weeks after I have left you. I am writing to you now, in the cabin where we were happy together. . . . When she has gone ashore with the letter, I will let the hulk drift to sea. When I am sure that even I could not swim back, I will open the sea cocks.

"'Dr. Gaines will tell you why, Mike. He will explain about my heart. I don't understand his words too well, but it seems that a part of it does not work any more. So I must leave you in a few months, no matter what. And I can't stay that long, unless I take to my bed.

"'I've guessed as much for some time. Now that I'm sure, I know there's just one thing to do. . . . You see, no one has ever really cared for me but you, Mike—and I won't be a burden to you, even for this little while.

"'So I'm just saying good-by, darling—and taking myself out of your life. Don't think it's hard for *me,* Mike. You don't need me any longer. I guess you never did, really, though you did a fine job of covering up. Please don't think that I'm blaming you for anything. Or regret a single minute of the life we had together. . . ."

He looked up from the sheet. "She knew, it seems. I didn't think——"

"Read on," said Felippa. "She was happy, even when she knew. How many women could say that and mean it?"

He went back to the letter, reading the last few sentences slowly:

"'You gave me more than I deserved, from the beginning. I won't borrow another moment of your time. The rest belongs to the lady at Punta Blanca—to the child that must be yours.

"'God guard you, Mike. And thank you again for being.'"

There was no signature, no sense of a faltering pen. The last "i" was dotted with schoolgirl precision, the last "t" crossed with a firm stroke. Michael stared at the white sheet of foolscap as though he could not believe its reality even now.

"How *could* she know, Felippa?"

"How does any woman know, when her man belongs to another?"

"I'd give anything if she'd never known."

"No, Inglés. Being a man, you are romantic. Being a good man, you would spare those who are—close to you. A woman is made of other clay. A wife like this one can die happy only if she believes your happiness will continue. Only if she senses that another woman will someday fill the void she is leaving."

"Don't ask me to take comfort in that now."

"She could have gone in no other way. I am telling you that she went without regrets."

"What of me? Can I go on living without regrets?"

"There is no other way to go on living," said the witch.

"I'll regret her always."

"In your secret heart. But a man's secret heart should be the sanctuary for his past. When it becomes his future as well, that man is better dead. Go to the River of May. Your future is there. Your home is there."

"I can't go alone."

"You will not be alone. You will have a wife to give you strong sons. She waits now, with your first son at her side. She is wondering how soon you can put aside your grief and come to her."

Michael looked at Felippa with wide-open eyes. When he spoke again, his voice had a new resonance, a new confidence, as though the witch had charmed him from himself at last.

"Is this another of your prophecies?"

"Have my prophecies failed?"

"Does this—this new wife come with her slaves, or alone?"

"She comes with twenty black freedmen."

"What of Punta Blanca?"

"Punta Blanca is only a name now. It goes back to scrub, at her orders."

"Will she marry me if I ask her hand in marriage?"

"She has always been your wife. Being only a man, you could not know that until now."

They faced each other one more time beside Dimity's grave. Felippa watched his shoulders square. She read the new light in his eyes and smiled quietly at that knowledge. She brushed his cheek again with her fingertips as he knelt to kiss the fresh mound at their feet.

"Go with God, Americano."

"I hoped you'd call me that," he said, and left her quietly.

Felippa waited under the live oak to watch him go through the gates of Bosquebello. Then she followed slowly, with her eyes on a distant point no other eyes could see: a bank above a wide blue river, where a house was rising in a grove of yellow pine; an arch of green against the sky, where a woman and a child stood waiting, hand in hand.